Her pupils were open as wide as saucers.

"Sweetie?" Jay touched the cap sleeve of his wife's baby-doll blouse. "You feel all right?"

Slowly, she turned to face her husband. "Yes, I do. I feel just fine. How many times are you gonna ask?" Her voice rose. "In fact, I feel great. I've never felt better." She was yelling now. "I've never felt this great in my whole life!" She sank her fingernails into his forearm. "How the hell do *you* feel?"

From the table by the door, a low laugh escaped Kohl Thacker. A woman at the next table began to snicker. Another started up. Soon the entire room reverberated with laughter.

Hazel glanced around the dining room: this was not funny *at all*. More like frightening. Watching these people she'd known all her life become sudden strangers, she recalled how Sean had asked her yesterday "Where did I go?"

At that, she felt the mountainside tilt beneath her feet....

ELIZABETH VOSS's

debut novel, *The Winslow Incident,* is a
Daphne du Maurier Award Nominee for Excellence
in Mystery/Suspense. Her short stories "Treats for
Adeline" and "Hawkin Rhone" were published in
2012. She is a member of the International Thriller
Writers.

Elizabeth grew up on a forested island in the U.S.
Pacific Northwest, a curious place of dilapidated
cabins, forgotten graveyards and creatures prowling
the woods. She lives in Santa Monica, California, with
her husband and frequent co-author Peter Tackaberry.
Together, they are at work on a second novel.

THE
WINSLOW
INCIDENT

ELIZABETH
VOSS

W❂RLDWIDE®

TORONTO • NEW YORK • LONDON
AMSTERDAM • PARIS • SYDNEY • HAMBURG
STOCKHOLM • ATHENS • TOKYO • MILAN
MADRID • WARSAW • BUDAPEST • AUCKLAND

For Peter Tackaberry,
co-creator of this story,
best part of my story.

Recycling programs
for this product may
not exist in your area.

ISBN-13: 978-0-373-06283-6

THE WINSLOW INCIDENT

Copyright © 2011 by S. Elizabeth Voss

A Worldwide Library Suspense/July 2013

First published by Five Star Publishing in conjunction with Tekno Books and Ed Gorman.

Printed in U.S.A.

THE WINSLOW INCIDENT

I find myself considerably discomposed and disordered—full of notions. Poor N. Burt cut his own throat. We hear great talk about witchcraft.
—From the Diary of Stephen Williams, Longmeadow, Massachusetts, 1716–1735
(*Poisons of the Past*, Mary Kilbourne Matossian)

Don't touch me! Stand back! I am dead, do you hear? I am dead. I have snakes in my stomach! They are burning burning burning.
—Charles Veladaire, Pont-Saint-Esprit, France, 1951
(*The Day of St. Anthony's Fire*, John G. Fuller)

Blood is pouring from the sky: We are going to drown. I see a river of bodies. I see a town of ghosts.
—Aaron Adair, Winslow, Washington, 2010
(*A Plague of Madness*, G.F. Olson)

PROLOGUE

I'M NOT WELL, he admitted.

Fearful of making a sound, Veterinarian Reed Simmons sat rigid in the dining room chair he'd wedged against his front door. From that vantage point he could make out the patch of brown grass that constituted his lawn but not the vehicle he heard roar up.

His rifle rested across his knees.

This intrusion could only spell trouble. Since Simmons' visit to Holloway Ranch that morning, followed by the realization that he too felt peculiar, he'd had his suspicions. And if those suspicions turned out to be correct, he did not want to be involved in any capacity.

Nothing I can do about it anyway. He shuddered so violently his teeth clacked together.

Footsteps on the gravel driveway, as loud as fireworks, advanced toward the porch. Simmons could identify the condition if not the cause: hyperacusis, his sensitivity to sound growing more and more painful as this interminable day wound on and on.

I'm not well, the thought crept back into his worried mind.

A dog began to bark…and clamor and claw around the porch.

Simmons cringed, which sent his forehead throbbing again. *How did I cut my head so severely?* Images flitted through his mind: the red truck, crashed in a roadside ditch; his bloodied face reflected in the bathroom mirror, hands fumbling to dress the wound. Now gauze stuck to the gash, making the area even more tender and sore.

If only that were the worst of it.

"Doc Simmons?" a young female voice sliced his eardrums and encouraged the dog to bark louder. "We need your help."

Hands trembling, the vet gripped the rifle. Just as he'd feared, they were coming for him. And why? He wasn't an MD. *I wish we had a real doctor on this godforsaken mountainside—*

A thunderous knock erupted inches from his ear, piercing his skull like a spike.

He sprang from the chair.

Holding his gun, he crouched in the middle of the living room and twisted this way and that—the barking coming from every direction at once—until he realized, *I can't see.* Where were his glasses?

Floodgates opened and panic the likes of which he had never known washed through his core. *I'm not right! There's sure to be others. Bound to get worse. What should I do?* His mind was a book he struggled just to open, written in a language he no longer understood.

There—he recognized the vague shape of his spectacles on the foyer table and dashed to retrieve them. Donning the glasses brought the world back into focus, brought him instantly back in control.

"All right, then," he decided, feeling angry that they expected him to save them when really the situation was quite hopeless, wasn't it?

He kicked away the chair and wrenched open the door to find the girl poised to knock and plead again.

Trick or treat, he half-expected her to say.

Instead she gasped and drew back from the doorway, a reaction that told him *he* was the trickster in a monster mask.

A growl replaced the barking, a sound so menacing it

startled Simmons. Because there wasn't a dog in Winslow that wouldn't recognize the vet's scent.

Truth is, Simmons realized, *I don't recognize myself.*

He looked down.

Beside the girl, the Irish setter drooled copious amounts of saliva onto the porch.

"Mad dog!" Simmons screamed. "Mad dog!"

The girl shot the vet a look of terror before bounding down the porch steps, the dog at her heels.

Simmons walked to the top step…slowly. *What's the hurry?* he thought. *No one in Winslow is going anywhere. Not anytime soon.*

The girl made it to the driveway with the dog running protective circles around her.

Simmons raised his rifle and took aim.

PART ONE

Day One of the Heat Wave

HAZEL WINSLOW QUICKENED her pace up the hill, each anxious step churning up dirt. A shadow's length ahead of her, Patience Mathers braced her back against the NO TRESPASSING sign and raised a hand to cover her mouth, revulsion spoiling her flawless features.

"What's wrong?" Hazel asked, her heart batting away at her chest like a bird caught in the house.

Patience let her hand fall from her face. "They're dead," she said.

"Who's dead?" Hazel crested the rise and saw for herself— and her mouth flooded with thin saliva. Dusk washed the hundred-acre pasture an agreeable orange. Tall weeds spun sparks of sunlight. The sky hung heavy with the sinking sun. *It'd be pretty,* Hazel thought, *if it weren't for all those dead cows.* Half a dozen corpses littered the pasture: bloated bellies crushing grass, legs jutting out at odd angles, black masses of flies feasting.

"What the hell?" Sean Adair said.

Hazel jumped at her boyfriend's voice behind her. She spun to face him, and they gaped at each other in astonishment. The dying light created a halo around Sean's long brown hair, and he looked sun-kissed and sturdy, as if the mountain air agreed with him.

Paler and lankier, as though he lacked some vital nutrient,

Hazel's cousin Tanner Holloway skidded to a stop next to Sean and made a grave face at her. "Uncle Pard is *screwed*."

Hazel gestured at the carnage with a sweep of her arm. "You said they were sick, Tanner. Not—"

"Sicker than we thought." Tanner smirked. "Apparently."

"This is bad." Patience sank to her haunches on the dirt road and clasped her hands together as if praying that she, too, would not suddenly be struck swollen and dead.

There was no breeze, yet Hazel could sense the stench of death. Scanning the pasture, she whispered, "What happened to them?"

Tanner flipped straight blond surfer hair out of his face. "Mad cow disease."

"No way." Hazel flashed on the steak and eggs she'd eaten during the midmorning lull in her shift at Rose's Country Crock.

"No way," Sean said. Hazel had served him a cheeseburger for lunch.

Patience rose to her feet and swung toward Hazel, her beautiful dark eyes seeking reassurance from her best friend. "Mad cow?" she said.

"Okay, they don't know yet," Tanner admitted. "Doc Simmons was out poking and prodding the poor dumb beasts all morning. Now Uncle Pard's waiting for the vet to come back with test results. But I do know one thing." His pale blue eyes brightened. "They are damn worried—and that was *before* any beef went belly-up."

Feeling hot and grimy, Hazel gathered up her long hair and knotted it into a sloppy, strawberry-blond bun. Fanning the back of her neck with one hand, she scrutinized her cousin, uncertain if she trusted him. They were all seventeen, but unlike Patience and Sean, Tanner Holloway was something new. Two weeks ago he'd been shipped up to their uncle's ranch for the summer to straighten out and fly right. And experience had taught Hazel that the Holloway side of her family kept secrets like thieves hoard plunder. Certainly her mother had, and took nothing but secrets with her when she left. Hazel turned from Tanner, unhappy to be reminded that her mother hadn't chosen to take her along either.

Silently she counted cattle carcasses: three nut-brown cows huddled in the shade of the aspens; a steer felled before the bridge spanning the creek, his enormous head dunked halfway underwater. But fifty feet away near the split-rail fence surrounding the pasture, a red cow stood chewing her cud—alive and kicking and flicking her switch. And close by, a calf romped around in a patch of clover. Hazel started toward the animals, curious why they seemed okay when the others were clearly not.

Sean grabbed her by the hand. "Don't go near them. You don't know what's wrong."

"You're the one who wanted to come here, remember?" she snapped and writhed free. But as soon as she recognized the hurt in his amber-colored eyes, a familiar remorse struck. She smiled in a way intended to say, *Sorry.* "I won't get too close. Promise."

She pulled away from him and headed for the pasture. As she approached the fence in a cloud of dust bothered up by her black Converse, she flapped the front of her baby-blue T-shirt to get some air circulating against her skin. By late afternoon the sun had swallowed the entire Pacific Northwest mountainside; now it was digesting it. Blowing out her breath, she waved a hand in front of her face to fend off the swarm of gnats that were losing their tiny minds to the heat.

"You're an idiot, Winslow," Tanner yelled.

"Hazel, come back!" Patience sounded alarmed.

Yet when Hazel glanced over her shoulder, she found all three crossing the road toward her, Patience wide eyed and Sean grimacing as though he had a bad taste in his mouth.

At the fence, Hazel noticed that the red cow's hind legs were trembling. Suddenly both legs buckled.

"Whoa!" Hazel cried and leapt onto the lower fence rail. Out of instinct, she reached for the cow, arm outstretched, and her fingertips skimmed stiff hide as the animal dropped to the grass. The long-lashed creature emitted a pitiful moo, struggling to rise on legs that refused to cooperate.

Coming up behind Hazel, Sean wrapped his arm around her waist. "That's not too close?" He pulled her off the fence and plopped her indelicately on the ground. "Let's go."

"Wait, Sean," she said. But by the time she turned around, he was already headed back toward their motorcycles, his head bowed in a way that tugged at her heart.

"You shouldn't have touched it." Tanner sounded like he was enjoying himself. "It's probably contagious."

Hazel frowned. "Cow sicknesses don't spread to people that way." But as she watched the animal struggle, she began to feel less certain. She glanced sidelong at Tanner. "Do they?"

He scoffed. "Guess you'll find out."

The calf that had been playing in the clover tottered up, nudged the cow's neck with his nose, and gave a sad bleat. Then he scampered deeper into the pasture, not slowing until he put fifteen feet between them as if he, too, were suddenly worried about contagion.

"This is bad," Patience repeated. Between strands of long black hair hanging in her white face, she eyed the animals with obvious gloom. "And that ring around the moon last night meant it's sure to rain soon." She flung back her head to search the sky. "I hope our rodeo isn't ruined."

Hazel couldn't care less about the rodeo, but she did feel sorry for the animals—and realized this meant serious trouble for their uncle. She squinted at Tanner. "What did Doc Simmons say?"

Tanner shrugged. "Only that they might've gotten into something they shouldn't have." He knocked Hazel's forearm with his elbow. "Think it'll be half-priced rib eyes at the Crock tonight?"

Ignoring him, Hazel crouched and held her hand between the fence rails toward the calf. "Hey, buddy," she said softly.

The reddish-brown calf stared at her for a moment before opening his mouth to say, "Blat."

She realized then that the calf wasn't right, either. His muzzle was coated in something sticky-looking and the tips of his ears looked flaky and sore. At the sound of horses clomping across the wood bridge, the animal gave a frightened toss of his furry head.

"Later." Tanner was already walking away.

"Wait for me." Patience scrambled after him.

The calf studied Hazel with huge wet eyes. A tuft of red hair stuck up on top of his head as if he'd just woken from a long nap.

"It's all right, little guy," she said. "Come here."

On his rickety legs, the calf started toward her, just as Sean yelled, "Get out of there!" from what sounded like far away. But the horses seemed closer now: heavy hooves pounding soft grass. The white, crescent moon-shaped markings on the calf's face made her think of rings and rain and the rodeo in ruin.

"You're a good boy, aren't you?" she murmured. "Gonna grow up to be a prize Holloway bull."

The animal was less than ten feet away. He picked up his pace, small rump swaying, tail swishing to-and-fro. Then he raised his pink nose and gave her a friendly bleat.

Hazel wondered why it sounded like someone was running in the dirt. "That's a good—"

"Get back!" a man's voice boomed. "Keep away from it!" Thunder cracked and the calf's face exploded, showering her in bits of blood and hide. For a stark moment Hazel thought she'd been shot too and toppled backward. Grabbing hold of the rough fence rail to keep from falling, she felt her palm fill with slivers.

"Hold your fire, Clark!" the man shouted. "That was *the* most asinine, half-cocked move! You're damn lucky you didn't shoot her."

Hazel's eyes were locked on the calf, crumpled on his side before her, silent and still. Blood erupted from the hole where moments ago there had been one large brown eye. Through a second hole in his skull, brain protruded.

She felt panic and vomit and tears all rising at the same time and heard that sound again of shoes slapping dirt right before Sean grabbed her up and away from the fence. Then she was running back down the road so fast her body got ahead of her feet for one long scary moment and she nearly tumbled to the ground.

Tanner and Patience were already tearing off on the red Kawasaki, with Patience tucked behind Tanner, screeching like a mouse clutched in the talons of an owl.

Heart hammering, Hazel clambered over the cattle gate after Sean, swinging her legs over the metal bar and landing next to their Yamahas in an explosion of dirt.

Three ranch hands on horseback were bearing down on them fast.

Fear fought with relief when Hazel realized it was her Uncle Pard leading the charge. Then she saw the fury steaming off him and fear won that battle.

After reining his horse to face Kenny Clark and Old Pete Hammond who followed, Pard held up his hand and yelled, "I'll handle this." As soon as they turned their horses to head back, he rode up to Hazel and Sean where they stood panting and sweating on the other side of the cattle gate.

Pard Holloway was a big man rendered even larger astride

his horse, pointing down at them with a finger that seemed huge. "You will not breathe a word of this. Not. A. Word. Understood?"

"What's wrong with your herd?" Hazel asked. Despite her ragged breath, she sounded calmer than she felt. "Why did Kenny shoot that calf?"

"That's not your concern, Hazel." Her uncle started pointing again. "And I will not allow you or anybody else to trespass on *my* property and interfere with *my* business. Matter of fact, trespassing is a punishable offense. Go ask your father." He reached into his back pocket, retrieved a blue bandanna, and flung it to her. "And clean yourself up before you catch something."

She let the bandanna flutter to the dirt. Her father always warned her to steer clear of his brother-in-law's ranch; now here she was: spattered in bits of baby bull, her hand full of splinters, sick to her stomach after witnessing animal murder. When she realized calf blood was trickling down her bare arms, a whimper escaped her.

She forced herself to swallow hard and stand up straight. *"Something?"* she echoed her uncle. "If you don't know what's wrong, why are you killing them?"

"All right, listen up!" Pard shouted with such force that Hazel, Sean and the horse all started. "That calf was sick and we couldn't chance it spreading to the rest of the herd." He pushed up his hat to reveal eyes the same greenish-brown as hers, hair the same shade of reddish-blond—as if neither of them were willing to commit to any one particular hue. Then he narrowed his familiar eyes. "And I will not allow *news* of this to spread, either."

Hazel glanced at her blood-spattered arms before grimacing at him. "People will find out."

"I'll be damned if I'll let that happen. You know why?" He gestured at the sky; the answer so obvious, surely it was written there. "If we lose our reputation, we lose *everything*. Not just my ranch, but this whole damn town. Right now I've got this under control, but you two have to promise me you'll all keep your mouths shut."

"Whatever." Sean shrugged before he kick-started his motorcycle to life. "We're outta here."

Hazel nibbled at her bottom lip, distraught over the animal remains stuck to the front of her shirt. Looking back at her uncle, she raised her voice to be heard over the bike's engine: "It's not safe to eat the beef, is it?"

"Dammit, Hazel!" Pard threw up one massive arm. "Repeat that and I promise you I'll dig up that mess between Sean Adair here and Hawkin Rhone."

Hazel and Sean swapped haunted glances.

"Going on five years now, I believe," Pard continued, leaning down toward them with his forearm against Blackjack's mane. The horse looked smug, Hazel thought, showing them his yellow teeth and breathing hot foul air in their faces.

Pard added, "That whole sorry business was never actually settled up. Was it?"

When Hazel looked at Sean again, his mouth moved but nothing came out.

A burning sensation crept across her scalp, and she caught herself chewing her lip—a habit she had fought hard to break ever since that day at Three Fools Creek when she witnessed Hawkin Rhone bite clear through his own tongue.

She stomped up to the gate and yanked the horse by the bit. Blackjack's head snapped back into her uncle's chest, the animal's frightened eyes rolling her direction. "You do that," she yelled, "and I'll tell everyone in Winslow—everyone down in the whole valley—that your beef is poison!"

Pard pushed her back a couple of feet with the bottom of his boot against her shoulder. "Don't force me to tell Zachary Rhone what really happened. Or about how your father lied. Because you know, sheriffs can lose their badges over a helluva lot less." Pard glanced at Sean before he drew closer to Hazel and whispered in a conspiratorial tone, "Not to mention what might happen to your friend, here. How's a boyfriend in prison sound?"

Feeling herself begin to shake, Hazel shoved her hands into the pockets of her shorts and turned her back on her uncle, stupefied that he was threatening them. "Who cares about your cows and your shit-filled ranch anyway?" she said, instantly aware of how weak that had sounded. She climbed on her own motorcycle and kicked and kicked the starter until the engine finally sparked.

"Good," Pard shouted while Blackjack reared from the buzz of both engines. "We've got a deal. You stay out of my business and I'll stay out of yours."

Instead of heading back the way they had come earlier from Ruby Creek, Hazel and Sean blasted the opposite direction up Loop-Loop Road toward town. After a minute of riding flat-out, they were forced down into the ditch in order to get around a white truck parked across the road.

It wasn't until they had skidded around the west gate that Hazel stole a glance over her shoulder.

Her stomach sank.

From that higher vantage point, she could see that there were more than a mere half dozen. Strewn across the pasture like passengers from a plane crash, at least fifty head of Holloway cattle lay dead.

"BE GENTLE!" HAZEL CRIED.

"Be brave," her grandmother said, even as her mouth turned down in sympathy.

They sat side by side in high-back chairs at the walnut table in the formal dining room, Sarah Winslow digging splinters out of her granddaughter's hand with a sewing needle and pair of tweezers.

To distract her mind from the operation and slaughtered animals and threats of blackmail, Hazel studied the fresco painted on the ceiling. She stared at swans and fountains and ladies with parasols, at all the things Winslow never was except on the plaster ceiling of her great-great grandfather's home. One man's fruitless stab at bringing civilization to an uncivil mining camp, she supposed. The Winslow stood four stories high, counting the round room at the top of the tower where the ghosts resided. Built in 1889, the fifteen-room, Italianate-style mansion was too fancy for its own good, and as caretaker, Sean's father had to do constant battle with the elaborate roof and ancient plumbing.

"Ouch!" Hazel jerked her hand away after her grandmother probed her pinkie with the needle. "That's gentle?"

Sarah took firm hold of her hand again. "Only a few more."

Hazel clenched her teeth as her grandmother pulled a splinter from the tip of her finger.

Eyes concentrated on her task, Sarah said, "Are you planning to tell me what happened?"

Hazel studied her grandmother's smooth cheeks and thick silver hair, hoping she would look that good at sixty-two. "Well, let's see. I saw your boyfriend, Cal, at the Fish 'n Bait. He told me to tell you he'll pick you up at one sharp tomorrow to escort you to the rodeo. He promised not to smell like trout."

"Thanks for the warning." Sarah laughed—a warm cackle that always reminded Hazel of fall leaves underfoot and made her feel in safe territory. And the idea of her grandmother hooking up with worm-loving Cal made Hazel laugh, too.

But Sarah turned serious again, asking, "And…?"

"And I tripped and fell in the woods," Hazel replied.

Sarah glanced up, raising the dark eyebrows that packed extra punch in contrast to her light hair. "I'll wait until you're ready then."

Hazel tried to frown but it felt more like wincing. She had never lied to her grandmother before, and it made her feel polluted and gore-splashed all over again. She had come to The Winslow to get cleaned up and calmed down. After sneaking a shower in an empty guest room—rinsing blood from her arms and picking pieces of calf hide out of her hair—she had donned one of Sean's T-shirts over her shorts and sought out Sarah to perform splinter surgery. Until she was in better shape, she had to avoid home and her father because she couldn't tell him what had happened. As sheriff he'd be forced to report the sick and dead cattle to the proper authorities. Then her Uncle Pard would make good on his threat. And then her dad and Sean would both go to prison.

"My brave girl." Sarah pulled away the tweezers. "Shall we take a break?"

Hazel hadn't realized she was crying; now she felt tears running hot and itchy down her cheeks. Only she wasn't sobbing from the pain, it was due to blossoming panic. Sean had protected her that day at Three Fools Creek, so now it was up to her to protect him.

But a new fear had begun to gnaw at her—the fear that she might prove sadly incapable of protecting anyone at all.

SATURDAY MORNING
STEPSTONE MOUNTAIN RANGE

Day Two of the Heat Wave

FRITZ EARLEY STEERED his flatbed truck around the final curve up Yellow Jacket Pass and the simple truss bridge came into view. Along the ridgeline, the early morning sun lit lodgepole pines like candles on a birthday cake. *Tinderbox,* Fritz thought as he bounced over the cattle guard.

He always felt uneasy crossing the bridge. Not that it was so far across; but it was a gut-dropping distance *down*. He imagined that one day the weight of his fully loaded delivery truck would collapse the bridge and send him plunging, falling end over end before he slammed into the Lamprey River. There the twisted wreckage of metal and his ample flesh would careen downriver until it wedged against the bank to await grisly discovery by some unlucky kid or angler.

So he whistled relief when he popped out the other end of the bridge and passed the familiar sign.

Welcome to Winslow
(Pop. 255)
"Jewel of the Stepstone Range"
Home of Holloway Ranch

Rather than keep to the main route leading downtown through a tunnel of quaking aspen, Fritz turned south onto Loop-Loop Road and headed for the ranch. He preferred to get Pard Holloway's delivery over and done with first since the ranch boss was always hollering at him. Then he could finish his deliveries and grab a bite at the Crock before he had to re-cross the chasm and start the long drive back down the mountain.

But halfway down Loop-Loop Road, Fritz had to slam on his brakes to avoid T-boning Maggie Clark's white Chevy truck parked across the middle of the road. He was surprised to see Maggie—sole Holloway Ranch cowgal—leaning sentry-like against the passenger side. More surprising was that the middle-aged woman's usually wild hair was reined into a ponytail so tight it looked painful. That and the fact that she was wielding a rifle.

After Fritz eased to a stop, Maggie set her gun inside the Chevy's cab and then came around to his open window. "Need to unload into mine." She cocked a callused thumb toward her four by four truck. "I'll take it overland."

"What's doin'?" Fritz asked, worried about what Maggie's new hairdo and brandishing of weapons could mean. Did this woman—known to round up cattle and sling chow with the same brutal efficiency—feel threatened? Or was she the one doing the threatening?

Squinting in the direction of the ranch did her crow's-feet no favors. "Road's washed out up ahead."

Fritz leaned forward against the steering wheel as far as his belly allowed, and peered through his bug-splashed windshield at the dirt road beyond Maggie's truck. He had been up this road just last week. And it hadn't rained in over a month.

HAZEL'S HOUSE
PARK STREET

"I DON'T HAVE time for this, Dad." Hazel threw her spoon and cereal bowl into the kitchen sink with a clatter. "I'm late for work."

All night she'd been haunted by images of calf brains leaking into pasture grass and Sean in handcuffs that sliced into his wrists and the badge ripped from her father's shirt. So this morning she was feeling, as her grandmother would say, burnt around the edges.

"You don't start work till eight. Don't you think I know that?" Her father set his own bowl on the counter. Cereal was as elaborate as breakfast ever got around their house. Hazel noticed that he had barely touched his and the flakes looked soggy and bloated. "Now, where were you last night?" he asked.

"Can't you find somebody else to interrogate?" she said. "You're the sheriff—shouldn't you be out protecting the town or something?"

He opened the breadbox and pulled out a loaf, all the while giving her his look that said, *I don't know what to do with you.* Then he warned, "I'd better not find out you bought pot from those carnies."

"You're completely paranoid!" She couldn't handle this right now. Pretending last night never happened was hard enough, she didn't need extra grief from him today, especially considering that her evasiveness was for his sake.

His and Sean's. She spun out of the kitchen, griping, "Quit harassing me."

He followed her into the living room. "I wouldn't be 'harassing' you if you'd come home at a reasonable hour."

The knot in Hazel's stomach just kept growing. After she had crept home from The Winslow and snuck quietly (or so she'd thought) up the staircase to her room, it had been past one in the morning. Now she glanced around at the overstuffed furniture in their Victorian house, and felt like she was suffocating.

Continuing to avoid her father's dark blue eyes, she said, "I was at Patience's house helping her with her rodeo outfit." A lame lie, but she was too nervous to invent a better one. She'd never lied to her father before, either. Not about anything important anyway. More inner pollution—she was beginning to feel downright toxic.

"How was I supposed to know where you were? When you were coming home?" He ran a hand through his short hair, making it stick up in dark spikes all over his head. "*If* you were coming home. You could've been lying dead in the ravine for all I knew."

That's a lovely image, she thought. "You're always worrying about things that never happen. Relax, Dad—take a pill."

He stared at her without saying anything else. It was his way of making her think about the things she'd said, to consider her next words. And it always pissed her off. She bit down hard on her lip, battling the urge to tell him everything, resenting him because, really, wasn't he supposed to protect her and not the other way around?

Finally, she huffed in frustration. "I can just leave, you know." She slammed out the front door and stomped extra loud down the porch steps.

Then she glanced back and instantly regretted saying those words, words that for all she knew were the last her mother had ever spoken to him. For there her father stood at the open screen door, still holding the bread, looking at her with a crumbled expression.

Hazel flushed with shame for getting into it with him in the first place. This situation wasn't his fault; none of it was ever his fault.

She was considering how best to apologize when he shoved the loaf of bread into their big antique mailbox. "Dad!" She laughed. "You weirdo!" But then she saw the genuinely startled look on his face and her amusement fizzled out. "What are you doing?" she asked, concerned.

"What?" he said. Confusion clouded his features. He glanced back at the mailbox, and then he laughed, too, before retrieving the squished bread. "I wanted to make toast." Looking slightly embarrassed, he asked, "Do you suppose I'll have better luck with that in the toaster?"

"Probably." She noticed that he hadn't shaved yet, and his beard stubble and messy dark hair stood in stark contrast to his suddenly pale skin. "Seriously, Dad, are you all right?"

"I'm fine," he said, glancing away from her. "Go on, now—you'll be late for work."

Late? she puzzled. He'd already called bullshit on that one, but she wasn't about to argue against her own fib. Instead, she turned to go, silently vowing to make it all up to him somehow.

Add it to the list, she thought, of her growing litany of missteps and mishaps, secrets and lies.

The moment she placed one foot on the stepping-stones to cross the front yard, Jinx fell in step beside her. As usual, he'd been waiting for Hazel. The Irish setter was Winslow's dog-about-town who belonged to nobody in particular and who always managed to track down Hazel.

She glanced at him. The dog looked concerned.

"Not you again," she said.

He wagged his tail.

"You're not my dog, you know."

Wag wag wag.

"I've got enough problems right now," she explained as they continued together onto Park Street, "without having to worry about you, too."

Jinx listened intently, all floppy red ears.

She stopped walking in front of Patience's house next door, stooped down to his level, and cradled his head in her hands. He gazed at her adoringly.

"Do you understand? I'm blowing this one-horse town soon. And once I'm gone, I'm never coming back."

The dog cocked his head, looked at her quizzically: surely she didn't mean that, did she?

"That's right. No birthday cards, no phone calls, no visits just to see if you're even still alive."

His tail thumped on the sidewalk and her irritation dissolved. "Okay, let's go, you stupid dog." They resumed walking in the early sunshine toward Fortune Way. "But don't say I didn't warn you."

RHONE BAKERY
FORTUNE WAY

SEAN ADAIR SMELLED bacon frying. He knocked again on the flimsy metal frame of the screen door and heard small bare feet slapping against the floor.

"Sit down and eat your eggs right this minute," he heard Melanie Rhone say, "or else the rodeo is canceled for two little girls I know."

When Melanie pushed open the door it stuck halfway against the warped overhang and she had to hit it with her palm to get it the rest of the way out. Regarding him with curious blue eyes, she said, "Morning, Sean."

"Morning," he said, feeling self-conscious. In the three weeks he'd been working at the bakery, he'd never had a reason to go up to the house. But he'd caught Melanie staring at him from the yard more than once, and each time wondered why the former rodeo queen had married a man like Zachary Rhone.

Now Sean peered over Melanie's head into the kitchen. "Zachary around?"

When she shook her head, red curls danced. "He's on the pot. Can it wait?"

"I'm already late with deliveries."

"Okay. Wait a second." She released the screen door and it stuck midway again.

Sean didn't have to wait a second; Zachary was already right there, slapping the door back open. His crew-cut head loomed large, skin stretched tight across his cheekbones, and

Sean's heart commenced a fitful beat at his sudden certainty that even though they'd kept their mouths shut, Pard Holloway had sold them out anyway to Zachary Rhone.

But then Zachary said, "You are *way* behind schedule, mister."

Sean let out the breath he hadn't realized he'd been holding. And damn, that bacon smelled good. "I need you to come down to the bakery," he said.

The rift of disapproval between Zachary's eyebrows deepened. "Why's that, Adair?"

"Some of it looks like it didn't turn out right."

Zachary rolled his eyes skyward as if to say *Please, Lord, grant me patience in the face of this idiot.* "Criminy, Adair. *Taste* whatever the hell it is. If it tastes right, it's right."

Sean felt heat rise in his face.

Jabbing his finger toward Sean, the delivery van parked next to the bakery below the house, and all points in between, Zachary shouted, "I'd better see that van leave that driveway in twenty minutes!"

Sean slogged back across the porch and down the hill, wondering if—worst-case scenario and he did get busted—prison could really be much worse than working for this asshole.

When he reached the rear entrance to the bakery, he turned to look back at the Rhone house. Hunkered beneath the old apple orchard, the clapboard cottage had a sloped porch and sagging second story, as if the weight of Zachary's rotten temper was too much for the poor house to bear.

Sean turned around and kicked open the bakery door. "Screw him then," he told the loaves of bread he had abandoned next to the oven. He tore off a chunk of rye and shoved it in his mouth, chewing mechanically while he carried the tower of trays into the storefront and released them onto the prep counter with a bang.

Screw. Him. He exhaled sharply. He still had to package up the hot dog and burger buns for the rodeo barbecue before he could even head out in the van. *If the piece of shit even starts.*

At least Zachary wasn't breathing down his neck here, which gave him time to think. As usual, he thought about Hazel. Then he saw her out on the sidewalk, passing the window display.

Catching his eye, Hazel backed up and pushed open the door. The frosted stencil on the door's window read *Rhone Family Bakery ~ Since 1924.*

The Irish setter sauntered in with her, stopped short of the donut case and looked up at Sean with expectation. Hazel's long hair was loose and wavy, and her freckles were out because it was summer. Sean thought she looked pretty. Then again, he always did.

"Hey, doughboy," she said.

"Not for long," he replied, laying an arm across the top of the case. "Want a bear claw?"

"Wait—why not for long?" She looked stricken. "Does Zachary know?"

"No, no—Pard kept our deal, as far as I can tell. But Zachary's completely drunk on power. Seriously, I can't take it." He retrieved a cake donut from the case. "How about you, Jinx?"

The red dog whined, *definitely,* picking up first one front paw and then the other in a little dance of high hopes.

"That's not a good idea," Hazel said. She looked down at the disappointed dog. "Sorry, buddy."

Sean pitched the donut into the trash bin. Jinx rushed over, rooted it out, and chowed down.

"I give up," Hazel said. Then, softly: "I'm pretty sure my Uncle Pard will keep his end of the bargain if we do the same. He has no reason to cause trouble for us."

"Did you tell your dad?" Sean asked.

She shook her head hard, eyes steeled with resolve.

He lowered his voice: "What should we do about the barbecue?"

"Nothing, Sean." She gnawed at her lower lip; her eyes conflicted now. "They test the beef. My uncle won't let any diseased meat get out."

An unpleasant buzz started up in his stomach. "Are you sure?"

"Yes." She looked pained. "He'd never risk losing his Prime grade. Now let's quit talking about it before *everybody* knows." She glanced worriedly at the dog, as if he'd overheard and might later spill the beans.

"You're right, you're right," Sean agreed, and then remembered he'd better get his ass in gear. "Come on..." He grinned at the girl he'd been in love with all of his life. "Do deliveries with me."

She thought for a moment, staring straight at him. Sometimes her eyes looked almost brown; today they were emeralds. Finally, she shrugged. "Why not."

PROSPECTORS WAY
SILVER HILL

———————————————

SWEAT WIGGLED DOWN Patience Mathers' back. *I hate this dress,* she thought. The Victorian-era gown was heavy and scratchy, and cut into her rib cage. Despite her distress, she waited dutifully outside Matherston Miners Supply for her grandfather to finish collecting admission and give her the go.

Turning her back to the antique dolls with their too-long eyelashes that were staring at her from inside the display window, Patience realized just how hard it was going to be at the rodeo later to pretend that everything was okay. That there weren't dead cows or rings around the moon or her best friend covered in brains and blood. Last night Hazel told her that since Patience had been able to pretend all this time that she never saw what happened at Hawkin Rhone's cabin, she could find a way to pretend she never saw bad things happen at the ranch, either. It had sounded convincing at the time.

This morning, Patience wasn't so sure. This morning, it felt like tempting fate all over again.

A sudden wave of nausea hit her. Taken by surprise, she wrapped her arm around a pillar for support and bowed her head, wishing she hadn't put so much butter and syrup on her French toast at breakfast, and breathing deeply until the sensation passed.

An old gray couple exited the store and shuffled past, kicking up dust as they headed over to join the other tourists assembled at the timber-framed entrance to Prospectors Way, anxious for the tour to begin. Unlike the paved rectangle of streets defining downtown Winslow, the one road running through the old silver miners' section of town was bare dirt that always left Patience with a mouthful of grit.

Her grandfather filled the doorway beside her. "Looks like that's everybody," he said, sounding pleased at the turnout. Benjamin Mathers' features were clustered tightly on his face, and his round head perched close to his shoulders, giving him an owlish appearance.

Patience had always been grateful that she didn't take after him. "I'm melting," she said, tugging on her high collar. "Can I give them the short version?"

"All right, Patience." Her grandfather looked hot and uncomfortable in his costume, too. "But don't leave out the murder in the Never Tell Brothel. They always love that part." Then he scowled at her right wrist. "How many times must I ask you not to wear that? It's not true to the period." The old man shook his head as if it really did spoil everything. "Your grandmother would not approve."

Patience had been fiddling with her chain-link bracelet, her fingertips nervously stroking the golden horseshoe, the wishbone, a tiny four-leaf clover, seeking protection in the lucky charms she had begun to collect soon after her Gram Lottie died, to defend herself from further blows of fate. Not wanting to argue with her grandfather, she tucked the bracelet up under her long, tight sleeve—she never dared take it off and didn't understand why he even bothered to ask.

As she walked over to the group of fifteen or so tourists, she looked them over to see if any were likely to tip. Always the men, and nearly always they told her, "You look like Scarlett O'Hara," when they slipped her a five or a ten. She'd say, "Really?" as if she'd never heard that one before. And all the while their wife or girlfriend would be standing there like poor Miss Melly saying, "Come *on*."

When Patience reached the expectant group, she forced a

smile. "Howdy," she said with a cheerfulness she did not feel. "Welcome to Matherston Ghost Town." She turned to lead the way. "If you'll follow me, we'll start with the blacksmith shop up here on the right and the livery stable next door, where you'll see a collection of mining equipment, including the original Burleigh drills and rolling mounts…"

The *clomp-clomp, clomp-clomp* of thirty feet pounding the wooden boardwalk as they made their way past the false-front buildings further grated on her nerves.

She stopped the group in front of the Mother Lode Saloon, saying, "This was one of three saloons in Matherston." She led them inside through batwing doors and pointed to a poker table covered in ratty felt with barely discernable markings. "Story has it—"

Without warning, her train of thought left the station without her. She'd given the ghost town tour a hundred times, yet all of a sudden, she had no idea what came next.

The tourists were all staring at her, obviously growing impatient.

What's wrong with me? She felt a surge of panic. *Say something!*

"Story has it, dear?" the old gray woman gently prompted.

"Uh…uh…" Patience swallowed hard, concentrating on the poker table until it finally came back to her. "Story has it that no less than five men killed themselves after losing their fortunes at that table even quicker than they'd made them at their claims." She chased her rush of words with a long exhale, still reeling from her memory lapse. Yet she managed to finish. "And some say those souls have never left the Mother Lode, unable to rest until they reclaim their treasure."

A tourist kid made a mock spooked sound and two little girls fell into a fit of giggles.

Patience gave the kid her best evil eye before taking the group back outside, deciding then to cut the tour even shorter for fear that her brain might short-circuit again. "Our last stop," she continued, "is the Chop House Restaurant, which was said to have the thickest steaks and surliest service in the West, both courtesy of Holloway Ranch."

Suddenly Patience wished the ranch would just go away, wished it would simply slip off the mountainside in a jumble of barns and cows, and then she'd have so much less to worry about.

HOLLOWAY RANCH
LOOP-LOOP ROAD

TANNER HOLLOWAY SAT alone at the bench table recently vacated by the ranch hands, spooning in clumps of lukewarm oatmeal and considering his options (which, he had to admit, were few) when his Uncle Pard stormed into the mess building with fire in his eyes.

Oh shit, Tanner thought, shooting up and looking for the quickest route of escape.

Pard charged up. "Where have you been and what the hell were you thinking last night?"

Tanner pretended not to see or hear him, glancing casually around at the litter of breakfast dishes on the long table, his pounding heart undermining his efforts to stay cool. Busted. Again.

"You were sitting right here at mess yesterday," Pard said, jabbing one finger against the table, "when I told everyone to keep quiet until we can get a handle on things."

He stared at his uncle now, refusing to respond, uncertain if his voice would quiver.

Pard glared back, exasperated. "Then I find you and your cousin and her crew out in the pasture laughing it up at a damn near tragic situation."

Working up his nerve, Tanner strode to the head of the table and poured himself a cup of coffee. "I'd offer you some," he said, amazed that his hands were steady, "but it seems like you've had enough."

His uncle went redder in the face. "No wonder my brother wanted to get rid of you. You're nothing but a punk."

"Then I'm not disappointing anyone."

"You disappoint everyone."

"Hey, I didn't ask to be here—"

"And I didn't ask to have you here, but I've been trying to make the best of it."

"Make the best of it?" *Bullshit!* Tanner thought. *You've made it crystal clear you wanted nothing to do with me since the day they dumped me here.* His parents had barely stayed long enough to drink a glass of iced tea on the porch of the sprawling ranch house—Tanner and Pard eyeing each other warily the whole time—out of fear Pard would change his mind about taking his nephew for the summer. And Tanner had been surprised by the way his dad had avoided looking at him when he unloaded the duffel bag from the back of the Forester and said, "Be good, son." That was the first time in a long time he'd been called "son," and to Tanner, it had sounded odd and somehow final.

Now his uncle tried a different tact. "Listen, you're a smart kid. Make yourself useful."

"What should I do? Go warn the innocent townsfolk?"

Pard slammed his fist down on the table so hard coffee jumped out of Tanner's cup and his heart leapt in his chest. "Dammit! I've got problems here and don't need any extra aggravation."

"Okay, okay…" Tanner backed away, thinking, *You do got problems.* Then, to Tanner's relief, Kenny Clark swaggered in.

"We're ready for you, boss," Kenny said.

For reasons beyond Tanner's fathoming, the only thing Kenny seemed to love more than his job was his boss.

"Find any more dead?" Pard asked Kenny without taking his eyes off Tanner.

"Nope." Kenny appeared proud to report that, maybe thinking that the boss would figure Kenny Clark had played a hand in this good turn. "More sick, but no more dead."

Relief softened Pard's features and he swiveled to tell Kenny, "Good. Be right there."

Pard turned back to Tanner. "Look. I'm willing to pull in my horns this time. But don't cause me any trouble at the rodeo. It won't get you down the mountain any quicker, I promise you that. It'll only increase your sentence."

Kenny chortled at that while Pard leaned closer to Tanner. "You will do what the men tell you to do, and when you are not doing that you will keep out of the way. Above all, you will keep your mouth *shut*. Understood?"

"Yes," Tanner hissed in reply. Of course he understood. That didn't mean he'd do it.

THE DELIVERY
DOWNTOWN WINSLOW

FROM THE PASSENGER'S SEAT, Hazel watched Sean fight to keep the steering wheel of the bakery van straight. Sunlight pouring through the windshield lit up his eyes and kissed his hair. *How's a boyfriend in prison sound?* A shudder snaked down her spine. It sounded horrifying—that's how it sounded. At the ranch, her uncle had known precisely which lever to pull. Now, as she studied Sean's profile, she couldn't help but think for the hundredth time that he was too good-natured for prison, too young and too good-looking; she felt sick imagining what might happen to him.

Sean crammed the gearshift into second with a grinding sound. "How's your hand?" he asked.

"Sore." She examined her right palm. "Not so splintery."

He grimaced, then said, "I had to kick Aaron out of my bedroom last night." He took his eyes off the road to look at her. "Out of left field, he's convinced that Hawkin Rhone lives in his closet."

"That's strange…" She felt uneasy, as if merely saying the man's name might conjure him up. "I didn't think Aaron believed in all that." Sean's kid brother had always been more sensibly obsessed with bikes and bugs than with scary stories.

Sean's face darkened. "He believes now."

"It's just a coincidence." She managed to keep her tone light, despite the dread tunneling through her that her uncle had, indeed, resurrected Hawkin Rhone. "You know how it is," she continued. "It's fun for the kids to picture him out across the creek—old and toothless and scary."

"You're right," Sean agreed, though he looked no less troubled.

She suddenly became aware that she was kneading her left wrist; it still hurt sometimes. Forcing herself to stop, she sat back in the tattered bucket seat and took in the familiar sights of downtown Winslow and Prospect Park. A rectangle around which the town was neatly arranged, the park occupied a broad plateau beyond which Stepstone Range resumed its eastward rise. The park was absurdly big compared to the rest of the town. Led by her own family (so it was told), the town founders had been certain Winslow would thrive and expand. But after the price fell out of silver in 1893 and the mines were boarded up, anyone with any sense packed up and left to seek their livelihood elsewhere. Those who didn't had their own stubborn reasons for remaining on the remote mountainside, inaccessible save for the bridge that spanned the narrow Lamprey River canyon. It didn't seem to bother anyone but her that the nearest real grocery store was two hours away in good weather, the closest movie theater three.

The van clattered to a stop in front of Clemshaw Mercantile, a two-story wood-frame store that stocked everything from bullets to baby food. A tarnished plaque above batwing doors proclaimed, *Established 1888*.

Sean climbed out and opened the van's back door with a grating squeak.

Hazel turned in her seat to watch him head toward the store carrying two trays of bread.

Out front, Tiny Clemshaw looked up from where he was sweeping to shout, "You're late!"

"I'm only—" Sean started.

"You're late and they're all waiting for you." Tiny gestured with his broom at the nonexistent crowd, and would have bonked Sean on the head with the handle had Sean not ducked out of the way. "My customers do *not* appreciate being kept waiting."

Hazel saw sweat streaming down Tiny's face, pooling inside his collar, dripping from his nose. Sure, it was hot out, but it wasn't *that* hot yet.

Sean was glancing around. "What customers?"

"*My* customers—" Tiny looked around then, too, and his face registered sudden dismay. "They were right here," he muttered, his bluster giving way to uncertainty. "They were all right here."

Sean looked over his shoulder at Hazel in the van and silently mouthed to her, "What the hell?"

Tiny bumbled over to the store's entrance and held open the doors for Sean, saying, "They grew tired of waiting for you. But they'll be back." The man looked increasingly flustered. "Don't you think?"

"Uh, yeah…" Sean said. Backing into the store, he rolled his eyes at Hazel like *Cuckoo, cuckoo.*

She sighed, her stomach knotting even tighter. They had enough crap to deal with today; they didn't need Tiny Clemshaw freaking out on them, too.

When Sean jumped back inside the van, Hazel turned to him and frowned in bewilderment. "Everyone is acting incredibly weird today," she said.

"No shit!" He shook his head. "First Aaron, then Zachary, now Tiny."

"My dad's not right, either," she said.

Sean made a monster noise, *wro-hoo-hoo,* while holding out one arm zombie-style. "Maybe aliens are invading their bodies."

Hazel laughed, but then the thought of mad cow disease eating holes in people's brains made the idea seem less farfetched and far less funny. "Let's hope not," she said softly.

Sean got the van moving, turning right at the corner and then rattling down Park Street past the row of Victorians. Hazel always thought the houses were over the top, making spectacles of themselves like old ladies wearing crazy hats and too much makeup. Just past her own house, Sean turned right onto Ruby Road and then hung a quick left up the steep drive to The Winslow, the hotel described by one travel writer as, "An Old West treasure trove well worth braving the hazards of Yellow Jacket Pass."

"Sticky and gray," Sean was muttering.

"What?" Hazel said, realizing she'd been distracted.

Sean glanced at her. "You know what? Screw Zachary."

"Are you gonna quit?" she asked.

"Get fired, most likely." He blew out his breath. "He's such a dick."

She nodded. "What's his problem?"

"Beats me. When I went to ask him a simple question he bit my head off."

"I'll talk to Owen Peabody. Maybe he can use some help at the Crock."

"Cool. Or maybe your dad needs a deputy," he joked.

That didn't strike Hazel as funny. Hell, Sean would probably *be* sheriff once her dad retired. For as much as she always lamented it, she predicted Sean was never leaving Winslow, never leaving his little brother, Aaron, or their mother alone with their drunken father.

Sean parked at the base of the stone staircase cut into The Winslow's massive retaining wall and climbed the steps with a tray of bread. Then he headed around the side of the hotel to go in through the kitchen door, where Hazel imagined he'd find his mother preparing breakfast for the guests. Hazel was glad that Honey and Samuel Adair ran her family's hotel and that she didn't have to work there. There was way too much history in the place, and Hazel hated dragging the past around—it was too heavy.

"Hazel!" Aaron Adair shouted, barreling down the steps so recklessly that Hazel was certain the seven-year-old boy would stumble and plant his face in stone.

She flung open the van door and jumped down onto the driveway. "Aaron, slow down!"

He did not slow down, not until he smacked right into her. "I just saw another one," he said, out of breath. The boy was a miniature Sean: same light brown eyes, same soft brown curls. And he was looking at her with fierce intensity. "I just saw one who looks like Patience Mathers."

Not easily spooked, Hazel's sudden shiver caught her by surprise. Before she could ask Aaron what he meant, she noticed Sean descending the steps. She frowned at him to signal her concern.

Still breathing hard, Aaron continued, "And all night long another lady with blood gurgling out of her throat scared the bejeebers out of me."

Hazel's breath caught in her own throat. "How do you know about—" Then she stopped herself, realizing it best not to say any more. Fearing Aaron might hyperventilate, she cupped his small shoulders. "Calm down," she said. "Take a long, deep breath." Beneath her hands, she could feel him trembling. She shot another worried look at Sean as he joined them.

Sean squatted down until he was face-to-face with his brother. "Aaron, what's gotten into you?"

"They're *everywhere*," Aaron whispered, looking about to cry.

"Who's everywhere?" Sean asked.

Aaron glanced over his shoulder at The Winslow, then looked back at Sean with fear in his eyes. "The ghosts," he said. The tears did start then.

"No." Sean hugged his brother. "Those are only stories—you know that. There aren't any ghosts."

"But I seen them, Sean," Aaron said, voice muffled against Sean's shoulder. "All over the hotel." He pulled back from Sean, his expression grave. "I seen the lady who looks like Patience only she's dripping wet. And the other lady with the bloody neck."

Hazel angrily wondered who in their right mind would tell Aaron about what happened to Patience's grandmother Lottie Mathers that violent night at The Winslow—a night Hazel had spent five years trying hard to forget.

Sean looked up at Hazel, clearly struggling with how best to handle the situation. After she gave him a helpless shrug, he stood and mussed Aaron's hair. "It's okay. I won't let 'em get you. I promise."

"Can you do that?" Aaron asked, wide-eyed and hopeful.

"Can I do that?" Sean mocked disbelief that he would even ask. Then he reached into the back of the van and came out holding a bear claw. "Let's start with this. Ghosts hate pastries."

"I hate those, too." Aaron pouted. "Nuts are gross and my stomach already feels yucky today."

"Now you're choosey?" Sean brought out another. "Apple fritter?"

"Yeah! I like apple." Aaron snatched the pastry from Sean's hand and darted away.

"You're welcome," Sean called after him. Then he shot an anxious glance at Hazel. "Now I'm really late." He rushed toward the driver's door.

After Hazel jumped back in, too, Sean started up the van and they headed down the drive. She watched the imposing mansion recede in the side-view mirror. Everyone perpetuated the notion that The Winslow was haunted. Good for business because tourists love a good ghost story. But having grown up in the hotel, Aaron had heard tales of ghosts in the tower his entire life and had never seemed afraid of them before.

"More weirdness," Hazel muttered. "Maybe the heat wave is making the whole town go strange."

PROSPECT PARK

HER BACK TO the fence, screams erupted behind Hazel from inside the House of Horrors each time a car rounded the third bend and the skeleton popped out of his grave. It had startled her the first time she rode through, but not the second…or the seventh.

From the ticket booth fifty feet away, a carny barked, "Every ride's an adventure!"

Where are they? Hazel wondered, the sun scalding her scalp the longer she waited. Her boss at the Crock had let her off early for the rodeo. It wasn't looking as though her friends were so lucky.

Looking past the ticket booth to the far side of Prospect Park, she watched two ranch hands complete construction of the rodeo stage by draping red-white-and-blue bunting across the front. Every summer the park was transformed into the rodeo grounds by installing tents, fences, corral pipes and aluminum bleachers. *We're going to burn our asses on those seats,* she thought.

Calliope music started up from the kiddie Go-Gator ride, apt accompaniment to Patience sashaying up. She wore short shorts and a pink tank top, black hair waving halfway down her back, and she pretended not to notice every male over the age of twelve ogling her.

Hazel glanced down at herself, at the cutoff jeans and loose T-shirt she'd thrown on without any consideration, and yanked off the ponytail holder strangling her own long hair.

"Let's go in," Patience greeted her.

"We have to wait for them," Hazel replied.

"No we don't." She tugged at the hem of Hazel's T-shirt. "It's more fun just us."

"We're waiting." Hazel searched Patience's porcelain-doll face for any sign that she might have cracked. But no shame marred her clear skin, no doubt clouded her thick-lashed eyes. Hazel had to ask anyway: "Did you say anything to anybody?"

"No!" Patience appeared taken aback. "You told me not to, so I won't."

"I'm sorry," Hazel murmured. Patience was right: questioning her loyalty was an insult.

Something behind Hazel caught Patience's eye. "They're here," she said, sounding disappointed.

Hazel turned to see Sean and Tanner approaching. Sean toted a brown paper sack just the right shape for a twelve-pack he must've swiped from the Mercantile. When they reached her and Patience, Hazel glanced at the line of tourists baking in the sun at the entrance gate. She started in the opposite direction, saying, "Let's sneak in by the goat pen."

As they casually climbed over the fence and passed eager kids manning 4-H livestock displays, Hazel hoped a new attraction might've shown up this year, like a lobster boy sideshow or pickled punk display. But glancing around, she saw only more of the same: squealing piglets and mean goats, caramel apples sure to give the little kids massive bellyaches, crafty goods and antique farm gear, and rides trucked in and operated by carnies much scarier than an actual turn on the Tilt-A-Whirl or Octopus.

"I'll catch up with you," Patience called over her bare shoulder, making a beeline for the fortune-teller's tent. Decorated with moons and stars, the hand-painted sign out front challenged: *Discover What Lies in Wait—If You Dare.* Daring, Patience disappeared through the clatter of beads that curtained the entrance to the dark tent.

Hazel wondered how many visits Patience would pay to Madame Marcelle this year, and how much mumbo jumbo it would take this time around to quiet the grim expectations that were Patience's constant, chatty companions.

Sean slung an arm across Hazel's shoulders and steered her toward his mother's dessert stand, with Tanner pulling up the rear. And after talking Honey Adair out of three bulging slices of blackberry pie, they made their way to the nearest shade beneath an ancient oak that overhung the duck pond.

Sean plopped onto the low wall surrounding the pond and barked, "Scram!" at the two Rhone girls playing beneath the tree. Ducks scattered as if he'd meant them.

"You're big fat fatheads," said seven-year-old Violet Rhone. "So there." She concluded by sticking out her tongue, bright pink from the cotton candy she was chewing.

"So there," echoed five-year-old Daisy Rhone, accentuated by a swing of her hips.

"That the best you've got?" Hazel laughed. She babysat the round-faced, redheaded sisters on the rare occasion Zachary Rhone took his wife, Melanie, down to Stepstone Valley for a special night out.

Daisy tugged on the front pockets of Hazel's shorts with her little hands. "We're gonna be in the rodeo parade. Will you watch us? You have to!"

"I will, I will!" Hazel promised, prying off Daisy's sticky fingers and then scooting her away with a few pats to her behind. "But you'd better be good," she warned the lingering girls in the most menacing tone she could muster, "or else the bogeyman will getcha."

The sisters took off running, flapping their arms and screaming, "Hawkin Rhone! Hawkin Rhone!" until Daisy ran smack dab into Old Man Mathers' midsection.

Ben Mathers fumbled and his hot dog hit the dirt. Then he glared at Hazel as though it were her fault. Hazel was used to it. Anytime anything bad happened, Mathers blamed a Winslow—even before the death of his wife Lottie. But after that, it had only gotten worse.

He threw up his hands as if to say, *Why do I even bother,* before he marched back to the hot dog stand, his spindly legs poking out of the Bermudas belted just below his chest.

Tanner's laugh was high-pitched. It annoyed Hazel and when she glanced at Sean, his pinched expression told her it bugged him, too.

"Is that Hawkin Rhone?" Tanner asked after he'd caught his breath.

"No." Hazel watched the old man wrangle a free replacement out of the hot dog vendor. "That's Patience's grandfather."

Tanner sat down next to Sean on the low wall. "Then who's Hawkin Rhone?"

Hazel looked at Sean but his face was unreadable—all pie chewing and no emoting. She sank down to the cool grass and sat cross-legged, facing the pond. "He used to be town baker until there was this incident," she told Tanner. "Then he was banished to live out his days across Three Fools Creek. But that was all a long time ago," she added. "He's been dead for a long time."

"Then why's every kid in Winslow so scared of him?" Tanner asked.

She glanced at Sean again, who pretended to pay no attention. "He's a restless spirit." She fluttered her fingers like *ooowheeooo.* "He'll getcha for filching apples out of his orchard." Hazel always found it odd that Violet and Daisy, especially, seemed to savor living in a constant state of dread of their grandfather's ghost. She prayed they would never know what haunted really felt like.

Several ducks moved back in, lingering not too close but

on the lookout for leftovers, while an irritating tune looped from the Gravitron across the pond.

Tanner spit a mouthful of pie to the ground and then sniffed at his slice. "Does this taste weird?"

Sean inspected his. "It's all right, I guess." He forked in another mouthful.

"Here ya go, Jinx," Hazel said, holding out her untouched slice to the approaching Irish setter. Despite competition from one brave duck, the dog snatched it off the paper plate. After the two seconds it took him to devour it, he stood panting berry breath in her face. "No more." She held up empty hands.

Jinx decided to perform his doggy duty by chasing away the ducks in a chaos of barking and quacking. Then he loped over to Sean, tried his best to look deserving, and licked his chops.

"Not this one, buddy." Sean tore into his pie with exaggerated relish.

Jinx chuffed in indignation before giving up, resigned to sprawl on the grass next to Hazel.

Tanner began tearing off chunks of piecrust and chucking them at the ducks. "So what's the deal with Patience? Is she unclaimed goods or what?"

Sean was rinsing his hands in the pond. "All yours, man."

"I just might get me a slice of that country pie," Tanner said. He had a growing fan club in the ducks, vying for the last of his food.

Hazel grimaced. "Country pie?"

Sean affected a Western drawl: "Round these parts we refer to little gals like Patience Mathers as low-hanging fruit."

"Not low enough to go out with Kenny Clark twice," Hazel reminded him.

"Yeah, but remember what happened the last time we were in Stepstone? We weren't at Gino's long enough to get our pizza before she took off with some skate punk to the back-seat of his Nova."

"I suppose she does allow herself to be easy pickins," Hazel admitted. "Sometimes."

"Sounds like my kind of girl." Tanner grinned wider than Hazel cared for, making her instantly regret that she'd told him anything at all about Patience. Tanner reached for the paper bag, saying, "Let's drink this beer before it gets any warmer."

Digging into the bag after Tanner, Sean retrieved two cans and handed one to Hazel just as she noticed Patience returning from the fortune-teller's tent looking rattled.

"Hey, juicy fruit," Tanner called to Patience.

Hazel sat up and slapped him hard on his bare arm while Sean made a noise somewhere between a snort and a laugh.

Patience ignored them; her eyes were fixed on Hazel and she came in close to her face. "Madame Marcelle says something's itching to be set in motion."

"Patience!" Hazel rolled her eyes and pushed her away. "Stop looking for more trouble."

"Yeah, enough with the prophecy shit already," Sean said.

"In threes," Patience blurted as if she simply had to get it out. "They'll come in threes."

"Enough," Hazel said. Already on edge, she didn't need Patience's superstitious hooey added to the queasy mix. They had plenty of real problems on their hands; why invent more?

"Okay, okay," Patience surrendered. Settling primly on the grass, she accepted a beer from Tanner only after first glancing around to make sure no one was looking.

"Maybe it's Hawkin Rhone itchin' for you." Tanner made clawing motions toward her neck. "Scritch scritch."

"Get away!" Patience cringed.

Tanner shrugged. "You're the one who brought it up."

She made a sour face at him. "I'm talking about what the future holds. Not the past."

"I know exactly what the future holds," Hazel said. "I'm leaving this rotting leftover of a town."

Tanner burped and crumpled up his beer can. "I'm with you—this place totally sucks."

"You've only been here two weeks," Sean said. "What the hell do *you* know?"

"That here is *nowhere* and that nobody gives a shit what goes on up here." He tossed his can toward the garbage bin and missed just as Kohl and Tilly Thacker walked by. They cast him twin shaming glares. "Not that anything does go on that I've seen."

"How can you say that?" Hazel asked. "Sometimes we get deliveries from Darryl the mail lady *and* Fritz Earley the grain guy in the very same week." She pitched her can and made it into the bin.

Tanner smirked, popping open another. "You could all eat each other over the winter and nobody would even know until the pass thawed."

"You're right." Patience's eyes went wide and she took a noisy sip. "That's scary."

"Don't listen to him," Sean said. "He's completely full of shit."

"A Donner Party waiting to happen," Hazel muttered. Jinx twitched in his sleep beside her. She rubbed his soft belly and whispered, "It's only a bad dream, boy."

"You just don't know yet," Patience told Tanner, one hand on her hip. "We've got a lot to offer here." She gestured wide.

"Are you offering me something?"

Flustered, she looked to Hazel for help. "I just meant…"

"All right already," Sean said. "Give it a rest. Let's finish these beers and go on a ride."

"Can't." Patience rose and repositioned her shorts. "I have to go change for the rodeo."

"Knock 'em dead," Hazel told her as she was leaving.

Tanner stood and announced, "I gotta get ready, too."

"What for?" Sean asked.

Tanner hitched his thumbs through his belt loops and cocked his head. "I'm ridin' in this here rodeo."

"You're *joking*," Hazel said.

"Nope. Calf-roping contest. Uncle Pard's letting me use his horse. Says Blackjack'll know what to do. I just gotta hold on and swing the rope around the little cheeseburger's neck."

Hazel blew out her breath like *oh, boy,* while Sean scoffed. Tanner turned and started to walk away. "I've been practicing," he said.

"Break a leg!" Sean called, and Hazel noticed Tanner's stride stiffen.

Sean handed her another can, which she took and held against her hot forehead.

"Think the Tilt-A-Whirl will make us puke after all this beer?" Sean asked.

Placing her can against his cheek because he looked overheated, too, Hazel said, "Every ride's an adventure."

IT WAS DIFFICULT for Hazel to decide who was the bigger blowhard: her father or her uncle.

First her dad took the stage above the rodeo field. Looking hot as blazes in his uniform, he droned on for a good five minutes, welcoming the out-of-towners and espousing Winslow's many glories harking back to the boom days of the town's founding in 1888. Shamelessly he tossed words like "grit" and "mettle" and "pluck" all over the oval ring.

They're already here, Dad, thought Hazel. *Enough with the sales pitch.*

Then, dressed in parade chaps and his customary scowl, her Uncle Pard wrested the microphone away and lectured on a vanishing way of life and the joys of freshly slaughtered beef, until finally: "It's great y'all got out here to support us. Now enjoy the show!"

"Get *on* with the show already!" Sean yelled from beside her.

They'd jostled their way onto an area of the bleachers with a modicum of shade but it was still hot and Tilly Thacker sitting on the other side of Hazel smelled like damp laundry.

Hazel swiveled to take in the sweating crowd of tourists and what looked to be every soul in Winslow and thought, *What am I doing here?*

Turning forward, she placed her cheek against Sean's shoulder and whispered, "I wonder if Doc Simmons figured out what's wrong with the cattle yet. I don't see him here, do you?"

Sean shook his head just as Rose Peabody, Hazel's boss at the Crock, squeezed by, struggling to maintain the integrity of her flimsy cardboard drink tray. She lost the battle and splashed cola on Hazel's legs.

"Wonderful," Hazel said, feeling cold, sticky soda dribble down her calves. "That feels great."

"I'm so sorry, Hazel!" Rose cried, looking even more like Olive Oyl than usual with her skinny arms bared and her dark hair gathered in a low, fat bun. "I've been really light-headed all day." She shook her head as if to clear it.

"It's all right," Hazel said. "Please just sit down before you lose the rest of it." Though Hazel rolled her eyes, it was impossible for her to ever be truly annoyed with Rose. No matter how many times a day Hazel had ventured into the Crock that first summer after her mother left, Rose had never failed to give her a gentle hug and an extra-large scoop of rainbow sherbet.

Now, as Hazel watched Rose maneuver toward an open seat, she grew concerned; Rose didn't look so good and Hazel worried she might faint and go tumbling down the bleachers, her bony Olive Oyl limbs knocking people in the head all the way to the ground.

Sean was wiping soda from Hazel's thighs with the hem of his T-shirt. "Think the ants will find us soon?" he asked.

Before Hazel could fully contemplate that possibility, drums started up from behind the stands. From the stage, her father announced, "First, some local talent."

"If you want to call it that," Hazel said.

"Whoa," Sean said, "check her out."

The crowd cheered as Patience rode her appaloosa mare, Trixie, onto the field. Patience was outfitted head to toe in American cowgirl regalia: pure-white hat, red-suede vest festooned with silver stripes, and fringed blue chaps studded with rhinestone stars.

"She's really outdone herself this time," Hazel said.

"Freak," Sean said.

As her horse galloped around the ring, Patience beamed, shiny eyes scanning the crowd.

"Bouncing in all the right places," the guy in front of Sean felt the need to say out loud.

"Giddy up, cowgirl," his pal added.

"Can you believe these smooth talkers don't have dates?" Hazel said loud enough that they both turned around to glare at her. She scowled back; she always bristled when jerks like these two salivated over her friend.

After Trixie performed a high-stepping, back-and-forth sort of dance that Hazel knew had taken Patience a month to perfect, the horse cantered up to the stage steps where Patience dismounted gracefully enough.

Next, the rodeo clown shuffled onto the field to the accompaniment of the Stepstone Valley High School band's jerky rendition of Queen's "We Will Rock You."

Hazel stared in disbelief: Zachary Rhone as the clown? She'd always considered the baker to be wound way too tight. So tight, in fact, that he'd always scared her a little, as if at any moment he might snap into sharp, angry pieces. Made scarier still, thanks to her Uncle Pard's threat looming over them that he'd tell Zachary what really happened to his father. Yet here Zachary was, garbed in gigantic patched overalls and a bright red wig. She turned to Sean. "What's he doing as the rodeo clown?"

"Got me." Sean's brown eyes narrowed. "Not a funny bone in that guy."

Violet and Daisy Rhone were on the field now, too, along with a squadron of other little girls. Several were armed with pom-poms, others had batons; all were dancing offbeat to the music.

"Looks like Patience has some competition," Sean said.

The band members marched around looking miserable, sweating it out beneath tall hats with yellow plumes. Behind them, Ben Mathers and Cal from the Fish 'n Bait and a few other old fogies wearing fezzes goose-stepped onto the field carrying Washington state and American flags.

"Are we the only locals who aren't in this show?" Hazel asked, shifting in her seat. Her bottom was already aching from the metal bleacher, and thanks to all that beer, her bladder felt ready to burst.

Sean pushed hair off his forehead and smirked. "Nobody in my family is."

"Lucky you," she said. But as she watched her dad clapping along on the stage, in his element, her humiliation gave way to relief at the sight of him so much happier than he'd been that morning.

Then everyone simmered down while Winslow's favorite bartender Marlene Spainhower gave "The Star-Spangled Banner" her all…and erupted in cheers at her short-winded conclusion.

With the opening pomp out of the way, her Uncle Pard again took the microphone. "Today I'm proud to announce that my own nephew will be first up in the calf roping competition. Let's all give a big hand for Tanner Holloway on Blackjack!"

A few scattered claps sounded across the bleachers while Pard took off his hat and wiped his face with a blue bandanna. Hazel recognized that bandanna from last night, and thought her uncle was doing a bang-up job of pretending all things were precisely as they should be in Winslow.

She looked over at the bucking chutes to see Tanner mounted and ready with a loop of rope in one hand, another in his mouth. His right hand gripped the saddle horn for dear life.

"This, I gotta see." Sean sat forward, a sadistic grin on his face.

The cowhands released the calf and swung open Tanner's chute gate but Blackjack just sat there until Kenny Clark smacked him hard on the rump. Then the horse bolted—kicking out behind and getting elevation—and Tanner instantly lost hold of the rope and saddle. He slid down and off the side, still hooked to the animal by one foot caught in the stirrup, dragging in the dirt until Blackjack finally shook him free and chased after the calf.

Tanner pushed himself up from the dirt, humiliation washing over his face.

Hazel pressed her fingers to her forehead. "Uncle Pard should've known that would happen."

"No kidding. I almost feel sorry for him," Sean said. "Almost."

Clown Zachary tried to escort Tanner off the field but Tanner shoved him away and hobbled off on his own, the crowd laughing at the spectacle of Blackjack still pursuing the calf.

"And my uncle wonders why I show no interest in being a rancher," Hazel said.

"All right," Pard shouted overly loud into the mic. "Simmer down, folks. Up next we've got Holloway Ranch buckaroo Kenny Clark. Let's show 'em how it's done, Ken."

At only nineteen, Hazel's least favorite ranch hand already bore the leathered face of the older cowpokes. She had no doubt the filterless cigarettes Kenny smoked helped that look along. But the weirdest thing to her about the Clarks was that they weren't even from Winslow—they *chose* to move here.

Kenny shot out of the chute, lariat swinging high above his head, and lassoed the calf in seconds. To the cheers of the audience, he leapt off his horse, picked up the calf and slammed it down on its side. Then he tied three of the terrified creature's bony legs together with his rope. Triumphant, Kenny stood to face the crowd, sucking up the applause.

"Not much of a match," Hazel said, flashing on the furry little calf from last night and the way his blood had turned the white crescent moon markings on his face a deep red.

"Yeah, Kenny's the kind of guy who gets off on torturing small defenseless animals," Sean said.

"And shooting calves," Hazel added. "Psychopath."

By the time Kenny's mother, Maggie Clark, finished the trick-riding routine she performed every year, the rodeo had been underway only half an hour but already dust was everywhere and Hazel could barely make out what was taking place down on the field.

Tilly Thacker leaned close to Hazel, her stench wafting in with her. "Anabel Holloway was the best trick rider we ever had in Winslow." She gave a pitying sigh. "The best."

Hazel crinkled her nose and recoiled from Tilly against Sean, her blood beginning to boil. What right did this nosy old bat have telling Hazel anything about Anabel Holloway?

Apparently overhearing, Sean put his arm around Hazel and pulled her closer. Too hot and agitated for comfort, she shrugged him off.

Following the applause for Maggie, it got quiet again, the dust settled, and Pard announced the bull-riding contest. "Some of you already know Indigo," he said, "and that there's never been a rider this boss couldn't toss. Now let's see if we can't break that downright disgraceful four-second record and get us a real eight-second ride! Are you ready?"

The audience cheered and whistled.

Indigo chuffed and snorted in his chute as the bull rider lowered himself onto the animal's broad back. Hazel had heard someone in the Crock say that he was an out-of-town cowboy trying his luck with this bull of some reputation; none of the local ranch hands would ride him twice.

After the cowboy adjusted his rope, he gripped it hard with his gloved right hand. His left arm hung balanced in the air. When he nodded to Old Pete, the chute gate flew open.

In a clang of cowbells the bull shot straight up before he slammed down and out of the chute, whipping the cowboy back and forth. In defiance of his incredible bulk Indigo bucked high again and the cowboy's feet flew into the air. Somehow the cowboy recovered and held on.

Going on three seconds now, it looked as though the cowboy was about to break the infamous record when all of a sudden Indigo cracked his tremendous body sideways and simply shuddered to a stop, leaning precariously as if gravity might get the better of him and send him crashing to the dirt.

After a moment the bull lurched forward, taking each step gingerly as if he weren't certain the ground would hold him. Hazel and Sean exchanged stunned looks while the audience dropped dead silent.

Clearly unsure as to what to do, the cowboy remained on the bull but looked nervously around the ring while the animal continued its slow, cautious advance.

Weaving around in his clown barrel, Zachary danced in front of Indigo, occasionally darting closer to kick the bull on the rump, trying to provoke the creature into more spirited action. When even that didn't work, Old Pete rode up on horseback and pulled the cowboy off the bull. Zachary then scrambled the confused man off the field while Old Pete headed toward the stage to consult with Pard, who had shut off the mic but could still be heard shouting, "What the hell is going on?"

Hazel looked to the front of the stage where her dad suddenly seemed smaller...and much farther away. In the silence it struck her how bright everything appeared; how exposed the fifteen-hundred-pound bull looked standing stock-still now in the stark sunlight.

And then Indigo's legs began to shake.

Alarmed murmurs rose from the crowd, like sound sleepers woken in the dead of night.

"Oh, no," Hazel whispered. The bull was trembling exactly as the red cow had yesterday before she crumpled to the grass. Watching the solid bull shake, Hazel feared the whole mountaintop just might crash down on their heads next.

She looked at Sean, who was shaking his head as if to say, *This is* not *good*.

"Sit tight, folks," Pard commanded from the stage. "We've got it handled."

Old Pete rode up behind Indigo and the bull twisted around, lowered his massive head, and lined up his horns with the oncoming horse. Kenny Clark came at the bull from the side and tossed his rope, but he overshot the horns and the rope looped around the animal's neck instead. Rather than drop the rope, Kenny pulled it tight. Though his rope was clearly digging into the bull's neck, he pulled even tighter. Then another ranch hand charged in from the opposite direction and roped the bull by the horns.

After Pete repositioned his horse behind Indigo, Kenny and the other cowboy turned their horses hard, yanking the bull forward while Pete hounded his haunches, and the horses began to pull Indigo off the field in a bawl of protest.

Shouts of outrage erupted from the bleachers. Many stood

and craned their necks. And a collective gasp sucked all the air out of the park when Indigo's front legs buckled and his powerful chest hit the dirt. His back legs gave out next and his body collapsed to the ground in an explosion of dust.

Even then, the cowboys did not release the ropes. Instead, they dug in their spurs, urging the horses on, dragging the bull by the horns and the neck.

"Sheriff oughta do something," Hazel heard a man say. She looked at her father, who stood uncharacteristically paralyzed. Only his eyes moved, following the bull.

Blood wept from Indigo's neck where rope chafed flesh and the bull twisted and struggled to get to his feet with those cowbells still clanging like mad.

Clown Zachary danced in front of the bleachers, trying to distract the audience, failing to accomplish anything except looking like the complete idiot that he was.

Hazel glanced around at the crowd. It was clear that while they knew the bull wasn't right, they also felt this treatment was very wrong. Boos and empty beer cups rained down on the field until the audience finally lost sight of the bull behind the corral. But everyone could still hear Indigo bellowing.

A shot cracked, and after the horses whinnied, all was quiet again.

Until Pard Holloway's voice boomed in the stunned silence. "Everything's fine, folks. Stay where you are."

But people were leaving, heading down the bleacher aisles toward the exit, grumbling and tossing trash.

"Hold on," Pard ordered. "We'll just take a quick break here. Get things tidied up. So go ahead and grab a cold one but get right back to your seats. Saddle bronc riding is up next."

It was no use; Hazel could see it on their faces. Everyone felt hot and unsettled, and the animals were beginning to smell rank.

Sean turned to her. "That was fucking harsh."

"Yeah…" She looked first at him, then at the stage where her dad still stood dumbstruck.

And a strange look crossed Patience's face right before she shot forward and vomited all over the stage, splashing the outfit she'd fussed over for weeks along with the Sheriff's shiny shoes.

"Oh, my God," Hazel gasped. "What's wrong with Patience?"

Sean made a disgusted sound before running the back of his hand across his mouth. "I hope it's not catching."

Beside Hazel, Tilly complained, "I feel sick, too."

"It's that Holloway beef," Tilly's husband, Kohl Thacker, said loud and clear. "Heard his animals have come down sick at the ranch."

Tiny Clemshaw stopped next to the Thackers in the aisle, gesturing at them to keep it down. Then discreetly, as if he didn't want the passing tourists to overhear, he leaned in and said, "It's worse than that." He glanced at the tourists again before adding: "I'm no friend of Holloway's, but we best keep this to ourselves, you know, for all of our sakes."

Hazel turned to Sean and silently mouthed, "They know." Relief washed over her. Though it didn't bode well for her uncle, at least now she no longer had to hide what she knew.

But then a cold fist clenched her heart. Taking Sean by the hand, she whispered, "*How* do they know?"

His eyes widened.

And Hazel shuddered in sudden panic. "Will Pard blame this on us?"

SATURDAY AFTERNOON
ROSE'S COUNTRY CROCK
FORTUNE WAY

As soon as Rose Peabody swung open the door, Winslow locals piled in and filled all of the Crock's thirty-odd seats. Nearly everybody ordered catwiches: Owen Peabody's famous fresh-fried catfish sandwiches.

Left with an hour's wait for a table in the Crock, most of the tourists decided to head out of town and grab a bite down Yellow Jacket Pass in Stepstone Valley. Those with more pressing hunger wandered back to Prospect Park and the Holloway Ranch barbecue tent, where they ate beans and brownies and Maggie Clark's corn bread. Nobody felt much like eating burgers.

SATURDAY NIGHT
MATHERSTON GHOST TOWN

OUTSIDE THE MOTHER LODE SALOON, Hazel parked her motorcycle next to the other two—horse-style in front of the hitching post. The waxing moon slung low over Silver Hill illuminated the tumbledown buildings on Prospectors Way, while the stagnant air trapped the day's heat. Still feeling disturbed over all that had happened at the rodeo, Matherston seemed to Hazel—for the first time—genuinely ghosty.

She scooted off her bike and hustled up to the boardwalk, worried that dallying would enable a pack of ghouls to descend upon her as surely as a swarm of mosquitoes.

Unlike downtown Winslow's ornate Italianate architecture, the old miner's section of town consisted of simple wood-frame structures bleached gray by the sun. Some of the buildings leaned left, some right, or as with Holloway Harness and the Chop House Restaurant, caved in straight down the middle. Long-faded signs and advertisements had been painted directly onto siding and overhangs: *Hank's Boarding House / Hot Baths—10¢ ~ Towel and Soap Free.*

No fussing or mussing here, Hazel thought as she pushed her way through the saloon's batwing doors. Matherston had been all about business, once: mining and assaying, shoeing horses and repairing wagons, and the serious business of boozing, gambling and whoring.

Hazel joined Sean, Patience and Tanner at the long pine

bar, where a hand-painted sign above the rifle rack ordered: *Check all Guns with Bartender.*

Sean lit a lantern with his lighter while Tanner doled out warmish cans of beer.

Holding a can toward Patience, Tanner said, "Quite a show you put on today." When she didn't take the beer, he slammed the can onto the bar and slid it her way. "Drink up—carbonation helps when you're sick to your stomach."

She groaned and pushed the can away.

"You're one to talk, Tanner," Hazel said. "Who made a bigger ass out of himself today, really?"

He scowled. "I don't want to talk about it."

"Okay, so quit hassling her." She turned to Patience. "How do you feel now?"

"Better. Not great." Putting a hand to her forehead, she tilted back her head and in an overdone Southern accent declared, "Ah'm sufferin' a toucha the vapors."

Hazel laughed. "Seriously—did you eat something that made you sick?"

"I'm not sure. It could've been the heat and the smells and Indigo screaming like that." Patience sighed in disgust. "I still can't believe I barfed in front of our whole town."

Tanner slowly shook his head. "Eating a burger was a big mistake. Why'd you do it?"

"She didn't." Sean sounded fed up. "Veggie burger, maybe."

"I don't eat anything that has a face," Patience said.

Hazel had been weighing whether or not to broach the subject with Tanner. Finally, she said, "I wonder how everybody in town found out about the cattle so quick."

Tanner stared at her as if she were dense. Then he stuck his finger on her upper chest. "Um, that would be…you." Hazel's heart stuttered as his hand moved past her to point at Sean. "And you."

Sean smacked his hand away. "Bullshit."

Patience shrank back as if worried the accusatory finger would taint her next.

"Does Uncle Pard think that?" Hazel asked, her heart refusing to settle into a steady beat.

"Hell if I know." Tanner was scrutinizing her face. "You didn't blab?"

"No." She grabbed the sleeve of his T-shirt. "So don't *ever* say that we did."

"Why didn't you?" He flicked away her hand, then narrowed his eyes at her. "What's Uncle Pard got on you, anyhow?"

Hazel avoided looking at Sean and Patience, avoided speaking the name that echoed in her mind: Hawkin Rhone. Instead, she said, "He told us he'd have us drawn and quartered if we said a word. And scatter our body parts around the pasture for a vulture feast." She shrugged unconvincingly. "He'll do whatever it takes to protect his ranch."

"No kidding. I can't believe they shot Indigo," Tanner said with zero emotion. "Wish they'd shoot that glue bag Blackjack next."

Patience rubbed her hands up and down her bare arms as if she felt cold, only it was still at least ninety degrees out. "What's the matter with all the cows anyway?"

"Who knows?" Tanner said. "And who cares?" He popped open another beer.

Hazel took a long swig from her own, hoping the alcohol would dull the edge on her increasingly sharp dread. "Doc Simmons hasn't figured out what's wrong yet?"

"Nope. He was poking around the pasture all morning. Picking weeds and scooping up shit." Tanner chucked his can through an empty window frame. "Why doesn't somebody just bulldoze this whole crappy place?"

"Can't do that." Patience blinked hard, as if incredulous that he'd even suggest it. "Where would the spirits go?"

"What spirits?"

"Don't ask," Hazel said, grateful for the change to a less frightening subject.

"Dead miners." Sean seemed relieved, too. "Badass son-of-a-bitch ghosts. You do not wanna mess with 'em. Believe me."

"Screw those dead miners." Tanner wrenched off a piece of wood from the lip of the bar and pretended to throw it toward the casket-sized mirror hanging on the opposite side.

"Don't do it!" Patience reached for his arm. "It's bad luck!"

"Bawk, bawk," Sean made like a chicken.

Tanner swiveled away from Patience, pulled back, and flung the wood hard. They all watched the clouded mirror crack, hold for a split second, then shatter into scores of pieces that plinked noisily to the wood floor.

Sensing Patience's distress, Hazel put a hand on her friend's shoulder.

"Oh…" Patience whispered. "Oh, no."

"What?" Tanner raised his hands in mock innocence.

Patience placed her fingers over her lips and slowly shook her head.

"Don't tell us," Sean said, flicking his lighter on and off. "Three years' bad luck."

"Seven," Hazel corrected, desiring to lighten the mood. "But is that seven for Tanner or seven divided by the four of us?"

Patience stared, unblinking, at the dark rectangle of wallpaper where the mirror had hung.

"Guess those ghosts'll be haunting me now," Tanner tried to joke with Patience and when that didn't work, he looked at Hazel with *whoops* written all over his face.

"There'll be no hiding from them," Hazel confirmed. Thanks to recent reminders of horrors past, she feared those words just might be true.

Patience spun to face Tanner. "You should've listened to me. It'll be worse than that."

Accustomed as Hazel was to the dire predictions of Winslow's rodeo queen, she still felt bees in her stomach. Hazel looked behind the bar at the fragments of mirror still clinging to soiled wallpaper, alive with the light of the lantern, and heard Patience add, "For all of us."

SUNDAY MORNING
FORTUNE WAY

Day Three of the Heat Wave

FRETFUL, HAZEL HAD hardly slept the night before. And two restless nights in a row had left her feeling dazed and disoriented, as if she were lost at sea. Strolling along in the early sunlight, she tried to convince herself that it was quite simple, really. Vet Simmons would figure out what was wrong, give the cattle medicine, and everything would go back to normal. Simple.

She popped into the Mercantile to pick up groceries for her grandmother and boxes of Lemonheads and jawbreakers for herself. She had it bad for candy—the harder the better—and her dad kept warning her that she was bound to crack a tooth. Walking down the humming, refrigerated aisle, she placed milk, eggs and ice cream into her basket. Her grandmother loved dairy, which maybe explained how she'd managed to get so old without ever breaking a hip.

After Hazel made her way to the front of the store, she spotted Aaron Adair and his buddy Tim Hotchkiss. Both stood staring into the big freezer next to the cash register, paralyzed, it seemed, by the enormity of the decision at hand. Sundae cup or ice-cream sandwich? Drumstick or Rocket Pop? The wrong choice certain to lead to a torment of unfulfilled desire. She noticed that Aaron was also holding a half-eaten glazed donut, which she suspected he'd procured from Sean at the bakery.

"Gonna give yourself a bellyache," Hazel said, walking up to the boy.

Aaron glanced at the donut in his hand as if he'd forgotten he was holding it. Then he announced to no one in particular: "I'm going home."

Timmy tore his eyes away from the freezer treats. "Why?"

Alarmed, Hazel took a step closer to Aaron. "Is something wrong?"

"I don't feel so good." He dropped the donut to the floor. "I see floaty things."

"Okay—hold on a sec." Hazel reached for his hand. "I'm going to The Winslow, too."

But Aaron was already rushing for the store entrance with Timmy calling after him, "Are we still goin' fishing later?"

Anxious to follow Aaron so that she could make sure he made it home all right, Hazel hurried her purchases up to Tiny Clemshaw at the cash register.

Tiny Clemshaw was a rangy, middle-aged man with a cotton ball of a face: no distinct features, everything just melded together in confusing white fuzz. "That it?" he asked.

No "Good morning," no "How are you today, Hazel Winslow," just "That it?" And she noticed he looked extra pasty today. But his was the only store in town so there was no avoiding him.

"That's it," she said and dug into her pocket for yesterday's tip money and pulled out a handful of crumpled singles.

"Thirteen-sixty then," Tiny said, tossing her items into a paper sack with uncharacteristic carelessness. Eggs on bottom, milk on top.

She noticed then that skinny streams of sweat were running down from his forehead, tracing the blue veins in his temples. "Are you all right, Tiny?"

"Thirteen-sixty," he repeated and a fat drop of sweat slipped into her grocery sack.

As she opened her mouth to protest, Tiny said, "And ask your father to come round next time you see him. Somebody's been busting into my cooler and stealing my beer."

Oops, Hazel thought. Maybe she'd just forget to mention that to her dad.

As it turned out, she never did get a chance to not mention it.

THE GHOSTS OF WINSLOW

THE TROUBLE AARON was having keeping the handlebars of his bike straight was only one of his problems. His stomach was churning and he was determined to make it home before he threw up. When they were in the first grade, Timmy barfed in Prospect Park after too many spins on the merry-go-round, and the other kids had never let him live it down: "Look out— he's gonna blow!" Aaron didn't want to be teased like that, too.

Peddling like mad up Fortune Way, he spotted his Uncle Jim heading into the Buckhorn Tavern. Uncle Jim always used to let Aaron ride on his shoulders, making the boy feel tall, too, and Aaron was just about to call out to his uncle when he caught himself...because Uncle Jim didn't belong here anymore.

Just keep quiet. Aaron broke out in a sweat. *Just get home.*

He pedaled faster, panting and sweating like crazy, trying not to crash his bike; he could barely see straight, let alone steer. Suddenly Uncle Jim appeared in the middle of the road, gesturing at Aaron to slow down. Instead, Aaron sped up, swerving at the last moment to dodge his uncle's spectral grasp.

Speeding recklessly, he carved the street corner and raced up Civic Street. Up ahead, the gurgling lady with the blood gushing out of her neck was slowly making her way up the walkway to the library. Just as he feared, she stopped to stare straight at him as he approached. He could turn around—but Uncle Jim was back there. So he rode faster, racing past the lady before she could sprint down the walkway and embrace him in her bloody arms.

What are they doing out here? Aaron wondered, both amazed and horrified. *How'd they get loose?* Then, an even more disturbing thought: *Did someone let them out on purpose?*

At least he was almost home. But when he popped onto Ruby Road, his relief gave way to terror. He turned his bike sideways, nearly laying it down, and skidded to a stop.

Less than ten feet away, a red-haired wolf blocked the road. The creature lowered his huge head and started for Aaron, orange eyes glowering at the boy, big paws slapping the street.

Aaron glanced over his shoulder, desperate for an escape route.

His heart froze midbeat.

Not only was the gurgling lady coming up fast behind him, so was Uncle Jim's ghost. Worse still, the other lady had joined them, the one who looked like Patience Mathers except her white skin was wrinkled and her dark hair and long dress were sopping wet.

Aaron did the only thing he could do. He closed his eyes. He closed his eyes and willed them all to go away.

It didn't work; he could still hear them, growing louder, getting closer: the wolf's claws scraping loose blacktop, the bloody lady gurgling, the drowning woman dripping, and his Uncle Jim asking, "Whatsamatter, boy? Don't you wanna ride?"

THE WINSLOW HOTEL

WHEN HAZEL ARRIVED at The Winslow, she was relieved to spot Aaron's bike at the base of the porch steps, carelessly pitched on its side, handlebars askew. Apparently Aaron had made it home safe, if not entirely sound.

Jinx bounded down the steps from the porch to join her. The red dog looked guilty somehow, his eyes a little too gleeful, his tail wagging a bit too hard.

"What have you been up to?" Hazel asked.

Jinx kept mum, choosing instead to sniff at Aaron's front bike tire.

"I better not find out you were chasing Aaron on his bike," Hazel warned the Irish setter. "Or terrorizing Ajax or Boo or any other cat."

The dog's expression changed to one of such profound innocence it was impossible to argue with him. "Okay, I believe you," Hazel said, quickly adding, "this time."

Since she needed to unload the groceries, Hazel walked through the side yard and then directly into the kitchen, where she found her grandmother at the big stove working over her cast-iron Dutch oven, pulverizing apples into applesauce. Sarah Winslow glanced up wearing the same look of delight she always donned to greet her only grandchild.

"Aaron's not feeling well," Hazel said, feeling uneasy herself because she'd rather be any kind of sick than sick to her stomach. She plopped the grocery sack onto the butcher-block countertop before remembering that Tiny had packed the eggs on the bottom.

"I know," Sarah made a sympathetic face. "He barely made it through the front door before he got sick in the lobby. Didn't you see Honey cleaning it up?"

"Luckily, no."

"Honey's under the weather, too. Maybe the entire Adair family ate something off." Sarah glanced around the kitchen as if the guilty dish might reveal itself.

"I don't know about Honey," Hazel said, "but it wouldn't surprise me if Aaron got sick from eating one too many treats this morning."

"That boy's sweet tooth *is* out of control." Her grandmother spied the box of candy peeking out from the front pocket of Hazel's shorts. "Like somebody else we know."

"Please," Hazel said. "Lemonheads are practically fruit." She stuffed the carton of ice cream into the freezer of the large fridge, shoving vegetables and fish to their proper place in the unreachable back.

Her grandmother came over and pulled the ice cream back out, squinting to read the label because she didn't have her glasses on. "Why'd you buy me this?"

"Because you love rocky road." Hazel took the carton from her and pushed it back in.

"You love rocky road." Whenever Sarah smiled, her bright blue eyes disappeared.

Hazel placed her hands on her hips. "What are you implying?"

But Sarah looked concerned now. "Your father told me he's having trouble with Pard Holloway again."

Hazel's stomach dropped. Had her father found out what happened at the ranch between her and her uncle? How much did her grandmother know? She decided to test the waters before giving her grandmother any information that could make her victim to the same blackmail. "True. Dad didn't want the carnies at the rodeo this year. Said he's had it with their rusty rides and rigged games, that they're not in the best interests of our town. And Uncle Pard said, 'You've got it exactly wrong, as usual, Winslow.'" Hazel deepened her voice in imitation of her uncle: "'Anything that brings in tourist dollars is in the best interests of this town.'"

Sarah shook her head, clearly distressed. "I'm telling you, dear girl, this business at the ranch bodes ill." She took Hazel's right hand and turned it up to inspect the red marks left on her palm post–splinter surgery, seeming to sense that there was a connection. Then Sarah raised her eyes to Hazel's: "Tell me what happened at the rodeo."

"I saw Ben Mathers," Hazel replied matter-of-factly. "Eating a hot dog."

"And?" Sarah asked as though she didn't have all day.

Hazel hesitated, then said, "And something went wrong with Indigo. They had to put him down."

"The bull, I know about. What I want to know is what, exactly, all of this has to do with *you*."

The look on her grandmother's face told her that she was giving her a chance to come clean. And since everyone in town already seemed to know about the cattle crisis—thanks to Tanner's gigantic mouth, she strongly suspected—was there any point in continuing to lie? She just had to leave out a few key details. Like her Uncle Pard's threat. Like what really happened that day five years ago at Three Fools Creek. Like why Hazel was so terrified, deep down, that the incident was rising to the surface like a long-dead catfish: spectral, slippery and foul.

SUNDAY AFTERNOON MATHERSTON MINERS CEMETERY

THEY SAT IN the shade of the granite wall, sweating into crisp yellow weeds. No one in town could recall who built the long squat wall around Matherston Cemetery, or why. It resisted memory; its white face wiped clean each time the snow came. There were no messages written on the wall that afternoon.

Hazel swiveled to admire Sean. The sun lit his eyes a warm color, like the bourbon they'd swipe from his dad when Samuel was so drunk he'd never remember he hadn't been the one to polish it off. Only now, with Sean's blank stare and sweaty face, he appeared feverish.

"Uh, oh…" she said. "Are you feeling sick too?"

He barely turned his head to look at her—too much effort, apparently. "Just hot, I guess."

Looping the front hem of her T-shirt through the neck, she fashioned it into a halter-top. Sean watched her perform this operation with interest. Then she swabbed the sweat pooled on her belly with her palm and wiped it on her shorts. That seemed interesting, too. She leaned back against the wall with a sharp sigh. "Does anybody even care that we're broiling to death up here? And with the stomach flu or something equally nauseating going around on top of that?"

"I don't think anybody gives us much thought between rodeos." He yawned hugely. "Do you suppose that's the end of the Winslow Rodeo?"

"Probably. Quite a finale."

"Do you suppose that's the end of Holloway Ranch?"

"It'd serve my uncle right, wouldn't it? Trying to keep it quiet only makes the whole situation worse. Obviously, it's impossible to keep secrets in this town anyway. I bet if he brought more vets up they'd figure it out. I wonder if anybody down mountain has heard yet."

"Doubt it. Seems like people are whispering today. Like if they talk too loud they'll hear it in the valley. Have you noticed?"

She nodded. "It's creepy." For all she knew, her uncle had something hanging over the head of every citizen of Winslow. It wouldn't surprise her. Maybe he'd been collecting instruments of blackmail for just such an occasion. "Like ghosts sharing secrets," she said.

Sean grinned at her. A lazy, sultry grin. "Are we ghost hunting this summer?"

"Only if you ante up the good candy."

"I can do a lot better than candy." A slight smile played across his features.

Suppressing her own smile, she touched one corner of his lips where they turned up. Then she kissed that mouth she knew almost as well as her own. When her tongue touched his, the heat of him shocked her.

She pulled away and placed her hand against his forehead. "Sean—you are so hot!"

He took her hand and tugged her back to him, eyes teasing. "Then where are you going?"

She sprang to her feet, held her hand down to him, and hauled him up. "We need to douse you in Three Fools Creek."

He blew a hot frustrated breath in her face…then he turned his back and bolted.

"Wait!" she called, chasing after him through the graveyard, laughing. "Wait for me!"

IN THE STINGY bit of sunshine the tree canopy allowed to pass, the surface of Three Fools Creek shimmered. "It's *too* pretty," Hazel decided.

Nodding, Sean poked at a mound of wet leaves with a stick. "Foolish to fall for it."

For beneath its sparkle, the creek raged. Three miners had drowned trying to cross the creek at high water after a wet spring like this. But unlike Hawkin Rhone, the miners had been buried proper in Matherston Cemetery.

Hazel stepped back to study the boulders that jutted up along the bank like crooked tombstones. When she looked at Sean again he was staring at Hawkin Rhone's cabin across the creek. In complete collapse now, the old prospector's shack was barely visible beneath a patient blackberry bush.

"Why did we go over there?" she asked.

He shook his head. "Seemed like a good idea at the time."

"Wish he'd stop haunting us."

"Don't worry." He reached for her hand. "Curse is on my head, not yours."

She pulled away, wagging her finger at him in a mock scold. "That's right, Adair—it's up to you to keep Hawkin Rhone in his grave."

He blinked at her. Then he gave her a long, puzzled look before saying, "You're right."

"What are you talking about?"

"I'm going over there," he said, his face marked by distress now.

His expression made her extremely uneasy. "We agreed we'd *never* go back."

"I have to. I have to make sure."

"Make sure what?"

"That he's still buried."

She spun him by the shoulder to face her. "I was only kidding. What's wrong with you?"

He stepped closer to the turbulent water. "I'm going over."

"You're out of your mind. This is *not* funny. Let's go."

"Hold on. I'll make it quick." He took off his tennis shoes and moved down the muddy bank.

She shot a glance at the crumbled cabin, knowing that her dad and Dr. Foster had buried Hawkin Rhone not far from the porch. Reaching for Sean, she said, "Okay, ha-ha, joke's over—"

An explosive splitting sound from behind them caused both to whirl and face the woods.

After listening for a silent moment, Hazel asked, "Rifle shot?"

Sean scrambled into his shoes, the violent sound evidently bringing him back to his senses. "Sounded more like a tree snapping."

Another sharp crack issued, this time from the place up the creek where the water ran black—closer now to where they stood straining to hear and see into the dark woods.

Her heart pounding, Hazel grabbed Sean and whispered, "Bigfoot."

"Like hell," he said too loud.

"I'm telling you, there have been all sorts of sightings lately."

"Not here."

"Why not here?"

"Hey, Bigfoot! Hazel Winslow wants to meet you!"

"Shush!" She smacked his arm. But he'd succeeded in making her feel silly rather than scared. She looked him in the eye. "I think *you're* afraid."

He smiled at her. "Maybe."

"Don't worry—I'll protect you."

"Your record isn't so good."

"I will. Promise." She gestured across her chest: "Cross my heart and hope to die."

A fish jumped in the creek behind them, making a plopping sound that startled them both.

Sean pulled her tight. "Protect me, Hazel!"

She shook him off and turned to go. "You need psychiatric help," she decided.

"I got your psychiatric help right here," Sean said.

Hazel swiveled back to find him lighting a joint. After a guilty yet brief consideration of her father's warning that they'd better not've bought weed from Cyclone Clyde, she plucked the joint from Sean's fingers. "You know, I think I feel a touch of insanity coming on, too." She took a deep hit and passed it back to him. Then, from her back pocket, she pulled the bottle of eye drops she always carried and gave each eye a squirt. "I have to get back," she said. "I'm working dinner shift." She took up the trail.

"Just admit it," Sean called after her, "you've always needed me to protect you."

She continued down the path for a few moments before realizing that he was no longer behind her. Turning around she found Sean several yards back, leaning against a lodgepole pine, arms folded across his stomach.

She ran to him and tried to catch him by the arm but he slid down the tree into a crouching position.

Squatting before him, she asked, "What's wrong?"

His long brown hair was suddenly drenched in perspiration. She pushed it off his forehead while he looked at her with swimmy eyes, as if he couldn't get them to focus.

"Sean—what's the matter?" she asked.

He ran his tongue across his lips, then: "Where did I go?"

THE RHONE HOUSE

ZACHARY RHONE NEVER sat on the porch swing, yet here he was: swinging and whistling and feeling so happy. No—that wasn't the right word. *Joy.* He felt full of joy. *And why not?* he mused as he looked over at his daughters. *My darling baby girls.*

Violet and Daisy sat on the steps clapping and slapping hands and singing, "Say say my playmate, come out and play with me, and bring your dollies three, climb up my apple tree…"

Even the cat seemed happy, Zachary noticed, lolling in a shady spot by the clothesline.

Melanie came out the screen door from the living room, where she'd been resting on the couch ever since they returned from the rodeo yesterday. "I still don't feel well," she said.

She has the bluest eyes, Zachary marveled. Blueberries. He leapt up and grabbed her around the waist, dancing her around the porch.

"Slide down my rain barrel *(clap-slap)* into my cellar door—"

Suddenly Violet groaned, "Ewwy yuck!"

Daisy was throwing up, while Violet backed away in disgust.

Zachary simply stared for a long moment. Then it struck him that this was quite hilarious. "That's funny, right?" he asked Melanie, but she was already shuffling back into the house.

Once Violet and Daisy both began to cry, all of a sudden it wasn't so funny anymore.

And Zachary wondered, *Who's going to clean up this mess?*

SUNDAY EVENING
ROSE'S COUNTRY CROCK

OUTSIDE THE CROCK, up and down Fortune Way, and as far as Hazel could see into Prospect Park, there wasn't a soul in town.

She gazed at The Winslow hunkered on the hill rising beyond the opposite side of the park. After she'd left Three Fools Creek and delivered a deliriously queasy Sean home to the hotel, Hazel had watched the last of the guests pack up their cars and head out, trying to beat nightfall for an easier time navigating Yellow Jacket Pass. Fully occupied before the rodeo, now entirely vacant, The Winslow would receive occasional guests over the rest of the summer and early fall, hopefully enough to keep the roof patched and taxes paid for another year. Then once the snow came and the pass required chains and hours of treacherous driving, they would close up the hotel until spring, save for the second floor quarters of her grandmother and the Adairs, and Samuel Adair could take to drinking in earnest.

She looked left over to Park Street.

Nobody.

With the rodeo over, she had expected the place to empty of all the tourists and carnies.

But where is everybody else? She raised her eyes to the blank sky. Usually townsfolk would be rehashing events: who made how much selling what, who got drunk and busted by

her father for conduct unbecoming, and who took top prize
or suffered worst injury at the rodeo.

Only now, downtown Winslow had become as much of a
ghost town as Matherston.

She turned from the front window to face the dining room:
nobody in here, either. Maybe the stomach flu really was
going around.

The interior of the Crock was early rustic gingham-style,
and like all of the original structures on Fortune Way, had
rough-hewn paneled walls, wide plank floors and tall multi-
paned windows.

"An embarrassment of Old West architecture," Hazel once
heard a tourist say.

An embarrassment, all right, she had thought.

Hazel jumped when a voice broke the silence directly behind her: "Are you still open?"

She turned to find James Bolinger towering in the doorway. Nearly six feet tall at only fifteen, he still hadn't grown
all the way into his hands and feet, like Jinx when he was a
puppy. And he sported studded leather wristbands and a dyed
black Mohawk. Despite his best efforts to look tough, James
was still one of the gentlest spirits in Winslow.

"Hey, Hazel," he said, and then smiled sheepishly, his eyes
bright behind heavy kohl liner.

"Hey," she said. For whatever reason (perhaps the time he
happened upon her skinny-dipping in Ruby Creek), she was
the love of the poor kid's life, and she always tried her best
not to encourage him.

"I need something to settle my stomach," he said.

"What's wrong? Do you have the stomach flu?"

"I don't know. I feel pretty bad. And my parents locked
me out of the house."

"Why would they do that?"

"I have no idea." He glanced down as if he were embarrassed that they had. "They've been acting like total freaks all day."

"Who hasn't?" Hazel said. "Here, sit. I'll make you some toast."

"Thanks." He shuffled over on his clown feet and collapsed into the chair she had indicated. In the sunlight streaming through the window, she could see the green around his gills.

She hurried to the waitress station. After she popped a couple of slices of rye into the toaster, Rose Peabody careened out of the bathroom wearing the same pale shade of green as James.

Rose wiped her face with a bar towel. "This is the nastiest bout of food poisoning I've ever had."

No wonder the place was deserted—not because of stomach flu, but food poisoning. Hazel was glad she hadn't eaten whatever was causing it, and instantly realized that it couldn't possibly be related to bad beef. Rose hadn't eaten beef since they found that first mad cow in Canada several years back, but Hazel had eaten steak just two days ago and felt fine.

"Does Owen have it, too?" Hazel asked.

Rose nodded once but then stopped as if the motion worsened her nausea. "He's so sick he took to bed right after church this morning."

"What do you think it's from?"

"Don't know…something at the rodeo? Didn't come from *my* kitchen. I know that much." Confusion washed over her face.

"What is it, Rose?"

"Did I eat one of Missy's apples?"

"Missy? Missy who?"

Rose gazed at her a moment before placing two clammy hands on Hazel's face. "You're like a daughter to Owen and me."

Uncomfortable with this sudden intensity, Hazel tried to pull away but Rose held fast.

"Like the daughter we never had. I hope you know that," Rose said.

The toast popped up, startling them both, after which Rose rushed back to the bathroom.

Hazel's heart fluttered as she buttered the toast. And when she took the plate into the dining room, James was gone, the chair pushed back in as if he'd never been there at all.

She looked down at the toast, picked up a slice and was about to take a bite when the sound coming from Rose in the bathroom spoiled her appetite. She returned to the waitress station to toss the toast and plate into a bus tray. As she did, she glimpsed Ben Mathers pushing into the Crock. She scurried deeper into the waitress station, wishing that if she hid there, he'd just go away.

No such luck. "I'll take coffee!" he shouted from the dining room.

Hazel scoffed—only Ben Mathers would drink coffee during a heat wave. "I'll have to brew some," she grumbled. After she got a pot going, she dragged her feet into the dining room to where Patience's grandfather sat at his usual table, looking anxious, as always.

"Do you want something to eat?" she asked, hoping he didn't because Rose obviously wasn't up for making anything. That would mean Hazel—the worst cook around, as her father would attest—would have to prepare his order, and Mathers complained even when the food was good.

"Two eggs. Over easy. Side of sausage." His staccato manner suggested that she wasn't worth the trouble of complete sentences.

Without spending any more of her own words on him, she left Mathers to stew in his impatience. In the kitchen, she fried up eggs, buried them in salt, and nuked some sausage, all the while curious about the old man's blood pressure. Then she returned to the dining room and set the plate in front of him with a clatter. "Enjoy," she said in her best monotone.

His bushy gray eyebrows shot together at the bridge of his beakish nose. "Any day now, Miss Winslow."

"Any day now *what?*" she asked, her hackles raised by his threatening tone.

"Coffee," he chided. "Remember?"

Grudgingly, she fetched the pot of freshly brewed coffee and returned to his table. When she went to fill his cup, he grabbed her by the left wrist. "Is that hot?" he asked.

"Yes." She shook him off and poured coffee to the very brim; he'd never get the cup to his lips without spilling. That was the wrong wrist for him—or anybody else—to grab, ever again, and her blood began to boil even hotter than the coffee.

"And I don't want to see you with my granddaughter anymore." Mathers poked at the eggs with his fork. "How many times must I repeat myself?"

"Don't waste your breath," she said. He needn't bother repeating himself, though he seemed to enjoy doing so. Once was more than enough.

You Winslows are treacherous, he had told her five years ago—right after his wife, Lottie, died—when Hazel was just a terrified girl shaking on his doorstep, who only missed her best friend and wanted to help her through the grief of losing her grandmother. But he'd refused to allow Hazel to see Patience, yelling, *Stay away from us, you devious girl!*

Now Hazel marveled at Mathers' ability to carry such a heavy grudge for so long, without so much as stooping beneath its weight. She was tempted to ask him how he managed when she heard someone coming up behind her.

"Rose," Mathers said, looking past Hazel. "You need to teach your employee some manners."

"That is it, Benjamin Mathers!" Rose said in her best *I'm*

not messing around here voice. "You're the one who needs to learn some manners. You, sir, are eighty-sixed." She pointed to the door. "Out!"

After the old man groused his way outside, Rose closed up. What was the point? James and Mathers aside, they'd had no customers in over two hours and Rose's condition was only worsening.

When Hazel left the Crock it wasn't dark yet, making the empty sidewalk along Fortune Way all the more eerie. She noticed that nobody was in the Buckhorn Tavern either except the bartender, Marlene Spainhower, who sat on a stool behind the bar watching baseball on the TV that hung in the corner. And Clemshaw Mercantile was shuttered up tight. Unusual also since Tiny Clemshaw squeezed every dime possible out of the day before closing up—never before nine o'clock in the summer.

Rounding the corner, Hazel suddenly wondered, *Where's Jinx?* She hadn't seen him since that morning at The Winslow. It wasn't like the dog to make himself so scarce. She truly hoped he didn't have food poisoning, too, courtesy of all the people food she allowed him to snack on.

Things weren't any livelier when she turned onto Park Street. She passed Ben Mathers' mansion first and could see no activity there. Then she went past the Ambrose and Foster homes. Nobody lived in those anymore. That was the way it would be for Winslow…a slow lingering death as the town emptied out one house at a time.

Upon reaching her own house at the corner of Park and Ruby Road she considered continuing to The Winslow to check on Sean. But then she noticed her dad heading down their front porch steps.

"What's up, Dad?" she asked, surprised when he got closer to see how sweaty he was. And the way his hand trembled when he put on his hat disturbed her.

"Melanie Rhone reported a wolf lurking about their property. Angling for their cat Boo, I suspect, but she's worried about her girls," his voice sounded forced.

Like his throat hurts, she thought. And his deep blue eyes were bloodshot. "Dad, are you okay?" She placed her sore palm on his forearm, which felt cold. So why was he sweating like that?

"I'm fine," he said. "Go on in." Then he added, "Stay out of trouble. And lock the door."

"Why?" They never locked their doors.

"Just do it, sweetheart." He started away from her, down the stepping-stones.

"But you don't have your gun!" Inexplicable panic struck her. He looked vulnerable, and she was suddenly overcome with worry. "Don't go, Dad."

"Everything's fine," he said. "Go inside now." Then he was gone down the sidewalk.

Hazel climbed the steps to the porch and stood for a while—puzzling over the idea of a wolf in Winslow since she'd never heard about any here before—until the hot dead quiet gave her the creeps. She hustled inside the front door and locked the deadbolt.

SHE FOLDED HERSELF into her mother's old overstuffed rocker in the living room. The chair had brought Hazel comfort when she was small and felt alone. So that now, even though its rose-print fabric was worn and torn, and its innards stole every opportunity to escape, she wouldn't let her dad get rid of it.

Dark out but still too warm to sleep, she rocked back and forth, worrying about why it was taking her dad so long to shoo a wolf away from the Rhone place, hoping it didn't turn out to be the Bigfoot she and Sean had heard in the woods that afternoon.

Urgent knocking started up from the back of the house and then she heard the kitchen door whine open. *So much for locking up.* She sat forward in her chair, heart thumping like mad.

A moment later Patience appeared in the foyer. From the light in the hallway, Hazel made out the look of alarm on her friend's white face. "I need to see Sadie," Patience said.

"What's wrong with you?" Hazel rose from the rocker. Patience's jittery eyes and the way she rubbed her arms as if she were itchy and cold at the same time further unnerved Hazel.

"I need to see Sadie," Patience repeated. "I had the worst nightmare ever."

Patience rushed over to the photograph taken at the 1889 Prospector's Day picnic that hung on the wall at the foot of the staircase, and pointed to the dark-haired girl that looked a lot like her—her great-great aunt. Patience turned back to Hazel, eyes panicky. "Sadie keeps telling me to come into the pond even though I told her I can't swim."

"You wouldn't have nightmares like that if you'd just let me teach you how," Hazel said. "I swear, Patience Mathers, you're going to learn to at least dog paddle this summer, even if it kills you."

Coming up beside Patience, Hazel peered at the black-and-white image, at Sadie center stage in Prospect Park. "The Fairest of the Fair," Hazel said softly. As evidenced by the bouquet in her hands, Sadie Mathers had just been crowned. And she had that spooky pale-eyed stare resulting from the long exposure required to take the photograph.

"The Fairest of the Fair," Patience repeated in a voice so strange that Hazel turned to look at her.

Patience's features suddenly shifted, as though she'd just remembered something crucial. Then she whipped around toward Hazel, her frantic face just inches away. "It's happening," Patience said.

"What is?" Hazel asked.

"It's happening again, Hazel. And it's our fault again."

"No, Patience." Hazel felt her stomach fill with lead. "That was just a stupid game."

FIVE SUMMERS AGO, when Hazel and Patience were twelve years old, Hazel's grandparents threw a dinner party in the formal dining room of The Winslow. Having no interest in that dull event, Hazel and Patience had rushed through plates of macaroni and cheese in the kitchen nook, anxious to get started on what the musty old book that Hazel had discovered promised to be a more thrilling venture.

After heaping their plates in the sink, the girls climbed the winding servants' staircase, on tiptoe at first to minimize the volume of each creaking, bare wood step, then abandoning all restraint and racing up to the fourth floor of the hotel's tower.

At the top, Hazel stopped on the staircase landing and whipped around, sloshing water out of the large glass she held tight with both hands. "Do you have the egg?"

One step behind her, Patience nodded, a sly grin animating her doll-like features.

"Good." Hazel continued into the circular room, well aware that The Winslow's ghosts resided there. But she wasn't afraid of the ghosts then. Back then, she had no reason to be.

Right away Hazel determined that the spookiest spot was in front of the floor-to-ceiling stained-glass window and she headed for it, Patience on her heels. They positioned themselves cross-legged on the hardwood floor, each facing the other. Ceremoniously, Hazel placed her grandmother's crystal glass in between them, then she lit three candles to set the atmosphere and ensure the full effect, all the while feeling sneaky, feeling as if they were about to do something they really shouldn't.

Patience placed the egg against the rim of the glass, poised to crack. "Here goes."

"Hold on!" Hazel grabbed her by the arm. "Remember—just the white."

"Okay, okay." Patience carefully cracked open the egg and held it above the glass, transferring the contents back and forth between half shells until the yolk separated and the white slipped into the water. She glanced up at Hazel through strands of dark hair. "Are we supposed to chant or anything?"

"The book didn't say to." Hazel shrugged. "But go ahead if you want." She gathered up her own long hair before leaning forward to watch the egg white mingle with the water.

"How long till it tells our fortunes?" Patience whispered.

Hazel scratched her nose, staring into their homemade crystal ball. "Guess we'll know when we see the future. Like the girls in Salem did." She heard a commotion in the dining room three floors below. Her grandfather must have told a really good joke.

The egg white sank to the bottom of the glass and Patience leaned closer, face screwed up in concentration. "Should we ask it a question?"

"Oh, great and wise crystal ball—" Hazel started.

"Wait!" Patience splayed her fingers as if to say, *Hold on everybody.* "That sort of looks like…no…" Suddenly she jumped to her feet as though something had bitten her on the behind.

"Do you see something?" Hazel asked.

Patience pointed at the glass, her face stretched in fright. "Don't *you?*"

The din rising beneath them increased. It sounded as if somebody had decided to rearrange the furniture in a hurry. "I don't see anything." Hazel wanted to, but she didn't.

"It's there," Patience insisted.

"Where?" Hazel stared hard at the egg white, increasingly distracted by the noise from downstairs. She lifted her head to look at her friend. "What do you see?"

Patience's skin had gone even paler. And when she spoke, Hazel could barely hear her above the clamor emanating from the first floor.

"What did you say?" Hazel asked.

"It's a coffin," Patience repeated.

Hazel scoffed and tilted the glass back and forth, swirling the egg in the water. "You're just saying that 'cause that's what the bewitched girls saw."

"Am not!" Patience clutched her hands to her chest. "Hazel, what does it mean?"

Hazel stood to look her in the eye. "It didn't look like a coffin to me."

"I don't like this game." Patience pursed her lips.

Hazel rolled her eyes and turned to leave, wondering why she ever thought this stupid trick would work, let alone be fun.

The crashing sounds coming from the dining room didn't seem so bad once the screaming started.

Hazel spun back to Patience, whose face mirrored her own shock. Another scream from downstairs spurred her to grab her friend's hand. "Let's go!"

On her way to the door Hazel kicked over the glass and spilled raw egg and water across the wood floor. Fighting not to slip, she rushed for the stairs, panic striking in bright flashes of ugly imagination: her grandparents held hostage by a gun-wielding maniac, her grandfather's head crushed by a falling chandelier, her grandmother running around with her hair on fire.

More voices joined in the screaming and shouting as both girls hastened down the staircase. When Patience knocked into her from behind, Hazel flew down several steps, arms flailing in thin air, before her hand found the railing and she regained her footing.

After the girls landed on the ground floor, they raced

through the kitchen, pushed open the swinging door to the dining room—and stopped dead in their tracks.

Chairs lay overturned. The table was littered with broken porcelain. And Hazel's grandfather had Lottie Mathers' arms pinned behind her back, while Jules Foster held a knife to the woman's throat.

"Stop!" Patience shrieked. "What are you doing to my Gram?"

Lottie tried to jerk her head away, straining to break free, her mouth gaping in a silent scream.

"Hold her still!" Jules shouted. Sure and swift, he plunged the knife into Lottie's neck.

Hazel and Patience both screamed as blood spurted Jules in the face and then splashed the others crowded around.

A cold meat smell touched Hazel's nose just as Lottie's blood rained on a platter of rare roast beef on the table, and Hazel swooned on her feet.

"No no no!" Ben Mathers howled, rushing at Jules. "You're killing her!"

Hazel's grandmother Sarah shoved both girls back into the kitchen, where they created red footprints across the tile floor, reminding Hazel of the wounded deer she and her father found the winter before, gut shot in the woods and leaving crimson, cloven hoofprints in the snow.

Before the dining room door swung shut, Hazel glanced back into the room.

Blood: dripping from the low-hung crystal chandelier, pooling on the white tablecloth. The screaming had stopped. Everyone stood frozen, stunned faces fixed on Lottie, who lay in her husband's arms, glassy-eyed, a wet red bib growing on her chest. Moaning, Ben Mathers rocked his wife as if her life depended on his keeping her in motion. Instead, each back and forth movement created a sodden smacking sound that made Hazel want to scream again.

Then the door slammed closed in Hazel's face and Patience grabbed her hand, squeezing it so hard Hazel feared her bones would break.

"This is our fault!" Patience whispered feverishly. "We made it happen. The coffin—"

"Don't say that!" Hazel couldn't handle another helping of horror; she was full.

Hazel's grandmother kept pushing the girls outside through the kitchen entry, repeating, "Shush, shush," as if the only thing wrong was their refusal to be quiet.

Patience stopped on the back steps and seized Hazel by the wrists. "Don't tempt fate, my Gram always says." Her eyes sparked with panic. "Oh, God. Oh, God."

"It's *not* our fault." Hazel tried to raise her hands to cover her ears.

But Patience held fast, mewled hysterically. "Tempt fate and your worst fears come true."

IT WAS AFTER that that Patience had begun to collect her lucky charms. Now she stood in Hazel's foyer on the verge of tears, working that bracelet, her fingertips compulsively stroking the tiny talismans. "It *is* happening again," Patience insisted.

"Listen to me," Hazel adopted a firm tone. "Nothing like that is going to happen now. Don't even start thinking like that."

Patience's expression remained bleak. "Tanner shouldn't have broken that mirror."

Hazel frowned. "That's just a silly superstition. Besides, you told me you buried the broken glass outside in the moonlight like a good little witch. Didn't you say that wards off the evil spirits?"

"Wards off bad luck," Patience corrected.

"Then you're safe, right?" Despite Hazel's attempts at reassurance, she sympathized with her friend. Not only had they sorely tempted fate again, this time they'd taunted it—practically dared it.

"I feel really, really weird, Hazel." Patience's tears welled higher. "I threw up in front of the whole town. Everything's ruined. I ruined my best chaps and everyone saw me, and my gramps is mad that I embarrassed our family."

"It's just food poisoning." Hazel backed up a step, her heart suddenly racing. "Lots of people have it. You'll be okay tomorrow."

"No I won't. I'm *sick*." Patience looked desperate. "And I'm scared."

Hazel wondered again how Sean was feeling. "It'll be okay. Don't worry." She tried to keep calm for both their sakes. "Everything's fine," she said, realizing how hollow that sounded. "We're all fine."

SILVER HILL

SEAN AND TANNER perched on the water tower platform, the highest point in town, with the lights of Winslow spread out below them like a Lite-Brite missing most of its pegs.

Sean hadn't been feeling too good since he and Hazel left Three Fools Creek. His stomach was slippery and it seemed as though his heart was beating too fast, the blood pumping around his body with sickening speed. His mom and Aaron were sick too, taking turns in the bathroom, and the sound of it had made Sean feel even worse.

So when Tanner came by inviting him to go have a smoke, Sean had said okay, figuring that the weed would settle his stomach and slow the pounding in his chest. The fresh air couldn't hurt, either, especially if he ended up retching anyway—who wants to stick their face in a toilet?

He watched Tanner roll the joint. After Tanner licked and sealed the paper, he held it up for Sean to admire. Sean had known instantly that he didn't particularly like—and definitely didn't trust—Tanner Holloway. But whatever, it wasn't like there were a lot of other guys his age to hang with around Winslow.

Sean decided that it might be useful to know what Tanner was capable of. "What'd you get busted for back home, anyway?" he asked.

"A little of this." Tanner waved the joint. "A little of that."

"You miss home?" Sean was starting to hope that he did and would go back there soon.

"Nah." He lit up, took a hit, passed it to Sean. "It sucks,

too," he squelched, holding the smoke, "just in a different way." He let out a billowing breath. "More chicks, though."

"That's cool, I guess." Sean took a hit, eyes narrowing. He could see how some girls might go for Tanner, but he struck Sean as the kind of guy who'd sell out a buddy for a six-pack.

Reaching into his pocket, Tanner retrieved a cell phone, flipped it open, waved it around.

"What are you doing?" Sean scoffed.

"Thought I might get reception up here." He glowered at the unreceptive phone.

Sean pointed straight ahead. "Happen to notice that mountain?" He pointed the opposite direction. "What about that one?" Turning forty-five degrees: "Or those?"

Tanner slapped the phone shut and crammed it back in his pocket. "Fucking boondocks. How can you stand it?"

"I don't know." Sean shrugged. "I've always lived here."

"Too bad for you, man. So what's up with you and my cousin?"

"Not much," Sean replied through a huge exhale.

"Bullshit!" He laughed. "You're so far gone on Hazel it's embarrassing."

Sean felt his face heat up. "What's it to you?"

"Nothing, I guess. Just hate to see a friend get suckered that's all. Like I said—embarrassing."

Friend? Sean did not like this conversation. At all. He carved the ash and took a deep hit before handing back the joint. "What the hell are you talking about?" he asked.

"Now Patience, on the other hand..." Tanner ignored his question. "Low-hanging fruit. Isn't that what you called her?"

"She's a trip." He coughed. "I can tell you that. And don' hotbox that joint."

"So what?" Tanner hit too hard again. "She's hot. Screw it—I'm goin' for it." He held the joint back toward Sean.

"No thanks, man." He shook his head, which set it to spinning. "Had enough."

"Lightweight." Tanner took one last hit before he stubbed out the joint on the bottom of his lighter.

They sat back against the metal tank and Tanner started jabbering again. Sean could barely hear him through the buzzing in his ears, but it sounded like he was saying something else about Hazel, something about her playing him…then Sean felt it coming and shot up and rushed to the platform railing. Leaning out as far as he dared, he threw up over the side—threw up a lot, and it was hot and disgusting but he felt better with it finally out.

He turned back to Tanner, swabbing his mouth with a shaking hand. "Damn. I don't feel so good." He wiped his face with his T-shirt.

"Too stoned?" Tanner jeered.

"Fuck off," Sean said, and then stumbled toward the ladder.

Even though his stomach was in turmoil and his throat and eyes were burning, he started down the side of the water tower. His hands felt sweaty and slick on the ladder rungs that he hardly saw through watering eyes but he hurried down anyway because he knew he was about to hurl again. Partway down his right hand lost hold, then both feet slipped, and he dangled for a moment, nervously wondering how far away the ground might still be, until his left hand surrendered to gravity and he was sent hurtling through the air.

Sean hit the dirt with an impact that jarred his bones. Then he leaned forward, hands on his knees, and gagged. But there was nothing left to come out except a trickle of yellow bile. Now his throat really burned like hell when he dry-heaved again. "Shit," he said in a voice so quavering that he made himself even more nervous.

He reeled over to his motorcycle and tried to start it up. On the fifth kick he put all of his weight into it and the bike finally sparked, but then he sat there idling, blinking to clear his vision. *Is there something in that weed?* he wondered.

No, he'd felt crappy all afternoon.

But now his heart was as sick as his stomach. *Am I making a fool out of myself?*

His confusion was sudden and total. *What did Tanner mean?*

Is Hazel just playing me?

Sean started slowly down Silver Hill, not taking the bike out of second gear, hoping to make it home without wiping out.

THE WINSLOW

Aaron Adair heard the guest lady crying, and once he reached the second-floor landing, he saw her. She sat on the top step of the red-carpeted staircase, face buried in her hands, sobbing in a way that scared him, scared him almost as much as the blood-gurgling lady had last night. *Gurgle, gurgle, gurgle,* she'd kept on, until finally he'd had to turn on his light and read *Treasure Island* till he was too tired to be scared of anything anymore except one-legged, one-eyed pirates.

Coming up behind her, Aaron wondered why she was crying. Maybe she'd been left behind when all the other hotel guests took off that afternoon. He stood at her back, feeling as though he was intruding somehow, as if he'd caught her telling a secret nobody should hear.

"What's wrong?" he asked.

She didn't answer, but her shoulders shook with sobs. Tears fell to her lap with the same soft sound as water dripping from leaves after the rain stops.

"Don't worry," he said. "They'll come back for you. They'll remember they forgot you here."

When she lowered her hands to her lap, Aaron noticed the rings on her fingers. Three, with bright stones that reminded him of jujubees. And her tears kept dripping. He realized the carpet around them had grown wet and squishy beneath his antsy feet.

"Can't you see it?" she suddenly asked in a voice full of breath.

That made him even more anxious. Still behind her, he

couldn't see her face, and he suddenly worried that if he did, he wouldn't like what he saw.

"See what?" he asked, not really wanting to know. Maybe he should just walk away, go back and hide in his safe bedroom down the hallway in his family's quarters.

But before he could escape, she lifted her head as if to look around the hotel. Then she sighed, a long, sad sigh. "Can't you see that this place is dying."

Aaron reached down to touch her, to comfort her, and to tell her to stop talking like that because she was making him really, really afraid.

He leaned forward, expecting his hand to land on her shoulder. Instead, his hand went straight through her and suddenly the staircase yawned wide before him, willing him to tumble down.

At the last moment, his hand grasped the banister.

She had looked so *real*. Blinking hard, the boy suffered a realization that turned his blood cold. *I can't tell them apart anymore.* How was Sean supposed to protect him if he couldn't even tell the living from the dead?

On shaky legs, Aaron ran.

And all of a sudden, he no longer felt the floor beneath his feet, no longer felt anything at all, in fact. Looking down from above, he could see himself running along the hallway.

His body, that is. His body was still running—he just wasn't inside it anymore.

MONDAY MORNING
FORTUNE WAY

Day Four of the Heat Wave

A FAT WET catfish splatted onto the sidewalk before Cal's feet.

He watched it squirm on the worn wood, watched it gasp with its whiskered mouth.

Cal sniffed the briny air. "I'll be damned."

He looked up to the sky as several more showered down and clattered heavily against the roof of the Fish 'n Bait. Awe-struck, his jaw dropped. *It's raining fish.*

He glanced down at the creature struggling for its life on the sidewalk. "I'll be damned."

Damned or not, what Cal saw—was *certain* he saw, was townsfolk up and down Fortune Way scramble for shelter as the sky darkened, thunder bellowed, and fish poured from the heavens.

Arms outstretched, Cal tried to grab hold but they wrig-gled out of his hands to land in the street with sickly plops. *I'll be damned,* Cal thought right before a catfish hit him on the head.

AWASH IN SUNSHINE, Hazel turned onto Fortune Way to see Cal sitting on the edge of his roof, fishing into the space between the Fish 'n Bait and Buckhorn Tavern. When she got closer she saw bartender Marlene Spainhower crouched in the dusty passageway tugging on Cal's line.

Cal raised his rod and reeled in the line, shouting, "Whoa, whoa!"

Marlene squeezed her face together to suppress the laughter that shook her petite frame. Then she noticed Hazel and put a finger to her mouth, *Shush*.

What the... Hazel marveled. After she had finally calmed down Patience last night, her dad had returned from his wolf hunt at the Rhone place looking even more shook up than when he'd left. Without a word he'd walked past them in the living room and into the kitchen where Hazel heard him take a bottle from the cupboard and scrape a chair away from the table.

"I'd better go now," Patience had whispered, the sheriff's strange behavior clearly refueling her fear. Then she'd left for her house next door while Hazel listened to her dad fill his glass.

The pit of dread born in Hazel's stomach at that moment had grown so much overnight that she wasn't surprised this morning to see Cal perched on the bait shop roof, fishing the dirt. Wasn't surprised to see Hap Hotchkiss pushing his lawn mower down the middle of Fortune Way. And wasn't surprised when she walked into the Crock to find it already packed and noisy. They weren't even supposed to open for another hour— Hazel had decided to come in early to set up for breakfast in case Rose was still sick.

Hazel wove her way around the tables—it seemed as if the whole stinking town was crammed in there—asking people to scoot in their chairs so she could get to the back where she found a pale and harried Rose Peabody at the coffeemaker just pushing Brew for a pot of decaf.

"What's going on?" Hazel asked, following Rose through the swinging kitchen door.

"Order up!" Owen Peabody pounded the bell twice even though they were standing right there.

"We had over a dozen people waiting for us to open." Rose was seriously flustered. "Last night, nobody. Today, everybody!" She grabbed two plates and headed back to the dining room.

Owen plopped more bacon onto the hot grill and it spat back up at him.

Hazel leaned both arms on the warm metal counter and watched him add a scoop of butter to a short stack with sausage and eggs. She always thought Owen looked like Popeye, especially around the oversize jaw, and since Rose looked like Olive Oyl, they made a perfect match.

"You feeling better, Owen?" Hazel asked.

"Right as rain, m'dear." He cracked open two eggs on the already full grill, not bothering to pick out bits of shell.

"You sure?" she said. He didn't look right as anything. A sheen of sweat covered his big arms and had soaked through the T-shirt covering his barrel chest.

"Never better." Owen grinned at her.

That gesture unsettled Hazel deeply. It was not his usual good-natured grin, but rather a manic-looking, teeth-baring gape. "Owen," she tried, "maybe we should close up?"

The counter was covered in plates of The Special. He spun the order wheel and looked at the sole ticket. "Okay." He rubbed his hands together. "Three more specials."

"Owen—you're cooking up the same order."

"Two by two by two." He flipped pancakes prematurely and battered the bacon.

She plucked the ticket off the wheel. "This is from yesterday." Hazel remembered taking the order from James Bolinger and his grandfather Gus yesterday morning because James— growing boy that he was—had bashfully ordered *two* Two by Two by Twos and then left her a hefty tip as a token of his adoration. "You already cooked this order, Owen."

"Look. I'm doing my job here. Please do yours and get these out while they're still hot."

Hazel had hoped things would get back to normal today; clearly things were not headed in that direction. Feeling topsy-turvy, she considered suggesting again that they close up, but decided to hightail it out of the kitchen instead once she saw Owen pick up his huge chef's knife.

After hastily tying on her frilly yellow work apron, she carried two plates of food into the dining room and set them on the table near the waitress station, where Jay and Julie Marsh sat looking confused.

Jay managed to stop pulling on his moustache long enough to acknowledge her. "Thank you, Hazel." He turned to his wife. "Try and eat something, Julie. It'll make you feel better."

Julie gave Hazel an odd look before squinting at her plate. "Are there potatoes?"

"I can get you some hash browns," Hazel offered.

Julie made a repulsed face. "I hate potatoes."

"Then I won't get you any hash browns?" Hazel looked quizzically at Jay.

"It's fine, Hazel," Jay said. "Thank you."

When Rose brushed by, Hazel followed her to the toaster. "Did you order any specials?"

"I can't remember." Rose covered her mouth with her hand and dashed for the restroom. Toast popped up loud. "Butter that, will you?" she called back, muffled, before disappearing.

As Hazel slathered the bread, she thought, *What the hell?*

Returning to the kitchen where Owen was flinging food all over the place and again to the dining room to deliver more plates, Hazel repeated this back and forth for twenty minutes before deciding she needed to go find her father and tell him what was going on. Ignoring demands for coffee refills, and wondering what had become of Rose, Hazel pushed her way out of the Crock onto the sidewalk.

The Peabodys' chocolate Lab was out front chasing her own tail. Molly spun in an endless circle, whimpering because she couldn't quite catch it.

"You're not very smart, are you?" Hazel asked the dog, feeling slightly guilty for doing so because Molly was Jinx's girlfriend.

Hazel looked over to the corner of Fortune Way and Civic Street, at the squat brick building that was once Mathers Bank but now served as the post office and the seldom-used jail. In fact, nobody had been incarcerated there since her dad busted Tiny Clemshaw a few years back for driving while intoxicated. Her dad's office occupied the southeast corner and she could see all the windows shut up tight. *Where is he?* He'd been gone when she woke up—something that'd never happened since her mother left. Now she had no idea where to even look for him.

Two doors down the opposite direction, Ivy Hotchkiss stood with her hands on her hips looking up at Cal on the roof of the Fish 'n Bait. "Come on down," Ivy told Cal, "before you hook somebody in the eye." And across the street in Prospect Park, Ivy's husband Hap Hotchkiss mowed pine needles with his gas-powered lawn mower.

This is food poisoning? Hazel marveled. *What did they eat?* Again she hoped that she wouldn't get it, too.

She noticed Patience sitting statue-still on the porch steps of her Grandfather Ben's mansion on the corner of Park Street. She appeared to be staring at the playground area in the park… as if waiting for Hazel or Sean to return victorious from the ghost hunt so they could finally eat the rest of the candy.

Wondering how Sean felt today, she decided to walk down to Rhone Bakery to check on him as soon as Rose came out of the bathroom. She was tempted to split right then but for some reason felt compelled to stay and help the Peabodys.

Perhaps because last night an overwrought Rose had chosen to inform her that she's like a daughter to them.

I've been taken emotional hostage, she realized, remembering how those Olive Oyl eyes had shone with such sympathy and affection after Hazel was abandoned by her mother.

Just as a car accelerated onto Fortune Way, she spotted Jinx trotting across the street from the park, heading for where she stood in front of the Crock. "Jinx, no!" she shouted. "Wait there!"

When the dog took this as encouragement and picked up his pace, Hazel stepped into the street and waved her arms, shouting to the oncoming car, "Stop, stop!"

The El Camino lurched to a halt just in time for Jinx to saunter in front of it on his way to the sidewalk. Molly the chocolate Lab whined in greeting to her boyfriend.

Hazel waved to the driver. "Thanks."

Kenny Clark, Holloway Ranch's youngest yet crustiest cowpoke, leaned out his window. "You better tie up that mongrel. Next time he won't be so lucky."

"Thanks, asshole."

Kenny narrowed his eyes. "Trespass at the ranch again and I'll shoot first and let somebody else ask questions later."

"You already shot at me, you dumb-ass! Does Friday night ring a bell? Poor helpless calf? Shoot anywhere near me again—even threaten me again—and I'll have my father haul your ass to jail."

"Oh, look out…" He pretended to gnaw on his fingernails. "The *sheriff.*" He made an even uglier face. "You Winslows think you own this town."

"Own it? If we do, it's for sale. Cheap. Got any money?" She gave him a facetious smile.

His middle finger said it all as he gunned his engine and peeled out.

She responded in kind before looking down at Jinx. "What's the matter with you? You're gonna get yourself run over."

He wagged his tail and licked his snout and saliva flew onto her bare calves.

"And you're really slobbery today, you know that?" She gave the red dog a few pets on the head.

He complained *more, more* when she stood back up.

"Sorry, gotta get back to work."

He whimpered again before he and Molly turned and padded up the sidewalk toward the Buckhorn Tavern…maybe they could score a hot dog there.

"Not open yet," she called after them.

She glanced back at the bank building. Where was her father when she needed him?

Determined to convince the Peabodys to close the Crock and urge everyone to go home until things got sorted out, she pushed open the restaurant door, unleashing the usual riot of bells.

In the dining room, all eyes were on Kohl Thacker. The tall bald man stood on his chair, sweating and excited and running down items they might have eaten in common. "Who had corn dogs?"

A few hands were raised.

"Okay then—who ate burgers?"

More or less the same. Hazel glanced around to see if any Holloway Ranch cowhands were present. There weren't. Ranch hands rarely ate in town.

Kohl wrinkled his bare forehead. "Sick cattle, sick people?"

"Rose doesn't eat beef," Hazel said. "And she's in the ladies room, sicker than anyone."

"Oh." Kohl sounded disappointed. "Okay then, how about catwiches?"

Hands were raised all across the dining room.

"I knew it." Kohl slammed his fist against his palm. "It's always the fish that goes bad."

Gus Bolinger broke in. "I ate no catfish, so you know squat, Thacker. And my guess is we'll all be feeling better in no time, so how 'bout we just leave it at that."

Looking defeated, Kohl sank to his seat while everyone turned their attention back to the food in front of them. It was then that Hazel realized nobody was actually eating anything. Just poking at their plates. She headed for the kitchen to tell Owen not to cook any more food, to tell him to get out here and flex his Popeye muscles and make everyone leave so she could go look for her dad.

As she was passing the Marshes' table, Julie exploded the sunny side of her eggs with her fork and a look of repulsion washed over her face. Julie gasped and pushed the plate away, quickly covering the offending yolks with her napkin. Hazel doubled back to remove the plate.

"What's wrong?" Jay asked his wife.

Julie stared at him with a helpless expression.

Just as Hazel reached for the plate, Julie looked at it in squinty-eyed terror and flipped it over. Food spilled across the table and Hazel's patience snapped—she'd had it with these people and their freakish food poisoning. "Why'd you do that?" she said.

Gently, Jay said to Julie, "Settle down, sweetie."

"There was something on my plate," Julie said.

"What?" he asked.

Hazel looked at the mess she would have to clean up. "Your breakfast?" she suggested.

"Something else…" Julie replied.

Hazel lifted the edge of the overturned plate. "Let's see: eggs and bacon and pancakes. Nothing horrible, nothing moving."

"Please," Julie said.

Hazel picked up a piece of bacon, examined it, then held it out to her. "Just good food."

"Please, Hazel!" Julie's eyes brimmed with tears.

"Sorry," Hazel said, realizing she'd gone too far—even if Julie was undeniably irritating.

"It's not your fault, Hazel," Jay said. "We were up all night. Didn't get a wink of sleep."

"It's okay." Hazel grabbed a bar towel and began consolidating the food strewn across their table.

Meanwhile, the dining room grew even noisier.

Concentrating on her coffee cup, Julie's pupils were open as wide as saucers.

"Julie?" Jay tried.

She remained fixated on her cup. When Hazel picked it up to wipe beneath it, her eyes followed the cup up...and then down again.

"Sweetie?" Jay touched the cap sleeve of his wife's baby-doll blouse. "You feel all right?"

Slowly, she turned to face her husband. "Yes, I do. I feel all right. I feel just fine. How many times are you gonna ask?" Her voice rose, "In fact, I feel great. I've never felt better." Yelling now, "I've never felt this fucking great in my whole fucking life!" She sank her fingernails into his forearm. "How the hell do *you* feel?"

Hazel jumped back while the noisy Crock went dead silent. Jay glanced around for some sort of help but everyone averted their eyes. Hazel felt as uncomfortable as he looked.

From the table by the door, a low laugh escaped Kohl Thacker. Then he let loose with a full belly laugh, gasped for air, laughed some more. A woman at the next table began to snicker. Another started up. Soon the entire room reverberated with laughter.

Tension twisted Julie's face before it lifted and she released hysterics of her own.

Jay gave a halfhearted, "Heh heh," while looking at Hazel as if to ask, *Are they outta their ever-loving minds?*

Hazel glanced around the dining room: this was not funny *at all*. More like frightening. Watching these people she'd known all her life become sudden strangers, she recalled how Sean had asked her yesterday, "Where did I go?"

At that, she felt the mountainside tilt beneath her feet.

She left the towel and the mess and dashed into the kitchen where she found Owen in the cooler, muttering, "Bacon, eggs, cheese, milk." He grabbed a handful of sausage off the shelf, sniffed it, dropped it to the floor.

"What are you doing?" Hazel asked.

Startled, Owen spun around and she noticed that his pupils were huge, too. "Something's wrong," he said.

Turning back to the shelf he poked at a package wrapped in white butcher paper, meat most likely. Then he picked up the bundle and examined it. "A definite possibility," he said before flinging it to the ground.

He strode out of the cooler, not bothering to close the door, and went over to the toaster oven. There he tore open a plastic bag containing a loaf of bread. He shook his big head. "This is wrong."

"What do you mean?" She moved next to him and looked at the pieces of bread strewn across the cutting board. "What's wrong?"

Owen held up a slice in the bright sunlight flooding the kitchen to reveal a slight grayish hue. "See?" He looked at her with an expression of wonderment. "It's the water, Hazel, it's gotta be. Something's wrong with the water. And it's gotten into everything." His face went ashen. "Including us."

SEAN

THAT SUN IS BLINDING ME, Sean thought, placing his hand across his forehead like a visor.

He ducked into Clemshaw Mercantile and swiped a pair of sunglasses off the circular rack next to the front door. Once back outside he donned the shades and realized that he couldn't recall it ever being this bright or hot so early. Waves of heat rose from the sidewalk, blasting him like when the door is finally opened on a car that has sat in the sun all afternoon.

At least his stomach felt better than last night. But while the nausea had departed, an uneasiness had moved in that he didn't really understand. Actually, he was having trouble understanding *anything* today. Everything felt different somehow, as if somebody had changed the channel during the night. Or more like it was the same show, only a different episode. And everything sounded louder. Maybe that was why the headache that'd been looming since early that morning had now arrived in full. No matter, Sean continued on rubbery legs toward the bakery, despite the nagging thought that he should just go home, get into bed and stay there for a very long time.

In the back of the bakery he found Zachary Rhone staring into the big oven. The place was immaculate, not a speck of sugar or flour dotted the countertops or floors. And there was no bread rising, no donuts frying, no buns cooling. Sean said, "Sorry I'm late—"

Zachary shot up so hard Sean worried the man might jump right out of his skin. And Sean noticed that Zachary's face looked craggier, as if his bad temper had etched itself deeper into his complexion overnight.

After what felt like forever, Zachary finally said, "Go home."

"I've been sick," Sean said and his brain pounded against his skull in agreement.

"I know," Zachary said quietly, and his stony eyes seemed to drill all the way past Sean's aching eye sockets right into his sore head.

"You know?" Sean asked.

"Don't say anything to anybody."

"Huh?"

"There's no need to say anything." Zachary's eyes were as dark and shiny as black marbles. "To anybody."

Oh, shit... Sean's stomach clenched.

"Just go home."

Sean noticed then that Zachary was trembling and he felt more than glad to get away from him.

After he stepped out of the bakery and into the shock of sunlight, he saw Melanie Rhone hanging laundry on the line. He shuffled up to her despite his thudding head because she waved to him and he liked her and he felt sorry for her.

Pale as the white sheet she'd just pinned up, Melanie smiled weakly. "Did you get the food poisoning, too?"

"Yeah, we all did. Except my dad." Sean tried to sort it all out, what it had to do with sick cows and Hazel and Hawkin Rhone, but his brain felt like taffy. All of his thoughts were stuck together in one gooey heap. Whenever he tried to peel one off, it would just stretch out until it lost its meaning entirely.

"...wasn't anybody's fault, I'm sure," Melanie was saying. "Probably just some mayo got left out too long in the sun."

Sean realized he hadn't been paying attention to her. "Where're Violet and Daisy?" he asked. It struck him as unusual that the girls weren't in the yard; they were never far from Melanie.

"Inside. Their daddy says they have to stay—" Melanie gasped and her blue eyes flew wide open.

"Thought I told you to go home, mister!" Zachary seized Sean by the back of his T-shirt and jerked him away, choking him with his own collar. Then he turned Sean around and let go with a hard push to his shoulder. "That's my *wife*—you have no business talking to her! Keep away from my wife!"

"Okay, okay…" was all Sean could muster as he stumbled down the lawn and off the Rhone property. *Not coming back,* he decided then. Never.

Once back on Fortune Way he felt as though he'd never been there before. Everything was in its place but the Old West–style storefronts now struck him as ridiculous. Laughable. He guffawed just for the hell of it and Tiny Clemshaw, now standing guard in front of the Mercantile, glared at him, which made Sean wonder if the shopkeeper had seen him steal the sunglasses.

The sound of Sean's tennis shoes slapping the wood plank sidewalk was so loud he couldn't believe people weren't rushing out to see what all the ruckus was. He laughed again. A humorless, one-note laugh: "Ha." He stopped to peek through the window of the Buckhorn Tavern—it looked invitingly dark and cool inside but wasn't open yet. The sun beating down on his back felt like fire so he moved on.

Then he called up to Cal on the roof of the Fish 'n Bait, "Having any luck?"

"Nibblin' this mornin'," Cal replied. "Shy ever since."

Sean heard Rose's Country Crock before he saw it—the swell of excited voices and the clink-clank clatter of cups and plates and spoons. The sandwich board listing the day's specials (often written in Hazel's sloppy handwriting so you were never actually sure what they were) was not in its usual spot on the sidewalk.

Reaching the doorway, he was relieved to spot Hazel amid the crowded tables. But he was afraid to go inside—too loud and too bright—so he waited there until she finally noticed him and came over.

"Hi," she said, a bit out of breath. Her eyes were extra green today, he noticed, her hair especially reddish gold.

"Hey." He felt better already seeing her.

"Everyone's freaking out here," she said, looking kind of freaked out, too. "Did you go to work?"

"I think Zachary fired me. I don't know what's going on."

Some maniac in the kitchen was pounding the pick-up bell.

"Sean…" She looked at him with concern. "Are you getting sicker? Do you feel worse?"

"I don't know."

Somebody who sounded like Owen Peabody called from the kitchen, "Hazel? Hazel?"

"You look really bad," she said. "You should go home."

"I don't want to. Why does everyone keep telling me to go home? I want to see you." Nothing had ever been more necessary.

"Ha-zel!" yelled the Owen-maniac.

Sean reached for her hand.

That bell kept ringing.

That fucking bell.

She gestured at the dining room with the hand he wanted. Needed. "I don't have time right now."

Suddenly Sean felt crushed beneath the weight of his humiliation. "I *always* have time for *you*."

"Hazel, Hazel, Hazel!"

"Sean, why are you—" she started.

But he yelled, "I've always done everything for you and you don't even give a shit!"

"That's not true!" She looked shocked by his sudden hostility.

"Why do I waste my time on you?" he asked.

People in the Crock were staring at them now.

"She loves me, she loves me not," Sean bitterly sing-songed. *Do you know how fucking confusing that is!"* he screamed at her, certain that his head would split open right then and there, his taffy brain plopping out—*splat*—onto the white linoleum.

"Sean."

"Do you think I'm an idiot?" he screamed some more. "You're jerking me around!"

"No, I'm not!" she cried. He turned away from her and she grabbed him by the arm. "What do you want from me, Sean?"

"I want you to leave me alone, Hazel." He shook her off. "Just leave like you've always wanted to."

HAZEL STOOD ON the sidewalk outside the Crock for a long time after Sean was gone, because everything he'd said to her was absolutely true.

LATE MONDAY MORNING
THE WINSLOW

Pulling up to The Winslow, Ben Mathers was surprised to find it looking so innocuous. This was his first visit in five years so he'd had plenty of time to work it up in his mind, and he'd expected the hotel to wear its malevolence brazenly.

He climbed out of his brown Valiant, walked to the foot of the steps, and stopped to look up at the structure: old-growth siding, flat rooflines with elaborate brackets supporting deep cornices, and windows as tall as late afternoon shadows. Nothing to suggest anything sinister.

The place is clever, he thought. *It hides.*

Ben shook his head, irritated by his own trepidation. He needed to keep his mind on what he was doing here. Swallowing the fear, he forced himself to walk up the stone steps.

He paused to catch his breath once he reached the level front yard, leaning against one of the pedestal gas lamps that flanked the walkway. An enormous birch tree still occupied the northeast corner of the yard, shading the hotel in summer, branches laden with snow in winter. He'd remembered that right.

Evan and Ruby Winslow's mansion had been converted into the town's only hotel after the Silver Hill Hotel in Matherston burned to the ground in 1918. Same year the Spanish flu stole away half the town. *Most likely Evan Winslow himself struck that match,* Ben had always thought.

That got his ire back up. He marched through the yard to where the path concluded at wide steps leading up to the columned front porch, then took each stair one at a purpose-ful time. After Ben passed beneath the double-arched entry, he reached the twelve-foot black walnut doors and placed his hand on the silver knob. Then he hesitated.

Not because the door was locked…but because things had happened here.

He stared down at his feet, shod in sandals with thick leather straps. *My Lottie would not approve,* he thought, and a wave of dread poured through him.

"Get a hold of yourself, Mathers," he said out loud and the sound of his own voice gave him the strength he needed to push open the heavy door.

He glanced around, eyes darting left and right, up and down…looking for what? What did he expect to see? Floating apparitions? Blood? All he saw was the red-carpeted stair-case with its silver stair rods and the brass statuette adorning the newel post.

Moving through the lobby into the ballroom, it felt as if it had been a hundred years since he'd sipped his last gin and tonic in there. He could almost smell the juniper scent of the booze and remembered resting his arm across the mantle of the carved marble fireplace, watching the others drink their cocktails in the reflection of the gilt-framed mirror. Now he was afraid to look into that mirror. *I don't want to see.* He backed out of the ballroom. *I don't want to see.*

Ben waved his hands in front of his face as if clearing away cobwebs. He needed to stay focused on the reason he'd come to this place: he needed to find her. Time to settle up with Sarah Winslow.

He didn't have to look far. When he turned around she was standing beside the newel post. She looked older than the last time he'd seen her. He supposed that he did, too. It didn't feel as though his heart was beating anymore.

"Get off my property," she said. Her light eyes reflected resolve, nothing more.

He stood his ground, but suddenly his bladder felt very full. "I demand to know what's wrong with this town." Something was wrong all right, and anytime something went wrong around here, it was a sure bet that a Winslow was behind it.

"I'm warning you, Mathers."

Funny, he hadn't noticed the shotgun resting against her side until now. *Painfully full...*

"You're not going to shoot me, old girl."

"You sure about that?" She raised the gun to her hip.

He was not at all sure. And he could no longer ignore his urgent need to relieve himself. "You had better hope nothing worse comes of this, Sarah Winslow."

As he moved toward the door, she swiveled with the shotgun to keep him covered. "You'd better hope not, either. And you'd better not come back here."

He careened out the door and hurried as quick as he dared back to his car. When he reached the Valiant, he scrambled in and drove fast down the driveway. Then he slammed on the brakes three quarters of the way to Ruby Road. Ben jumped out, raced to the side of the drive, and unzipped his shorts. As he stood urinating into a thatch of ferns, he looked up at the hotel.

It wasn't hiding anymore. The Winslow watched him through arched windows, mocking him, forcing him to remember—and daring him to do something about it.

HOLLOWAY RANCH

SITTING ASTRIDE BLACKJACK, Pard Holloway surveyed his acreage and worried.

Worried, *What the hell is happening to my herd?*

Worried, *Where the hell is Doc Simmons?*

And it promised to be hot again. *Is that it: the heat?*

Then he wondered how much this nightmare was going to cost him above and beyond the market value of each head lost.

He figured he'd lost sixty-five head total. About the same number were sick, but hanging in there. So far. And his men had found no more dead since Friday. While a relief, that made the whole damn thing all the more confounding. Each time he ran down the list of possibilities, he was left more perplexed than the time before. The symptoms, variations in severity, rapid onset: none of it added up to anything Pard had ever seen or even heard about. In fact, if he didn't know better, he'd think his animals had been poisoned.

He was likely to strangle Doc Simmons whenever he finally decided to show back up, but only after the vet told Pard what was the matter with his cattle, why his prize bulls were buckling like newborn calves. All night Pard had fought the panic that threatened to spill over like the creeks at high water. If Simmons didn't figure this out soon, it might be too late to save the rest of the herd. And depending on whatever the hell this turned out to be, Pard stood to lose his herd *and* his reputation. And if that happened, that'd be the end of Holloway Ranch.

Pard was not a rich man but he did well enough. The ranch

had been in his family for nearly ninety years but it was he
who'd grown it from bare subsistence to a full-blown money
making operation when he'd made the name Holloway syn
onymous with Prime grade beef. Now his beef was shipped to
upscale restaurants and high-end markets across the country

And Pard was dead certain about one thing in this whole
sorry mess: news about sick cattle would spoil those refined
appetites for his goods. For good.

At least he'd scared the kids quiet Friday night. (And dam
mit if Hazel didn't look just like Anabel when she was mad
Eyes flashing that same fierce green, those long coltish legs
kicking at the dirt.) But then there'd been that regrettable in
cident with Indigo at the rodeo. So now, on top of everything
else, Pard had to worry about the other townsfolk squawk
ing. He hoped they'd have enough sense to keep quiet—for
the common good. They had, after all, done this dance before

While Pard found that somewhat reassuring, he still wor
ried that someone was bound to slip up. In which case Pard
may as well take out a billboard on Yellow Jacket Pass: Some
thing is *very* wrong up at Holloway Ranch.

He sighed so loudly that Blackjack craned to look at him

Patting the horse's neck he said, "It'll be all right." Then
he nudged the animal with his boot heels to get him moving
across the narrow bridge. Once they reached the opposite side
of Ruby Creek, Pard nudged harder and Blackjack broke into
a gallop across open pasture.

I'll do what it takes to put an end to this, Pard thought.

Story over. Period.

But what precisely—*Dammit!*—was this all about?

He found his ranch hands talking and smoking outside
the main barn. They constituted fifteen weathered cowpokes
ranging in age from nineteen (Maggie Clark's boy, Kenny
to seventy-two (Old Pete Hammond, who was curing ham
and churning butter on this land before Pard was even born)

He knew he had the complete loyalty of these men. Though they resented his heavy hand, their livelihood depended on Pard keeping the ranch afloat and for that they respected him.

Noticing him riding up, they gathered and turned their attention to the boss.

Pard remained on Blackjack. "Listen up! I want you men to separate the ailing cattle from the rest and as you do, check them from muzzle to switch for cuts, lesions, screw worms, bugs, grubs, ticks, fleas, blisters and warts. Check their piss, shit and every hole in their body for discharges of pus, snot, and blood or any other damn thing. Herd the healthy to the north pasture. Sick go south. Move it out!"

TANNER

His UNCLE HAD assigned him to keep an eye out for Doc Simmons since they wouldn't be finished separating cattle until
late afternoon at best. *Good riddance,* Tanner had thought and
took the opportunity to go back to bed. His uncle kept getting
him up so early. And he was sore from being dragged around
by that bastard horse at the rodeo.

When Tanner first arrived at the ranch and was assigned
a bedroom on the second story above his uncle's room, his
first thought had been that it was going to be hard to sneak
out at night. Now he knew Pard didn't give a shit what he did
so long as it didn't harm his precious ranch or dent his sterling reputation.

So that morning, without a second thought, Tanner had
crawled back into bed and fallen fast asleep and dreamt of
heifers and steers and his Uncle Pard riding around barking
orders and looming large like Moses parting the Red Sea.

A buzzing noise from the direction of the main barn woke
him. He looked at the clock: 12:20. That was more like it. He
grabbed his blue trunks off the floor and threw them on with
a T-shirt. It was hot already, which was the only drawback he
could see to sleeping late: not easing into the heat.

After he left the house, he wandered toward the buzz until
he found Doc Reed Simmons at the far end of the barn.

Using a circular saw, the veterinarian was cutting open the
head of the bull killed at the rodeo. He finished the cut and
with a lot of effort and cursing pulled off the top of the skull
and tossed it aside. It landed on a hay bale with a soft plunk

For a fascinated moment, Tanner watched Indigo's lid—horns erect, ears slack—drip red into yellow hay. "That's nasty," Tanner said.

"Don't sneak up on me like that!" The bony and bespectacled vet looked seriously startled and wielded the circular saw as if he just might use it on Tanner's head next.

"Have you figured out what's wrong?" Tanner kept his distance from the agitated man.

"That's what I'm trying to do right now." Doc Simmons pushed up his glasses with a gloved finger, leaving a bloody mark on the bridge of his nose. He then made some wet snips inside the head.

Tanner found himself intrigued by this autopsy. "Haven't found anything yet?"

"Acutely inflamed gastrointestinal tract."

Tanner glanced at the bucketful of guts next to Simmons' blood-spattered galoshes.

"Could be the bull got himself into marsh marigold," Simmons continued, "or lupine."

"What're those?" he asked, though it seemed like the vet was talking more to himself.

"Toxic plants." *Snip snip.* "Ate some jimsonweed maybe."

"Is it serious?"

The vet looked at him as if he were an imbecile. An annoying imbecile. "Dead serious. Or haven't you noticed?" When the vet adjusted his glasses again, Tanner noticed that his fingers shook.

Tanner wondered if the vet was always this nervous or just when he had to deliver bad news to Pard Holloway. "I was wondering if—"

"Look, kid, I'm busy here!" Doc Simmons plunged both hands into the head cavity, twisted, and pulled out the brain with a loud *schloopp.*

"Fine, take it easy…" Tanner had wanted to ask if the ani-

mals being sick had anything to do with Patience puking at
the rodeo and Sean and his family getting sick, too. Clearly
now wasn't the time.

So he left Doc Simmons in the barn and turned his attention to the troublesome question of why his left leg hurt so
much. Plus he felt extra-miserably hot today. Walking back
toward the house, he scanned the acre after acre of pasture
surrounded by split-rail fencing. The boonies. No DQ, no cell
phone reception, no signs of civilization whatsoever. He may
as well have been on the fucking moon.

In the empty kitchen of the empty house, he ate some cereal and then felt seriously bored and decided to take the dirt
bike into town and try to scare up some action. The Kawasaki
was the only good thing on the ranch. It was Kenny Clark's
but Maggie said he'd outgrown the bike and Tanner could use
it if he wanted. That was before Maggie got all pissed off at
him. Whatever. It never took long.

DOWNTOWN WINSLOW WAS as lame as ever until he spotted
Patience Mathers all by her lonesome in Prospect Park, sitting
on one of the swings, not swinging but spinning lazily, using
one foot as a pivot. Tanner rode his bike right into the park,
tearing up grass, and parked it next to the kiddie-go-round.

The park felt desolate with the rodeo attractions and car-
nival rides packed up and gone. And after cutting his engine
it was quiet except for a duck quacking and flapping along
the wall surrounding the pond as though it wanted to take off
but couldn't get up the momentum.

Patience watched him approach with a tight look on her
face, as if she might jump up and bolt out of the park at any
second.

"Want a push?" he asked when he reached her.

He could tell she didn't trust him; why should she?

"Okay. But not too high." She pulled up her feet.

After untangling the chains to get her headed straight, he came around behind her. She wore a strapless pink top and he thought how easy it would be to hook his thumb on it and—oops—pull it down. But he thought better of it when he saw that her back was covered in scratch marks: stark red against her alabaster skin. So instead he pulled up the swing by the chains and let her go. When she swung back to him he placed his palms beneath her shoulders and pushed.

"Not too high," she repeated.

Her skin was cold to his touch. *Zombie,* he thought. Here he was, sweating it out in the midday swelter, and she felt kinda...dead. That made him want to push her hard. And when she yelled at him to stop, he pushed even harder. But then she was screaming at him so he grabbed one side of the swing and yanked her to a sideways stop. "Sorry," he said.

She sniffed hard. "You shouldn't've broken that mirror."

"Sorry," he lied again. He stood above her, holding on to one chain.

She looked not so good: holding fast to the swing with both hands, tilted forward in the seat, staring straight ahead.

"You looked hot in that cowgirl getup at the rodeo."

Her face was really white. She scratched at her cheek, creating red welts there, too.

"That vest, especially. You looked damn good in that."

No response.

He stared down at her, calculating, then: "You're the most beautiful girl in Winslow."

She raised her head to look at him.

"You know that, right?" he said. Her pupils were huge: Raggedy Ann eyes. "You're the most beautiful girl I've ever seen." He squatted down in front of Patience, grabbed both chains of the swing, and pulled her toward him. "Anywhere. Ever."

She stared at him, black-eyed, for a long time, until finally: "Really?"

"Without a doubt." Their faces were close now.

"You liked my outfit?" Her breath was on his face.

"You looked amazing."

But then something skittered behind her dark eyes and she said, "You're just after country pie."

"What are you talking about?"

She tried to pull away from him by backing up with both feet. "I know you said you were gonna get a piece of me."

"Who told you that?" he asked through gritted teeth, holding tight to the swing.

"I'm going home now." She tried to twist out of his grasp.

He could feel her panic rising. "Who told you? Hazel?"

"Maybe." She strained against his grip.

"Fine." He released the chains and stood but didn't step back. "Hazel told me something about you."

She pushed the swing aside and backed away from him. "What?"

"That you're easy."

"She didn't say that."

"Easy pickins were her exact words. Low-hanging fruit."

"Hazel would never say that." She spun around and ran.

"Skate punk? Backseat of his Nova?" he yelled. "Ask her if you don't believe me. And while you're at it, tell her Sean isn't putting up with any more of her two-faced bullshit, either."

"You never should've broken that mirror," she cried without looking back. "Nothing good will come to you!"

"Obviously." Tanner watched Patience, and his only chance for getting some tail in this backwoods, race out of the park, and wondered how he was going to make Hazel Winslow pay.

TANNER HAD BEEN back for a while by the time Pard returned. From the kitchen where Tanner sat eating more cereal, he heard his uncle plod up the front steps and tear open the door. His nerves twitched as he waited for Pard to find him, which took all of three seconds.

"Did you see Doc Simmons?" Pard sounded out of breath.

"Yup," he answered without looking up from his bowl.

"And?"

He glanced up then to see his uncle looking as if he might smack him. "And Simmons doesn't look so good himself," Tanner replied. "Nobody does."

"What are you talking about?"

"Everyone in town is sick as hell."

"What kind of sick?"

"The puking and shitting kind."

Tanner saw alarm register on his uncle's face for a split second. But then Pard seemed to catch himself. "That's got *nothing* to do with us. Do I make myself clear?"

"What if it does?"

"We're not sick, are we?"

Tanner thought for an instant about his aching leg. "No."

"Then if people in town are ailing, it must be *from* something in town," he reasoned.

Tanner suspected he was trying to convince himself more than anyone else. "Like what?"

"Could be anything. Bad fish from the Mercantile, spoiled coleslaw at the Crock."

"Cows don't eat coleslaw." Tanner couldn't help himself.

His uncle's eyes took on a queer look and Tanner was sure he would get a smack after all. So he was surprised when instead Pard agreed, "No, they sure as hell don't." But then he grimaced at his nephew. "Are you hurt, kid?"

Tanner realized he was rubbing his leg. "You care? Why'd you make me ride Blackjack?"

Bootsteps pounded the porch, followed by somebody banging on the front door.

As Pard strode out of the kitchen he muttered, "Better be that scrawny-assed vet."

But after Tanner heard his uncle wrench open the door, he recognized Kenny Clark's voice: "We found Simmons' truck wrecked in a ditch off Loop-Loop Road. But no Simmons."

HAZEL

HAZEL WAS DESPERATE to leave the Crock so she could race to The Winslow where she hoped she would find Sean, but Owen begged her to stay and help him since Rose refused to come out of the restroom. After Sean had walked away from her, she'd felt like her heart had been ripped out and she knew she wouldn't feel better until she saw him again, until she made things right with him.

When Owen finally evicted everyone from the dining room around three, Hazel tore off her yellow Crock apron and dashed out.

Cutting through the park, she popped a few Lemonheads into her mouth. In an effort to avoid the food poisoning, she'd been eating nothing but candy. In fact, the last real food she'd consumed was cereal yesterday morning. She felt starved but figured that was better than getting sick and acting like a freak.

The whole thing reminded her of when she was nine years old and had mononucleosis—the sore throat and nausea so severe she barely ate for a week.

"Who have you been kissing?" Dr. Foster had teased. He passed away two years ago after falling off a ladder onto his brick patio, and there hadn't been another doctor in town since.

With the mono, she had been stuck in bed forever and would have gone crazy with boredom were it not for Sean, who bought a new comic book for her every day at the Mercantile, using up his entire allowance.

Now that he was sick, she owed him. Maybe not comic

books, but at least the comfort of her promise that no matter what, they could work this out.

As she left the park, Hazel glanced up at the water tower on top of Silver Hill. She'd had no water since Owen claimed there was something wrong with it. Of course, thinking she mustn't drink it made her insanely thirsty. Owen could be wrong, but why chance it?

When she reached The Winslow, she grabbed a can of orange soda from the fridge and chugged down the whole thing in five long gulps. Stomach sloshing, she then headed up the servants' staircase.

Nobody was around in the Adairs' quarters…and alarm rose as she searched the empty rooms on the second floor. Things were so off kilter she wouldn't have been surprised if everyone simply vanished off the side of the mountain, or if skeletons popped out of the closets like in the House of Horrors.

She finally gave up and started down the formal stairway, where she met Sean's mom walking up. Honey Adair looked as if she'd just gotten out of bed: mascara smudged, brown hair tangled, sundress wrinkled.

Hazel stopped. "I'm glad to see you."

Without so much as a glance, Honey continued past her up the staircase.

Did Sean talk to her? Hazel wondered. *Is she mad at me?* She headed back up the stairs behind her and tried again: "I wanted to see how Sean is feeling."

"Sean?" Honey asked with a dazed look on her face.

"Your son."

"He's a good boy."

"Well, yes, but how is he feeling?"

Honey paused near the head of the staircase—hand resting on the banister, one foot on the upper stair, the other hanging back yet—and appeared to consider the question.

Impatience nudged Hazel. "Have you seen him?"

"I can't see him anywhere, can you? I think he's invisible now." Honey turned to look at Hazel. "Thank you for asking, Anabel."

Honey completed her ascent and headed down the hallway, leaving Hazel to stand there dumbfounded for the second time that day by a member of the Adair family.

But Hazel knew Sean wasn't in the hotel; invisible or not, she would sense him. She descended the wide, red-carpeted steps, skirted past the ballroom, and went out through the beaded-glass back door, where she found her grandmother on the porch that ran the entire length of the rear of The Winslow. In the shade of an ancient oak, Sarah sat facing the woods with a shotgun lying across her lap.

Ordinarily Hazel would have found that strange.

She plopped down beside her grandmother with an exhalation that belied her age. Then she stared at the gazebo planted in the corner of the yard like some oversize, over-decorated birthday cake. The structure always annoyed her. Too fussy. She longed to take an ax to all of its gingerbread details.

Instead, she asked her grandmother, "What are you doing with that gun?"

"Your father says there are wolves about," she replied. "Never saw a wolf in Winslow myself, but he seems sure."

"You saw him today?" Hazel still hadn't seen him since last night. That, she did find exceedingly strange.

"He visited earlier." Sarah peered into the woods. "But I haven't seen him since. I never was able to keep track of that boy. He'd hide in the woods for hours on end even when no one was playing seek."

"That's funny…" Hazel felt distracted, wondering where her dad was now. And what about Sean? Where had he disappeared to?

"Guess he felt safe out there."

Hazel turned to look at her grandmother. "Safe from what?"

"Your mother, I suppose." Sarah laughed. "Anabel and Nate were just like you and Sean—always chasing each other around."

"I know," Hazel said, and that's what had always scared her. If Sean kept chasing *her,* would she have any choice but to run all the way out of Winslow and—*poof!*—disappear, too?

Her mother used to drive a little car they called The Lemon. Hazel had always thought it was because it was yellow, but later her dad told her it was because the car had a transmission no man could fix. Hazel could never remember the exact moment her mother got into The Lemon and left, but she could never forget that soon thereafter she'd discovered all the newly empty spaces—in the house, in her heart—that her mother had formerly occupied. And afterwards her dad would drop her off at the hotel every morning where Honey Adair made pancakes with blackberries from the side yard, which Hazel and Sean would eat in the kitchen nook. But she hated coming over to play because Sean would chase her around the long porch and pull her hair.

"It's because he likes you," Honey would say.

Doesn't feel much like "like" to me, Hazel always thought.

Sometimes Patience would come over too, so her mom, Constance, could *take a break* and the five-year-old girlfriends would gang up against Sean and chase him around the giant oak, threatening to kiss him. All the while Hazel pretended her mother would be coming to pick her up like she always did after she'd just gone down the mountain to do a big grocery shop. But she never came. Instead, her dad would return for her in the afternoon and take her to the Crock for a snack of pie and coffee for him and rainbow sherbet for her. Hazel would sense him willing her not to ask where her mother had gone, so she never did, because as long as she didn't ask, she didn't have to know that Anabel was never coming back.

"You look tired, Hazel," her grandmother said now.

"I am." Suddenly she felt exhausted and slouched down in the roomy wicker chair. *I'll close my eyes for just a minute,* she thought, and then she dozed on the shady porch, dreaming about wolves and little girls in braids and Sean running away from her, into the sun.

When she woke, she found her father sitting beside her in place of her grandmother. She had to squint because while she'd slept, the sun had changed position and now violated the shade of the porch. It was too warm on her skin but her dad's expression as he sought something beyond the tree line made her sit still so she could watch him.

It took only a moment for her to decipher the look on his face. Worry. Deep, black worry. He wore his uniform and, unlike last night when he'd gone to the Rhones' house, he now had his revolver nestled in its holster.

That further unsettled her. With his rifle always locked on the rack inside his Jeep, he didn't usually feel the need to carry his handgun. Despite the sun shining right on him, he looked chilled.

He must have sensed her awake because he turned his head to look at her. "Welcome back, my Hazel." He smiled at her with such tenderness it made her heart hurt.

She smiled back, feeling safe for the first time that day. "Thought you'd gone missing," she said.

But then he gave her a look that stole her sense of relief at having finally found him, and made her feel anxious again. "Dad, what is it?"

He ran a hand over her head to smooth sleep-mussed hair. "You needn't be concerned."

"Too late—I'm already concerned." She sat forward and eyed the woods. Though she couldn't see the water, she could hear Ruby Creek traversing the forest on its journey westward, running down through Holloway Ranch to its final meeting with the Lamprey River. She returned her gaze to her father. "Everyone's acting so weird."

"Something isn't right," he agreed, resuming his own scan of the woods. "Something's out there."

"Wolves?" she asked, confused.

"Something worse," he said.

And she felt a dark splotch of fear spread slowly through her like a drop of warm blood in still water.

MONDAY NIGHT
RHONE BAKERY

ZACHARY RHONE HAD no idea how long he'd been in the bakery staring into the oven, but it was dark out now. He remembered Pard Holloway stopping by for a while, and he remembered Melanie coming in a couple of times. But he couldn't remember why they'd interrupted him.

He could hear Violet and Daisy outside in the yard skipping rope and chanting, "Not last night but the night before, twenty-four robbers came knocking on my door."

Struggling to ignore them, Zachary continued to stare into the big bread oven, on the verge of figuring it all out. If only he concentrated a little harder, he knew it would come to him. Though he felt no heat, he saw flames dance, heard fire hiss his name.

His daughters chanted faster: "And this is what they said… to…me! Ladybug-ladybug, turn around. Ladybug-ladybug, touch the ground."

Ice-cold fingers tapped Zachary on the chest: the fire had a question for him. He leaned closer while the frozen fingers wrapped around his heart, chilling his blood.

"Shall we bake a cake?" asked the flames.

Zachary wiped at the sweat dripping from his forehead into his eyes. He knew this was important—if only he could pay attention.

But his girls were so *loud.* "Ladybug ladybug, fly away home."

"Bread buns rolls for everyone," the flames taunted.

So hard to concentrate. He spun on his stool, putting his back to the oven, and shouted, "Can't you girls be quiet for one minute and let. Daddy. THINK!"

Faster, faster they shouted, "Your house is on fire, your children will burn!"

Flames sprang from the oven, snatching at Zachary's arms and neck.

I only turned my back for a second! he lamented before breaking free of their fiery grip.

Pinwheeling up from the stool, he saw a contorted, monstrous face in the window. "What are you?" he screamed at his own reflection. "What do you want from me?"

He backed away and slammed against a shelf, upsetting a sack of flour that burst open when it hit the floor and sent a grayish plume rising in the air.

I can't breathe! Zachary choked, feeling his way out of the bakery. *It's killing me.*

BUCKHORN TAVERN
FORTUNE WAY

"JUST CONSIDER IT, is all I'm saying," Owen Peabody was saying, although nobody appeared to be listening when Pard Holloway entered the Buckhorn Tavern.

Mounted game heads and antique horse gear festooned the bar's wood-paneled walls. And townsfolk were parked on every last cowhide-covered chair and bar stool. *What the hell are all of you doing out?* Pard puzzled. Even Tiny Clemshaw was there, sucking on a bottle of beer. Pard hadn't seen Clemshaw take a drink in years. Not since Nate Winslow arrested him for plowing down Meg Foster's poodle Pepé on the sidewalk of Park Street.

"That rotting old water tank," Owen continued, seemingly undaunted. "Bacteria multiplying like gangbusters. Slime." He shuddered. "Toxic slime." Owen paused as if for reaction, but everyone remained engaged in their own spirited conversations. "Just consider it, that's all." Looking deflated, Owen sank down onto the stool next to his wife, Rose, at the bar.

Pard maneuvered around Laura Dudley and Ivy Hotchkiss dancing to Creedence's swampy "Susie Q" on the jukebox, and took the bar stool between Tiny Clemshaw and Kohl Thacker. Then he motioned for the blond, pixyish Marlene Spainhower behind the bar.

Marlene sauntered over to him in tight jeans and tighter cowgirl shirt. "Hi ya, Pard," she greeted him brightly. Marlene and Pard had an arrangement. They'd had it for years. It worked well enough.

"What's all this?" he asked her over the din, gesturing at the crowded bar.

Shriekish laughter spurted from the table by the jukebox. She shrugged as if to say, *Who knows?* and drew him a draft. "People have been acting peculiar all day, seemed drunk before they had their first."

"Have you seen Doc Simmons?" Pard asked. Earlier, Pard had pounded on the vet's front door but there had been no answer and Pard hadn't had any luck finding him anywhere else. Pard was seriously worried that the vet may have injured himself when he totaled his truck and was wandering the woods, bleeding from the head.

"Simmons?" Marlene glanced around with green eyes. "Not scraggly hair nor skinny hide." She set the glass in front of Pard but he made no move to pick it up.

Instead, Pard turned his attention to Kohl Thacker who sat mumbling beside him. "What's that you say?" Pard wanted information.

"The sickness," Kohl raised his voice, then knocked back the rest of his bourbon and banged the glass down on the bar.

Pard's unease grew. "What sickness?"

"The sickness we got!" Kohl yelled and the bar got quiet, the only sound the *chick chick* of the ancient jukebox as it loaded the next forty-five.

"And what exactly is it?" Pard asked in a measured tone designed to encourage Kohl to keep it the hell down.

"It's spreading, that's what it is!" Kohl squawked and murmurs rolled through the tavern.

After talking to Tanner, Pard had figured he'd better come into town and see for himself exactly what was going on. Now he assessed this situation as *not good*. Maybe worse. His visit to Zachary Rhone at the bakery had been none too encouraging either, the baker at present being a few slices short of a loaf.

From the jukebox, Peggy Lee spoke, "I sat there watching the marvelous spectacle…" while Julie Marsh walked to the head of the bar as if called for her turn to speak.

"I have been feeling poorly, not very well," Julie announced before returning to her table where her husband, Jay Marsh, sat sweating into his beer.

"It's the strangest feeling I've ever had," Ivy Hotchkiss said.

"It is a most peculiar feeling," Rose Peabody agreed. "Sometimes I feel fine and then—"

"The Government!" Laura Dudley looked convinced. "It's a secret military experiment."

Owen shook his head fiercely. "It's gotta be the water. We drank it. The cows drank it."

Pard strode to the jukebox and pulled the plug. "We all need to settle down." He looked around the tavern and felt his impatience shifting toward anger. "You've got food poisoning, plain and simple. Right, Rose?"

From the bar, Rose stared at him and neither agreed nor disagreed, just looked weary.

"All we have to do is ride this out," Pard continued.

"Is that so?" Gus Bolinger said from the far side of the bar. "I'd like to know where Sheriff Winslow is. What's he got to say about all this?"

"Nate must be sick," Marlene replied. "He's made himself scarce today."

"Now, Gus," Pard managed to keep his tone agreeable, desiring no wrangle with the Korean War hero. "You know we've got no need for the law. Haven't we always taken care of our own?"

Tiny Clemshaw shot up, jabbed his finger in Pard's direction, and knocked over his beer bottle with his elbow. "It's your fault!" he blustered. "You've been wantin' to be rid of us for a long time, and now you've gone and poisoned us with your stinking, rotting meat!"

Pard stormed over and shoved Clemshaw back down onto his bar stool so hard it was a wonder the stool *and* the man didn't snap. The storekeeper was always on the prod but he usually showed Pard respect. Not tonight.

"All right, Holloway." Gus rose from his bar stool. "No need to get rough."

"Pard," Ivy piped up from right beside the door, looking ready to bolt if need be. "Most of us did eat beef at some point over the past few days."

"Is it mad cow disease?" Kohl asked, fright wrinkling his pale face.

"Oh, for Pete's sake, Thacker." Pard spat out his breath in aggravation. "My cattle eat organic grains, so mad cow isn't even a possibility. Besides, it takes *years* for symptoms of BSE to develop in humans, not days."

"Oh, no." Laura looked shocked. "It's anthrax, isn't it?"

Pard inhaled deliberately slow and let everyone fidget while awaiting his reaction. "Enough!" he finally boomed and the people nearest him shrank back from the force of it. "I'll be damned if I'll stand by and let you ruin this town with your half-cocked speculating. Don't you see? Rumors like that spoil tourists' appetites. Even the simple truth—food poisoning— will be enough to ruin our reputation. *Forever.*" He glared around the room, challenging anyone to argue with that.

No one dared.

Until Tiny Clemshaw, full of piss and vinegar and abnormal daring, said, "Won't be carryin' Holloway meat in my Mercantile anymore, I can tell you that much."

Pard felt a nearly overwhelming impulse to haymaker the man into next week. Instead, he reined in his fury and said, "Disparaging my good name is as good as destroying your own."

Tiny brayed.

"Don't come crying to me, Clemshaw, when you've got no livelihood. Listen up, all of you—I'm trying to do you a favor."

"Pard's right," Marlene said. "Think about it—this could really hurt us next season."

"Aw, hell," Gus said. "The tourists come more for blackberry pie and Lamprey River trout than Holloway rib eyes."

"What is *wrong* with all of you?" Pard pressed his fingers against his forehead. "They can get those things a lot easier down in Stepstone without having to brave the pass. And I bet those folks down in the valley will be more than happy to soak up our lost tourist dollars."

Tiny narrowed his eyes at Pard. "What are you hiding?"

"Not a damn thing! Not a single cowhand is sick and we eat beef nearly every damn day."

"But what about your dead cows?" Ivy asked. "What about Indigo?"

"Enough about my herd! You're barkin' at a knot! Cattle get sick—it happens. Stop trying to connect invisible dots."

No one would meet his eyes now.

"Look," he continued, "we need to work together here. Let's not allow things to get blown all the hell outta proportion." Everybody looked sheepish and uneasy, so he figured he must finally be getting through. "And we need to keep a lid on this or else we'll end up like Hawkin Rhone with an orchard full of apples no one will touch at any price. Is that what you want?"

Heads were shaking.

"Didn't think so," Pard said.

"It almost feels the same as then, doesn't it?" Ivy said.

"Like when Missy Rhone—" Kohl started.

"All right, all right." Pard gestured at them to quiet down, though he couldn't help but think, *Same family, two of the worst things that ever happened to this town.* He shook his head. "No need to flog that dead horse. Now let's all go on home and stay there until this blows over."

He turned back to the bar and took a long draw from the glass. "Thanks for the beer, Marl," he said.

"Anytime." Marlene was looking at Pard with concern.

Or maybe that look held the first stirrings of distrust, Pard couldn't be certain.

The crowd parted to let him out of the tavern. After he burst through the batwing doors and into the hot night air, he heard the jukebox start up again. Across the street in Prospect Park, Hap Hotchkiss was doubled over—one hand on his belly and the other pushing back his hair—losing his biscuits to the pine needles. And in front of the Fish 'n Bait next door to the Buckhorn, Cal was rearranging plastic letters on his *Today's Special Critters* board.

"What the hell are *you* doing?" Pard wanted to know. Usually Cal closed up shop by noon.

"Folks'll be in early for bait and tackle."

"What folks?"

"Gonna be lots of anglin' around here from now on."

"Why's that?"

"Seeing as we can't eat your beef anymore and we've got all these fish storms."

All argued-out, Pard left Cal to his task, thinking, *This situation is not good at all.*

BAM, BAM, BAM! Somebody knocked with startling force. *Bam! Bam!*

Nate Winslow heard the windows rattle as he hurried through his living room to the entry, one hand on the grip of his gun. With his other hand, he jerked open the front door just as Pard Holloway was about to pound it again.

"What can I do for you, Pard?" Nate asked, feeling worn out and not up for a fight with his brother-in-law. It took great effort just to stand there, holding on to the door, and suddenly Nate wondered if his outward appearance betrayed how truly bad he felt inside.

Pard brushed past Nate into the house, knocking him away from the door. "You need to do something about this right away, Sheriff."

Plunking down onto the staircase, Nate tried to guess which *this* Pard meant. Pard always said the word *sheriff* with such derision. *As though it tastes bitter on his tongue,* Nate thought.

Looming over him, hands on hips, Pard said, "These people of yours are fixing to make things a whole lot worse than they already are."

"People *are* worse," Nate agreed. Then he could tell by the perplexed look on Pard's face that he hadn't responded correctly to what he'd said. What had he said? Already, Nate could not remember. His stomach gave another sickened lurch.

Pard stood for a moment, staring at Nate, appearing to consider. Finally, he cleared his throat. "You're right then, Winslow," he said with an air of conclusion. "We need to quarantine the town."

Have we been talking for a while? Nate wondered. Hadn't they just gotten started? He felt as though he'd definitely missed something.

Pard stabbed a finger down at him. "And do it quick or you'll send the whole place into a panic."

"Shouldn't we consult a doctor first?" Nate tried.

"Doc Simmons can handle it." Pard dismissed further discussion with a flick of his hand. "Besides, phones are out. I'm guessing another rotted-out pine split in two and took out the line again. Damn bark beetles."

Alarms clanged in Nate's head. *A veterinarian is going to handle this? What if things get as bad as they got with Missy Rhone?* He began to protest, "But a quarantine requires—"

"Listen, *Sheriff,* time is of the essence here. I've taken care of my ranch and quarantined my cattle. Now it's your job to take control of your town. Or else I'll do it for you."

"We need to get the authorities up here." Nate was certain this was what they needed to do. Right away. Why hadn't he thought of it before? When had all this started anyway?

"We *are* the authorities, Winslow, and we clean up our own messes around here. Always have, always will. You know that better than most."

Nate grappled with the implications of Pard's statement. "What are you saying?"

"A helluva mess that was, too." Pard rocked on his heels and whistled.

Nate endeavored to maintain a semblance of control, when really he felt like crawling into a closet and shutting the door. They had all agreed that summer that no one would miss the old man. That there was no point in Sean Adair getting into trouble—what was done was done. They'd all agreed on that. And Nate and Dr. Foster had buried the body the full six feet deep.

Only now Nate sensed Hawkin Rhone clawing at the earth.

Pard cleared his throat again. To get Nate's attention, Nate supposed. "Just so we're clear, Sheriff—that radio of yours quit working, too. Because I'd hate to have to dredge all that up again, truly I would. Especially since Jules Foster isn't around anymore to back your version of it."

"Are you threatening me, Holloway?"

"Threatening?" Pard feigned a look of surprise. "No, just applying a little leverage, Winslow, to keep you herded in the right direction. Hate to see you stumble off a cliff."

All at once Nate realized he didn't want to be in charge anymore. *What if I can't handle it?* With sudden panic, he understood that he was too sick to handle anything. Maybe he should just let Pard take over. *He's okay, isn't he?* So hard to tell. Nate massaged the muscles aching in his arms while his pulse raced and his stomach flopped around like a hooked eel.

"So what's it gonna be, Sheriff?" Pard glared at him while Nate struggled to muster a response. "A quarantine then? Good idea. No one in, no one out. Effective immediately. Your orders, Sheriff."

Pard left then, evidently satisfied Nate wasn't going to give him any trouble.

Feeling incapable of rising from the step, worried they may have woken Hazel in her bedroom upstairs, Nate laid his head across his arm and hoped things wouldn't get any worse—and that the past would stay buried across Three Fools Creek.

FIVE SUMMERS AGO
MATHERSTON MINERS CEMETERY

AFTER THE GHOSTS began to stir in the tower of The Winslow that summer Hazel turned twelve, but before her grandfather's heart attacked him in the sunny bedroom upstairs, she sat with Sean inside the granite wall surrounding the cemetery. There were no messages written on the wall that day either.

Hugging sunburned knees, curious how long the corpse beneath them had lain buried, Hazel leaned forward to consider the epitaph burned onto a pinewood cross gone crooked with age, and planted at her feet:

Here lies Dinky Dowd
Not another breath was he allowed
By order of The Hon. E. Winslow
1889

She looked at her twelve-year-old friend Sean slumped against the wall beside her, and worried they would run out of dead townsfolk and candy money soon.

Their tenth straight day of ghost hunting had been launched that morning after they pestered Patience's grandfather for a dead man's name until finally Ben Mathers challenged them to find Dinky Dowd. When Patience became spooked during their fruitless search of the grassy church cemetery, she quit the game, and Hazel and Sean had raced across town to the weedy silver miners' graveyard. Since Sean was first to spot Dinky's grave, he'd won the prize of taffy and Jolly Ranchers they'd bought at Clemshaw Mercantile and stashed at the playground for later. But Hazel knew Sean would share with her, unless Patience ate it all first. More than once they'd met back up in Prospect Park and found Patience waiting for them on the red merry-go-round, wrestling with a mouthful of the rightful victor's taffy.

Now, after contemplating Dinky's corpse decaying beneath their feet, Hazel decided, "Hanged is a lousy way to die."

Sean pitched a rock at Dinky's grave marker before turning his light brown eyes on her. "Hanged is what happens when you knife George Bolinger through the heart in the Never Tell."

"Shot. In the gut." She rubbed her own unscathed neck. "I hope I never get hung."

"Try not to kill anyone in Winslow."

"I'll try. But even if I did, I don't think my great-great-grandfather would sentence me to hang."

"Somebody would," Sean said.

Squinting past the scatter of other graves to the empty space beyond the edge of the canyon, Hazel wondered what would happen if it rained too hard and the hill gave out in a wave of mud. Maybe all the markers and coffins and bones would stream over the precipice and splash into the water below. Maybe the whole stupid town would slide into the Lamprey River.

She inhaled warm, pine-sap-tinged air, and then blew out her cheeks. "I wish it'd rain."

"Never rains in July," he said, fishing around a droopy foxglove for more rocks to throw.

She glanced up between the branches of the purple-leaf plum tree, its leaves black against the heat-washed sky. "Never," she sighed. Abruptly she rose and brushed stickers

off the back of her shorts, feeling hot and ornery, and thinking that a grilled cheese and brain-freezing chocolate shake
back at the Crock were starting to sound pretty good. "I'm
bored of ghosts." She nudged Sean's foot with her own. "Let's
do something else."

He stood to face her. "Dare you to jump in Three Fools
Creek."

She looked her best friend in the eye. "I'll take that dare."

"Bullshit."

"What will you give me if I do it?"

"Don't matter. You won't."

"What will you give me?" she repeated.

"I'll give you whatever you want." He narrowed his eyes
at her. "What *do* you want, Hazel Winslow?"

"MAYBE THIS ISN'T such a good idea." Hazel swatted a skinny
alder branch out of her path.

"Don't think about it." Sean placed his hand between her
shoulder blades and gave her a soft shove. "Just go."

They crunched down a trail covered in dried pinecones
while the air grew thick with the rising heat and the scent of
warming resin. And the deeper they continued into the woods,
the more Hazel wondered if she'd completely lost her mind.

After the path disappeared beneath a tangle of ferns, she
tripped over a fat tree root. To keep from falling, she grabbed
an overhead branch and pitchy pine needles rained down on
her head.

"Yuck!" Hazel clawed her fingers through long waves of
hair. Then she spun to frown hard at Sean. "What if he's over
there?"

"Maybe he'll invite us for lunch." He shrugged, grinning.
"Squirrel soup."

She couldn't help but laugh. "You truly are the village
idiot, I swear."

When she turned around again, Sean plucked more needles out of her hair and off the back of her shirt. Despite the uneasy feeling roiling her stomach, she plodded forward, regret building with each step that she'd taken his dare.

By the time she reached the banks of Three Fools Creek, Hazel was sticky, scraped up, and dead sure that they were *both* village idiots for coming here. She glanced upstream to where scant sunlight permeated the dense tree canopy and the creek ran cold and black. Edging cautiously closer, she peered into the rushing water.

Sean bumbled up and nearly knocked her in. "See three fools down there?"

She pointed at their wavering reflections. "Only two."

Nervously chewing her bottom lip, she lifted her gaze to the ramshackle prospector's cabin across the creek. Its rough-hewn log siding was grayed and peeling with rot, roof warped and moldy beneath the monster blackberry bush consuming the structure.

"Do you really think he did it?" she asked.

"Doesn't matter." Sean swiped at the gnat buzzing his ear. "Way Ben Mathers tells it—"

"And tells it and tells it…" She rolled her eyes.

He laughed before continuing. "Mathers says, guilty or not, he's a mean sonofabitch and everyone in Winslow was glad to have a good reason to run him out of town."

Studying the cabin, Hazel wondered aloud, "Maybe it was an accident."

Sean grabbed her by the elbow. "Let's go over and ask him."

"Ssh! He'll hear us."

"Scaredy cat. You took my dare, remember?"

"To jump in the creek, not go over *there*."

"Look—he's not home. He's gone hunting or something."

"Hunting children." In the shade of the pines, Hazel got goose bumps beneath her sweat.

"C'mon." Sean stepped down the bank.

"Don't." She reached out to pull him back.

Dodging her, he tore off one tennis shoe and plunged his foot into the water. "Last one in has to be rodeo queen."

"Dang you, Sean Adair!" She kicked off her sandals and knocked past him into the creek. Chill water reached above her knees as she waded across with care. Unlike Ruby Creek where they usually swam, this creek bed harbored jagged logs and slick rocks—bumpy and mean, threatening broken ankles and concussed heads.

Splashing in beside her, Sean whispered, "We'll steal something to prove we were here."

Hazel gaped at him. "Now we're *stealing* from him?"

Huffing in agitation, she climbed out of the creek up the opposite bank and crossed into a world silent, brambly and weirdly wet. She spun in a slow circle, taking in the dusky woods, the tumbledown cabin, the smell of damp dirt—and her skin crawled with paranoia. "Let's get out of here," she hissed.

But Sean was already on the cabin's slanting porch searching for a souvenir. A huge pair of buck antlers hung above the door and he jumped up, grabbed onto one branch, and swung in midair for a moment before crashing back down to the disintegrating floorboards.

"Nice try, Tarzan." Hazel joined him on the porch and peeked through the cabin's only window. Dark inside, she made out the shape of a chair next to a potbellied stove, little else.

"How's this?" Sean asked.

She turned to see him holding a raccoon pelt by the tail. "Eww! Put that down."

"His name's Bandit." He swung the stiff hide in front of her face.

"Gross! Get away!" She smacked Sean's arm then whirled around to head off the porch. Mindful of being barefoot, she stepped gingerly along the splintered boards, which protested at even her slight weight. "I'm leaving."

"Don't go. Bandit likes you—"

Hazel made it one step off the porch and onto the dirt at the side of the cabin before Hawkin Rhone seized her left wrist. Soiled and crumbly as a long-buried corpse, he yanked her close.

"I warned you children!" the old man howled in her face with breath reeking of decay.

Suddenly blind to everything except his black mouth, she tried to scream but could force no breath past the cold slab of terror choking her—certain that he was about to bite off her head with his remaining rotten teeth and roast it in his pot-bellied stove.

"Sean, help me!" Hazel gasped. She recoiled and kicked at Hawkin Rhone's towering, bony frame with her bare feet. "Let me go! *Sean!*"

The man tightened his grip around her small wrist. "Warned you!"

Her scream finally burst free and she kicked at him again while her arm exploded in pain and her heart skittered around in her chest like a trapped animal.

"You didn't listen!" he shouted and more rancid air escaped his lungs and poured into her screaming mouth. "None of you listened!"

"Where are you, Sean?" Hazel looked up to the sky through pine boughs that seemed to be spinning then back at the man's craggy face just inches from her own and feared she might pass out and never come to again. She finally landed a kick with the heel of her foot against his gnarled right knee but it wasn't enough to make him let go.

Instead he wrenched her arm harder. "No more apples till spring! Hear me?"

She sobbed, "Please—" Then Hazel heard her wrist snap

with a sharp sound that instantly coated her terror in nausea. "Stop!" she cried. "Let go!"

But still he clutched her broken wrist. The pain shot up her arm into her neck and her fingers tingled in a way that made her feel weak and the stink of him made her gag. "Sean," she wept, "help me."

"I told my children," Hawkin Rhone rasped softly now. "Told Missy and Zachary to stay out of the orchard." His eyes filled with tears; his sorrow spilled down his creviced cheeks. "She didn't listen." He squeezed Hazel's ruined wrist. "Why didn't you listen to your father?"

She cried, too, at the pain that came in ever-greater waves, fearing she'd soon drown in it. Strangled by sobs, she could barely speak. "Sean—I need you. Where are you?"

At last he was there, sneaking up behind Hawkin Rhone from the rear of the cabin with an expression of terrified determination. Half the man's size, Sean leapt up on a stump before swinging the split pine log like a baseball bat against the back of Hawkin Rhone's head.

The old man's head snapped forward and his upper teeth sank into his tongue. Raising his head, he attempted to speak but the teeth were stuck clear through. As he tried to pull them out by working his jaw up and down, blood streamed from both sides of his mouth, while Hazel and Sean shrieked unintelligibly—primal shouts of triumph and horror.

Slick with blood, Hawkin Rhone's teeth finally slid free of his nearly severed tongue. And his face was a swirl of confusion as he put a hand to his cracked skull and sputtered in red, "Wha?" Then he began to turn toward Sean.

"Again!" Hazel screamed.

Sean swung and connected squarely with the bewildered man's face, log meeting flesh with the revolting sound of cartilage and bone collapsing beneath unyielding wood.

Sprung free of the man's grip at last, Hazel shrieked again, exultant now. With her good arm, she reached for Sean where he stood—log raised and ready—and dragged him away from Hawkin Rhone, who was now only a slack heap in the dirt.

They splashed recklessly across the creek and retook the trail, crushing barefoot through sharp pine needles, not stopping to look back or consider what had happened, just running and shouting until they rounded a corner beneath a spray of hemlock and Hazel smacked hard against Patience. Both girls cried out before falling onto a painful bed of pinecones.

Sean skidded to a stop and shot a look over his shoulder, as if wanting to make sure that the madman hadn't given chase.

Hazel struggled to get upright, feeling battered and traumatized. The wind knocked clear out of her, she gulped futilely before catching enough breath to half say, half sob, "Oww, crap."

Patience didn't look surprised to see them. Instead, she looked about as guilty as a cat with feathers stuck to its fur. She was chewing—taffy, Hazel had little doubt—her right cheek ballooned out chipmunk-style.

Sucking more air into her deflated lungs, Hazel managed to gasp at her, "Were you following us?"

Nodding, Patience's eyes went wide.

Hazel stood up on unsteady legs to point down at her. "Did you see what happened?"

More chews, another nod, an audible swallow.

"You can't tell anybody what you saw."

"Ever," Sean added, his breath ragged.

When she didn't respond Hazel grabbed her by the hair with her good hand and Patience screeched like a bat. "Promise, Patience Mathers! Cross your heart and hope to die."

"Cross my heart!" Her voice was taffy garbled. "Hope to die!" At that, Hazel let go and Patience got to her feet, rubbing her scalp where Hazel had pulled out a smattering of long dark hair.

Hazel noticed Sean's eyes dancing a panicked jig: looking from the path to the treetops and into the woods. He glanced down the trail once more before pulling Hazel against the trunk of the hemlock. "Do you think he's dead?"

Holding her throbbing, shattered wrist against her belly, Hazel whispered, "I hope so." With the shock subsiding, the shaking began, and suddenly she felt very cold.

"What if he's not dead?" Sean's face was crumpled up just like after the time Kenny Clark kicked his ass up and down the wood plank sidewalk in front of the Fish 'n Bait. "Can we just leave him there, in the dirt, bleeding to death?"

"Yes," she said, fighting the urge to start crying again.

"I don't know, Hazel…"

"Yes, we can."

He passed a hand hard across his mouth, then: "We have to go back later and bury him."

"No, Sean." She heard the creek complain as the first fat, dirty drops of rain fell from the summer sky. "We're never going back."

DEAD OF MONDAY NIGHT

HER UNCLE PARD'S pounding and yelling had woken Hazel up and sent her heart racing. Now she couldn't get back to sleep. She'd been restless and barely dozing anyway. It was still hot and she never slept well with just a sheet on; it made her feel vulnerable. And through her windows—opened in the vain hope a breeze might kick up—she heard a lot of ruckus outside.

Her clock said 2:35.

She tried to throw off the sheet but it was tangled with her feet and she kicked at it, annoyed, until finally free of it. Then she went to her bedroom window facing Prospect Park and leaned on the sill. To her surprise she saw not just a few drunks shuffling noisily home from the Buckhorn Tavern, but dozens of people wandering the streets. She leaned farther out the window to look down Park Street, and then up toward Ruby Road. Some houses had lights on inside, including The Winslow.

Hazel glanced at the clock again—2:36. Then, for the thousandth time that night, she wondered where Sean had disappeared to.

Turning her attention back to the street she saw Tiny Clemshaw and Ben Mathers deep in animated discussion, their dander clearly up. Bits of their conversation wafted up to her: "Held accountable for once," and "Get away with it again." But Hazel could make no sense of their words.

The men shushed and huddled together conspiratorially when Jay and Julie Marsh walked by. Oddly, Julie was bundled up in a pouffy down jacket. Jay's arm hung protectively across her shoulders.

Then Hazel noticed Jinx sitting next to the elm, looking up at her with hope in his eyes. He barked twice and startled Tiny and Ben, who looked over but then quickly resumed their heated conversation.

Fishing around her floor she came up with cut-offs and her black tank top—the one with the big rainbow across the front. A stupid shirt. When her dad gave it to her on her last birthday she'd thought, *He thinks I'm still a little girl.* But now it was the only thing sort of clean. She threw it on along with the shorts, stuffed her bare feet into her tennis shoes, and headed downstairs.

In the foyer, she heard her dad arguing in a sharp, hushed tone and figured her Uncle Pard hadn't left after all. But when she looked into the dark living room, she saw that he was alone. "Dad?" she whispered.

Her voice must not have registered because he continued talking bitterly to himself.

Unnerved, it took her a moment to shift her attention to the scratching sound coming from the back of the house. Imagining it to be Jinx, she made her way to the kitchen and flipped on the light.

Then she hesitated, suddenly afraid to go to the door and answer that scratch, because Jinx had never behaved like this before.

The scratching took on greater urgency and her heart sped up.

What else could it be?

Shaking off her fear, she forced herself to the door.

After snapping open the shade, all she could see was her own reflection—big eyes, big rainbow—so she leaned close to the window and peered into the darkness.

A heavy crash against the glass sent her springing back.

She scanned the kitchen for a weapon, her heart bouncing around in her chest.

When she looked back at the door, there was nothing there.

Until Jinx jumped against the glass again. This time he remained standing on hind legs, front paws pressed against the window, eyes rolled halfway back in his head in pure doggy fright.

Exhaling relief, she rushed over and opened the whiny door and he fell in. Scampering across the tile the dog cast a furtive glance behind him, as if terrified that something were about to give chase into the kitchen. And after Hazel slammed the door shut, Jinx looked relieved, too.

She put her back to the door, squatted down to him, and stroked the soft hair on his head. "What's the matter, boy?"

The dog shook nose to tail.

"There's nothing to be afraid of—"

Behind her the door was shoved open with such force the old hinges didn't just whine, they screamed.

Jinx yelped as Hazel spun up and around in one fell swoop to face Patience: wild-eyed and breathing hard, her dark hair all a jumble, looking like some crazed, beautiful witch.

"We have to undo it," Patience said, struggling for breath.

"What are you talking about?" Hazel's chest tightened while Jinx whimpered beside her.

Patience narrowed her eyes at the dog. "We have to undo it." She looked back at Hazel. "Or else three more will die."

Jinx growled at Patience then, deep in his throat, and Hazel glanced down. The dog's hackles stood on end...and she felt the hair on the back of her own neck creeping up.

ALL THE WAY to The Winslow, Patience kept pulling at her shorts and tank top as if they were chafing her skin. Then she would scratch at her arms, leaving welty red streaks up and down them. "Stop that," Hazel ordered her, the sound of it driving her mad.

But Patience told her, "I can't—there's something under my skin."

When they reached the base of the hotel's steep driveway, Hazel stopped and took Patience by the shoulders. "Listen. You really don't want to do this."

"We *have* to do this." Patience gave her a look of total desperation.

But Hazel felt certain that what they were about to do would prove to be a huge mistake. Just like the first go round. "Why now—of all times—do you want to come back here, Patience?"

A violent shudder shook Patience's frame. "Don't you understand, Hazel?" She glanced up at the hotel and trembled again. "It's the only way for us to set the past right. And to make sure it won't happen again." She looked back at Hazel. "To stop it from happening *right now*."

Despite Hazel's continued pleading, there had been no talking Patience out of it.

So here they sat, cross-legged, before the tall, darkened window in the circular room at the top of the tower, the crystal glass positioned between them. Hazel watched Patience summon her courage—she could almost *see* the waves of dread passing over her friend's face.

"Let's get this over with," Hazel whispered. She wasn't sure why she whispered; nobody appeared to be around. But it seemed best to leave whoever or whatever might be undisturbed.

"Okay…" Patience said through a shaky exhale. Then she cracked the egg and worked the innards and shells until the white slipped into the water. As the egg sank, she sucked in her breath.

Nothing. No coffin. No sign of ill fortune. No discernable

shape at all. Hazel hoped that would put an end to this. It was starting to feel claustrophobic in the tower. She looked up at Patience, who was staring into the glass, skin ghost-white, eyes ink-black.

Raising her wide eyes to Hazel's, Patience asked in a hushed voice, "Do you see anything?"

"A slimy egg white." Hazel suddenly felt swallowed by claustrophobia and unable to contain her irritation. "And you being a freak. I'm leaving now."

"No you're not!" Patience snatched up the glass and threw it against the window. Water splashed back on them but the glass didn't break. Instead, it cracked a 120-year-old pane of red stained glass before it bounced to the floor. Patience shot up and pointed down at Hazel. "You're glad I'm sick!"

Hazel was taken aback. "Why would I be?"

"You're jealous of me!"

Hazel stood to face her. "You are seriously deranged. Get a grip."

"I know what you said!" Patience's shrill voice cracked.

"Oh?" Hazel placed her hands on her hips, surprised that it felt almost good to be fighting with her. "And what was that?"

"That I'm easy pickings."

Hazel didn't reply. She was busted; what was there to say? So she stood her ground and stared at Patience, her next door neighbor since they were squirming babies, and thought about how she'd like to punch Tanner Holloway right in his gigantic mouth the next time she saw him. Finally, she said, "At least I warned you about Tanner and his creepy country pie fantasy."

That reminder did nothing to dampen the flames of Patience's outrage. "You're a backstabber! And Sean's not taking any more of your bullshit, either!"

She'd never heard Patience use those words before. Clearly they were Tanner's. *Or Sean's,* Hazel realized with a sinking heart. "Where is Sean?"

"How would I know?"

"When did you see him?"

"I didn't, Tanner told me. Why didn't you help me bury the broken mirror?"

"When did Tanner see Sean?"

"Does it matter? It's too late."

"What does *that* mean?" Hazel felt cold despite the smothering heat in the tower.

"If you don't bury the glass beneath the moonlight, the bad luck comes. In threes they'll come, Madame Marcelle told me. You know you should've listened to me."

"Settle down, Patience."

"The cows sensed it coming—what a bad sign. Indigo knew and now I know. Gram Lottie says the cows knew and I threw up over everything in front of everybody and Gramp is ashamed at such a display and he said, 'No Mathers should make such a spectacle of themselves,' and he asked what the devil is the matter with me anyhow?" Patience placed her hands over her heart. *"I don't know!"*

"Calm down!"

"What's the matter with me, Hazel? I thought you were my friend, I always thought that, but when I told you about the ring around the moon you—"

"Patience! Stop!"

"—didn't listen. I tried to warn you and now look. Now I'm sick everybody's sick and it's too late. The cows are dying the mirror's broken the ring is red and that's three only that's not all Sadie says—"

Hazel slapped Patience across the face. Surprisingly, that felt good, too.

HAZEL TRIED TO steal more sleep in the lobby of The Winslow where she'd taken up position on the sofa in case Sean came home. When she heard heavy boot steps outside followed by a loud thump on the porch, she slogged through her exhaustion to the door and opened it wide, too tired to be afraid of what she might find there. The body leaning against the door slumped into the entryway and came to rest on top of her bare feet.

She flipped on the light.

Owen Peabody. Not dead, she didn't think, but not moving, either.

She watched Old Pete Hammond and Kenny Clark climb into Pete's truck and jostle back down the driveway. "What the hell is going *on?*" she yelled at the taillights.

By the time Hazel found Sean's dad, Samuel Adair, and they half carried, half dragged Owen into the lobby and up onto the couch, Rose Peabody, Ivy Hotchkiss, Gus Bolinger and Kohl Thacker were in the lobby, too. They all looked upset and disheveled.

"What are you doing here?" Hazel asked them. She felt raw from too little sleep, hungry because she was afraid to eat, thirsty from drinking nothing but soda.

"They said we have to stay here." Rose stood looking down at Owen on the sofa. She didn't look concerned or even curious. She just looked.

She's detached, Hazel realized with dismay. *Unhinged.*

"We said we wouldn't go." Kohl's eyes had a feral glint to them. "Not with them."

"They rousted us out of the Buckhorn Tavern like cattle." Ivy was on the verge of tears.

"Why'd they bring you here?" Hazel asked her.

"Said since we wouldn't stay home, we'd run out of options. Said we had to go to the south pasture."

"Tiny Clemshaw's the only one who broke free," Gus said.

"Goes to prove Clemshaw's been right all along," Kohl said. "Holloway's got the most to lose so he's corralling us all here to keep us quiet."

"What's wrong with us?" Ivy asked. "Is everybody sick?"

"The ranch hands aren't sick," said Gus.

"I'm not sick," Kohl declared. "I'm perfectly fine."

Gus gave Kohl a sidelong glance that said, *Sure you're fine.*

"Who is in charge?" Ivy searched their faces. "Where's Sheriff Winslow?"

Owen woke up babbling, "Stay away from the water don't even shower in it everything has water in it—*everything.* The cattle drank water, didn't they? It looks clear but hides hideous toxins and microscopic amoebae—"

"Should we go down to the hospital?" Rose interrupted. "I think you need a doctor, Owen." She looked around at the others standing in the lobby. "I think Owen needs a doctor."

"Not tonight," Samuel Adair finally added his two cents. "It'll keep till daylight. Too risky driving the dark pass in your condition." With that he turned and headed up the stairs.

"If it's just food poisoning," Rose said, "then we'll all feel better in the morning." She tried on a hopeful expression.

Hazel could not stand to look at that forced face and turned away, thinking, *It's already almost morning, Rose.*

Then Kohl said, "Gonna get worse before it gets better. A lot worse."

Now the tears did let loose down Ivy's cheeks and a look of panic crossed Gus's face.

"Nobody's getting worse," Hazel said, "you're just tired." She knew she was. "Why don't you take rooms and get some rest. There're no guests left in the hotel."

They all just stared at her...unwilling to take direction from this mere girl.

Hearing silverware clink from the direction of the kitchen, Hazel abandoned the cause and rushed back to see who was there—hoping for Sean—surprised to find her grandmother at the table with Sean's mom, Honey Adair. Honey's dress was still wrinkled, her hair uncombed. With all the lights on against the dark night beyond the windowpanes, the women sat drinking port and not eating the wedge of cheese plated before them.

"Why isn't anybody sleeping?" Hazel complained.

Honey Adair looked at her with a completely blank expression...until instantly she brightened, as though somebody had flipped her On switch. "If everybody's up, I best get breakfast on." Honey rose and started banging around the kitchen.

Taking Honey's place across from Sarah, Hazel heaved herself down onto the hard oak chair. The fatigue made her feel weighty despite having eaten so little since yesterday morning. She leaned closer to the white cheese, poked at it (soft), sniffed at it (stinky), and decided against it. Instead, she sat back and blew out an exhausted breath.

Then she closed her eyes...and remembered Lottie Mathers' blood all over the dining room: on the chandelier, the tablecloth, the hardwood floor. Hazel had sworn she'd never eat in there again, never even go in there again if she could avoid it. That had only lasted until her grandmother threw her thirteenth birthday party in the dining room. Sarah had hung purple crepe streamers from the chandelier and covered the long table in colorfully wrapped gifts and pink-frosted cupcakes to prove that it was not the room or the furniture, but rather the guests and the menu that had wrought such horrors.

"Has Ben Mathers ever been back here?" Hazel asked her grandmother. She knew that until tonight, Patience had not stepped foot inside The Winslow in over five years, not even for Hazel's birthday parties.

Sarah scowled at the mention of Ben Mathers. "He paid me a visit just yesterday."

"Really?" Hazel asked, not at all surprised by the flash of anger that accompanied that news. "What did he want?"

"To threaten me."

Hazel shot forward. *"What?"*

"Don't worry." Sarah caressed Hazel's cheek, smoothed her hair. "I shooed him away."

Still fuming, Hazel said, "Grandma, tell me about Lottie Mathers."

"Charlotte Ambrose." Sarah sighed. "Lottie used to be an Ambrose before she hitched herself to Benjamin Mathers." She shook her head as if to say, *What a mistake that was.*

"Do you think the guests will want pancakes?" Honey flung open the refrigerator door. "I suppose I could make waffles."

"The guests are all gone," Hazel said. "Remember?"

Honey dropped a carton of eggs to the tile floor. "Well fine! If they don't want waffles, I'll give them grilled cheese."

Ignoring Honey, Sarah rose from the table and told Hazel, "Let's go into the other room."

"Grilled *ham* and cheese," Honey decided. "That's always good."

"Honey," Hazel said, following her grandmother through the kitchen. "Nobody's going to eat. Anything." Hazel pushed through the swinging door and entered the dining room behind Sarah, who then lowered herself onto a chair at the head of the table.

Hazel felt like standing. After she and Patience had raced down the servants' staircase to find out who was screaming in this room, they'd been whisked outside. But not before they saw the knife, and the blood that followed. That had been enough—and Hazel had never wanted to hear any of the other grisly details. Until now. Patience's escalating obsession now made Hazel want to know everything, made her want to know why this incident still felt so raw. "Patience thinks it's her fault her grandmother died in here. Hers and mine."

"I know." Sarah looked pained, as if she didn't want to talk or even think about it.

"And I've never understood why Ben Mathers thinks it's your fault."

Sarah folded her hands, looking unhappily resigned. "You had to be here."

"I *was* here."

"Only for part of it."

Before Hazel could change her mind, she said, "Tell me the rest."

Sarah sighed again, in a way that sounded sad. "Of course your grandfather was still with us then. Randall had just begun to carve the prime rib I had prepared, rare to perfection. For achieving that, he smiled at me in appreciation."

Hazel glanced around the dining room, imagining her august grandfather, Randall Winslow, still alive and playing host to Winslow's finest.

Sarah continued, "We heard you and Patience scuttling up the servants' staircase, and I looked at Lottie across the table, asked her what she supposed our little witches were brewing up this time. She laughed and agreed that you two had been whispering a lot about witchcraft. Then she'd cocked her head at your grandfather, saying, 'Who may we thank for this latest obsession?' I laughed, too, telling her that for once, it wasn't his fault. That you, dear Hazel, always so inquisitive, had discovered a book about the Salem Witch Trials all on your own."

Ruefully, Hazel remembered doing just that, and then immediately corrupting Patience with it.

Sarah seemed to be growing more distant, reliving that night. "Lottie had rolled her eyes, saying, 'Heaven help us— we'll all be deemed guilty of witchcraft.' Then she raised her face and cupped her mouth, shouting to you two on the upper floor: 'Don't tempt fate, girls!'"

Hazel winced, stung by Lottie's prescient reproach.

"And your grandfather's eyes were playful when he said, 'Truth be told, Lottie, all are guilty, but some are guiltier than others.' Just then Ben Mathers rejoined us from the kitchen, juggling a tray of drinks: vodka tonics for Jules and Meg Foster, and Scotch for Randall and himself. Lottie and I would stick with cabernet—were already, as I recall, well into our second bottle. Coming up behind Lottie, Ben had a puzzled look on his face. 'Guilty of what?' he asked. And Lottie shot out of her seat—as if seriously startled—bumping the drink tray with her right shoulder. Ben Mathers danced, tried to regain his balance. The tray tipped anyway and sent glasses flying, ice cubes bouncing off the table, booze cascading to the floor."

Hazel felt her stomach curling upward, much like it had that night.

Sarah's eyes were wide and bright, manic with memory. "I rose, saying, 'Lottie, what is it?' over and over. She was clutching one hand to her throat as if she were choking. Right before our eyes her lips puffed up and her throat swelled. Jules Foster rushed to her from the opposite side of the table while Ben backed away saying, 'Help my wife, help her, help,' until he fell backward over Lottie's upturned chair."

Hazel knew exactly where this was going; the play was about to reach the part where she and Patience had entered, stage right. Suddenly she regretted having her head filled with these new images—she had enough haunting memories already stored up.

But Sarah went on, "Lottie was wheezing, suffocating on her own swollen neck, while her arms flailed across the table, crashing decanters into soup urns, and shards of crystal and porcelain flew through the air and cabernet splashed the tablecloth, the ceiling, all of us in red."

If Hazel had not heard the crashing and seen the aftermath for herself, she'd have to think her grandmother was embellishing this horrific story.

"By the time your grandfather restrained her arms, Lottie's

face was purple and her eyes bulged. Jules picked up the knife and poked clean through her throat. If Lottie hadn't twisted at that exact moment, Jules wouldn't have hit her artery. As it was, blood poured out but no air flowed in." Sarah lowered her head and pressed her fingers to her eyelids. "It wouldn't have mattered anyway. It was already over."

"Why does Ben blame you?" Hazel asked. "We all saw Dr. Foster stab her."

"He *did* blame Jules Foster, until the coroner's report came back and confirmed that short of having a syringe full of epinephrine in his pocket, there wasn't a thing the doctor could've done to save Lottie."

"I thought she bled to death." Hoping to quell the memory of all that blood, Hazel kept her eyes on her grandmother.

"No, her death was due to anaphylactic shock—an allergic reaction to my escargot. Lottie had never had snails before, never dreamed she was allergic. So with Dr. Foster in the clear, Ben turned on me. He accused me—he continues to accuse me—of poisoning his wife."

"That doesn't make any sense. You and Lottie were close friends." Just then it struck Hazel as extremely strange that Patience told her earlier tonight that Gram Lottie says, *The cows knew.* She shook her head hard. "Why does it have to be *anyone's* fault?"

Sarah looked tired all of a sudden, her bright eyes dimming. "Ben couldn't accept the truth—there wasn't any blame in it. And he *needed* that blame to help him through it."

Hazel's anger reignited as she recalled the cruel words and harsh glares that had constituted Ben Mathers' ceaseless campaign against her family ever since. Placing her hand on Sarah's arm she asked, "Grandma, what's happening now?"

"Looks like we're headed for another bad patch," Sarah said. "Like when—"

"Get out! Get out!" Honey yelled from the kitchen.

Hazel rushed back into the kitchen to find Honey chasing Jinx, dangerously whipping a saucepan through the air while the dog struggled to find traction on the tile.

"Stop, Honey!" Hazel darted past her and flung open the back door so that Jinx had a route of escape.

The dog's floppy ears lay plastered against his head, tail tucked between his legs, feelings clearly hurt.

"I won't have wolves in my kitchen!" Honey gave Jinx a fuzzy-slippered kick to the ribs.

He yelped in surprise and pain before scurrying out the door.

"Have you lost your mind?" Hazel shouted at Honey before running after her dog.

When Hazel caught up to Jinx where he cowered at the front corner of the hotel she knelt and pet him, trying to calm him down. "You all right, boy?"

He was tense and low to the ground, frightened not only by Honey's mad chase but by the men who were shoving Jay and Julie Marsh through the yard toward the front porch. Julie tripped and fell and Jay knelt to help her. Kenny Clark clipped Jay aside and hauled Julie up by the collar of her down jacket and pushed her up the porch steps.

Jinx made a sympathetic sound.

"Please," Jay said, "we're fine. We don't need any help."

Help? Hazel thought. "Who's helping anybody?" she whispered to Jinx and the dog began to bark.

No use hiding, she came around into the yard to face Kenny and Old Pete. But she didn't know what to say because she didn't understand what she was seeing.

When Pete noticed Hazel, he ordered, "Under no circumstances are you to let them leave." Gesturing at Kohl Thacker pressed up against the bay window of the ballroom, his face staring out at them in frantic-eyed interest, Pete added, "We gotta assume it's contagious."

And with that Kenny gave Jay a final shove and waved the Marshes into the hotel.

Contagious?

The word bounced around inside Hazel's head; she wouldn't let it lodge there.

Guess we're not talking about food poisoning anymore.

TUESDAY DAWN

Day Five of the Heat Wave

BY THE TIME they headed out in the earliest light by which Hazel dared to navigate her dirt bike, there were twenty people assembled at The Winslow and they were running out of beds. Nobody was sleeping anyway. But Hazel was dead tired with a serious adrenaline hangover.

"Everything will be fine," she told Jinx over the engine buzz.

Jinx sat precariously balanced on the motorcycle tank between her legs, leaning back into her chest. This was slow going because steering was awkward and the dirt road rough, but Doc Simmons lived out a ways and it would've taken them too long to walk.

And the dog was sick.

At first she'd thought he was bruised thanks to Honey's kick in the ribs, but then she'd noticed the red in his weepy eyes and his incessant salivation—the yellow tank of the Yamaha was slick with dog spit—and realized he was suffering from something worse.

His front legs began to tremble and Hazel feared he'd slip off the bike. "Just hold on," she told him.

He nuzzled her under her chin with his nose and then chuffed mistily. His red coat was dirty and matted but that was okay and she nuzzled him back, recalling how they had all called him "Red" until Patience renamed him Jinx. The dog earned the name when he caused Patience to wipe out on the gravel driveway of The Winslow by darting right in front of her pink Schwinn.

Now he twisted his head to look at Hazel with wet, inquiring eyes.

"I know, boy," she murmured. "I know."

Chuffing again, he sprayed her face with doggie goop.

"Don't worry, Jinx." She didn't dare take a hand off the handlebars to wipe her face, even if what Jinx had really was contagious. "Doc Simmons will help us."

But a few minutes down Loop-Loop Road, Hazel spotted a red truck pitched halfway in the ditch to the right side of the road. Pulling up beside the truck she realized it was Doc Simmons' Ford. She peered through the cracked windshield into the cab, empty save for a few paper coffee cups and a worn leather case on the passenger's seat. Then she noticed the drops of blood dotting the dirt that led from the driver's door up and out of the ditch.

Dread clutched at Hazel and she wrapped a protective arm around the dog.

"Come on, boy." She pulled away. "Let's see if we can find him."

Doc Simmons' place was painted barn red; a low hedge framed his dying lawn.

Hazel pulled up the driveway, and Jinx leapt off the bike and scrambled onto the porch before she could even park. The dog had turned agitated, barking, looping around the porch.

She felt uneasy, too, and she climbed the porch steps hesitantly, hugging her arms, suddenly less certain that she wanted him to be home.

"Doc Simmons?" she called out.

Jinx's barking was the only response.

"We need your help," she said, her apprehension growing. There was no doorbell, so she knocked once on the door.

Then she heard furtive movement inside the house, followed by incoherent muttering that told her Simmons was not only in there, but likely sick.

Had Jinx not needed help, she would have fled. Instead, she raised her hand to knock again.

Through the lace curtain covering the door's window, she made out a man kicking aside a chair.

When he opened the door, her worst fears were confirmed. Jinx growled.

The man barely looked like the Doc Simmons she knew. His face had transmogrified into a grotesque mask. And along with the rifle he held, he looked dangerous.

"Mad dog!" he screamed. "Mad dog!"

Hazel spun and ran back down the steps, Jinx on her heels, and jumped on her motorcycle.

She had never started her old YZ on one kick before and thanked her lucky stars that this time she had as she flipped it around in a spit of dirt and gravel and hauled ass down Doc Simmons' driveway.

Just after she carved the corner of the driveway and turned back onto the road—her rear tire spinning out until she recovered and opened up full throttle—she heard a sound, like *pfftt*.

She had time to worry, *Where's Jinx?* before he ran right in front of her.

She pulled up on the handlebars and jerked hard to the right, begging gravity to let up *just this once.*

Jinx never even yelped when the front tire of the bike came crashing back down.

Then she was down, too, the full weight and force of her body plus the bike bearing down on her right elbow with a shatter and shock that blacked her out.

HOLLOWAY RANCH

TANNER KNEW SOMETHING major must be going down when his uncle busted into his room and told him to get his ass up before the sun was even shining.

Ignoring the dull ache in his leg, Tanner scrambled into some shorts and his Sweet Leaf rolling papers T-shirt, the one that almost got him kicked out of the state fair until he promised to wear it inside out.

He hustled downstairs and outside. And what he saw out there next to the barn was pretty interesting.

Against the sun just coming over the mountaintop, the light still fuzzy across the ranch, fifteen cowboys sat on horseback. He was nervous and excited to see that they all carried rifles.

His uncle rode up and put a hand down to him. "Come on, kid, this'll put hair on your chest." When Tanner took his hand, Pard yanked him up onto Blackjack's back behind him.

Tanner didn't feel fully awake yet except for his nose smelling the horses as they rode behind the rest of the men in the direction of the south pasture, in silence until Pete Hammond reined back his horse and waited for Blackjack to catch up. Tanner noticed that his uncle's right-hand man was looking a lot older and even more grizzled than he had just yesterday.

When they pulled alongside, Pard asked Pete, "Notify Sparks?"

"Yeah, told him what to expect. Nate Winslow, too." Then more quietly Pete said, "It's a waste."

"Got any better ideas?" Pard asked.

"Find Simmons, run more tests, figure out for certain what

it is. Could be lichen like in '58. Or arsenic leached into the creek."

Tanner noticed that Pete pronounced creek as *crick* like an old fart out of a shitty Western.

"You're talking days," Pard said, "weeks maybe. What if it *is* hoof-and-mouth?"

"You know it's not."

"I've got no choice but to nip this thing in the bud, Pete. Because if I don't and it spreads to the rest of the herd—then *word* will spread and I'll be out every which way there is."

"Best to know for certain, is all," Pete said.

Pard lowered his voice even further. "Half a herd can be replaced. Hell, even the whole herd. But once a reputation's ruined, it stays ruined. I promise you it'll be a stain that won't come clean."

"Your decision." Pete rode back up to the rest of the men.

For once Tanner kept his mouth shut. Their demeanor told him that now was not the time to be a smartass. Seeing that huge bull Indigo at the rodeo—twisted and bleeding from the neck while being dragged behind the corral—had been enough to convince Tanner that once the ranch hands decided to get down to business, they didn't screw around.

When they reached the south pasture Tanner was expecting to see something harsh, but not this. The cowboys were working a herd of fifty or so sick cattle into a trench that looked to have about the same dimensions as an Olympic-size swimming pool. With dogs yipping at their hindquarters, some of the cattle could barely walk their legs shook so bad, and many gave out completely once they were in the trench and the dogs withdrew. Next to the backhoe, a bulldozer sat at the ready.

As soon as all the cattle were in, the bulldozer driver pushed a heap of dirt into the mouth of the trench. The cattle bellowed. There was no way out for the animals, and the whole scene was almost more than Tanner could stomach.

After they dismounted Blackjack, Pard handed Tanner the reins. "Walk him over and hitch him with the others. Tight. Understand? And come right back."

Tanner dragged the resistant horse through the grass toward several others tethered to the railing of the wood bridge. "You messed up my leg, glue bag," Tanner told Blackjack. But he couldn't muster any energy to curse the animal further because he wasn't sure he was up for whatever was about to happen. He didn't like that *I've made up my mind to hell with all of you* look on his uncle's face, didn't like the reeking fear of those cows.

By the time he rejoined his uncle at the trench, a dozen men had gathered at the edge and were staring down at the confused animals.

Kenny Clark stood tensely in position where the opening had been filled, rifle pressed to his cheek.

Pard yelled over to him, "Hey, Ken, take it easy. Hold up a minute."

"Okay," Kenny said, eager as hell. "But I'm ready whenever you say go, boss."

Tanner moved close to Pard. "Simmons said he thinks it might be something they ate. What if that's all it is?"

When his uncle swung his head to frown at him, Tanner instantly regretted saying anything. What did he care anyway? He wished he could leave.

"Drastic situations call for drastic measures," Pard replied, all business, no bullshit.

I don't want any hair on my chest, Tanner decided.

Watching the last of the cowboys assemble at the edge, Pard shouted, "Looks like we're ready, men." Then a look came into his uncle's eyes—uncertainty maybe but Tanner couldn't be sure—before he commanded, "Fire away!"

With pained expressions, the men shot down into the mass grave. Quickly cocking their rifles, they shot again while the cattle made horrible sounds. A stampede ensued, but there was nowhere to go and the big animals tried to clamber over each other and up the sides of the trench, necks outstretched, hooves scrambling to find purchase in the soft dirt.

The men cocked and shot faster.

Tanner wanted to turn away but felt pinned to the spot, paralyzed by what he was witnessing. There was a lot of blood.

After what felt like a long time, the shooting slowed. When at last it stopped, Old Pete and a few others scattered around the trench and leaned out and doused the dead animals in gasoline.

Before Tanner grasped what was happening, his uncle handed him a length of board, the tip of which had been dipped in the fuel. Pard lit the makeshift torch and shoved him by the shoulder toward the trench. Tanner didn't know if he could do it, he didn't *want* to do it, but then all the cowboys were looking at him and his uncle gestured with eyes that said, *Get the hell over there!*

So Tanner walked to the edge—hoping his knees didn't give out and he didn't puke from the putrid smell the dead cattle gave off—and tossed the torch into the trench.

Nothing…until *whroosh* followed by a fast-growing plume that smeared the dawn sky black. And soon the ghost cries of the animals hanging in the air were drowned out by the obscene crackle of the fire.

When they returned to the house, he grabbed a few things and then jumped on the Kawasaki and tore out of there. Before he hit Loop-Loop Road, he looked back the way he'd come. It was the last time Tanner ever saw Holloway Ranch.

MATHERS MANSION

PATIENCE SAT ON the mission-style bench on the wide front porch of her grandparents' house, talking to the ghost of her Gram Lottie.

She preferred spending time here rather than at her own house because her grandparents paid her a lot more attention than did her parents, who always treated her as an afterthought. Once on vacation they'd stranded her at a gas station when they assumed she was asleep among a jumble of jackets and blankets in the backseat of the car, when in fact she'd gone in to use the restroom. They were completely unaware until a highway patrol officer pulled them over and informed them they'd left their child behind a hundred and forty miles ago.

Now Patience gazed down at the sidewalk. Her Gramps Ben had gone over to Clemshaw Mercantile for what seemed to be the tenth time that morning.

"Gotta get stocked up," he'd said. "Never hurts to be prepared."

That made movies play through her mind of earthquakes shaking the wood frame stores until they collapsed and their windows exploded into the street, of fires racing down Park Street and all the houses ablaze with flames shooting out their rooftops, and floods uprooting the big trees in the park before swallowing the town whole.

And although the porch was swaying somehow, she was frightened to leave it—it seemed more dangerous *out there*. Too hot, and too many people around, talking loud, looking at her.

Of course, she'd been happy when Gram Lottie came out from the house to keep her company. She always made Patience feel safe. Plus it had been so long since they were together, so long since that awful night when Patience and Hazel tempted fate at The Winslow and Gram Lottie died and was taken away forever. At least, Patience had thought it would be forever.

But now Gram Lottie was telling Patience things that made her feel anxious. How much she looked like her Great-great Aunt Sadie, and how Sadie had died too young.

Patience touched the charms on her bracelet while bits and pieces of the Prospector's Day picnic photograph in Hazel's foyer flashed through her mind: dark hair, white skin, spectral eyes.

"Everyone knows Evan Winslow drowned Sadie Mathers when she refused his affections," Lottie Mathers told her granddaughter. "He lured her to The Winslow, he suggested they take a walk…"

Patience wished her grandmother would talk about something else, something nice. This was giving Patience a very bad feeling in her belly. Like when Hazel slapped her. Why did she do that? Patience put a hand to her cheek to stop the stinging she still felt.

"Obviously his workers covered for him, he paid them well," Lottie continued. "So he *got away with it*. And went on to marry Ruby Waring. Had to bring his bride all the way from San Francisco so she wouldn't know what a monster he was—and nobody dared to tell her."

Lottie paused and Patience hoped she was finished.

She wasn't. "After that everyone forgot about poor Sadie Mathers, except her faithful brother, Sterling, who had suffered to discover her in that pond with a look frozen on her face, not of peace but eternal torment."

Patience's thoughts swirled around…whirling colors. Her

brain one of those gigantic, sticky, multicolored suckers you buy at the fair. She wanted so much just to close her eyes and see nothing, think nothing. But doing so only made it worse because then images of dead cats and hanging men and people screwing flared in her brain like lightning strikes.

So she opened her eyes again and looked at Gram Lottie, who didn't look quite right, either. In fact, she scared Patience a little. *No, a lot.* She shivered.

"They buried Sadie in Winslow family ground," Lottie told her. "Right above that deep pond, atop the rise that overlooks the whole mountainside, because it's such a beautiful spot."

The word *mountainside* went spinning through Patience's mind on a brown ribbon. *Beautiful* was turquoise. She scratched at the ants crawling beneath her skin. The scratches burned. Her silver bracelet felt cold against her wrist.

"And that felt so *wrong* to her brother, Sterling, that she should be interred everlasting to the land of her murderer, that he went back and dug her up and reburied her behind the church next to a little oak sapling—young and tender, like her."

Gram Lottie would not stop. Patience didn't even bother to try and make her stop. Patience couldn't stop shivering, either.

"Sterling Mathers never let Evan Winslow forget that he knew what Evan had done to his sister. So when Evan thought enough time had passed that he could get away with it again, he killed Sterling, too, in the very same spot, and left your grandfather Ben to be raised fatherless."

Patience's mind spun so fast now that her grandmother's words became a blur.

"And they tried and they tried to fill in that pond, but it just kept coming back up wet with the blood and the tears of the Mathers family."

Patience could not listen to another word and although the steps were undulating and difficult to navigate, she dared to leave the porch.

FORTUNE WAY

IT WAS TOUGH to make out what Tanner Holloway was saying to him. Sean could see words sliding out of Tanner's mouth but they were so slippery he couldn't grab hold of them.

Hand outstretched, Sean finally caught the word *ranch*... then *fire*.

But he didn't want to think about that. Really, he didn't want to think about anything. Not even Hazel. Because they'd had that fight.

Was that today? he marveled.

No, yesterday.

It'd been a long two days.

Freakishly long. And freakishly hot.

Where have I been? he wondered. He'd taken off his shirt somewhere and lost it, but managed to hold on to the shades he'd swiped from Clemshaw Mercantile.

Now he could *hear* the sun beating down on their heads where they stood on the sidewalk in front of the Mercantile. And Tanner was saying something about a bucketful of bull guts in the barn and cows eating marigolds and jimsonweed.

Sean couldn't remember the last time he'd eaten. It didn't matter—he wasn't hungry. Maybe he'd never eat again. *That'd be interesting.*

He tried to focus back on Tanner but the picture kept shifting. *Hold still,* he thought.

Then Sean heard himself talking: "I tried to tell him. I tried and Melanie knew I was trying, not making time with her—even if she is pretty—while he was on the pot and I was already late with deliveries. But he wouldn't listen. You are *way* behind schedule, mister! Violet and Daisy eat your eggs! Screw. *Him!*" He felt as though his brain had just barfed.

"Tell him what?" Tanner's mouth seemed gigantic, like he could swallow Sean's head whole if he wanted to.

So Sean stepped back from him.

The mouth opened wide again. "Tell him what?"

Sean searched his mind for what that question could possibly mean. "What?"

"*What,* you dumb fuck?"

"It smelled good."

"What did?"

"The bacon."

Tanner gave him a strange look.

"Don't say anything to anybody, he said."

Tanner looked even more perplexed.

"I should've tried harder?" Sean didn't actually want the answer.

"Let's split, man."

"Can't."

"Why the hell not?"

"People are sick."

"So?"

"It's worse than food poisoning."

"No shit, Sherlock."

"Worse than mayo got left out too long in the sun."

"All the more reason to split."

"Gonna get sicker."

"What's it to you?"

"Gray and sticky. Tasted okay but it wasn't okay. Don't say anything to anybody."

"You are completely fucked up, Adair. What about you, juicy fruit? Wanna go for a ride?"

Suddenly Patience was right there. *Has she been here the*

whole time? Sean had no idea. Her hair was piled up on top of her head and she was wearing practically nothing; her collarbone looked exposed and fragile. *Like little bird bones,* he thought.

She stared at him with dark eyes, stared at him as though she knew what he was thinking.

You are *beautiful,* Sean thought. Or maybe he said it out loud; he wasn't sure.

He leaned closer to Patience, to get a better look because the picture of her kept shifting, too. But then Tanner's sudden laughter was so high-pitched and loud in Sean's ear that he became annoyed and pulled back.

"I'm going ghost hunting," he informed Patience. "See you at the merry-go-round." And above the calamitous sound he created pounding away from them down the wood-plank sidewalk, he called back to her, "Don't eat all the candy!"

What seemed like a lot later (but who really knew?) he sat against a wrought-iron fence inside the church cemetery. His head hung down to his chest like a man defeated. He couldn't remember whose headstone he was looking for. And if he couldn't remember, he would lose the ghost hunt. And if he lost the ghost hunt, then he could never go back to the park. And then he'd never see Hazel again.

But something else was bothering him.

There are a lot of things bothering me, he thought.

Deciding it best to concentrate on one thing at a time, he rose and trudged back up the hill to look over the grave markers once more. He started with the oldest headstone first: Sadie Mathers' grave, shaded beneath the canopy of an enormous oak.

Not her, Sean thought and moved to the next granite marker.

Sterling Mathers ~ 1892
Tears gather upon the grave
of one sent young to slumber

Not him.

Sean stood for a moment, hanging on to a low, scraggly oak branch. *Who am I looking for?*

At last it came to him.

Hawkin Rhone.

So this wasn't the right place at all. Where was that?

Sean probed his memory but it was slow going because his head still felt thick. It would come to him. It had to.

Hustling out of the church cemetery, he tried to remember all the places in Winslow that were good for ghost hunting.

Because he needed to talk to Hawkin Rhone right away.

About poison.

THE RHONE PLACE

ZACHARY RHONE WANDERED around the apple orchard looking for his mind. He had lost it earlier, and couldn't seem to find it anywhere.

Moving between rows of trees, he noticed their branches had grown skinny and mean. Nobody wanted to tend the orchard. *Look at it.* Zachary swallowed in disgust. If his mind was hanging around out here, he was not going to be very happy about it.

The orchard makes people do things. A shudder snaked along his spine.

Out of the corner of his eye, he caught movement down by his house. Tendrils of dread wrapped around his heart. *The wolf is back,* he decided, and the tendrils tightened their grip.

He needed to get down there. He needed to protect his wife.

But leaving the orchard proved difficult; the trees were lonely and loath to let him go. When at last he broke free, he sprinted downhill, half-blinded by sunlight, wholly mad he had begun to suspect, running and tripping and falling his way to her.

In the backyard next to the clothesline, Melanie writhed and thrashed in dandelion-infested grass. Zachary raced toward his wife only to skid to a dead stop five feet away.

She wore her favorite sundress, the blue one that matched her eyes.

Snakes slithered in and out of her mouth.

Revulsion poured through Zachary. "Melanie—don't look

at them," was all he could manage, as if the godless creatures would leave his sight if only *she* would close *her* eyes.

Yet he couldn't tear his eyes away, either, and he watched as she convulsed, bluest eyes rolling back into her head, red hair drenched in sweat, soft hands clutching her throat.

Then he understood: *She can't breathe.* On the heels of horror arrived panic. *They're choking her!*

He dashed to the chopping block next to the bakery, hesitating only a moment before he wrested the ax from the stump and rushed back to where his sweet Melanie lay.

She reached up toward him, pale fingers splayed. "Help me," he thought he heard her say.

Panting hard, he stood spellbound while his lungs constricted until he felt as though he were suffocating, too. He wanted to look away, the snakes were that obscene, but he could not—he had to save his wife.

When he raised the ax above his head, her eyes went wide, favoring him with oceans of blue.

RUBY CREEK

IF SHE HADN'T had to walk back into town, Hazel would have never found her father. But her right elbow was shattered and the Yamaha's front forks were bent, so riding the bike was no longer an option. Had it been, she wouldn't have taken this shortcut and run into her dad's Jeep parked in the middle of the fire road. Nowhere to be seen, she figured he must be in the forest.

Usually the woods were inviting this time of morning, the sun lighting the pines on high, leaving the trails in shade. Only now things felt spooky and she was hesitant to leave the bright open fire road for the dark of the trees. After all, there'd been those snapping sounds in the woods around Three Fools Creek Sunday afternoon. Loud snapping sounds.

Stop being so stupid. She forced herself to plunge into the woods.

As she plodded along the trail, the pain in her arm forced her to relive the impossible things that had happened at Doc Simmons' place. After she had come to on Loop-Loop Road, the first thing she wondered was how long she'd been unconscious. The second was whether Simmons would come over and shoot her as she lay in the dirt, watching the sun finally rise above the ridgeline.

Now she was frightened to even consider how severely she might be injured. Nothing had ever hurt this much. Her face was wet so she knew she was crying, her nose running, though she was barely aware. For it was all she could do to keep moving forward rather than curl up into a tight little ball and surrender to a bed of cool ferns.

She came upon her dad patrolling beside Ruby Creek. He didn't look surprised to see her, nor did he seem concerned about the blood on the shredded elbow she cradled against her side. Instead, he asked her, "Can you smell that smoke?"

"You can see it." She turned and pointed west to where a black cloud diffused into the clear sky.

"Coming from Holloway Ranch. That's what I thought."

Hazel's heart leapt with sudden hope. During the summer months, Sparks Brady manned the forest-service fire look-out deep in the woods south of Winslow. Her dad took her once to see the seventy-foot-tall wooden tower with its 360-degree view of the forest and its brass Osborne Firefinder instrument in the center of the cab. "Do you think Sparks will respond?" she asked.

"Pard's men gave me a heads-up." He peered southward. "So I'm sure they notified Sparks, as well. You know your uncle—no loose ends."

Of course not, Hazel thought, while her heart sank in disappointment.

When her father looked back at her, he frowned. "Were you out all night, young lady?"

"Dad!" She shook her head at him as if to say, *Let's start over, here.* "We need to figure out what's going on. The phones are dead and so the internet's down, too. And Rose and Owen and Honey and a whole bunch of others are acting sick and weird at The Winslow and they asked after you and when I went to get Simmons he—"

"I haven't seen them for some time now." He looked over first one shoulder toward Dead Horse Point, then the other in the direction of the bridge. "All night, in fact."

"*Dad.* What's wrong with you?"

"But they're here, Hazel." His eyes searched a stand of

bristlecone pine across the creek. "Waiting for me to let my guard down."

"Dad," she whimpered, "I'm hurt."

He stared at her with a blank expression, not seeming to comprehend. "Doc Simmons can fix you up."

"No, he can't!" Cold panic stabbed her. "I think he's hurt because he wrecked his truck. He has a dark crusty bandage on his forehead and he's acting totally insane."

Her father grimaced as if he found that image distasteful. "A head injury is nothing to fool around with."

"I know, Dad! Now listen to me, we need to get help up here."

"Can't do that now," despair suffused his voice. "Isn't any way to do that now."

"Why not?"

"We need to take care of our own."

"What are you talking about?"

"Can't let anybody in. They'll only stir up trouble for us."

"Then let's get in the Jeep and go!" She'd never been more frustrated or in greater pain.

"I can't leave." Confusion washed over his face. "What will happen if I leave?"

"Then I'll go," she told him, and suddenly felt very alone.

"You're just like your mother."

She felt as if she'd been gut punched. "How can you say that to me?" She would have rather been gut punched. "She left me, too, Dad."

He placed his hand on her shoulder, sending bright new spikes of pain up and down her arm. "You won't leave me, will you?" He sounded so afraid.

She looked at her father standing in his rumpled uniform, shaking head to toe in the early morning sunshine, and promised, "No, Dad, I won't leave you."

HAZEL FOLLOWED RUBY Creek up toward The Winslow, the scent of pinesap growing with the warmth of the day, the ache in her elbow deepening with the exertion of hiking, the strength of the promise she just made to her dad weakening in the face of her nagging desire to flee and never look back.

But one-armed, she couldn't drive the Jeep, and she couldn't think of any vehicle around town she could manage. She racked her brain, *Who has an automatic?*

The creek beside her answered with a useless roar, telling her all it knew about high water after the wet spring, but nothing about transmissions.

Then she realized that even if she found an automatic to borrow, it was unlikely she could handle the sharp curves of the pass using only one hand to steer. Defeated, before she'd even turned the key.

She glanced up at the towering pines, their branches like the spokes of enormous wheels, and wished she could fly away instead, skip the pass altogether. *Because everyone's in a bad way, so we need help, and Simmons is worse than no help.*

"He's a fucking lunatic," she told the trees.

She crunched down the trail and thought about Old Pete saying that they have to assume it's contagious, and figured if she was going to get it, she would've gotten it by now. From what little she'd gleaned out of the lessons Gus Bolinger had taught on European and early American history, it seemed to her that when contagious disease sweeps through a town, not every citizen falls to the fever—some are spared to change soiled sheets and swab sweating brows.

Hazel swabbed her own sweating brow with the hem of her tank top.

If it isn't food poisoning, she wondered, *what is it? What's making everybody climb out of their skulls?* She looked to the blank sky, hoping a few answers might fall from it.

Only it wasn't everybody. Not her—at least not yet. And Samuel Adair wasn't sick, or her grandmother. Certainly Kenny Clark seemed in fine form yesterday, almost running over Jinx and telling her the dog wouldn't be so lucky next time. *And he wasn't,* she thought with renewed anguish.

There was no question Jinx was injured; now she could only pray that his injuries weren't fatal. After the crash, she'd scraped herself up off Loop-Loop Road and gone to him. "It's only a bad dream, boy," she'd sobbed to the unconscious dog—the same soothing words she always whispered whenever he twitched in his sleep. Unable to carry him, she'd had no choice but to leave him there, but not before promising to come back with help, not before begging her dog to please, please wake up from this really, really bad dream.

The creek was rushing in the opposite direction Hazel walked. It would've been nice to get in, rinse her bloodied arm, cool off…but she felt that she needed to keep moving.

She wondered if Tanner had it. She hadn't seen him since he broke the mirror in the Mother Lode Saloon Saturday night. Her Uncle Pard wasn't sick, either, or at least he hadn't sounded like it when he was yelling at her dad last night.

Something skittered in the ferns beside the trail and Hazel jumped half a foot off the ground.

Just a bird. A bird. A stupid little bird.

Taking a deep breath, she tried to calm her thudding heart. *Get a grip.*

She hurried down the path, her mind racing ahead of her feet. Had any of the tourists who visited over the weekend come down sick? *If it's worse than food poisoning, then people will go to the doctor, right?* Maybe somebody would figure out that they'd gotten it in Winslow. Maybe somebody was on their way up right now.

I can't count on it, she conceded. Then she'd have to find someone who seemed okay and get them to drive down to the valley. Samuel Adair, maybe.

If only she could just pick up a cell phone like everyone else in the civilized world. *Wouldn't that be nice?* she thought bitterly, glancing at the mountaintops that surrounded them on each side.

Leaving the creek, she took the path that led to the backyard of The Winslow, her elbow throbbing mercilessly to the beat of her heart. When she reached the gazebo and heard a car turning around in the driveway, she dashed around front. *Somebody's driving,* she thought. *That's good.*

Halfway down the stone steps, she realized it was Kenny Clark, who must've noticed her in his rearview mirror because he slammed on the brakes and the El Camino went sliding in the gravel for a few feet. Then he backed up to where she now stood at the base of the staircase.

"What the hell are you doing here?" she yelled at the back of his head through the open rear window. Kenny's hair was tight and curly tight and reminded her of cheap carpet. "This is private property—didn't you see the sign?"

He leaned his head out the side window and gestured with his thumb toward the hotel. "You'd better get up there with the rest of the sickos."

"Screw you, Kenneth."

"Whoa!" He opened his car door. "Those are awful big words for a gal whose big boyfriend doesn't seem to be anywhere around for once."

Glancing down, she spied a nice-sized rock a couple of feet away. She picked it up with her good arm and hoped that he made her use it.

"But then Sean Adair is really just a big pussy." He stepped out of the El Camino.

Kenny and Sean had gone at it before, back when Sean was still scrawny and Kenny beat the crap out of him in front of

Cal's Fish 'n Bait. Suddenly Hazel hated Kenny Clark more than she'd ever hated anybody or anything in her entire life. She took three rage-filled strides toward him, holding the rock behind her, ready to swing at his head. *C'mon*...

"Or should I say, Sean Adair is pussy-whipped?" He was only four feet away now.

She didn't care that he could come over and flatten her with one punch or worse, tweak her wounded arm. All she cared about was wiping that smirk off his face. "If you say one more word about him, if you even say his *name,* I'll smash this rock into your ugly mouth."

And Kenny must have believed her because he backed off. That or he was scared she had the sickness and didn't want to get too close. Either way he couldn't come up with anything else to say to her (*because he's a complete dumb-ass,* she thought) and he got back into his El Camino and gunned it down the driveway.

She threw the rock after him, but her arm was tired from the weight of it so it just landed in the gravel with a thud as she watched him tear down the drive and whip right onto Ruby Road.

Then she sank down to the driveway and cried.

Cried because her elbow hurt like hell and she was scared bone chips would travel her veins and lodge in her heart. She cried for Jinx, her sweet dog who never deserved to be shot at or have a motorcycle crash into his furry little body. She cried for her dad, who she feared was losing his mind and his nerve and who knew if he'd ever find them again. And she cried for Sean, who was sick and missing and she missed him and had only herself to blame for that.

After a while she had nothing left in her so she let out a shaky sigh, got to her feet, and headed for The Winslow. Crossing the yard, she went around to the side kitchen door, the way Sean always entered the hotel. Maybe she'd find him sitting at the kitchen table, happy to see her, as though nothing had ever happened…

Instead, Sean's father, Samuel Adair, sat at the table drinking from a bottle of bourbon. Honey Adair had been busy cooking; every pot and pan in the kitchen was in use. What looked to be pancake batter coated the countertops, the floor, the copper hood above the stove.

"Has Sean come home?" Hazel asked Honey.

Honey was concentrating on something inside the kitchen sink. "Why won't you cook?" she said, oblivious to Hazel.

But Samuel was looking at Hazel bleary-eyed. "If you see Sean, tell him to hightail it back here. His brother's been asking for him."

Hazel suddenly felt afraid for the small boy. "Where is Aaron?"

Samuel made a noise, "Blaah," and took back to his bottle.

"Whoops-a-daisy," Honey said.

Hazel turned to see that Honey had started a fire in the sink. Hazel dashed over and cranked on the tap, running cold water over flaming newspaper, burnt bread and melted butter. Gaping at Honey, Hazel struggled to keep exasperation out of her voice. "What are you doing?"

Blank-faced, Honey blinked at Hazel. "Making toast."

"Stop cooking, Honey, before you burn the whole place down." She took the matchbook from Honey's hand and glanced at the cover. Beneath a pig in a bib eating ribs, it read, *Stepstone BBQ Grill*.

Hazel shoved the matchbook into her pocket and turned back to Samuel. "Now where's Aaron?"

"Upstairs," Samuel said.

"Upstairs? Alone?" Hazel longed to smack Samuel upside his soggy head, but instead shoved past him to the servants' staircase.

She found Aaron in the Adairs' quarters. She could sense his fear as soon as she entered his bedroom. "It's Hazel, Aaron."

He peeked out at her from beneath his Seattle Seahawks bedspread. The bed was lumpy. When she pulled up the spread on one side, she found Spiderman and X-Men action figures crowded in with him. She sat on the edge of the bed and tugged down the covers enough to see his face. Those expressive eyes, that soft brown hair—he looked so much like his big brother that the mere sight of him made her heart ache miserably.

She could barely make out his amber irises because his pupils were so dilated. "You all right?" she asked.

He shook his head, *uh-uh*.

"A lot of people are sick." She touched his cheek: burning hot. "Sean, too."

"I can't keep inside," he whispered.

"You can't keep inside what?"

"My body."

Hazel gasped. Then she tried her best not to sound spooked. "Where are you now?"

"Above my bed."

She glanced up as if she might see his spirit hovering there. "Well, okay, that's not so bad," she said as though this were an ordinary occurrence.

"Before, I was outside," he said.

"Outside your room?"

"Outside the hotel. All over the place. I don't want to go back—it scared me."

"Did you see Sean out there?" she asked and immediately questioned why she had.

"I can't find him." He looked as sad as she felt. "I looked everywhere."

"Me, too." After she struggled to give Aaron a soothing smile, they shared a sigh.

"Should I go look again?" he asked, his fever-flushed face screwed up in frustration.

She could tell he didn't want to go anywhere and suddenly she was terrified that if he went too far, he'd be unable to find his way back. Whenever Sean finally returned, he'd ask, *Where's my little brother?* And she'd have to confess that she let Aaron float up and over the mountaintop and now he's lost to them forever…all they're left with is a shell of the boy.

"Listen to me, Aaron." She shook him harder than she meant to. "You have to get back in your body. Right now!"

"I'm so tired," he said and looked it, so she figured he wouldn't stray far for a while.

Shoving aside Wolverine and Cyclops, she eased onto the bed beside him.

It was then that Hazel realized she'd never known what tired truly is. Positioned on her side so they'd both fit on the twin bed, she laid her injured arm lightly across the boy's chest to keep in his soul while they both slept.

HAZEL WOKE TO music coming from the ground floor of the hotel. She wasn't sure how long she'd been asleep but it must have been awhile because the light in the room was different. *It's late morning now,* she figured, *maybe noon.*

She couldn't bend her arm. At all. And, damn, did it hurt.

After she half climbed, half fell out of the bed, she went down the hallway and into the Adairs' pink tiled bathroom, praying for something strong in the medicine cabinet. All she found was orange baby aspirin. She chewed five and took two more back to Aaron's room where she roused him and made him take the tablets. Then she dragged a beanbag chair over next to his bed, plopped down in a crunch of pellets, and tried to come up with some sort of a plan.

Not a single thing came to her.

Nothing.

Aaron appeared to have fallen back asleep, but his breathing was rapid and shallow.

She grabbed a small T-shirt slung over the desk chair and held it up: lime green with a caped and toothy vampire climbing out of his purple Chevy van. A single word was emblazoned beneath his pointy-booted feet: *Vanpire.* Pulling the collar over her head, she eased her damaged arm through one sleeve and pulled the rest of the shirt around her arm to create a sling. It would help, she hoped, but for the moment she longed to scream from the tender agony of having jarred her miserable elbow. To keep herself from crying out and waking Aaron, she squeezed her eyes and mouth shut, digging her fingernails into the palm of her left hand and curling her toes inside her tennis shoes.

After a painful while she realized that as much as she wanted to stay with Aaron in the safety of his little boy room, she needed to get moving. She extracted herself from the beanbag and stood beside his bed.

"Aaron," she whispered so quietly it would be a wonder if he woke up. She supposed she didn't want him to. "Stay here, just stay put."

"Don't go, Hazel," he said in a thick voice. "I'm scared."

"There's nothing to be scared of," she lied.

"Is so. Ruby Winslow and Uncle Jim are here, and the lady with blood gurgling out of her throat." His mouth turned down. "And more are coming, too. New ones. They told me so."

That gave Hazel chills and her hand shook a little when she touched his forearm. "Listen to me—they're friendly ghosts. Like Casper, you know? He's nice, right?" Hazel had never taken The Winslow's ghosts seriously before; she was beginning to now.

"Don't go," he said.

"Don't worry, Aaron, I'll be back. I swear."

Then she left him there, alone with his ghosts, when she shut the door behind her.

On her way out to the hallway, she glanced into Sean's bedroom. His bed was unmade, one corner of the sheet flipped over where he'd gotten up. He always slept calmly, the sheets and blankets hardly messed up. Whereas she slept restlessly, her bedding twisted and falling off to one side in the morning as if she'd done battle with it during the night. Every time she'd been in this bed with Sean, she'd managed to make a jumble out of it, too. *I miss you,* she thought as she turned away, feeling horribly homesick even though her house was just around the corner.

The music drifting up from the first floor grew louder as she approached the stairway landing; a lone guitar playing a lonely tune. Loud voices also carried up from the ballroom. The long room was the largest single space in the hotel—in the entire town—so it was little wonder people had congregated there. *That or the cowhands are sequestering the "sickos."*

She shivered when she reached the top of the red-carpeted staircase.

Since Winslow had never built a town hall or courthouse, every town-wide meeting, frontier justice trial, and resolution of neighborly dispute over the past hundred-plus years had taken place in the ballroom. It was tradition. And it was here that in 1889, after less than fifteen minutes of jury deliberation, Judge Evan Winslow sentenced Dinky Dowd to hang for the murder of George Bolinger.

The last town meeting to convene had been to discuss water-tank maintenance. The tank was an old rust bucket and her dad worried the water was poisoning Winslow's children with dangerous levels of lead. Of course nothing had been resolved because the town had no funds, which made Hazel think that Owen might be right after all.

Humming along to the music, Hazel cautiously descended

the wide staircase. She felt crusted-over tired and unprepared for any more surprises. She didn't want to see more skeletons jump out of their graves; this ride was already getting scarier the longer she rode.

"Aiii!" someone screamed from deep inside the ballroom. "It's a hundred and fifty degrees in here!"

As Hazel walked across the black-and-white tiled lobby, her heart picked up the beat of the song Marlene Spainhower's brother, Caleb, played on his guitar from the sofa upon which Hazel had slept last night. Ivy Hotchkiss danced around the black tile star located dead center in the lobby. His playing was smooth, her dancing was not—an aimless flailing about.

When Hazel reached the ballroom, she hesitated beneath the arched entryway while her mouth went dry and her heartbeat lost the tempo and turned erratic.

It *was* hot in there. But that wasn't all.

Jay Marsh stood in the middle of the room beneath a chandelier, ripping at his shirt and gasping, "Too hot! It's too hot!" Julie Marsh sat at her husband's feet examining her left hand. Not moving, just staring at that hand as if she'd never seen it before, as if it revealed the very mysteries of the universe. Laura Dudley and Marlene Spainhower huddled together on a velvet couch near the fireplace, giggling at each other like little girls sharing a delicious secret. Rose and Owen Peabody were curled together on the opposite sofa, neither moving now.

Hazel blinked, and blinked again, yet still he stood in front of the fireplace: Kohl Thacker, buck-naked but covered from bald head to bare toe in a cruel-looking rash.

"I'm telling you, it's typhoid fever," Gus Bolinger insisted from the green wing chair he occupied next to the bay window facing the front yard.

"I'm telling *you* it's the beef," Kohl hollered at him. "Why else would Holloway burn down his ranch?"

"You don't know that's what happened."

"And you don't know it's typhoid fever."

Nobody's taking care of them, Hazel realized.

Suddenly Kohl bolted to the far side of the rectangular ballroom and ran back and forth in front of the floor-to-ceiling windows that looked out onto the woods. "Trapped!" His voice rang shrill. "Trapped like rats and left to die!"

Gus Bolinger stood up from his chair. "For the last time, Thacker, *shut up!*"

"It's just *too* hot!" Jay grabbed Julie up by the precious hand and marched her out of the ballroom. Passing Hazel in the doorway, Jay whispered, "Don't stay."

Hazel realized that sweat was running off her forehead and down her jawbone. The fans whirring in each corner of the room did nothing to relieve the stuffiness. Rather, the fan blades wafted about unpleasant odors. She wished Rose or Owen would move—even a little.

Gus started as if to beat a path to the doorway after Julie and Jay, but then his legs buckled and he collapsed to the wood floor with a pitiful sound reminiscent of the red cow at Holloway Ranch Friday night. An old man, Hazel hoped he hadn't broken anything. She wondered where James Bolinger was right then, if he knew his Grandfather Gus was here. The two had always been close. But the last time she'd seen James, at the Crock Sunday evening, he hadn't looked so good himself.

Hazel moved toward Gus, intending to help him up.

Kohl had his nose pressed against the window now, watching Jay lead Julie through the backyard and into the woods. "They're gonna get them." Kohl turned to face the occupants of the ballroom. "Holloway's gonna get them for sure."

That was when Laura Dudley started convulsing.

I can't stay here! Hazel stopped. Spun around. *I can't look at these people anymore!*

She raced out of the ballroom and tripped past Caleb and Ivy in the lobby. When she reached the main entry, she heaved open a heavy walnut door, burst across the porch and yard, and ran down the stone steps and onto the gravel driveway.

Several yards down the drive, she cut off into the trees and made her way back to the trail leading to Ruby Creek—running away from the hotel, away from the sickness, and away from the certainty that she was about to lose control of her body or mind at any moment, too.

Pounding the trail, a plume of dust rising and a bolt of pain shooting through her arm with each thwack of her tennis shoes, it occurred to her that she hadn't run this hard since that day five years ago when she and Sean ran away from Hawkin Rhone's cabin.

Halfway to the creek she heard a noise in the woods. She slowed to a jog. Most likely a raccoon or deer. Or maybe—

She stopped to listen.

"Jinx?" she asked hopefully. "That you, boy?"

Nothing.

Deer, she told herself, *harmless fawns with downy tails.* She listened for another minute while her heartbeat slowed and there was only silence in the woods.

Until a rustle…followed by the distinct *crunch crunch* of dry pine needles being crushed against the forest floor.

She bolted.

More snapping and crackling—louder now so that she could hear the sounds even over her panting and footfalls.

She ran faster, thinking, *Fucking Bigfoot! I've got enough problems here!*

Nearing the creek now, legs aching and lungs burning, she looked over her shoulder.

Nothing there.

But then she rounded a curve and found two small figures directly in her path. She slammed on the brakes and skidded through the dirt, trying to keep her balance with one good arm. To avoid plowing the girls over, she leapt off the trail and smashed through ferns and pinecones for several more steps before finally stopping herself with a hard slap of her left palm against a tree. *Please don't let that wrist snap again,* she prayed.

Violet and Daisy Rhone looked raggedy and unkempt. Hazel couldn't ask what they were doing out here, all she could do was lean against the tree trunk and wheeze.

Trying desperately to keep hold of her squirming gray cat, Violet hissed, "Stay still, Boo!"

Daisy stared at her feet, wringing her hands. When the little girl glanced up, Hazel saw that she was flushed and feverish like Aaron. Acting shy, Daisy asked, "Can you babysit us?"

It was then Hazel realized the girls' dresses weren't just dirty: they were spattered in blood. She flashed on Patience a few days ago at Holloway Ranch saying, *This is bad.*

We had no idea, Hazel thought now.

"We'll be good," Daisy added and then gave Hazel a small scared smile.

Hazel's heart broke a little more. Unless things got better soon, she doubted she'd ever be able to put all the pieces back together again.

"Of course I can babysit you." She tried to sound less freaked out than she felt. "I'll take care of you." But immediately she worried, *Where can we go?* Her grandmother could look after them, couldn't she? Things were creepy at the hotel but it was confined to the ballroom. *So far,* Hazel thought, then out of necessity pushed it from her mind.

Hazel's sense they were being watched was extreme—her scalp tingled with it. Though the only sounds she made out now were the buzzing of insects in the midday heat of the damp woods and her own ragged breathing. She looked first at Daisy sucking her dirty thumb, next at Violet struggling to keep Boo on board, and decided to steer them back toward The Winslow.

They all hurried up the path; Hazel had no trouble rushing them along. Maybe the girls also sensed they weren't alone. Or Hazel's fear was contagious. Both sisters' hair had come loose from braids—tousled red curls framed dirt-smudged faces. And the blood on their yellow sundresses had dried dark and crusty. So whatever happened, happened a while ago.

"Are you hurt?" Hazel asked despite her reluctance to find out. What would she do if they were?

No, the girls shook their heads while Hazel exhaled in relief.

But then whose blood was that? *Maybe it's animal blood,* Hazel tried to convince herself. *A pig's.* Then, *What's the matter with me? Why would I even think that?* Hazel felt her loose ends unraveling even further.

"Look at the porcupine!" Daisy squealed, pointing into the woods.

"Where?" Hazel saw no porcupine. She'd never seen a porcupine.

"By that rock, silly-willy. It's the hugest porcupine ever!" Daisy laughed in delight. "It's bigger than our house!"

But there was no gigantic spiky creature in the woods, for which Hazel was grateful.

"Knock it off, Daisy," said Violet. "There's nothing there. I told you a zillion times."

Daisy shrugged as if to say, *It's not my fault you're too stupid to see it.*

Violet seemed healthy and fine, Hazel noticed, if scared, which made Hazel wonder how one sister could be affected by this illness but not the other. And why were the girls running around in the woods by themselves? Where were Melanie and Zachary?

"Violet, are your parents all right?" Hazel asked.

"Daddy's not well." Violet's tone was grave.

"Is that what he told you?" It didn't sound like something Violet would say, and it gave Hazel the creeps.

Violet balled her small hands into tight fists against the poor cat's belly. "That's what Hawkin Rhone told him."

HAZEL HAD HOPED to find her grandmother when they reached her quarters down the hall from the Adairs' rooms on the second floor, but Sarah Winslow was nowhere to be seen.

With some difficulty, Hazel used her good arm to strip the girls and stick them in her grandmother's bathtub—in hot water, despite the heat. Then she wadded up the filthy dresses and threw them down the seldom-used laundry chute.

Wiping her hand on her dirty shorts, she studied the plump gray cat hunched on the hearth. Boo looked belligerent. "Good kitty," Hazel said with zero conviction.

The cat cast a baleful glare at her before he darted beneath the bed.

Rummaging through her grandmother's armoire, all Hazel came up with for the girls to wear were Sarah's formal gowns from long ago, when she'd been on the petite side. With an uncharacteristic pang of nostalgia, Hazel recognized them as the same dresses she and Patience used to play in. Patience had always loved to play dress-up. Perhaps because Hazel had no mother to emulate, it didn't interest her as much. Sometimes she'd play along as a bribe to get Patience to go with her to explore the ponds or the mines afterward. But once everyone started making a fuss over *how beautiful little Patience is,* dress-up stopped being any fun at all for the freckled and weedy Hazel. After that, no matter how much Patience begged, Hazel refused to play it anymore.

Maybe I should look for Patience, crossed Hazel's mind. *Maybe I was too hard on her.*

It would have to wait. She needed to sort things out. Her impulse was to lay low until everything died down. Only things weren't dying down; things were ramping up. The clamor rising out of the ballroom below reminded Hazel of the crashing sounds in the dining room the night Lottie Mathers died. The din also made her think of the shrieks she'd heard coming from riders in the cars ahead of hers the first time she rode through the House of Horrors, warning her that surprisingly scary things lay just around the bend. Suddenly her stomach felt slippery and loose…an upset feeling she hoped was due to disagreeable memories and not the sudden onset of the mystery sickness.

Shaking off her anxiety-induced stupor, she tossed the dresses onto the bed and returned to the bathroom to help the sisters wash their hair.

When she saw their narrow shoulders and skinny arms, Hazel thought, *Nothing bad can happen to you. Nothing.* Their biggest worries should be over losing at hopscotch or their Otter Pops melting too fast—not getting sick, not getting soaked in blood.

While the girls splashed each other and sang a silly song, Hazel rinsed their hair and again wondered where Melanie and Zachary could possibly be without their young daughters.

Realizing she was not too clean herself, Hazel wiped her face and then her armpits with the wet washcloth. Thus freshened, she pulled the girls out of the tub and toweled them off, their red curls drying quickly in the warm air pushing through the bathroom window.

After ushering them into the bedroom, Hazel held up first one then another sleeveless dress. "Green or blue."

"Blue," said Violet. Patience's favorite, too.

"Blue!" said Daisy.

"I've only got one blue."

"Daisy can have it." Violet placed a protective arm around her sister's shoulders.

Hazel smiled at Violet. "You'll look better in green anyway."

She helped the girls into the gowns, which hung long and loose on their tiny frames. Standing back to assess her work, she declared, "Lovely."

"What about jewels?" Violet asked.

"Why not?" Hazel retrieved a rosewood box from the top shelf of the armoire and decked them out in her grandmother's rhinestones.

Leaving the girls to admire themselves in the mirror, Hazel went into the bathroom and searched through the vanity cupboards. "Thank you, Grandma," she said when she spied the bottle of Percocet. Her grandmother always kept something around for pain because Winslow had neither doctor nor pharmacist. Once Sarah had frowned at Hazel and told her that you just never know what you might need until you need it, now do you?

Hazel popped a Percocet into her mouth and stuck her head under the running faucet. After the pill and water splashed into her hollow belly, she thought, *I need to eat something soon.*

Then she realized how unbelievably stupid she was. Unbelievably. Stupid.

The water. Owen. That rusty old tank on top of Silver Hill.

Too exhausted to contemplate it further, she collapsed onto the pink chaise lounge beneath the window and willed the drug to kick in. *Please stop the throbbing long enough so I can think...*

The painkiller quickly worked its way through her empty stomach and into her bloodstream, and she finally felt some relief when the insistent throb became a less demanding ache. All she wanted was to pop another and sleep for a while. But she knew she must disengage herself from that cozy chair and try to figure out why and what next.

Hadn't her grandmother started to explain something last night? Before Honey went after Jinx?

She pocketed a few pills before dragging herself back

into the bedroom and telling the girls, "I have to go find my grandma. You stay up here and lock this door behind me— don't let *anyone* in except me or my grandma. Okay?"

They didn't answer. Daisy wasn't even paying attention, dazzled instead by the sparkling red of the garnet pinky ring she wore on her thumb.

"I'll bring back something to eat," Hazel said, having no idea what that could safely be.

Violet wagged her small finger at Hazel in a scold. "Daddy says don't eat any bread."

"Why not?"

"It's moldy."

Daisy made a face. "We don't like moldy bread."

"Nobody does," Hazel agreed. "I'll find some cookies and we'll have a tea party, okay? You're safe up here."

It sounded reassuring and she hoped like hell it were true, especially with the way Violet was looking at her, unconvinced. Even Boo looked skeptical.

"BENJAMIN MATHERS CAME 'round again," her grandmother informed her.

"Ignore him," Hazel said. They sat alone at the small oak table in the nook off the kitchen, but she could hear Honey Adair making a racket at the stove to the accompaniment of Samuel's incoherent grumbling. The smell of broiling meat made Hazel's stomach growl. "Ben Mathers is the least of our problems," she added.

"Perhaps." Sarah sighed. "We'll see." She leaned closer to Hazel. "Did I ever tell you about the afternoon Sadie Mathers drowned in the deep pond?"

"No," Hazel said, though she could picture the pond Sarah meant. There were three ponds on The Winslow's grounds and she'd been warned to stay away from all of them ever since she could remember, especially the deep pool next to the family plot. Now she understood why, as she imagined the puffy body and pasty white face of poor Sadie Mathers floating below the surface of the still water. "You never told me but I'm not sure now is the time, Grandma."

"It was July the eleventh," Sarah began in that slow, formal way she began every story. "The first Prospector's Day, 1889. Your great-great-grandfather Evan Winslow was in love with Sadie Mathers."

What does this have to do with anything? Hazel thought. "This isn't the best time—"

"Of course that was before Ruby was in the picture."

Hazel gave up. There was no stopping her grandmother once she got started. "Did Sadie love Evan?" She couldn't imagine it: a Winslow and a Mathers. Impossible.

"That's something people disagree on. But on this particular day Sadie accompanied Evan here while the celebration was ongoing in the park. The house was still under construction and he wanted to show her the frescoes newly arrived from Europe."

"The dining room ceiling?" Hazel asked.

"Yes, now stop your interrupting."

Hazel sat back and just listened. She was surprised she'd never heard this story before and wondered if Patience knew it.

"By several accounts," her grandmother went on, "they were standing in this very room when one of the workmen, a stonemason from Norway, confronted Evan over plans the architect had revised, whereupon the furious architect stormed in and an argument erupted. Naturally, wanting no part of it, Sadie whispered to Evan that she was going back to the party in Prospect Park. 'Wait, I'll escort you,' he told her. Before he could, he was again distracted by the hysterical Norwegian and Sadie slipped away from him."

Sarah paused, looking pensive, and Hazel wanted to scream, *Then what?*

Finally, Sarah said, "It wasn't long after they realized she'd gone missing before her brother, Sterling, found her drowned in the pond."

Hazel briefly wondered if her grandmother was losing her mind, too—why else tell this terrible tale? Of course now she had to know the ending. "What happened to Sadie?"

"Nobody knows. Aside from being drowned, of course, her body was unscathed. No signs of violence or a struggle. Speculation ran wild: accident to suicide to witchcraft even. But Sterling maintained that Evan murdered Sadie in a rage born of unrequited love. And the more Sterling persisted, the more certain Evan became that *Sterling* had killed his beautiful sister for quite the same reason. Evan's name was cleared as soon as his workmen attested to the fact that he'd been with them the entire afternoon. Sterling refused to believe it, would never let it go. And several years later, out of unrelenting grief or implacable guilt, Sterling Mathers took his own life with a Colt .44 to the temple at the edge of that same damned pond."

Hazel cringed. How many people had died out there? Were there other bodies hanging around in the deep pond, hair tangled in tree roots? And besides that, how much decomposing bodily fluid had seeped into the pond over the years from the overgrown family plot above, the unofficial—and likely illegal—graveyard that had held the bones of every dead Winslow since the late 1800s?

Shaking her head to try and dispel the images, she remembered Patience's nightmare where Sadie invites her to come into the pond. *"I don't know how to swim,"* Patience tells her. *"Neither do I,"* Sadie says. So Hazel realized that Patience must know the story. "Why are you telling me this, Grandma?"

Sarah tucked back into place a lock of silver hair shaken loose during her animated yarn. Then her expression turned even graver, bright eyes darkening. "Bad blood is flowing again."

Hazel felt dread moving in for a long stay now—thick and deep. "What do you mean?"

"Blame will be placed."

"But nobody even knows what's wrong."

"That never stopped them before."

Hazel didn't want to hear any more.

Sarah folded her hand over Hazel's. "Worst part is, once placed, right or wrong, blame is hard to shake."

Unease chilled Hazel to the bone when, for the first time in her life, she saw fear in her grandmother's eyes. Suddenly Hazel felt as though the world were washing out from under her. That if she made a move to get out of the chair she'd be swallowed whole because she had no leg left to stand on.

"You must leave," Sarah said.

"How can I?" Hazel indicated her arm in the T-shirt sling.

"Find a way."

TUESDAY AFTERNOON

It DIDN'T TAKE long for Hazel to pinpoint exactly where the high-pitched whine of the dirt bike had terminated. When she spotted the motorcycle parked next to the porch of Ben Mathers' mansion on Park Street, disappointment skidded through her: It wasn't Sean's Yamaha; it was Tanner's Kawasaki.

She was halfway up the walk to Mathers' porch when Tanner came out the front door, not bothering to close it behind him. He carried a paper sack, which Hazel guessed to be their joint venture. Every summer since Jay Marsh first introduced them to Cyclone Clyde, Hazel, Patience and Sean could count on the carny to bring them decent weed. This time Tanner had gone in with them on a bag and they'd stashed it here because even if Ben Mathers found it, he wouldn't know what he was looking at. Samuel Adair would, her dad definitely would, and pity Tanner if their Uncle Pard found it: he'd have his ranch hands draw and quarter his nephew in the center of Prospect Park. Over the past few days, Hazel had been so preoccupied that she'd forgotten all about the ounce they'd hidden in Mathers' basement.

Tanner paused on the top step with a *busted* look on his face, blond hair tangled from riding the bike. Then his usual smirk returned.

At least he looks normal, she thought.

He tucked the bag into the waistband of his shorts and continued down the steps. "Thought I'd better retrieve it for safekeeping. You know Patience's old gramps is gonna find it and smoke himself silly." Looking her over, his face tightened in apparent disapproval.

Self-conscious, she glanced down at herself: shoes covered in dirt, legs scraped, knees pasted with bits of leaves and gravel, sling encrusted with dried blood. "I look sick." She returned her eyes to his. "But I'm not."

His grimace held. "Good for you."

"What about you?"

"Me? I'm getting the hell outta here—there's seriously weird shit goin' on."

"Are you splitting now?"

"Hell yes, now." He looked past her toward the sound of a truck rumbling along Fortune Way. "They're quarantining us."

"Who ordered quarantine?"

"Who do you think?"

"Not my dad."

"Who else has the authority?"

"I don't know," Hazel admitted. Quarantine? She didn't like the sound of that, not one bit. It made her think of cruel scientists in hazmat suits prodding people into white windowless buses, sick people bleeding from their eyes.

She wanted to talk to her dad again, *needed* to talk to him. *But then he won't let me go,* she realized and her heart hurt even more. *Not if he ordered quarantine.*

Tanner got on his bike and started it up. "The weirdness is spreading fast. I just saw Tilly Thacker making it with Cal right on the sidewalk in front of the Fish 'n Bait."

Hazel shuddered, then felt grateful she hadn't witnessed that, too. "What was on fire at the ranch this morning?" The exhaust from Tanner's bike was making everything seem even hotter. "Did more cows die overnight?"

"Die? No. Killed? Yes." His rising voice revealed a hint of fear. "Fifty head slaughtered and burned to a crisp."

"You're kidding, right? Why? Did they figure out why they're sick?"

"Why wait? Once Uncle Pard's damage-control machine kicks in there's no stopping it." He revved the bike. "Which is why I'm outta here!"

They were shouting at each other over the Kawasaki's engine, so she walked closer to where he sat on the idling bike. "Take me with you."

"Get your YZ, why don't you?"

"Can't." She pointed to her wounded arm. "I have to ride with you."

"I'm not taking you anywhere."

"Why not?"

"You totally blew it for me with Patience."

"How could you think I wouldn't tell her? Especially when you were so creepy about it? She's my friend."

"Since when?"

He's right, she thought. She always kept Patience at a distance—her and everybody else.

"Oh, and screw you, Hazel."

"Fine. But you told her what *I* said, too, so that makes us even. I also have my suspicions you've been talking shit about me to Sean."

She could see him biting the inside of his cheek to keep from smiling.

"True?"

His half-assed shrug told her *yes.*

"Then we're more than even. Come on, Tanner, I need your help."

"Obviously."

They stared at each other, neither of them moving, neither flinching.

Until finally he said, "Get on."

She hesitated. "We can't leave without Sean. And what about Patience?"

"Forget her—she's completely wasted."

Hazel hadn't seen her since their fight in the tower of The Winslow last night, since she'd slapped Patience across the face. "Where did you see her?"

"In front of the Mercantile. Saw them both. Sean's wasted, too, and man was he all over her."

"I don't believe you." She wouldn't believe that. Couldn't. But suddenly she wasn't so sure she knew everything, wasn't so sure she knew anything.

"Whatever," Tanner said. "It's nothing to me, just thought you'd want to know."

Her foundation dissolved again. She hadn't seen Sean since *their* fight outside the Crock. Who was left to fight with? Another round with Tanner, she supposed. And things weren't even close to settled between her and Kenny Clark. "Do you know where Sean is now?"

"No, but I can take you by a piece of his artwork on the way out of town."

"What are you talking about?"

"I'll show you."

ON THE BACK of the bike, Hazel held on to Tanner with her left arm and rested her head on his shoulder. She was spent and it felt good to have somebody else in charge, for the moment anyway. She closed her eyes against the dust kicked up by the motorcycle's knobby tires.

The Percocet is wearing off, she thought as her arm resumed its miserable throb.

From memory of every twist and turn, she knew they were riding away from town on Winslow Road toward the bridge...

darker and cooler here, the trees reaching for each other across the road.

Then the Kawasaki pulled them uphill a ways, bouncing over slight whoops before coming to a stop. Tanner placed both feet on the ground to keep them upright, and cut the engine.

Hazel could barely lift her head she was so tired. And when she did, she couldn't comprehend what she was seeing.

They had stopped at the granite wall outside Matherston Miners Cemetery. It was tradition for townsfolk to write messages on the wall's white stone face: *Marry me Julie* or *Congratulations Class of '02.* And when they'd played ghost hunt as kids, whoever located the grave first would write *Found it!* so the other players knew to stop looking and meet up at the merry-go-round.

The wall had been clean when she and Sean were here Sunday afternoon. Now—chalked in scraggly, two-foot tall letters—there was a message: I'M SORRY—SA.

"I don't get it." She scuttled off the bike, knocking Tanner off balance, and walked to the wall for a closer look. Then she turned back to him. "What's Sean have to be sorry about?"

"Beats me."

"He didn't say anything when you saw him?"

"He told me it's worse than food poisoning."

"Everybody knows that."

"He said people are gonna get sicker."

"How could he possibly know that?" Hazel looked again at the writing on the wall, then back at Tanner. "What is going on?"

"I've got no clue. And I don't care."

Hazel fished a Percocet out of her pocket and dry-swallowed it. Then she plunked down onto a big boulder in the shade. "Okay, let's figure this out."

"No—let's *go*."

"No, wait a minute."

"We can figure it out on the way down the pass."

She didn't budge.

"Okay, dammit." When Tanner got off his bike she noticed that he was limping a little and sweating a lot.

She took a deep breath, then exhaled sharply. "I saw Gus Bolinger hit the floor of the ballroom just like that cow in the pasture Friday night. Same leg buckle, same sad sound on the way down."

Tanner wiped his face with the back of his hand and blew out his cheeks. "So?"

"So I'm not sick, you're not sick, Uncle Pard isn't, Kenny Clark isn't—is *anybody* at the ranch sick?"

"If you ask me they're all pretty twisted, even on a good day."

"Okay—so nobody at the ranch is sick. And Patience and Rose are vegetarians and *are* sick. So that definitely means people aren't sick because they ate sick beef."

"Right..." He joined her at the rock but remained standing and sweating.

"So whatever it is, it has to be something that affects both people and cattle because it'd be way too much of a coincidence if both came down with completely different ailments, yet with similar symptoms, at the exact same time."

He bobbed his head and rolled his eyes as if to say, *Can we hurry it up here?*

"So what does that leave? The heat wave? The water? Maybe Owen Peabody is right."

"But no ranch hands have it and we all drink the same water, don't we? It comes from that piece of shit tank up there—the ranch doesn't have a separate supply."

"Then what could it be?" She briefly nibbled on her bottom lip. "Something in the air? A bug?"

"Wrong again, genius." He blew hot breath at her. "We'd all have it by now."

She waved her hand in front of her face. "I suppose we would."

"Doc Simmons said Indigo had an inflamed something-or-other tract," Tanner said. "Some sort of gut problem. He thought the bull might've gotten into a poison plant like jimsonweed. But people don't eat jimsonweed and cows don't eat coleslaw."

"Huh?" She squinted at him.

"It's gotta be something people *and* cattle eat."

Hazel tapped her chin with one finger. "Zachary Rhone told Violet and Daisy not to eat any bread because it's moldy."

Tanner made a sour face. "Does moldy bread make people sick or does it just taste disgusting?"

"Makes me sick just thinking about it," Hazel said.

"But what does bread have to do with cattle? Cows don't eat bread, either, they're too busy gorging on grass."

"And feed, right?" she asked.

"I guess." He shrugged.

She glanced in the direction of the bridge. "Feed comes from Fritz Earley."

"What the hell's a 'fritz earley'?"

"He's the grain distributor from down mountain. Comes once a week to deliver feed to the ranch and—" Hazel's stomach sank. She pressed her hand against her mouth and shot to her feet.

"And?"

She let her hand fall. "And flour to the bakery."

"Moldy bread, moldy feed? Is that what you're thinking?"

"Oh, my God—Sean told me he tried to tell Zachary something."

"Me, too." Tanner wiped fresh sweat off his face. "He

rambled on and on about bacon and deliveries and Zachary not listening."

"Do you know what Sean was trying to tell him?"

"I tried to get that out of him but he wasn't making any sense."

"What did he say?"

"Something about mayo getting left out too long in the sun and turning gray and nasty."

Hazel remembered Owen in the kitchen of the Crock holding up the slice of slightly gray-tinged bread. "Not mayo," she told Tanner. "Flour. Sean must've been trying to tell Zachary there's something wrong with the flour but he refused to listen. He told me Zachary bit his head off when he tried to ask him a simple question." She scoured her mind—had she eaten any bread over the weekend? Not that she could recall. She usually tried to avoid carbs. "Do ranch hands ever eat stuff from Rhone Bakery?" she asked.

"Not that I've seen. Maggie Clark bakes up corn bread and biscuits at the ranch."

Hazel flashed on all the French toast and catwiches she'd served at the Crock over the weekend—to her father, Patience, so many others. "We have to warn people," she said.

"If the feed's bad," Tanner ignored her, "then what about the horses?"

"What about them?"

"Why aren't they sick, too?"

"Maybe they eat something else. Oats. Hell, I don't know— Do I look like a farm girl to you?"

"No, you look like a stoner chick. Which means no one's going to believe you anyway, so what does this matter? Let's get outta here."

She glanced at the wall. "I still don't get why Sean wrote that. It's not his fault."

Tanner looked unusually serious. "If you really think abou it, Hazel, it is."

"What?"

"He should've told Zachary. He said so himself."

"He tried."

"How do you know?"

"He told us," Hazel replied.

"Even if he did try, even if he didn't do anything on *purpose* it's still his fault."

"Don't say—"

"He knew the flour might be bad, but he delivered bread all the hell over town anyway."

"Tanner! Don't ever repeat that—*swear* you will never say that again!"

"Don't worry." He held up his hands as if to tell her, *Back off already.* "I'm completely out of here and I have zero inter est in what happens after I'm gone."

She shook her head. "There's just no way. If Sean though even for a second that the bread would make people sick, he never would've delivered it. Besides, he's sick too, isn't he? Why would he eat the bread himself if he knew it would make him sick?"

"Maybe he didn't know it'd make people sick. Maybe he just thought the bread would suck and the bakery would take a hit. A way to pay back Zachary Rhone for being such a dick But then he probably tried some bread and when it smelled and tasted okay, he figured that was the end of it."

"Still…would he risk it? I don't believe it." But wasn't ev erything unbelievable right now? And except for her grand mother and Violet, Tanner was the only sane person she'd talked to all day so it was hard to disregard what he was say ing.

"What's not to believe?" Tanner said. "You know how pissed he was at Zachary."

The bakery was ruined, that was certain. And Sean did tell her he thought he might get fired, told her Zachary was drunk on power and he couldn't take it anymore. Told her those things while they delivered the bread. Together. All over town.

She suddenly felt shaky. "No way. He wouldn't take that kind of a chance. I know him."

He narrowed his ice-blue eyes. "You sure about that?"

She thought about Sean shouting at her in front of the Crock and then disappearing off the face of the mountain like a shadow in shade. *No, I'm not sure about anything anymore.* Except for one thing: "We have to find Sean. We have to take him with us." If only she could talk to him. This was the longest she'd gone without seeing Sean since she'd been quarantined with mono.

"We don't have time," impatience edged Tanner's words. "Quarantine, remember? Besides, he won't go. I already tried, for the same reason I agreed to bring you."

"Why's that?"

"I don't know the way."

Hazel couldn't help but laugh. "Go over the bridge and head downhill."

"Shut up, I know that. After the pass—I can't remember from the drive up which way to go after that, it's a backwater down there, too. Do I turn left after Hatfield's tractor or right past McCoy's barn? And it'll be pitch-black by then."

"Okay, but—"

"We've got no time to argue, we have to go." He got back on the Kawasaki. *"Now."*

He was right. The bike had no headlamp and there was little daylight left to get down the mountain. She looked west toward the bridge. Just over the next hill…the way out, the way to help.

"You coming or not?" Tanner asked.

Without a word of acquiescence, she moved to get back on the bike.

Before she could, Tanner grabbed her by the wrist. "You do realize we won't be able to tell anybody what's going on up here."

"What are you talking about?" She tried to wrench free. "Why not?"

"Because Sean *told* me not to say anything to anybody. And *I* know how to be loyal."

The second Percocet was kicking in and it was becoming hard for her to think straight. And Tanner was holding and hurting her wrist just like Hawkin Rhone had. "But we have to get help. Isn't that why we're going?"

"No, we're going because everything's completely messed up and there's no reason to stick around."

"But if we can't tell anybody, then we won't be able to get a doctor up here."

"Don't need to—Simmons can handle it."

"If one more person says that, I'm going to scream!" She thought about poor Jinx and how Doc Simmons had shot at him. With her injured arm, she hadn't been able to carry the dog off the road and into the shade of the trees. Jinx was probably still lying there, baking in the sun. *What's wrong with me?* She suddenly felt sick and horrified. *How could I leave him like that? What if somebody runs him over?* She had to go back—right away—and give the dog water, help him into the shade, beg his forgiveness for leaving him.

Tanner squeezed her wrist harder. "If you tell, it'll be the end of this tourist trap. Did you think about that? Then what will the Adairs do for a living? Uncle Pard? And everyone else around here? What about your dad, the Sheriff? How's it gonna look for him? He'll lose his job for sure."

"You don't care about any of these people."

"*You* do?"

She wanted to screech at him to stop—to be quiet for a minute so she could think.

But he kept going. "And Sean'll go to prison or be banished or pitchforked or whatever the hell else happens around here."

"Why? It's not like anybody's died!"

His cool gaze chilled her. "Not yet."

Or as far as we know, crept into her mind. What if all sorts of people were dead? What if there were corpses stacked behind closed doors all over Winslow? Swollen bodies collecting flies like the dead cows.

Alarm electrified her every nerve. *Protect me, Hazel!* Sean had joked at Three Fools Creek on Sunday afternoon. *No joke now,* she thought, her heart racing.

Abruptly, Tanner released her wrist. "Now or never, Hazel."

"If we can't get help, then I can't leave," she said. "So I'm staying."

He scoffed angrily at her. "What good will that do?"

"Shut up! Shut up!" She placed her hand over her ear, panting in panic and frustration while a confusion of images flashed through her mind: Aaron floating around the hotel, chased by ghosts and waiting for her to come back like she swore she would; the Rhone sisters in their jewel-tone gowns, locked in her grandmother's quarters needing a babysitter because their parents have gone missing (or worse—that blood); Rose and Owen Peabody lying dead still on the couch in the ballroom; and the unprecedented fear she'd read in her grandmother's eyes.

Hazel shifted her feet in the dirt, widening her stance. "I have to go back to The Winslow. Nobody's taking care of them. They need me."

"Are you *serious?*" He couldn't have looked more incredulous. "Like you give a shit? All I've heard out of you since day one is smack on this—and I quote—'rotting leftover of a town.'"

As much as she would have liked to, she couldn't exactly argue with that.

"And quit pretending like you ever gave a shit about him, either."

"Stop it, Tanner. Just stop." Tears stung at her eyes. She had no idea where or how sick Sean was, and her grandmother's words kept pinging back and forth in her head: *Blame will be placed.*

Tanner scrutinized her for a moment before saying, "I'll take you to your mother."

Suddenly she couldn't find air as her resolve was knocked completely on its ass. "You know where she is?"

"Of course. Aunt Anabel stayed with us for a while after she split here. Had to give her my room, which sucked. But it's now or never, Hazel—a one-time-only offer."

He's bullshitting me, she thought. But what if he wasn't? She tried to read his eyes, but they revealed nothing except his impatience. "How do I know you're telling the truth?"

"You'll have to trust me. And we've got even less time to argue now. Let's go!"

Even if it were true, and even if her elbow really did require urgent medical attention, and even if her mother might—just might—be thrilled to see her, could she really just leave everyone here to fend for themselves? Could she really just leave them all baking in the sun?

"No." Hazel pictured her father patrolling the banks of Ruby Creek, trembling and paranoid, worried over whether his daughter would keep her promise. "No," she repeated. "I won't leave him, too. I won't leave any of them. How could I?"

For the first time, she understood what a horrible thing that is to do to somebody. And that it was pure fantasy to imagine that her mother would be happy if she showed up on her doorstep, as if, miraculously, Anabel might suddenly regret she'd ever left at all. Pure fantasy. "I'm staying," she repeated

Dramatically rolling his eyes, Tanner said, "You've got to be kidding me."

Hazel shook her head fiercely, shaking off a dozen years' worth of fear that when it came time to decide, she would have no choice. "I don't have to be like her. I won't do that to them."

He threw up his hands in complete exasperation. "You're outta your mind to stay here. So what? You're gonna be sheriff now? Good luck. And have a nice walk."

He started up the bike and peeled off, only to skid to a stop a few yards away and turn back to her. "Oh and by the way, Hazel," he yelled over the idling engine, "when you do find Sean, be sure to tell him Zachary Rhone is looking for him."

And then he was gone, leaving her standing outside Matherston Cemetery in the orange light of the setting sun, wondering what he meant by that.

Finally, she turned to trudge back into town for the second time that day, glad to be rid of Tanner Holloway once and for all, certain she'd made the right decision.

After all, she thought, *things are so bad, how much worse can they get?*

PART TWO

Trapped. Trapped like rats and left to die.

—Kohl Thacker

SUNDOWN TUESDAY

DON'T LOOK AT IT. Don't look. Zachary Rhone careened down the hallway on the second floor of his house. The light in the hall was strange—a thick amber.

It's so hot. I can't breathe. His hand went to his throat and he struggled for air. *Is the house on fire?* he panicked.

No, he realized and his throat reopened. *The sun is going down.*

The prospect of another dark night filled him with dread. He had not slept in days, and he didn't want to go through the long night alone.

Except there's him, he remembered but wished he hadn't. *He's worse than alone. Why won't he stay across the creek where he belongs?*

Losing his balance, Zachary smashed hard into the wall with his left shoulder. Plaster buckled. He barely registered the pain—every muscle in his body ached already. Deep. His bones were sore.

"Where am I?" he asked the wall. "What am I doing here?"

He spied something out of the corner of one eye. *Don't look.*

Standing in the bathroom doorway, he stared at the tub where his daughters always took their baths, their red hair tucked into polka-dot shower caps because Melanie didn't like the girls going to bed with wet heads.

All at once he remembered. *Looking for her. That's what I'm doing here.*

"Melanie?" he whispered.

Then he stood, uncertain, listening to his own rapid breathing.

"Melanie!" he yelled at the house, only to watch his shout bounce against the tile.

"Don't look at it," he said.

His voice sounded like his own and he found comfort in that. Maybe he hadn't followed him in here after all. But then Zachary was standing at the sink, the porcelain ice cold beneath his hands. He gazed into the mirror on the medicine cabinet. And there he was.

"Who are you?" The man in the mirror had tried everything to look like Zachary: same crew cut, same sharp jaw, same muddy eyes. "Why are you following me?"

Me. Zachary blinked hard. *The apple doesn't fall—*

There was no time to think about him right now. He pivoted away from the bastard in the mirror. He needed to find his wife.

I don't want to look at it.

But then he couldn't stop himself.

He looked.

At the blood.

At the blood on the wall and the floor of the bathroom… bloody handprints on floral wallpaper, bloody footprints on white tile. When he staggered out to the hallway he saw the blood there, too: smears of it along the wainscot rail, drips of it on the scuffed hardwood floors. Everywhere he looked, he saw red stains.

Standing at the top of the staircase, he howled, "Where is my wife? Where are my daughters?" His despair was profound, running as deep as his aching marrow.

Zachary looked down at his hands and slowly turned up his palms. Blood. *These aren't my hands.* Red, dirty, crusty-under-the-nails hands.

He realized he was crying, animal sounds coming from his throat, tears and sweat dripping off his cheeks. And he smelled himself—foul like an animal, too.

The apple doesn't fall far from the tree.

His eyes went to his feet: red splashes up and over his ankles as if he'd stepped in a pool of it. *Stop looking!*

He took the stairs down two and three at a time, marveling at his agility. After he crashed to a stop at the bottom of the staircase he bent at the side to peer cautiously into the living room. Nobody. But more red prints led toward the kitchen, the back porch, the rear yard.

"A killer on the loose," Zachary murmured. "A maniac."

He felt himself disassociate then, the foreboding so powerful he could no longer bear to be present in this moment, in this situation.

Bolting the opposite direction of the trail of blood, he tore out of the house and raced across the yard past the bakery, feeling *him* just on his heels, feeling *his* stale breath on the back of his neck. And Zachary did not stop running until he reached the cover of the apple orchard, where the trees sprouted no blossoms and bore no fruit.

I'll stay here. He spun in a slow circle, watching the surrounding trees turn dark against the dusk. *He'll never follow me here.*

To the nearing night Zachary Rhone pleaded, "Please, let the bear get him first."

SEAN ADAIR HELD his hands before his eyes and watched as fresh tremors seized them. Spasms had racked nearly every part of his body by now. Making tight fists to stop the trembling, he raised his eyes and refocused.

The world was a solid blind of orange, which made it tricky to differentiate between objects. Except for the crosses, lined stark on the rise against the deepening sky.

Though he had no memory of how he'd gotten here, he knew where he was: the Winslow family graveyard on the eastern slope of the hotel grounds, nearly overgrown with brambly bushes. The blackberries smelled overripe.

Despite its low-slung position the sun continued its assault. *I'm dried out,* Sean realized. His lips were cracked and his tongue felt rough. Gazing at the pond at the base of the boneyard, he weighed the wisdom of taking a drink. *Could I feel any worse?*

Not likely, he decided, and went to the edge of the pond.

Sean leaned down and scooped up a handful of warm, murky water, sending soft ripples across the pond. Cupping his hand to his mouth, he drank, relieving his parched throat. He reached for more—only to snatch back his hand when he noticed long black hair floating a foot below the surface. Enthralled, he watched the hair sway and fan out in the water.

He stepped away. "Just walk away," he told himself.

Instead, Sean picked up a fat stick and crept back to the water's edge. Against his better judgment, he bent forward and poked at the hair, upsetting the surface of the pond with a sound like falling leaves, creating small whitecaps on a miniature ocean. Then, working his stick beneath the mushroom of hair, he pulled up.

"Patience?" His voice revealed his sudden, sure dread.

A face rose slowly to the surface—a lovely, pale face.

"Holy shit." Sean felt instantly paralyzed. His heart stopped beating and his mind screamed, *Don't fall in!*

Her arm shot out of the pond, white and slippery, reaching for him, trying to pull him down into the dark water with her.

Sean fell onto his back, still gripping the stick, and the arm bone landed on his bare chest with a smack while the wet hair draped over his belly. He struggled to claw the hair off but the strands clung tight. Mud-thick revulsion poured through him and his skin crawled wherever she was touching him.

He screamed and scrambled up, finally figuring out that these horrors were attached to his stick. So he flung it. Neither bone nor hair, he could see now. Just a harmless sapling with dangling roots. It smacked into Ruby Winslow's headstone and slid down, coming to rest in a tangle with the blackberries.

"Damn…" Sean glanced down to see if his heart really had exploded out of his chest or if it only felt that way.

He walked over and kicked the pale sapling away from the marble grave marker, then he read the epitaph.

> *Ruby Waring Winslow*
> *Beloved Wife and Mother*
> *Not a thing we could do*
> *'twas the Spanish Flu*
> *1918*

Nearly hidden in the weeds, a shorter headstone stood several feet away. Curious since he'd never noticed the grave before, he went over and smashed down brambles with his foot and brushed away dirt, the granite grainy and cool to his touch.

His blood turned to ice when he saw the inscription: *H. S. Winslow.*

No, he thought.

Born 1993 / Died 2010

No. He backed away, refusing to believe.

Until he read the final line: *Our precious Hazel.*

No No No No No. His lungs clamped shut so tightly he was certain he'd never breathe again.

Dying flowers lay at the base of her headstone. Ugly pink carnations. *Hazel would hate those,* he thought. *Hate them.*

When he turned to run he stumbled over a mound of dirt and fell into freshly turned soil, his face inches from another engraved granite stone.

Aaron Samuel Adair
April 2003 ~ July 2010
Sleep, Little Lamb

"Oh, no." Sean shook his head violently. The mound was so small, so pathetically small. He pushed himself up and away from the headstone.

Turning his back on the graves, desperate to forget he'd ever seen these horrors, he pounded his thighs with his fists. "Wake up! Wake up!"

Only he wasn't asleep.

He kicked at brush and rocks, stirring up stickers and dirt. "I should've told Zachary. I should've told him, 'Screw your bacony breakfast and come take a look at this right now!'"

Sean glanced back at the headstones. "I didn't know," he explained. "How could I have known?" Remorse flooded him and he sank to his knees, drowning in it.

When a man cleared his throat, Sean lifted his head to find his uncle standing before him.

"What's got you so down, kid?" Uncle Jim asked, holding a bottle of whiskey by the neck just like he always had up until it'd killed him.

DOGS ARE DEATH. That Irish setter puppy showed up in town only one day before Patience's grandmother died. Nobody knew where he came from, and then her Gram was gone. But the dog stayed. Dogs are omens of death. And Jinx is Hazel Winslow's familiar.

"She's a bad girl, Patience," Gram Lottie said, "who plays games with people's lives."

"No," Patience disagreed, at the same time wondering if it might be true. And she wished the spiders would stop crawling on her, pricking her skin with the tips of their spindly legs. For hours she'd been sitting with Gram Lottie on the piano bench, their fingers poised but silent on the ivory keys. The charms hanging from Patience's bracelet clicked against the honey-colored wood each time her hand shook. "No," she repeated. "That's not true, it isn't." She reached out to touch Lottie, her grandmother's skin so dry it brushed away like powder beneath her fingertips.

"You told my fortune," Lottie spoke without breath, without warmth, without words. "You knew what was about to happen to me. And now you know what is going to happen next."

"It's not true." She refused to face Lottie now; her Gram would know Hazel had hurt her, would see the shame branded onto her cheek. Instead, she began to play her part of the duet and Lottie joined in at once and the music was beautiful, so beautiful, that she never wanted the song to end. When it did Patience said, "Let's play it again."

"Who are you talking to?"

Startled, Patience swiveled on the bench. She hadn't heard her grandfather come into the parlor and didn't understand his question.

"Who are you talking to?" Ben Mathers repeated. He wore a mask over his mouth, goggles over his eyes, a cap on his head, gloves on his hands.

He looked silly but even as she smiled at him, her stomach churned with trepidation. "Why do you have all that stuff on, Gramps?"

When she stood up from the piano bench he yelled, "Keep back! Close enough!"

"Why?" Patience felt crushed. Nobody cared about her. Not her parents, not her grandfather, not Hazel—*especially* not her. Like sisters, Patience had always thought. Until Hazel slapped her.

Cocking his head at her, he asked, "Why the devil are you wearing that get-up?" The mask made it sound as though Gramps Ben was actually in the next room. "You march home, Patience Charlotte, and get yourself cleaned up."

She glanced at the outfit she'd changed into earlier, humiliation burning her face.

"And who were you talking to?" he murmured through the mask.

Why did he keep asking that question? Couldn't he see? "Gram…" She gestured to where Lottie sat sideways on the piano bench, watching them with keen interest.

His eyes looked surprised behind his goggles. Then he backed farther away. "Patience, dear, listen. Your grandmother passed on. It's been five years. Don't you remember?"

Patience shook her head hard, deflecting his words away from her.

"The Winslows killed her. You remember that, don't you?"

Yes, Patience thought but refused to say it out loud.

"That place is vile." His mask twisted on the last word.

She glanced down at her charm bracelet, at the gold horseshoe Hazel gave to her on her sixteenth birthday, and at the four-leaf clover Hazel had given to her not long after her Gram Lottie died.

Then Gramps Ben said, "The Winslows mean this town harm, dear. Ruinous harm."

I told her! Patience's heart clenched painfully tight. Didn't she tell Hazel something really bad was about to happen? Madame Marcelle knew. *I knew. Why doesn't anybody ever listen to me?* Hazel should've never let Tanner break that mirror. And she didn't even help me take the pieces of broken glass outside to bury them in the moonlight. *Why didn't she help me?*

More baby spiders hatched beneath her skin; the pinching increased. "Gramps," she tried to steel herself, "is Hawkin Rhone back?"

YOU. ARE. THE SHERIFF. You. Are. In charge here.

Nate Winslow paced along the precipice at Dead Horse Point. He strode ten feet, stopped, then turned back in the opposite direction. When he lost his footing, dirt and pebbles cascaded down the side of the cliff until he recovered his balance and resumed pacing.

You're weak, he berated himself. *Weak and not performing your duty.*

Peering directly into the brilliant sun setting across the canyon, his gaze landed on the truss bridge. He blinked to erase the glare spots from his eyes…to clear his vision so he could see the bridge, so he could see what was happening down there.

Nobody's coming. He took a long, faltering breath.

Then his scalp crawled. Something was watching him.

His pulse burst wild as he whirled to face the woods at his back.

Nothing but trees. Incredibly tall trees. Even the young bristlecone pines towered, growing fast and skinny, reaching for their share of sunshine. He felt incredibly small.

Nate turned to look out over the canyon again, swaying at its edge, the Lamprey River rushing by below. It'd be better if he just fell over the side, he realized. Then it'd all be over. For he was certain his incessant retching had by now ripped open his stomach to leak its noxious contents and pollute the rest of his body. He felt as though his every cell had been injected with poison.

He wondered when he'd feel better. *If* he'd feel better.

He wondered if he was thinking straight at all.

He wondered if he'd completely lost his mind.

He thought of his daughter, Hazel, a tough girl but still only a girl, with a dusting of freckles and delicate features, and bright eyes that were all Anabel Holloway. Nate hoped Sean and Hazel were looking out for each other. Despite some occasional undesirable behavior, Sean was a good kid. And even though Hazel sometimes came home red-eyed from drinking and what else Nate didn't want to know, at least she'd never come home pregnant.

He wished his wife were here to help him worry through these things. What did he know about a seventeen-year-old girl? Anabel was the only girl he ever really knew—*thought* he knew—and now this one was enough like her to scare the hell out of him.

He'd given up looking for his wife a long time ago. Why look for somebody who doesn't want to be found? It'd finally dawned on him like a cold slap to the face what a fool he'd been making of himself in front of his fellow lawmen whom he'd enlisted in the search, in front of his townspeople, in front of his daughter.

Now he thought, too, about his mother Sarah and the rest of the townsfolk. If he felt this bad, might others be even worse? If they were, they would be vulnerable. They would need him to protect them. *It's all up to you. If you don't do something, people are going to get hurt.*

"Pull yourself together!" He shook his head to try and clear it, and in answer to his voice something stirred in the woods behind him.

Again he spun to confront it, drawing his revolver this time, and his boot heels sank into the loose dirt at the edge. Only vaguely did he register that he was about to tumble backward over the side of the cliff. He threw his weight forward by dropping to one knee and then he scrambled back up to take aim at the rustling.

After he fired off a round without consciously pulling the trigger, the sound of cracking branches and fleet footfalls over dry pine needles confirmed the creature's presence. Visually tracking its movement between the trees, Nate refused to get any closer.

Refused because the smell coming from the woods horrified him: it was the scent of a monster, of thick dank fur and hot rapacious mouths with long tongues.

Pulse quickening, he chastised himself for being so frightened. *It's only a wolf—and you're the one with the Smith & Wesson.* He looked down at his shaking hand. Suddenly the revolver felt burning hot, searing his palm, and he dropped the gun to the dirt with a dull thud and a splash of dust. And just as suddenly, he could not possibly have been any more disgusted with himself, disgusted with the worry and the weakness, with the debilitating fear.

Stooping, he picked up the revolver. The grip wasn't hot; it was never hot.

That was when the brown dog burst from the woods.

On muscular legs the chocolate Lab raced toward him where he teetered on the rim of the canyon. If he didn't move she'd plow him backward over the edge. If he did, she'd continue over by herself. He decided to make a stand because it was the Peabody's dog, Molly. A sweet dog.

Only she didn't look sweet when she came to a stop in the dirt eight feet away from Nate. Teeth bared, she growled low and deep.

"What's the matter, girl?" Offering her his left hand, he held the gun tight in his right.

The dog whined and for a moment Nate thought it was going to be okay, but then she snapped her head and jerked her body around as if she'd been bitten on her back. She darted away, yelping and leaping into the air and twisting again, before racing back in Nate's direction.

"What is it? What is it?" He could do nothing but watch helplessly as she ran in frenzied circles.

Abruptly Molly dropped into the weeds and Nate saw her struggling to get back up but her legs seemed to have given out on her.

He stepped slowly to where she lay, cautious not to startle her further, trying to reassure her. "It's all right, girl."

But as he got closer he heard her chewing, heard her biting on something hard, making loud crunching and grinding sounds. When he reached Molly he saw what was in her mouth.

A rock. She was gnawing on a fist-sized rock and her mouth was covered in blood and her teeth were cracking and falling into the dirt.

Nate took careful aim. One well-placed shot to the head.

Then he turned away from Dead Horse Point and marched resolutely in the direction of town. *I'll go back in. I'll face what needs to be faced.*

"DAMN THOSE WINSLOWS!" Dread stuck snugly in Ben Mathers' craw. He wished that Patience could be right, that Lottie really were here, because Lottie always knew how to ease his tangled mind. Ben was convinced that if Sarah Winslow's appetizer hadn't killed his wife, she would have found another way. He leaned over the steering wheel and through his goggles glared at The Winslow perched contemptuously on the hill, lording over the whole town.

He shook his head, reminding himself, *I warned her, didn't I?*

He shifted his focus back to the road. Prospect Park passed by on his left, the buildings of Civic Street on the right. He peered intently straight ahead. No longer accustomed to driving the Valiant, it required his full concentration. There hadn't been reason to go anywhere lately. For years, really. Not since Lottie was murdered. Bitterness twisted his gut. "I warned her."

But she hadn't listened. Now, not only were things worse, things were *much* worse. Fire at Holloway Ranch, his granddaughter suffering delirium, people beyond themselves—

A couple holding hands stepped out into the street in front of him. Ben slammed the brake pedal to the floor and the Valiant jerked to a stop. They were, he realized, buff-bare as the day they were born. But these were no babies.

When the man made a move toward the Valiant as if coming over to share something, Ben yelled, "Stay away from me! Keep away!"

The man (who looked a lot like Bowen Marsh only Bo had been gone for a while) held up his bare arms as if to say, *Okay, take it easy.* Then he retook the woman's hand and the pair finished crossing the street into the park.

Ben yanked down his mask to call after them, "Put on some clothes for decency's sake!"

He shook his head again. *Much worse.*

The sun was setting over the Lamprey River canyon, and he recalled the July when they were just boys and Bo Marsh and Randall Winslow and Hawkin Rhone hiked with Ben into the woods beyond Ruby Creek. It wasn't dark when they set out. That was later. When he was trying to find his way back. When he was trying to swallow the panic. When the night was choking up all around and the day was sneaking away from Ben just as stealthy and mean as the other boys had when they ditched him. He'd been lost for hours, way past terror by the time he finally came upon The Winslow. If his father had been around to teach him about things, he would've never let himself get tricked like that. Ben Mathers learned that day not to trust just anyone.

Now no one could be trusted, not even his Patience. When he'd looked at his cherished granddaughter's face he could see the sickness raging beneath her skin and behind her eyes.

As for Ben, he refused to get sick. Somebody had to keep a handle on things and Nathan Winslow certainly wasn't around.

Some sheriff he turned out to be. *The minute a real crisis hits the sonofabitch is nowhere to be found.*

That definitely did not help the nervous roiling in Ben's belly.

He dared another peek at the hotel. *I warned her, didn't I?*

Up ahead a pair of cowboys on horseback crossed the street and rode into the park. Ben didn't know what Pard Holloway might be up to, but had no cause to trust him either, and decided to steer clear. There was a menace to the cowhands even under normal circumstances. They carried guns.

Should I just leave? Should I just keep driving? Ben suddenly wondered, surprised that the idea hadn't occurred to him before then.

No, he decided and straightened up behind the wheel. *This is my town now.*

He realized he'd drifted over to the wrong side of the road and yanked the steering wheel hard right. Overcorrecting, he sent the Valiant smashing into a parked pick-up.

The jolt and noise were extraordinary.

For a stunned moment, Ben sat motionless. Then a smile formed on his lips.

He backed up his car at a diagonal to the Chevy and sat idling. Squinting through the sunset, he contemplated the dented truck bed. Then he glanced around. Had anybody seen? If the cowboys had heard, they obviously didn't care, for the street remained deserted.

Gunning it, he slammed into the truck again, collapsing the driver's door into the cab of the Chevy with a scream of metal and a hail of glass. The impact was astounding and the Valiant's engine abruptly died. The old man slammed both gloved hands against his steering wheel in a confusion of triumph and frustration.

Then, belly shaking and tears welling in his eyes, Ben Mathers laughed.

Pard Holloway wiped the sweat from his face with a bandanna. It smelled of horse. He liked that smell. He got along better with horses than people and didn't suppose there was much wrong with that.

Tugging the reins, he turned Blackjack left onto Ruby Road, glad to leave The Winslow behind. *They'll be okay,* he told himself. Just need to buck the hell up, is all. Lord knew he'd already sacrificed—a hundred head of cattle worth of sacrifice. And since he was starting to suspect that his initial gut instinct had been right all along and that his animals had been poisoned, that sacrifice might prove to be a complete waste. But one thing was for damn certain: no one was leaving Winslow until he found out exactly how this happened—and why.

Pard shook his head, fighting the persistent notion that townsfolk's wild paranoia and half-cocked speculating were affecting him more than he cared to admit. *Maybe this madness really is contagious,* he thought.

He peered up the street, wondering where the crash-'em-up derby he'd heard while he was up at the hotel had taken place, but he didn't see any wrecked cars along Ruby Road.

As they continued into the park, Pard found Blackjack's steady gait reassuring. Pard wanted to believe he had everything under control, yet he had his doubts. For one thing he still couldn't find Doc Simmons. Or his nephew. Or the sheriff.

At least that bastard sun was finally going down, blanketing the town in pleasing orange light. He let himself think then that everything would be fine. That it would all be over soon. *We'll wind up this sorry business and get back to the way things were.*

With no interest in ranching, the rest of the Holloway clan had left the mountainside and were now scattered around the state—around the country, for all he knew. And his niece Hazel had as much intent to stick around Winslow as a bucket of ice at a Fourth of July picnic. So, childless himself, Pard

hadn't planned on having anybody to pass it all on to. Except
now there was this kid—this smart-ass, skinny, *annoys-the-
hell-outta-me* kid. If he could somehow whip Tanner into
shape...but he had serious doubts. He hadn't meant for his
nephew to get hurt at the rodeo Saturday. If only Tanner had
held on like he'd told him to do. Clearly Pard would not be
making a buckaroo out of that boy anytime soon.

When he rode into Prospect Park he came upon Hap Hotchkiss pushing his lawn mower under the monkey bars. Out
of gas, apparently, since the motor was silent. Hap, hunched
over the mower handle and, sweating like a horse thief, nodded slightly as Pard passed.

Have to send a man out here to take care of him, Pard
thought. It was getting damn hard to keep track—

"Keep up the good work, Hotchkiss!" Jay Marsh ran by
bare-ass unshucked.

Pard watched Jay scurry out of the playground to the duck
pond, where half a dozen people had congregated. Some were
sprawled beneath the shady oak while others sat on the low
wall surrounding the pond. No one spoke when Pard rode up.

"You folks know we got quarantine on, don't you?" he said.

Nobody answered; few even looked at him.

"That means you're picking yourselves up and going home."

Nobody moved. That included the two ducks floating dead
in the pond.

"That means *now*." The end of his patience was very near.
He had enough problems at the ranch, didn't need more nonsense in town.

Jay had joined Julie Marsh (also unshucked from muzzle to
switch) where she sat in the shallow water. Pard dismounted
Blackjack and walked to the edge of the pond.

"It's hot," Jay informed him.

This was really too damn much. Pard put one foot up on

he low wall and leaned in. "Get out of that water, get some
clothes on, and get yourselves home."

"We're not bothering anybody," Jay said.

"You're bothering me. Get the hell out of there!"

Reluctantly the Marshes stood while Pard turned to address the others. "If you'll just do as I say, you'll all be fine."

"Your cattle weren't fine," Jay said from behind him. "You
planning to firebomb us, too?"

Pard reeled around and punched him just below the eye, and
Pard thought he felt the man's cheekbone give way beneath his
fist. Wearing a look of pure astonishment, Jay was flung flat
on his back into the pond. And when he sat up, blood-sullied
water cascaded from his nose. Looked a lot worse than it actually was, Pard speculated.

Julie's mouth opened wide, though nothing came out. At
first. Then an angry screech split the dusky air just as Pard
turned his back.

"This is about damage containment," he told the rest of
them. He strode back to Blackjack and swung himself up
into the horse's back. "And we can do this the easy way or
the hard way. Your choice."

He jerked the reins to turn his horse around and then rode
out of Prospect Park to the accompaniment of Julie Marsh's
furious sobs.

Pard had had enough. *Why won't they just cooperate?* he
thought. *For their own damn good.* He'd send his men to take
care of these people, to clean up this mess. Once they were
gone at the bridge.

TANNER HOLLOWAY WASN'T sure how it would all play out, but
the idea of riding off into the sunset sounded pretty good. And
he didn't know what he'd do once the sun went all the way
down and he was stuck on the pass in the dark. That didn't
matter yet. Getting out was all that mattered.

For now, that orange ball of misery was shining right in hi
eyes as he rode the Kawasaki toward the bridge. Whenever
he blinked, sweat dripped off his eyelashes.

Of course it'd been bullshit about taking Hazel to he
mother. He had no clue where Anabel Holloway might be
But it'd almost worked. She bit hard; he saw it in her eyes
Then he'd watched as she'd struggled with her desire to g
running to mommy versus her guilty need to stay and make
up for being such a disloyal bitch to Sean Adair. Poor dumb
bastard. At least Tanner had been able to set him straight abou
her. Sean and Patience both. Poor dumb Patience.

It'd also been bullshit about not telling anybody in Step
stone what was happening up here so Sean wouldn't get
busted. It was so *he* wouldn't get in trouble. Pard would kil
Tanner—douse him with fuel and toss him in the trench—i
he were the reason any of this got out.

Who cares anyway? he thought. *I'm so outta here.* His parents would have to take him back in. It wasn't his fault the
whole thing turned to shit. For once, it really *wasn't* his fault.

Wondering how much gas he had left in the bike, Tanner
glanced down at the tank as he crested the last hill before the
bridge. What he saw when he looked up again shocked him.

It's too late.

His heart sank. Too late to cross the bridge, too late even
to turn around because the ranch hands were all looking at
him with a lot of interest. Rifles at the ready, six men and one
woman stood in front of trucks parked across the near end of
the bridge, blocking off both incoming and outgoing traffic.

As Tanner puttered downhill toward the mouth of the
bridge he told himself, *Act like you meant to be here.*

When he came to a stop before her, Maggie Clark asked,
"Where you headed, kid?"

Kenny Clark stood next to her in his stone-washed jeans

and his lariat belt buckle. He unrolled a soft pack from the sleeve of his T-shirt and shook out a cigarette. "Yeah, where you headed on *my* bike?"

Jack-off, Tanner didn't have the guts to say out loud.

Tanner cut the engine and got off the motorcycle, thinking, *Damn, my leg hurts.* It felt swollen, and it crackled when he put his weight on it. Crackled. *Damn.*

To Maggie, Tanner said, "Uncle Pard wants me to help stand guard."

"I doubt that." She started to say more but then abruptly brushed past him, moving up to the road along with the other suddenly mobilized cowhands.

Tanner turned to see a station wagon lurching downhill toward the bridge, alternating between too much accelerator and too much brake. Tanner figured the driver must be seriously wasted.

The ranch hands leapt out of the way just as the car weaved dangerously close to the guardrail. In a squelch of tires the car jerked to a stop two feet short of the barricade.

Now Tanner recognized the driver: that tall, skinny kid with the lame black Mohawk. James Bolinger, he remembered. Obviously this was his first time behind the wheel.

The kid rolled up his window quick while a woman in the passenger's seat smiled pleasantly at the cowhands closing in on the station wagon, as if they were bringing her a root beer float.

Maggie tapped the driver's window with her rifle. "Turn it around."

James cranked the window back down. "But it's the only way out."

"Nobody leaves," Maggie said.

"Says who?" James asked.

"Sheriff. Town's under quarantine. We can't let you infect the whole valley."

"I'm not sick," James said, even as his face took on a guilty expression. Then he mumbled, "Not really."

"Not yet." Maggie gestured with her rifle. "What about her?"

The woman had gotten out of the car and was heading for the bridge railing.

"Mom!" James yelled. "Get back here!"

She leaned over the rail to peer down at the river. "It's so beautiful…"

"Go ahead, Emily," Kenny Clark said.

She spun around to look at him with eyes big and bright. "We are as beautiful as butterflies." Emily's smile turned to a look of puzzlement. "Time to fly?"

Kenny grinned at her and nodded. "Go ahead, Butterfly. Fly."

Emily turned back, grabbed the railing with both hands, and hoisted one leg. Then with one foot up on the rail and the other dangling above the pedestrian walkway, she hesitated.

"Mom!" James flung open his door and ran toward her just as she raised her trailing leg to fully stand on the rail, bobbing and teetering like a sprung jack-in-the-box.

James shouted, "Don't look down!"

At that, she looked down at the river and Tanner saw sheer fright strike her face right before James snatched her by one flapping arm and a trembling leg and pulled her off the railing.

Emily immediately squirmed loose from him and raced off the bridge, singing, "Free, free, you'll never catch me."

Looking panicked, James rushed back to the station wagon, scrambled in, and then swerved backward the way they'd come, while Kenny laughed and everyone else swung their attention to the sound of a vehicle grinding into low gear at the far end of the bridge.

A flatbed truck driven by a fat man approached in slow motion.

The cowhands stayed this side of the blockade until the moment the truck stopped several yards away, its driver confused by the obstruction. Then they stepped out with their rifles and were on the guy before he could think to slam it into Reverse and get the hell out of there.

Tanner was never going to get another chance like this. He jumped back on the bike and kick-started it with a foot that felt as if it might fall off anytime now.

In the two seconds it took him to decide that he should go back the way he'd come rather than try and squeeze around the trucks, Kenny Clark grabbed him by the hair with one hand and by his T-shirt with the other. The shirt ripped but the hair held as Kenny yanked him off the bike and slammed him to the ground. No sooner was he down than another cowboy picked him up and punched him in the gut.

Doubling over, Tanner caught a knee beneath his chin. His teeth clacked together hard. *That's funny,* he thought, *I actually see stars…*

"Enough," he heard somebody say through the blood rushing in his ears. He looked toward the voice, his focus swimming, and realized it was Old Pete.

They had the truck driver now, who was looking at Tanner with a mixture of sympathy and terror. Kenny came back at him and Tanner flinched away, but Kenny was on him and putting an arm across his shoulders, a brotherly gesture. And the asshole who'd sucker-punched him held out his hand as if to say, *No hard feelings.*

Not knowing how to get out of it, Tanner shook the calloused hand, all the while marveling, *What the hell? These people are seriously fucked up.*

He looked at the fat man again, trying to figure out who he might be and what he was doing here…and how soon someone would notice he'd gone missing because it was obvious they weren't planning to let him go, either.

The man's eyes darted around as if he weren't clear who was in charge here. Finally, they landed on Old Pete. "I need to talk to Pard Holloway," he said.

Kenny scoffed, his arm still around Tanner in a posture both possessive and threatening.

Old Pete whistled and rolled his eyes. "Pard's a busy man right about now, Earley. What's there to talk about?"

Tanner had never seen anybody look so nervous as this man Earley, and figured him for the grain guy Hazel had told him about. You could fill a gallon bucket wringing out his shirt. Then he realized that if moldy flour and feed really were to blame for all this, Fritz Earley *oughta* be scared shitless.

And he could see the man mentally kicking himself, *Why did I come up here?*

Tanner was kicking himself, too. *Why did I waste so much time dilly-dallying around with Hazel Winslow? I could've been—should've been—halfway down the mountain by now instead of getting the shit kicked outta me.*

And then he wondered who would be sorrier he didn't make it out.

TUESDAY EVENING

JINX WAS GONE, but Hazel's motorcycle was still there. Pitched in the dirt at the side of Loop-Loop Road, her Yamaha looked broken, beat-up—looked pretty much the way she felt.

"Jinx!" She whistled for him, producing more wheeze than whistle. "Come here, boy!"

No use, the Irish setter was gone, and she could only hope some sane and sympathetic person had happened upon him and was now nursing him back to health with hamburgers and hot dogs (his favorite). *Or buried him,* she couldn't help but think, and tears blurred her vision.

She forced herself to get moving, to leave Jinx yet again in the belief—delusional, she recognized—that he'd find her like he always managed to, every day, before all of this started.

Three days ago. She blinked hard against the tears, against her utter disbelief.

Just three days ago she'd fought with her dad about being out too late Friday night. How ridiculous. Three days ago she'd accused Patience of being completely paranoid, of looking for trouble. Three days ago Jinx was still wagging his tail. And Sean still wanted to hold her hand.

She glanced westward, squinting against the sunset. *Three days? Impossible.*

Walking up Loop-Loop Road, bugs stuck to her sticky skin and hunger churned her empty belly. She adjusted her arm in the makeshift sling and took a stab at mental imagery to distract her mind from the misery of her ruined elbow. She'd read somewhere that people endure surgery without anesthesia by concentrating on pleasant thoughts: beaches and waterfalls, kittens and puppies. So she willed herself to think about swimming in Ruby Creek with Sean, and her grandmother brushing her hair with the soft-bristled Bakelite hairbrush, and her father giving her a bear hug, the kind that squishes her rib cage and makes her beg for mercy.

But the pain was stubborn and refused to leave. So she carried it with her between the quaking aspens, up Winslow Road, back toward town.

Still hot despite the setting sun, the heat was cooking the grime deeper into her skin. She looked down at her feet carrying her along the dusty, pot-holed road and turned Tanner's words over in her mind: "I'll take you to your mother."

Now she felt foolish, ashamed even, that she'd even been tempted. After all, her mother knew where to find her. If she wanted to bother.

Swatting at the pack of gnats swarming her head, she questioned whether anybody had ever felt this lonely. Somebody sentenced to life in a Turkish prison, she supposed, or somebody shipwrecked and floating on a makeshift raft in the middle of the Pacific Ocean.

Can you hear me? she sent out a telepathic message to Sean. *Where are you?* Then she emptied her mind, open to his reassuring response.

No answer came. Instead, tears rose. But she would not let herself cry again—too draining. And she needed to think about what to do next.

"I have to warn people not to eat the bread," she told Sean, wherever he might be. "But if I do that, will I get you into trouble?"

Still no answer, telepathic or otherwise.

She continued anyway. "Zachary must know what's going on and why, because he told Violet and Daisy not to eat any bread." She scratched her nose. "But has he told anyone else?"

It was Violet's voice that answered her. "Daddy's not well," echoed in Hazel's mind.

Hazel kicked a pinecone out of her way. "Why the hell didn't Zachary listen to you, Sean? If he had, we wouldn't be in this stinkin' mess, now would we?"

Almost to town, she suddenly realized that she should've erased Sean's apology from the granite wall, and that she'd have to go back out to Matherston Cemetery at first light. "I swore I'd protect you, Sean. Crossed my heart and hoped to die."

In an instance of poor planning, the church cemetery was the first thing greeting visitors upon arrival downtown. The hand-painted sign directly preceding the graveyard (Rose Peabody's handiwork) read, Welcome to Winslow, and Hazel always thought *more dead than alive* would be an appropriate add-on.

More signs followed: *The Winslow → left on Ruby Road, Clemshaw Mercantile ~ Fortune Way, Cal's Fish 'n Bait, Rhone Bakery Since 1924,* and finally, *Rose's Country Crock* decorated with pie slices and a T-bone pointing straight ahead.

Hazel veered into the cemetery. The plots sat tiered up the hill, each section contained by a low retaining wall constructed of brick or granite and bordered by wrought-iron fencing. From the top of the rise, the small church kept watch over the dead.

The graveyard had another visitor, who glanced up from chewing grass next to the Mathers section of graves beside a huge oak tree. Hazel slogged up the hill and when she reached the oak, slung her good arm around a low branch and leaned against its cragged bark.

"Did you escape from the ranch?" she asked the cow mowing around Sadie Mathers' grave.

Chewing her cud, the cow stared at Hazel with enormous eyes.

"Good for you." Hazel looked up at the oak's massive branches; it had grown, evidently, since Sadie's brother, Sterling, dug her up from the Winslow family graveyard and reburied her beside the tree.

With the sun gone, the oak and headstones quickly turned dark; the cow stood silhouetted against the pallid sky. Hazel would have lingered there a while, had she not sensed things trying to wriggle to life beneath her feet. So she got her tennis shoes moving toward the church, where music played and candles flickered behind stained glass.

A white clapboard structure, the church was neither large nor fancy save for its colorful windows. Like the school, the community served the church on a rotating basis. With no permanent minister, sometimes Rose or Owen Peabody gave do-unto-others-type sermons, other times Ben Mathers preached hellfire and brimstone. Not because he believed it, Hazel always thought, but because he enjoyed it.

When she pushed open the door and walked into the church, she found the people inside sheathed in sweat. All the windows were shut tight, and every nook and cranny held lit candles that cast fast-moving shadows against the walls. Several people were on their knees praying. A woman played a dirge on the organ while another softly sang, but the lyrics didn't seem to match the tune the organist was churning out.

The atmosphere was so eerily thick that Hazel's gut instinct was to turn around and flee. Yet she remained rooted to the spot, transfixed by the fearful oration streaming from the pulpit, the force of it drowning out the singing and the music and the praying.

It wasn't Rose or Owen Peabody preaching. It was Ben Mathers.

"The devil challenges us in our weakness." The old man glowed, eyes greedy behind a pair of goggles. "Unless and until we atone for our misdeeds, we shall shed tears in great plenty."

"Amen." The organist nodded.

Ben Mathers lifted his goggles to look dead-on at Hazel. "Wrongs must be righted. Wicked acts atoned for."

A thin man standing before the pulpit shouted, "Atone, yes!"

"Atone," the organist agreed.

"Atone!" the thin man repeated. Then, slowly, he turned. Doc Simmons.

Hazel hadn't seen the vet since he shot at her and Jinx from his porch—and her rage against this man instantly overtook her. This man who would do nothing to help anybody. He who had hurt her dog, killed him maybe, and very nearly killed her.

"Atone for this, you lunatic!" Hazel shouted as she charged toward him past rows of pews.

The prayer-makers stopped praying and the singer stopped singing. But Ben Mathers droned on, "Without atonement there is no salvation. Without salvation there is no peace…"

Simmons noticed her then, adjusted his spectacles, and must've realized she was gunning for him because he dashed out the doorway to the left of the pulpit. This time, he had no rifle.

Hazel reached the doorway seconds later to find Simmons halted just outside, shrinking from the darkness back toward the church. She stood behind him, longing to strangle him, certain she could find the strength even one-armed, the fingers of her left hand twitching with the desire to sink her nails into the saggy flesh at his neck. But she needed answers. "Tell me what's in the bread that's making people sick."

After Simmons spun around, he leaned so far back from her she thought he'd topple over. "I don't know anything!"

"Don't mess with me, Simmons."

"Leave me alone. I don't know anything."

"Tell me. What is it?"

His mouth drew down in a grossly exaggerated frown.

"What?" Hazel reached her arm toward him.

He leaned even farther back. "Ergot."

"Er— What?"

"Ergot. Now leave me be, girl."

"No. What is it?"

"A mold, a fungus. Found its way into Pard Holloway's feed as sure as the sun."

"The flour, too?"

"Looks that way."

"Did you tell my uncle? Or Zachary Rhone? Anybody?"

Simmons shook his head rapidly back and forth.

"How long will this last? How long will everybody be sick from it?"

More head shaking.

"What are you going to do about it?"

He held up empty hands. "Nothing I *can* do, and that's the honest truth."

She leaned closer to him. "Is it going to get worse?"

He seemed to think his feet were stuck and he continued to pivot his torso away from her.

"Worse?" she repeated.

He gave a slight nod.

"How bad, Simmons?"

"Bad." He finally uprooted one foot and turned from her.

Watching him run into the night, she yelled, "My dad's gonna arrest you! Throw your ass in jail for dog murder and willful neglect of our town!"

It was then Hazel realized it couldn't have been her dad who ordered quarantine; it must've been her Uncle Pard. That, for whatever reason, Tanner lied. Her father would never order quarantine without first consulting with at least one real doctor. Ergot? At this point she couldn't be sure that it was something real and not just Simmons winding out. Either way, there was nothing contagious about this sickness and the last thing they needed was quarantine.

She wasn't aware that Cal from the Fish 'n Bait had come up behind her and was also watching Simmons scurry away until he said, "He'd better watch out for Indians. Scalping is a rough way to die."

When Hazel turned to look at Cal, he smiled at her...not a warm and friendly smile, but the smile of a madman that made her stomach flip over.

She hurried away from Cal and the church, into the darkness, heading in the opposite direction Simmons had fled.

Bad, she shivered.

The street appeared deserted, which was at once a relief and a worry. And while the air had cooled a few degrees she remained sticky and damp. If she weren't so scared of the dark she would've gone straight to Ruby Creek and jumped in with her dirty clothes on.

Once Dad feels better, she thought, *there's going to be some serious hell to pay.* Simmons, definitely. And Old Pete and Kenny Clark for dumping the sick at The Winslow. *Unacceptable.* And whoever was responsible for the blood on Violet and Daisy Rhone's dresses, they would have to pay, too.

Civic Street seemed especially sinister. Usually a benign collection of buildings, she now imagined things hiding behind dark windows and brick walls. Hiding and watching. Sick people and sasquatches, lunatics and wolves. The strong sensation that she was being watched sent the creeps crawling up the back of her neck. She picked up the pace.

Ducking into Prospect Park, she thought, *Six hours of darkness left, six and a half at the most.* That was one good thing about summer in Winslow: not dark till ten, light at five. Not well-acquainted with five o'clock in the morning, or six even, she knew that this particular morning she'd be relieved when the sun rose.

For now, the park was deep in silence and shadow. As she moved across the playground, she kept catching movement out of the corner of her eye. But when she'd turn to look, there was never anything there except for the swings, the little merry-go-round, monkey bars. She put the hustle on, anxious to pop out onto better-lit Park Street.

When she reached the duck pond, her foot encountered something mushy. Hazel shuddered and saliva flooded her mouth.

She glanced down in horror, certain she'd stepped on a body.

It was a pile of clothes: a sundress, a man's shirt, a squishy down jacket. She remembered Julie Marsh wearing that parka because it'd struck her as so odd. She poked at the clothing with her shoe, terrified she might uncover a body part—a toe or a finger, an entire hand.

Where is Julie now? Hazel scanned the dark park.

Silence and shadow.

Until an astoundingly loud crunch split the quiet, followed by the scream of metal scraping against metal. It came from Civic Street, where she'd walked just minutes ago.

When she turned to look, she saw a streetlamp falling. It hit the road in a shatter of glass and the light extinguished. Through the trees, she could make out vehicle headlights traveling slowly up the street toward Ruby Road. Then the vehicle picked up speed before slamming into a parked car in another cacophony of destruction. Her heartbeat raced out of control. Maybe she should've left with Tanner. *Did I make a mistake?*

"I think I made a big one," she whispered and hurried on.

She was nearly to Park Street when the ducks came after her. In a confusion of quacking and flapping, a dozen birds burst from the darkness to chase her the rest of the way out of Prospect Park.

When she reached the street she glanced back to find they'd all stopped at the edge of the park, evidently satisfied now that she'd left their territory, except for one large duck who continued to waddle toward her. "Get lost, you stupid duck."

The green-headed bird honked loudly before falling onto his side. Trying to right himself, he flapped a wing several times but then lay strangely still.

"I told you to get lost, not drop dead."

Staring at the bird, Hazel realized she shouldn't leave him lying in the middle of the street. But she didn't want to touch him, either. She went to the duck and gently nudged him with the toe of her tennis shoe. Dead as a dodo. Using the bottom of her shoe she indelicately rolled him off the road and onto the grass.

Studying the creature's dead eyes, she remembered Tanner feeding pieces of his piecrust to the paddling of ducks before the rodeo. Had this duck been among those that ate Tanner's pie?

She spun away, refusing to consider it any further. All she wanted to do was go home, find her dad there, and together, figure out what to do next.

But when she reached her house she remained on the sidewalk, afraid to get any closer. The house was dark—hostile in its emptiness. Clearly her dad wasn't home. *I'm not going in there alone.* A whimper sounded from her throat. *Was that me?* She didn't know what to do, or where to go. She turned in a complete circle, a sinking sensation in her belly. *Where is everyone?*

Reluctantly, she looked up at The Winslow. All the structure's lights were blazing, which she took as a good sign. At least there were people inside, maybe even somebody who wasn't sick. Besides, she needed to go back and check on Aaron, her grandmother, Daisy and Violet.

After she crossed Ruby Road, trudged up The Winslow's steep driveway, and climbed five stone steps to the yard, she stood in the yellow glow cast from the pedestal gas lamps—distraught to discover that her grandmother's hotel now looked menacing.

"What's changed?" she entreated its tall windows. "What are you trying to tell me?"

That I should've never come back here. She sensed the hotel watching her with its bay window eyeball as she continued through the yard. *That I should've left with Tanner.*

She was startled to encounter Marlene Spainhower tucked into a corner of the porch. "Why are you out here by yourself?" Hazel asked. Marlene smelled gamey and Hazel brought her hand to her nose.

"Best to keep to myself," Marlene whispered. "I don't want to get it."

It was obvious to Hazel that she had it. Even in the dark she could see that Marlene's pupils were open too wide, that her cheeks burned with fever. But Hazel couldn't tell her that. Instead, she went to the door and twisted the silver knob.

"You'll catch it in there," Marlene warned.

Hazel pushed open the heavy door and made her way through the lobby.

Ivy Hotchkiss still danced to Caleb Spainhower's weeping guitar, while another man crawled on all fours along the perimeter of the octagon-shaped room, eyes intent on the black tile border, mumbling, "Fits nice fits nice fits nice—" He ceased crawling. "A little off. Bring me my square and level." A rail-thin woman in a flower-print dress lay flat on her face on the red-carpeted staircase, as though she'd intended to head upstairs but collapsed in exhaustion after only three skinny-legged steps.

Somebody must be better by now, Hazel tried to convince herself.

She wiped damp palms on her shorts as she entered the ballroom. Brilliant light thrown from three crystal chandeliers illuminated the population of the long room—many more people than were here just hours ago. Heavy rugs from the lobby and hallways had been dragged in to cushion sore bodies from the hardwood floors. The podium used at town meetings was positioned at the back end of the room as if somebody planned to make a speech. It struck her as curious that there were no Mathers here. And nobody from Holloway Ranch.

Rose Peabody sat stick straight on the sofa by the fireplace—an improvement over the last time Hazel had seen her. She was staring at her reflection in the window, Owen no longer at her side.

Hazel picked her way across the ballroom and when she reached the velvet couch, she touched Rose on the forearm to get her attention.

Rose stiffened as if she'd been electrocuted and let out a surprised cry.

"I'm sorry." Hazel pulled her hand away.

"What are we doing here?" Rose said. Sweat-drenched hair plastered her head and neck.

"Don't you remember?" Hazel sat on the arm of the sofa.

"I don't remember."

"Are you feeling better?" *Please, please, please, say you're feeling better.*

"I'm seeing things." Rose was pale and perspiring and shaking, her eyes as big as saucers. "Horrible things, Hazel."

"They're not real."

"Black bears with no arms keep coming out of the woods to look at me through the window." Rose mewled helplessly. "I think they want to eat me so they can grow their arms back."

Hazel went to touch her again but quickly thought better of

it. "No, they don't, Rose. They're not really there." Yet Hazel found herself peering through the window at the dark trees.

Rose covered her eyes with her hands and moaned. "Wolves with heads as big as Molly's entire body. They keep their snouts low to the ground, sniffing around." She dropped her hands and looked at Hazel with desperation. "I'm afraid they'll smell me."

"Don't worry. They won't get in here. I promise." So many promises Hazel had made now. *They'll prove hard to keep,* she predicted.

Hazel worried then about Rose's chocolate Lab; when had Molly last been fed? She remembered Sean tossing dinner rolls to Molly and Jinx outside the Crock Saturday morning and she'd yelled at him that the rolls would make the dogs sick—Jinx especially since he had already eaten a donut.

Sick dogs. Rolls from Rhone Bakery… Suddenly she felt ill, too.

Hazel scanned the ballroom before asking Rose, "Where's Owen?"

"Owen," Rose repeated, not understanding it to be a question. "Why isn't the doctor here? Will you take me to the hospital?" Her eyes pleaded. "Will you, Hazel?"

Hazel didn't know what to say to her. Images flashed through her mind of Doc Simmons running bowlegged into the night, of Tanner pointing at Sean's apology on the granite wall, of her father slapping handcuffs onto Sean's wrists—he doesn't want to but he has no choice—while Sean looks directly at her and repeats, "I've always done everything for you."

Hazel tried to stop trembling. "Rose, I can't. My arm's messed up. I can't drive."

Rose's mouth turned down in despair.

"You'll feel better tomorrow." Hazel realized she was banking everything on that. They had to get better soon. It could only happen that way. "In the morning, you'll feel better."

Rose did not reply.

And Hazel could no longer look at her, into those Olive Oyl eyes, because those eyes would know Hazel wasn't telling her the whole truth. So she turned and walked away from Rose on legs suddenly gone to jelly.

Gus Bolinger hadn't moved since that afternoon from his green wing chair by the window. She'd never given much thought to him before, just another old guy around town. Except he had wild gray Einstein hair. James Bolinger's grandpa. He taught history at school because he'd fought in the Korean War and he walked with a hitch from the bullet he'd taken to the shinbone during the Battle of Bloody Ridge.

Hoping he might be feeling better, Hazel went to him and kneeled. "Mr. Bolinger?"

Quietly he was saying, "I can't see, I can't feel, I can't see..." He'd aged; the past few days had turned him into the spoils of an archaeological dig. And the anguish in his voice made her heart heavy. "I can't feel," he repeated.

"It's going to be all right." She patted his hand in what she hoped was a comforting gesture. "I promise." *Why the hell do I keep saying that?* Now if he stayed blind and paralyzed she'd feel guilty forever and surely he'd haunt her for breaking her promise.

The man slumped in the matching chair next to Gus suddenly sat bolt upright and hissed at her: "Can you hear that, little girl? They're breaking in. They're coming to get us."

I should've never come back. Hazel's heart began to thump so loud it was a wonder she could hear anything over it.

"Where are the children?" Sprawled on the floor before the fireplace, a woman was repeating a lament of her own. "Where are the children?"

Hazel glanced around; the woman was right. *There are no*

children here. She should find Aaron Adair and Violet and Daisy Rhone. *Right away.* Panic squeezed her lungs.

"Where are the children?" the woman cried again.

Kohl Thacker stopped running in circles beneath the center chandelier long enough to answer her: "Hawkin Rhone got 'em."

The woman wailed.

"All of 'em," Kohl added.

"Didn't we rid ourselves of him?" another woman asked.

"He's back."

Hazel's heart launched another small attack. No one ever proved Hawkin Rhone guilty of poisoning anybody, but he'd been banished from Winslow all the same. "People saying he did it is all that mattered," Sean had told her at Three Fools Creek a long, long time ago.

Alarmed, she dashed from the ballroom. *I have to get rid of the bread—all of it!* Where did they deliver Saturday morning? To Sean's mom, Honey, here at the hotel, to Clemshaw Mercantile, to the Crock. *Where else? Think, think!*

She raced through the dining room toward the kitchen, knocking over a chair along the way and imagining Ben Mathers watching in horror as his wife choked and suffocated to death before his very eyes. Harmless escargot to everybody but Lottie Mathers. For her, the snails were poison. For her, fatal.

Hazel burst through the swinging kitchen door to find Honey Adair clutching the edge of the countertop and crying soft helpless sobs. Owen Peabody was also in the kitchen, standing in front of the open silverware drawer next to the stove. Spoons were lined singly along the countertop and Owen pointed to each in succession as he counted, "five, six, seven, eight…"

Hazel went to his side. "What are you doing, Owen?"

He kept his eyes on the spoons as if not wanting to lose his place. "Taking inventory."

"Why?" Hazel asked, though she was grateful he'd taken up such a harmless preoccupation.

"Because as soon as the water stops poisoning us, we'll have to put everything back where it belongs," he explained, sounding impatient, as if he resented the interruption. "We'll need to know if anything is missing."

He resumed counting while Hazel thought, *It's people we're missing, not things.*

Seeing Hazel had somehow made Honey start to cry even harder. Hazel crossed the kitchen and hugged her as best as she could with one arm, and murmured soothing lies, "It's okay, it'll all be okay." Honey's sobs were contagious and Hazel had to force back her own tears. She couldn't break down now.

"Aaghh!" Owen fumed in frustration. Then he took a deep breath, let it out in a huff, and started again. "One, two, three, five, seven, eight, nine…"

Honey pulled away from Hazel. "My sons are missing."

"I'll find them." Hazel made yet another promise.

"Eighteen nineteen twenty-two twenty— *Aaahgh!* One, two…" The muscles in Owen's Popeye arm flexed as he pointed at each uncooperative spoon: *Lay there and be counted or I'll fix you.*

"Your grandmother," Honey said then, "watch over her."

Can seventeen-year-olds drop dead from heart attacks? Hazel wondered. She had a genetic predisposition. Her grandfather was only sixty-five when his hit. "Where is she?"

"Last time I saw her she was with Samuel."

A fresh bolt of panic struck. Before she'd left that afternoon she told her grandmother that she'd be back soon with help and ordered her to lay low until then. Now Hazel shot up the servants' staircase to the second floor. *Help, Grandpa,* she silently implored. *If you're up there guardian-angeling, Grandpa, now is the time to help us.*

When she reached the top step, she found Samuel Adair tearing it up, but Sarah was nowhere in sight. Obviously blind drunk, Sean's father swerved down the hallway, smashing into side tables and knocking off their contents, slamming into photographs along the wall, cursing with a passion. He carried a baseball bat. Sean's—she recognized it. She stared at it for a moment before realizing she was checking for blood, for signs he'd used it.

Noticing her, Samuel stopped dead. Then he squinted at her like a parody of a drunk, cocking his head this way and that as if it would sharpen his focus. "Ruby Winslow?" Holding the bat in swing position he took a few steps toward where she stood at the top of the staircase. "That you, Ruby?"

Hazel was afraid of that bat and those beet-red eyes. She couldn't step away because the stairs were behind her. If she wanted to run down she'd have to turn her back on Samuel and he was within striking distance now.

"Not Ruby," she managed to keep her voice steady, "Hazel. A real-live Winslow."

Samuel picked up a candy dish from the table and tossed it at her like a Frisbee. It bounced painfully off her hip and landed on the floor at his feet, not breaking but spilling mints across the Oriental rug. "Guess you're real." He didn't sound entirely convinced.

"You need to go sleep it off, Samuel," Hazel tried.

"Don't you tell me what to do." He took another step toward her.

"It's late, Samuel, really late. Time for bed." She took a step backward onto the staircase. Brained with a baseball bat would be a terrible way to go. She imagined it might take more than one swing. That or she might tumble to her death down the staircase. Either way, it would definitely hurt.

Running a hand across several days' worth of beard he said, "I *am* bone tired." Incredibly, he lowered the bat and turned away from her.

She was amazed he'd given in so easily and figured he must be even more stewed than usual. After he weaved back down the hallway and disappeared into the Adairs' quarters she began to breathe again. But there was always tomorrow—always more to drink—so still she would worry about that bat.

Somehow she'd have to get Aaron out of there. She looked down the hallway, then up at the ceiling. "Aaron?" she asked in the quietest voice. "If you're floating around out here and can hear me, go get your body and come back out to the hall."

She stood still for a minute, believing it might actually happen, that the little boy would emerge from their living room in his cowboy pajamas.

When he didn't, she resigned herself to wait until she was certain Samuel had passed out before going in to retrieve him.

She tiptoed down the hallway to her grandmother's rooms, praying that the girls had minded her and stayed put. She tried the door. Locked. Good.

She knocked softly. "Violet," she whispered through the keyhole, "it's me—let me in."

After much hushed discussion behind the door, the lock turned and Violet cracked it open barely an inch. Confirming it was Hazel, she opened it just wide enough to let her squeeze in.

Relief washed over Hazel. Here were all three: Violet, Daisy *and* Aaron. But she knew they couldn't stay. The hotel was too dangerous now: desperate people, drunks with bats, no place for kids. *They're so small and breakable,* Hazel thought, the girls in their silk gowns, Aaron in his short-sleeved pj's. None of them had on shoes.

The children had all the lights off and the kerosene lamp lit. In the winter the electricity always goes out in Winslow.

During the first storm and every storm thereafter. Now the
wick lamp that usually occupied her grandmother's mantel
sat on the outer hearth, casting yellow light upward onto their
innocent faces. Boo glared at Hazel from beneath the vanity.
Though the kids looked glad to see her, they kept their distance. In the flickering light of the oil lamp, Hazel figured
she must look a fright.

"Are you sick, too, Hazel?" Violet asked.

"No, no, I'm fine." She smoothed her tangled hair and hiked
up her drooping shorts. "Have you seen my grandmother?"

"Haven't seen anybody 'cept Aaron. Maybe she's hiding,
too."

"I hope so. Here, sit." Hazel positioned the three kids on
the chenille bedspread. "I'm glad you're all together. Listen,
we have to leave here."

Each nodded their head as though they already knew that.

"Remember how we play hide-and-go-seek?"

More grave nods.

"Let's play it now, only I'm going to count to one million
zillion so you need to stay hidden for a long time. Don't come
out till you hear me yell 'olly olly oxen free.' Just me. Understand?" Then she thought, *Brilliant. Now if something happens to me, they'll wither away in their hiding spots, waiting
for a call that will never come.* She chased the worry away.
No time for it now.

"You, Daisy, especially," Hazel continued, "stay put no
matter how spooked you get." Daisy usually came out of hiding as soon as she sensed anyone near her spot, the fear of
getting caught by surprise (you're it!) evidently worse than
flat-out losing the game. Gently, Hazel took the little girl by
the chin. "No matter what, okay?"

"Yes, Hazel." Daisy was more solemn than any five-year-
old in the history of Winslow. She ran her tiny fingers across
the raised pattern on the yellow bedspread. "I'll stay put."

"Good girl." Hazel placed a hand against her cheek. Then she looked at Violet. "I'm counting on you." She felt terrible placing such a heavy burden on her—a mere seven-year-old. It wasn't fair. None of this was fair.

"Should we hide in the tower?" Violet had accepted the responsibility, brave girl.

"No!" Aaron said.

"No," Hazel agreed. "Somewhere away from here, someplace you know better than anyone else."

Violet cupped her hand around Aaron's ear and whispered.

"Where's it going to be?" Hazel asked.

"Can't tell," Violet said. "That's not hide-and-go-seek."

Hazel smiled. "Fair enough. But stay in town, all right? I have to be able to find you. Is it a good place?"

"It is," Violet said and Aaron nodded in agreement.

Daisy and Boo continued to stare at each other.

"Good. Okay, then…" Hazel went to the door and opened it a bit, poking her head out. The hallway was empty. Not allowing herself any more time to think about it, any chance to change her mind or chicken out, she flung the door wide open and told the children, "Now. Go now!" She gestured with her hand, *hurry hurry,* then brought a finger to her lips, *sshhh.*

Violet was fighting with Boo, who had dug his nails into the rug when she tried to drag him out from underneath the vanity.

"Leave the cat," Hazel said.

"I can't!" Violet despaired. "He's counting on me!"

"Okay okay, but hurry up!"

Violet finally got the better of the cat and gripped him tight in both arms as she led Daisy and Aaron out into the hall.

Aaron stopped just outside the door and looked back at Hazel, his eyes filled with panic. "Aren't you coming with us?"

"No—now go!" And he started to cry when she scooted him away with a couple of pats to the behind. She watched them run the length of the hallway and then bob up and down the servants' staircase until their tiny heads finally disappeared.

Hazel had to sit down. She was going to be sick or faint or something similarly unpleasant. So she sat where she had stood in the doorway and cradled her head in her hand and worried, *Are they going to be okay? Please, please, let them be okay.*

And she still had no idea what had happened to her grandmother.

She rose to her feet and returned to the fireplace, where she carefully lifted the oil lamp and placed it back in its usual position on the mantle next to the photograph of Anabel holding Hazel on her lap, smiling at her baby while Hazel ogles the photographer (her dad, she'd been told). Turning the knob on the base of the lamp, Hazel extinguished the image.

Feeling altogether alone, she dragged herself down the hallway on legs heavy with fatigue…past photographs of the hotel through the decades that had been knocked crooked along the wall, past upset furniture, past Samuel Adair snoring loud enough it was audible through closed doors.

Rather than descend the staircase as the children had, she walked up the creaky bare-wood steps, the air surprisingly cool in the dim stairwell, until she reached the top floor of the tower—or Ghost HQ, as Aaron called it, as if all The Winslow's lost spirits regularly congregated here to conjure up new ways to spook him.

"Friendly ghosts," she addressed the round room when she entered. Was she trying to convince them or herself? *Both,* she concluded. She'd never been afraid like this before. Now it was the only emotion operating. "Friendly ghosts…Casper and Friends."

Why are there no ghost animals? she wondered as she continued into the room. Perhaps there are those who linger, not understanding they're dead. She hoped that Jinx wasn't one of them. That if he were gone, he'd already passed on to a happy place with a steady supply of hot dogs and unstingy girls who love him without reservation.

The crystal glass remained on the floor where it had bounced to rest after Patience threw it against the window last night. "I tried to warn you," Patience said then, "and now look. I'm sick, everybody's sick."

For once, Hazel marveled, *you were right.* For once— incredibly—her morbid imaginings had proven true.

She wondered where Patience was now. In fact, she didn't know where *anybody* was and wished Winslow had a loud bell or siren to call everyone together at a predetermined location in case of emergency.

She walked to the arched window, touched the chip in the red glass, and looked out over downtown Winslow. Taillights receded down the hotel driveway and a few vehicles made their way along Fortune Way. Otherwise, the town was still and dark. Figuring she must be a strange sight standing at the floor-to-ceiling window, she raised her left hand in a claw and opened her mouth in a silent screech for the benefit of anyone who happened to be gazing up.

A click issued behind her.

"Grandma?" She hoped.

Then she turned and stepped on the crystal glass, skidding on it for a moment until it cracked beneath her tennis shoe against the hardwood floor. When she regained her balance she thought, *That can't be good luck.* Patience would freak.

She bent her leg to inspect the bottom of her shoe, relieved to see that no shards of glass had punctured the sole.

Eyes searching the room, she asked, "Are you here, Grandma?"

Silence. Except in shadow, there was nowhere in the tower to hide.

Click.

Though not an especially loud or threatening noise, it disturbed Hazel enough to convince her to hightail it out of there. She had to recross the length of the tower to reach the stairway and was sure that whatever was clicking would reach out from the shadows and grab her by the hair and yank her back into its dark corner and do disagreeable things to her.

Friendly ghosts... Claustrophobia clutched at her as she kept moving toward the staircase that somehow grew farther away. *Friendly, my ass.*

Finally, she reached it—unclutched and unscathed—and ran down four flights of stairs, her feet barely resting on each step as she hastened out in a clamor. She didn't stop to talk to Honey or Owen in the kitchen or Rose in the ballroom or dancing Ivy in the lobby. Rather, she dashed out the open front door and pulled it closed tight, relieved to shut in the horrors of the hotel behind it.

Gone was Marlene.

Instead, a man-size shape lurked in the deepest pocket of the porch.

"You can't leave," his voice thundered and the wood slats creaked and groaned beneath his weight as he came for her. "Nobody leaves."

Hazel turned to run.

A lariat lay strewn at the top of the steps. She tried to avoid it but her forward momentum was irreversible and her feet immediately became tangled in the rope. Losing her balance, she crashed against the porch banister. When her rib cage connected with the rail, a fresh new pain introduced itself to her battered body.

I should've never come back!

She scrambled forward and then raced through the grassy yard and down the stone steps and onto the drive, feeling nips at her back the entire time, claws reaching for her hair.

She ran faster. Her ribs burned.

No wonder Dad's hiding, she thought. *The monsters in town are scarier than the monsters in the woods.*

She made a tight right turn onto Ruby Road, glad to be off the gravel and on solid ground, and begged her screaming legs to just get her home.

They obeyed. And dark and unwelcoming as the house was, she tore open the front door and then slammed and locked it shut.

She flipped on the entry light. With her good arm she leaned against the hall-tree and tried to catch her breath, her heart exploding in her chest.

Then she raised her head to look in the mirror.

The agony of her throbbing elbow and traumatized rib cage had caused her to go white. Sweat streamed from her forehead down her cheeks; her freckles stood stark in her wan skin. Her long hair was snarled and matted, her tank top filthy. She stared at the rainbow spanning her chest and thought, *This shirt is ridiculous.*

When she returned her gaze to the reflection of her face, she was jolted by the look of terror in her eyes—like the trapped raccoon her father once freed from the Mercantile's storeroom. The animal had been soiled in the pastel remnants of the Frankenberry cereal he'd torn open to eat, and his eyes were beyond panic; they were without hope.

Several long blinks did nothing to alter her manic expression.

"What if somebody doesn't come up to Winslow soon?" she voiced her worst fear to her reflection.

Then she glanced at the brass letter slot next to the front door. "What about the mail? Daryl comes on Thursdays…"

Cradling her arm in the sling, she sank to the floor—and a misery of dread spread over her like a filthy blanket.

Will we make it till Thursday?

MIDNIGHT

"WE'LL SNEAK THE back way," Violet told Aaron and Daisy. "It's the very best way."

They'd left the hotel by the side door (after Aaron tried to talk to his mommy in the kitchen but she didn't know him) and then hid in the trees 'cause they heard grown men out front stomping on the porch. When the men wouldn't leave, Violet gave up on going the front way and took them onto the dark path through the woods. Now she was paying attention like she knew she should 'cause she was in charge of them and couldn't get them lost.

Boo squirmed in Violet's arms but she held tight. "Be good, kitty, be good."

They were in Hazel and the Sheriff's backyard now and the house looked dark and mean and the moon was fat but not full, so they walked fast through the backyard and squeezed through the hedge separating their yard from Patience Mathers's house.

Patience Mathers is pretty, Violet thought. *Snow White kind of pretty.* But there was a feeling around her that always made Violet a little nervous and she never wanted her to babysit. Hazel was pretty, too, but in a different way and her eyes changed color depending on what mood she was in. That was what she'd told her and Violet believed it. Hazel was what it's like to have a big sister, Violet decided. Somebody to look out for you, somebody who's always on your side.

When she glanced at her own little sister beside her, Daisy gave her a big gummy smile.

You could use some front teeth, Violet thought but was polite and didn't say it out loud, because Mommy said if you don't have anything nice to say, don't say anything at all.

Lights were on in the Mathers's house and yellow beamed out into the backyard. Patience's mommy, Constance, worked in the yard a lot wearing her garden gloves with butterflies on them and there were little pots of purple and blue pansies around the back porch. *Maybe we should hide here.*

No— She remembered Hazel saying to hide someplace they knew better than anyone else could.

Stopping to think was a big mistake because Boo spotted Patience's cat Ajax under the porch and he growled and cried all in the same noise and let out his claws and scratched Violet's arms as he jumped from them and ran after the black cat.

"Boo!" she called. "Tict tict tict," she clicked with her tongue.

But he was gone. It was okay; Boo knew his way home. One time they were driving all the way down by Matherston Cemetery and they saw Boo walking up the side of Winslow Road. She didn't know where he'd been or what he'd been doing but when they stopped to pick him up, he was all wrung out, Daddy said, and he and Mommy smiled at each other like they had an adult secret.

Now they kept going through Patience's flowery yard then went very fast past the back of the Ambrose house because nobody lived there and it was dark dark dark.

It was the best way for them to go, Violet knew, only Daisy kept stopping and saying, "Look! Look!" If she said it again Violet was gonna sock her. She yanked Daisy's hand, the one wearing the red sparkly ring, and dragged her through Dr. Foster's backyard. He was a nice man, she remembered her mom saying, but nobody lived there anymore, either, and she wanted to get outta there quick.

"C'mon, Aaron," she told him. Even in the moonlight she

could see he was scared. "C'mon," she said again 'cause she couldn't think of anything else to say. Maybe he felt embarrassed because he was still in his pajamas.

Violet started to feel scared again, too… She didn't understand what was going on. Think happy thoughts, her mom always told her when she was afraid, like when she had to get a shot. So she thought about when Boo was a baby kitten (just a teensy pouf of gray fur), and about playing on the swings in the park for so long she would dream all night about swinging, and about her mommy tucking her and Daisy in at bedtime—snug as bugs in a rug—and she felt better.

It felt better to be out of the hotel, too. What was Mr. Adair so mad about, anyway? *Mrs. Adair is nice; she gives us treats even when it isn't a special occasion day. Sean's nice, too.* Violet knew that Aaron would feel safer if only he could be with his big brother. It was weird, she realized then, that Sean and Hazel weren't together like usual. Violet hoped that when she got older she'd have a cute boyfriend, too. Maybe Aaron, maybe Timmy Hotchkiss.

But Aaron's dad was really mean tonight. Violet could hear him yelling all the way down the hallway and when she heard a door open and then slam shut again, she leaned her head out into the hall and saw Aaron standing there all alone and told him, "Psst! Come in here."

She couldn't think about her own daddy right now, wouldn't let herself think about her mommy. "La-la-la," she sang loud to hide it away.

"La-la-la," Daisy echoed.

"As I was walking by the lake," Violet chanted and Daisy laughed. "I met a little rattlesnake."

Aaron gave her a funny look but she kept going 'cause it shut up Daisy with her "Look, look!" and kept Violet's mind off other things.

She and Daisy chanted together: "I gave him so much jelly cake, it made his little belly ache! One, two, three," they shouted as they ducked under the trees and into the next yard, "out goes she!"

Daisy giggled like crazy, just like whenever their daddy tickled her feet.

She's a good girl, Violet thought. *I'm a good girl.*

When they entered the last backyard on Park Street behind old Mr. Mathers's mansion, Violet shushed Daisy. Every light in the tall house was on, it looked like, all the way up to the attic. But she never even thought about stopping there no matter how bright it was. Because Ben Mathers was *not* nice—he yelled at them all the time, even when they were playing quietly.

He was yelling now, too. And wearing goggles and a funny hat.

As they tiptoed past the back of the house, Violet could see him through the mudroom window talking to some man whose back was to them (but it looked like Cal from the Fish 'n Bait maybe) and she heard Mr. Mathers yell, "How the devil else will we put a stop to this?"

And the other man, Cal maybe, held up his hands like he didn't agree but didn't want to fight about it.

"Why do we let them get away with it?" Mr. Mathers kept on shouting. "Time after time! It has got to stop!"

Violet looked at Aaron and he looked back at her really worried. This wasn't like when they dare each other to steal candy from the Mercantile or pretend Old Lady Winslow is a witch.

This is really *scary.*

"The shit's hit the fan," her daddy would say.

When they reached the back of the bakery, she noticed lights on upstairs in her own house…shining out from the bathroom and her and Daisy's bedroom. The front door hung open. She thought about hiding inside but then realized, *Isn't that the first place anybody'd look?*

Leading them up the rise in the opposite direction of the house, Violet resolved that when they made it there, they'd hide really good. Like Hazel told them to.

It's the best place to hide, she thought. *We play there every day. Nobody else, only us. So it's the very best place.*

She just hoped Hawkin Rhone wasn't anywhere around.

SUPPORTED AGAINST THE kitchen sink, staring at her reflection in the window, it occurred to Honey Adair that it was already dark out again. The days left quickly now and the nights stayed long. She didn't know how that could be. It was summer, so that simply could not be.

Yet it was, and behind the image in the window she recognized as her own, a slideshow played over and over: her husband, Samuel, threatening her temple with the hammer he uses to pound nails into loose boards on the porch, ink-black creatures as big as horses and with wings like bats skulking out of the Second Chance mine shaft, and her beautiful sons flung over the mountaintop, away from her forever.

When did I last see my boys?

She glanced briefly over her shoulder, at the disaster area the kitchen had become.

The hotel was displeased, she knew. With the infirmity and the malodor and the wailing, the hotel was displeased. Which was why Honey kept quiet, she didn't want The Winslow to notice her…didn't want it to see her like this, not taking care of it like she's supposed to.

If the hotel becomes wet with blood, she thought, *I'll never get it clean again.*

Blood—like the time Sean sliced through the web of flesh between his thumb and index finger on the pantry door's split hinge that she'd begged Samuel time and again to fix. She'd rinsed the wound in this very sink and, seeing how deep the gash went, bound up his hand and ran him to Dr. Foster's place. Later, after they'd come home with Sean stitched up, she'd gone back to the sink. She'd made navy bean soup for dinner that night and four bowls sat waiting to be washed.

The bowls were full of blood—her son's blood—and she'd gone weak and queasy with the helplessness of it then, too.

Where are my sons? she silently asked her reflection as visions of fire danced behind her.

THIS WAS FRITZ EARLEY's worst nightmare.

As soon as he'd hung up with Hank from Stepstone Feed Supply (Hank had chewed him a new one, all right), Fritz had jumped in his truck and headed for Winslow. Because between calling him a cheap bastard and a thieving sonofabitch, what Hank had to tell Fritz was chilling: he'd found ergot fungus in last week's delivery of feed.

Driving up Yellow Jacket Pass, vacillating over whether to stop first at Holloway Ranch or head straight to Rhone Bakery, Fritz had pleaded with the good Lord that if the fungus hadn't also infested the flour he'd delivered to the bakery, he would turn over a new leaf and become a better man. Clearly his prayers had come too late. Clearly Fritz would not be considered a better man anytime soon.

Now Fritz was jostling around in the back of an El Camino making its way along rutted Winslow Road. With every dip, he slammed painfully against the wheel well. *I should've told somebody I was coming up here.* Before shoving him into the truck bed, Pard Holloway's ranch hands had roughed him up enough to make him wish he'd told somebody he was coming up here and why. Anybody. His bruised eye and split lip pulsed with the question: *Why didn't I?*

Because you didn't want anybody to know, because you hoped to keep it quiet.

An accident, that's all, surely people would understand that? Everybody makes a mistake every once in a while. Only Fritz knew he shouldn't have bought that grain on the cheap, knew the deal was almost too good to be on the up and up. But a man's in business to make a profit.

Fritz touched his wounded face and winced. He was beginning to understand how much that inexpensive grain might really cost him, how quickly the price was rising.

There was going to be holy hell to pay once Holloway figured this out. On Fritz's way up to Winslow he'd dreaded dealing with Pard Holloway but figured he'd be reasonable once Fritz insisted on compensating him above and beyond any actual losses. Sure, Holloway was a hard bastard, but he was a pragmatic bastard at heart who understood the bottom line.

That was before Fritz had reached the bridge and saw what was happening up here.

The road surface changed to gravel and Fritz realized they were headed up the driveway to The Winslow Hotel. He wondered why they weren't driving to Holloway Ranch. "Where are we going?" he shouted at Kenny Clark and Pete Hammond in the cab.

Over his shoulder, Kenny said, "We're tossing you in with the sickos to see if you catch it."

Did I hear him right?

The El Camino stopped with a lurch that caught Fritz off balance and sent him crashing into the wheel well again. Then Kenny got out of the cab and leapt into the truck bed with a clomp of boots, the weight of him bouncing the truck up and down. He lunged for Fritz as if he might try to escape.

It was laughable. To where would he escape? There were woods on all sides, it was dark, he didn't know his way around, he was too fat to run fast or far, and he didn't have a Winchester like the one Pete was aiming at him.

"It can't be caught," Fritz said.

"Get up!" Kenny wrenched him forward by the arm.

"What do you think I was trying to tell you before you smashed my face in?" There'd been a blond kid at the bridge and Fritz could tell by his eyes that he got it, but he was battered, too, and had looked away.

"Shut up and get moving!" Kenny pushed him out of the truck and Fritz fell down into the driveway. The impact cut gravel into his hands and knees.

Fritz looked up at Pete and his rifle. "Do *you* understand me? It can't be caught."

"Guess we'll find out," Pete said.

Kenny jumped down into the gravel. "Get up there." He shoved Fritz toward the hotel. "And if we catch you anyplace else, we won't go so easy on you."

Pete cocked the rifle.

"I get it, I get it." Fritz stood but then stumbled again on his own and felt oddly embarrassed.

Kenny turned, muttering, "We'll be back later to collect what's left of you."

Despite that harrowing promise, Fritz felt relieved when Kenny and Pete got back in the El Camino and sped down the driveway. At least the beating was over. For now, anyway.

With nowhere else to go, he headed up the wide stone steps—only to stop dead in his tracks once he reached the top and the hotel revealed itself to him.

What is happening here?

Large red *X*'s marked the tall windows and doors of The Winslow. An age-old warning of plague that he knew meant stay away. And an inviolable order that the afflicted are to remain inside.

This was only the beginning of Fritz Earley's worst nightmare.

WEDNESDAY
3:00 A.M.

─────────────────────────────

THE PAIN IN Hazel's arm woke her just a few hours after she'd fallen asleep in the flower-print, burst-stuffing chair that had been her mother's favorite place to sit. She felt stiff and out of sorts.

Out of sorts. That was hilarious and she actually laughed a little. *Oh, we're all fine, thank you, really...just a bit out of sorts.*

With some effort she sat up. The mantel clock claimed it to be three o'clock. Nothing had changed except for the stiffness in her back from sleeping in the chair and new tenderness in her ribs where she'd cracked against the porch railing at The Winslow.

She dug into her pocket and came up with a few Lemonheads and her last Percocet. She swallowed the pill before popping the candy onto her tongue. When she chewed into the soft sourness, her mouth watered.

"Dad?" she called. "Are you here?"

Dead silence, until Hazel's stomach growled ferociously, the sugar and saliva teasing it back to life, making it think it had a chance at some real food. But she was still afraid to eat, afraid *everything* had become infested with the ergot.

She adjusted her sling where it'd slipped off her shoulder and sucked in her breath at the pain, wondering if she were bone-bruised or bone-broken or both. She wasn't up to poking around the wounded area to find out.

Scuffling sounds started up from outside, as if a number

of hurried feet were rushing up the stepping-stones toward the front porch. Hazel held her breath, straining to hear their hushed conversation over her own clamorous heartbeat.

When the footsteps reached the porch, the voices rose, high and hysterical, before erupting into maniacal laughter.

Terrified they were about to pound on the front door *(Did I lock it? I can't remember!)* or worse, break a window like zombies always seem to enjoy doing, Hazel shot out of the chair, prepared to bolt. But then the footsteps and laughter retreated back to the street, and she released her breath and placed a hand over her chest to try and calm her belabored heart.

A box of jawbreakers sat open on the table beside the chair; she'd been chomping on them Sunday night while she waited for her dad to come back from checking on the wolf at the Rhone's house. Now she grabbed the box and stuffed it into the back pocket of her shorts. Then she crept to the drapes and parted them just enough to peer outside.

Nobody there. No zombies waited on the porch, eager to eat her brains.

While she had slept, the shock from the horrors at the hotel had dulled—as if it were a movie she'd seen, not something she'd experienced. A fully messed-up, torture porn kind of movie that leaves you feeling damaged, that is the product of a damaged mind. Now with scary people roaming the streets, her dread had been fully restored, weighing heavy on her spirit. She dragged it out of the living room, across the entry, and into her dad's office.

Despite the hot stale air, the office had a cold feel to it, perhaps because none of the electronics were glowing or beeping, more likely because her father wasn't there.

She skirted the desk and plopped down onto the leather seat of her dad's wooden chair. After swiveling to face his computer she clicked the mouse to wake the machine. As it warmed up she willed the phone line to be working again. She needed information off the web. And she needed to send an e-mail SOS to the Stepstone Valley Sheriff's office—with a cc to the whole world.

While she impatiently tapped her foot, the modem made a lot of loud and labored noises but ultimately found no dial tone and gave up.

"Sonofabitch!" She picked up the telephone base unit and slammed it up and down until it started making broken chirping sounds each time it hit the desk. Then she swiveled this way and that in the chair, pausing only to kick at the desk. Finally, she settled down and glanced at the bookshelf.

After Patience's father's fudge shop went belly-up (Hazel always figured it was because he'd spelled it Shoppe), Hazel's dad had felt sorry for Chance Mathers when he came calling in his new salesman vocation and bought an entire set of encyclopedias even though the library had a perfectly decent collection they could reference anytime. Handy for the first time now, she jumped up, pulled the E–G volume from the shelf, and dropped it on the desk with a thud.

Returning to the chair, she opened the thick book. "Maybe this is actually mass demonic possession."

Then she realized that talking to herself was probably not a good development.

Uncertain how to spell it, she spent a few minutes flipping through thin pages and in her haste ripped through the biography of Ralph Waldo Emerson and a picture of an emu. Once she found what she was looking for, she switched on the banker's lamp, leaned forward, and read.

Ergot fungi are molds that attack wheat, rye, barley and other wild and cultivated grasses. Wet spring weather favors the infection of growing crops.

Mold—Hazel recalled Violet saying that the bread was moldy.

She skimmed down the page past all the $C_{33}H_{35}N_5O_5$'s and $C_{35}H_{39}N_5O_5$'s.

Ergotism, a disease of humans and domestic animals, is caused by excessive intake of ergot: in humans by eating breadstuffs made with infected flour, and in cattle, by eating contaminated grain. Acute and chronic ergotism is characterized by insomnia, mood swings, mental disorientation, delusions, hallucinations, fever, slow pulse, muscle aches and spasms, convulsions and gangrene of the extremities.

Chronic? She wasn't positive but thought that meant it might not get better—or at least wasn't going away anytime soon. Remembering how Doc Simmons had shaken his head when she'd asked him how long it will last gave her the chills.

She kept reading.

Great epidemics of the Middle Ages were caused by ergot poisoning, and outbreaks continued into the twentieth century. Ergotism broke out August 17, 1951, in the south of France, where people in the town of Pont-Saint-Esprit ate contaminated bread. Three hundred people were affected in the largest epidemic since the Russian outbreak of 1926. The disease has often been referred to as St. Anthony's Fire since those suffering from gangrene would pray to St. Anthony for relief from the burning sensation in their extremities.

Reactions depend upon the individual and amount ingested. Some become too weak to leave bed, while others exhibit superhuman strength. Delusions occur sporadically with lucid moments between. Some report having beautiful religious experiences, others, hellish visions of the apocalypse. In Pont-Saint-Esprit, a war veteran believed he was surrounded by his dead comrades, conversing with the ghost soldiers day and night. Another victim believed he could fly and after jumping out of a fourth-floor window, he rose and ran down the street on broken legs.

She slammed the encyclopedia shut.

Hellish visions. Dead comrades. Broken legs.

"We're screwed." Hazel's heart sank. "We are completely screwed."

Gangrene? Was that like leprosy? She didn't know, but it sounded bad. Gangrene. She decided not to look it up. Then she couldn't help herself. She reopened the book and flipped to the G section, cringing as she read.

Gangrene occurs when there is extensive tissue death and is characterized by severe pain and swelling. This often occurs due to compromised blood circulation. The most common sites are toes, feet, legs, fingers and hands. The skin is firm and sounds are heard when it is displaced or bent.

Her eyes flew across the page—no stopping now despite her revulsion.

Gangrene leads to the development of black skin with dead underlying muscle and bone turning red if the skin breaks open. As the tissue decays, there may be ulceration and discharge from the tissue that is rancid. If not treated, the infection can spread to the rest of the body.

"Oh, no no no no no…" Her stomach was backing up into her throat. This was too much to grasp. Soon everyone's appendages were going to start oozing and falling off? She imagined the wood-plank sidewalk on Fortune Way littered with blackened, foul-smelling hands and feet, and a town full of human stumps—a freak show for the tourists.

This was *way* too much to grasp.

Her eyes darted around the office. She hoped somebody might magically appear—Sean, her dad, her grandmother, her grandfather's ghost, her mother, anybody—because she sure as hell couldn't handle this all by herself.

Panicked beyond all reason, she snatched up the telephone handset and futilely pressed Talk. "Hello? Stepstone General Hospital? This is Hazel Winslow and we are in deep shit up here. Can you please send a doctor? Better yet, send a whole team. Everyone you've got. Right away. You see, we've all been poisoned by moldy bread."

Heart racing, she sprang from the chair and began to pace

furiously. "And I think my boyfriend is in seriously deep shit, too. Better let me talk to Sheriff Washburn now."

She kicked the chair and sent it crashing into the bookshelf. "Riley Washburn? It's Hazel, Nate's daughter. Listen, Riley, you have to promise me you won't bust Sean Adair, okay? I don't know why he wrote I'm sorry on the granite wall, and I don't know why Tanner Holloway told me to tell Sean that Zachary Rhone is looking for him, but do you really believe that Sean would let his little brother, Aaron, eat that apple fritter if he thought for one split second that it'd hurt him?" She paused to gulp some air. "You're right, Riley! There is no fucking way!"

She threw the handset against the computer monitor so hard the casing burst apart. Then she shouted at the pieces of plastic strewn across the floor, "Hello? Hello? *Hell-o!*"

She glanced around the room; nobody had shown up to help her. "Okay. Okay. I have to get out of here." She took a deep breath, pulled the bottle of eyedrops out of her pocket, and gave each eye a good squirt. "No more screwing around." She strode out of the office. "I'll figure out a way to protect Sean while I'm driving down. But I need to get help *now.*"

Then she remembered her right arm and paused to gaze at the T-shirt sling.

"So what?" she challenged the foyer. "I'll just get the Jeep into any gear and leave it—I can work the clutch if it starts to stall, screw the transmission. I'll be down the mountain by sunrise." *If I can steer.*

After plucking the spare set of keys off the hook, she swung open the front door. The three-quarters moon had risen in the clear sky, so it wasn't especially dark out. She doubled back anyway to grab her dad's aluminum flashlight off the hall tree. She instantly liked the heft of it in her hand. Returning to the doorway, she swept the yard with the flashlight beam, searching for zombies. All clear.

But then she hesitated at the top step of the porch, her confidence faltering.

It was a long walk back to where she'd seen the Jeep parked on the fire road that morning. And what if it wasn't there anymore? She'd waste a lot of precious time and still be no closer to leaving. Rose and Owen would let her take their Jeep but it would need to be parked at the Crock because the Peabody's house was way down on Loop-Loop Road by Doc Simmons's place. And even if it was at the Crock, that would mean going back to The Winslow to get the keys from them.

And I can't do that. Hazel shuddered. *I won't.*

She decided to check if Patience's parents next door would let her take their Dodge pickup. She hadn't seen Constance or Chance Mathers since the rodeo but she'd noticed lights on in their house. Maybe they weren't even sick. And maybe Patience would go with her. Though she was probably still sick, she could at least shift gears while Hazel worked the clutch, maybe even help steer if she wasn't too far gone on ergot.

As she started toward their house through the yard full of flowers, she heard animals growling. Her pulse sped up. It definitely didn't sound like wolves. Still, their tone held menace. She scanned the yard with the flashlight. Everything looked surprisingly normal, the yellow and red blooms on Constance's rosebushes shone bright as jellybeans in the beam of her flashlight.

More growls and Hazel discovered the source. Patience's jet-black cat, Ajax, and Violet's cat, Boo, were in a standoff beneath the dining room window, issuing low hateful rumblings. Clearly bad blood existed between these two—a feud for the ages.

"Stop it," Hazel hissed at them but that only set them off and they went after each other, rolling around in a tight ball, screaming in vengeful fury, tufts of black and gray fur shooting into the air. "Stop it," Hazel yelled at the spinning cat ball. "Stop!"

When they finally separated of their own volition she tracked Boo with her flashlight as he scampered around the side of the house. Ajax flew up a tree, sailed onto the roof, and was gone, too.

Then the porch light switched on and Hazel saw Patience's parents peeking through the colored glass squares in the tall window next to the front door.

She bounded up the porch steps and knocked, even though they were already looking at her. When they didn't open the door Hazel moved in front of the window, where they continued to stare out at her with wide eyes. They wore masks that covered their noses and mouths, and acted as though she couldn't see them—as if they could look and look at her but they themselves were invisible.

Hazel pounded the door. "Please, Constance, Chance. I need to talk to you." When they made no move to let her in she pounded harder, taking out all of her frustration on the carved walnut door. She considered breaking the stained-glass window. They'd never be able to replace it. *We'll never be able to replace a lot of things,* Hazel suddenly realized.

Finally, Constance responded, "If you stay back, we'll open the door. But you have to stay back."

After Hazel moved several feet away the door opened.

"We can't risk catching it, you see?" Constance said, her moving lips making the mask dance. "Why aren't you at home, Hazel? We're under quarantine."

"It isn't contagious. It's in the bread." Despite the masks, Hazel could read skepticism on their faces. "If you don't eat any bread, you won't get sick."

"Bread?" Constance said. She and Chance shook their heads, not buying it for a minute.

She didn't have time to argue with them. "I need to borrow the Dodge."

"Oh no, you don't." Chance's mask buckled on his face. "Not my truck."

"Wait—"

"Absolutely not. I've seen the way you tear around town on that motorcycle." Chance shook his head again. "Not in a million years, little miss."

She was wasting her time here. "Where's Patience?" Constance and Chance looked at each other with questioning eyes.

"Don't you *know?*" Hazel couldn't believe it.

"In the park?" Constance tried.

Chance shrugged his shoulders.

"Well that's nothing out of the ordinary, at least," Hazel said. "You're crappy parents to her. You've always been crappy parents."

"At least we didn't abandon her." Chance slammed the door in her face.

There was no point in trying to defend herself, or in telling him to go to hell, so she retreated from the porch and made her way past the rosebushes again. As she retook the sidewalk she thought, *They're not even sick—they're cowards.*

She stopped to glance back at their house, sealed up tight against the world, concerned only with protecting themselves.

And that infuriated her.

Hazel ran back through the yard and up the steps and the porch light went out just as she reached the door and swung the back of the flashlight against the ornate window. Glass imploded into the foyer, destroying the sanctity of their shelter, and Constance screamed and Chance shouted but Hazel was already racing away down the sidewalk feeling slightly better.

Once she reached Dr. Foster's house she shortcut a diagonal into Prospect Park toward the Crock on Fortune Way. Now she had no choice but to go and see if the Peabodys' Jeep was parked there. That first. She wouldn't let herself worry about having to go back to The Winslow unless it was actually there. Maybe the keys would be in it. Wouldn't that be lucky?

Walking through the park, Hazel shined the light before her feet to avoid stepping on any bodies. And when she reached the playground she scanned the flashlight across the swings and monkey bars. Then she lighted upon a slight figure crouched on the metal platform of the red merry-go-round: Patience Mathers.

As Hazel approached she saw that Patience was wearing her rodeo queen garb—white hat, fringed chaps, pony-hair boots—the whole cowgirl outfit. She played the light up and down Patience. Her red vest was soiled and when Hazel got closer, she could smell the dried vomit.

"Hey…" Hazel stopped a few feet away.

Only then did Patience look up with hollow eyes.

"Patience, are you okay?" Of course she wasn't, Hazel could see that. Her face was so drawn she looked like a corpse.

"I don't think so," she whispered.

Hazel put her hand over her nose and mouth, the smell of Patience's sick-encrusted clothes overwhelming her. "Wait here, all right?" she said through her fingers.

"Don't go!" Patience reached for her, panic igniting her eyes.

"I'll be right back, I swear." Hazel took off in the direction of the duck pond, trying to remember where she'd stumbled into the pile of clothes.

When she returned to the playground she helped Patience peel out of her clothes and into Julie Marsh's sundress. Even in the pale light of the moon, Hazel could make out the welts and scratches now covering nearly all of Patience's skin. "You have to stop scratching yourself," Hazel said. "Do you understand?"

"Okay," Patience said and dragged her nails along her right arm.

Hazel grabbed her hand away. "Don't do that anymore. *Don't.*"

"Okay." Patience sat back down on the little merry-go-round.

"What are you doing out here?"

"I'm waiting for you and Sean to finish the ghost hunt." She took on a pained look. "But there isn't any candy."

Hazel reached into her back pocket and pulled out the box of jawbreakers. She shook out a few and handed them to Patience, who put a purple piece in her mouth but then puckered her face as if the candy were sour. She spit it to the ground where her boots and dirty clothes lay in a heap and handed the rest back to Hazel.

"Nobody's ghost hunting right now," Hazel said.

"Sean is."

"How do you know?"

"He told me."

"Tanner said he saw you and Sean together." *All over each other,* she didn't add. "When was that?"

Patience whispered something Hazel couldn't quite hear.

"When, Patience?"

She said, "He wanted to kiss me."

"You're lying."

"He did, Hazel. He told me I'm beautiful."

"No, he didn't."

Patience looked up at her. "Yes, he did. In front of the Mercantile. Tanner Holloway was there too. You can ask him."

Hazel didn't have to. She sucked in a deep breath and closed her eyes. Maybe she'd just hold it till she passed out or better yet, died. She hated to think Tanner had told the truth about that. It meant she'd have to consider he was telling the truth about a few other things that she didn't want to believe.

"I didn't ask him to do anything, Hazel, I'm not easy pickin's."

Hazel finally exhaled. "I know you're not." She felt as though she were flailing underwater, out of air and unable to figure out which way is up.

"Tanner wanted to kiss me, too, after he pushed me too high on the swing but I wouldn't let him."

"Popular, aren't you?" Hazel popped a candy into her mouth to offset the bitterness. Jealous of Patience Mathers? She got that upside-down, inside-out sensation again.

Patience looked as sad as when Hazel had told her she couldn't come live with her after Hazel's mom disappeared. Patience offered to share her room and let Hazel bring all her stuffed animals and they'd be sisters. Hazel said she had to keep her daddy company at their own house but they could be sisters anyway. On every birthday after that Patience would sign the cards pasted with ribbons and stars and hearts she still handmade for Hazel, *Love, your sister P.*

"I didn't want him to," Patience said.

"I know you didn't," Hazel said. "I'm sorry."

"Something's wrong with Tanner." Her mouth puckered again. "He doesn't smell right."

"You don't have to worry about him anymore. He's long gone." But suddenly Hazel recalled how excessively sweaty he was at the granite wall outside Matherston Cemetery and for the first time realized, *Maybe he's sick, too.* Could he have made it down the mountain by himself if he were? Maybe that was the real reason he'd wanted Sean or her to go with him. *What if he didn't make it out?* The thought alarmed her for reasons she couldn't distinguish from all the other things making her anxious.

Hazel kneeled on her haunches to face Patience where she sat on the metal platform with her feet drawn up out of the dirt. "Have you seen Sean since you were all together at the Mercantile?"

Patience shook her head.

Then they were quiet for a long time. Hazel knew she should get moving but felt paralyzed, hopelessly incapable of doing anything she needed to do.

Finally, Patience said, "Did you know Hawkin Rhone is back?"

Goose bumps rose on Hazel's arms. "That's impossible—he's been dead for a long time."

But Hazel recalled Kohl Thacker saying the same thing in the ballroom of The Winslow while the woman by the fireplace cried, "Where are the children?"

"Gramps told me he's back," Patience said.

"As usual your gramps is completely full of crap." Hazel swallowed hard. "You *saw* what happened to Hawkin Rhone with your own two eyes."

Patience made chewing motions with her mouth as if she'd been conveyed back five years and now stood with a mouthful of taffy on the banks of Three Fools Creek opposite the rotting cabin, watching Sean crack Hawkin Rhone's head open with a pine log. She stopped grinding her teeth and stared at Hazel. "Sean's looking for him. I hope Hawkin Rhone doesn't find him first."

Hazel's heart constricted. "What are you talking about?"

"Gram and Gramps told me other forgotten things, Hazel, about you and your family."

"You shouldn't've listened."

"Things you should know," Patience continued, her expression disturbingly blank. "You didn't believe me before but you'd better now—terrible things are happening at The Winslow."

Hazel's heart clenched tighter. She was certain her grandmother was still somewhere in the hotel, along with Rose and

Owen Peabody and Honey Adair and the other defenseless sick people. But Hazel wasn't going back there without reinforcements. "Don't say another word. I've got enough problems without hearing more of Ben Mathers's nonsense."

"He said your grandmother killed Gram Lottie."

"More lies. And listen—don't eat any bread or donuts or anything from Rhone Bakery."

"And your great granddad killed Gramps's father."

"Did you hear me? No bread."

"And drowned Aunt Sadie in the pond."

"Enough!" Hazel suddenly felt nauseated. "Enough."

Patience took a shuddering breath. "Hazel, when am I going to feel better?"

"Soon," she said, despite the fact that Patience looked worse each time Hazel saw her. "Soon, I'm sure."

Patience stared at her filthy bare feet for a moment before glancing around the playground. "Where'd Jinx go?"

"I think he's dead," Hazel whispered, because saying it too loud would make it too real. "Doc Simmons killed him."

"You're crazy." Patience shook her head. "I just saw him."

Hazel shined her flashlight across the park. "Before I got here?"

"Just now. Under the monkey bars, watching you like he always does."

"*You're* crazy. I didn't see him."

"He looks different. Maybe you didn't recognize him. I hope he doesn't come back."

"I don't think he will." As Hazel sighed, defeat hung itself across her shoulders like a saddle. She looked at Patience and wondered if Doc Simmons was right, that there was nothing to be done and people were only going to get worse. "Do you want me to take you home?"

"No—we'll stay here and wait for Sean." Patience pulled

her knees up to her chest and hugged her legs. "We have candy now, so he'll come."

"I don't think he's coming, either." She reached over and pushed Patience's hair out of her eyes. "And I need to go and get help. I have to get down to Stepstone somehow so I can bring back doctors."

"Noooo, no no." Patience shook her head fiercely. "You're staying here with me."

"I can't."

"Please, Hazel, don't leave me, *please*."

"I have to, Patience, I don't have any choice."

"You do—you always have a choice. I need you, I'm sick. Help me, Hazel."

"I have to go. Me staying here won't help you. You need a doctor, Patience." Hazel turned her back.

"No! I need *you!*" Patience grabbed her sling from behind and Hazel twirled around and reflexively raised her left arm to strike her away. "Don't hit me again." Patience shrank back.

"I—"

"You never liked me. The only one you ever liked was Sean."

"You're wrong…"

"But he doesn't like you anymore."

"Stop it."

"You'll see."

"Shut up."

"Why did you slap me? You don't even care about me!"

"Stop it, Patience!" Hazel was certain she could not take one more awful word, one more harrowing sight, or one more dreadful thought before shattering into jagged pieces like that broken mirror in the Mother Lode Saloon.

Then her friend began to cry.

"I'm sorry," Hazel said softly. "Just be quiet and stay put.

Okay? I'll come back with help for you, Patience." Feeling overwhelmed and woefully ill equipped, Hazel walked away.

Leaving the park, she popped out onto Fortune Way in front of Rose's Country Crock. The screen door hung open but the interior held dark—an uninviting invitation. The Peabodys' Jeep was nowhere in sight, nor were there any other cars around. Yet an exhaust smell hanging in the dead air told her somebody had recently driven by.

Her pulse picked up when she noticed a light on next door in the old bank building where her dad's office occupied what used to be the teller area and the former vault now served as the lockup. *Of course he's here.* She smiled in relief, chastising her foolishness for not thinking to come here sooner. *He's here being Sheriff of Winslow.*

She dashed past the Crock, pounding the wooden boardwalk in her haste, and threw open the glass door stenciled, *Mathers Bank ~ Established 1888.*

Inside, she found an empty office, an empty chair and an empty spot on the table behind her dad's desk—a blank rectangle outlined in dust.

It's not here, either... Her spirits sank. The radio. *Damn damn damn! The radio's gone.* Of course her Uncle Pard had a radio, but there was no chance he'd let her get anywhere near that.

She took a huge faltering breath and then let it out slowly, trying to get her mind to stop snapping inside her head and her heart to stop pinging inside her chest.

A resolute clang sounded from the direction of the jail cell.

Hazel's breath caught in her throat. "Who's there?" she called.

"So dang hot!" A man's voice. "And all gone to pot faster than whiskers on crawdads."

She plodded toward the cell on feet suddenly grown as heavy and awkward as bricks. A fishing pole with a snapped line was leaning against the wall in the hallway leading to the vault. Several feet farther she stepped over the other end of the line, which had a dried-out worm skewered on the hook.

"Cal?" Hazel hazarded a guess.

"Yep. That'd be me."

She turned the corner and saw Cal from the Fish 'n Bait sitting on the cot in the jail cell, holding a foam cup on his lap. When she reached the bars she could see the squiggling worms inside the container. The door to the cell was closed. She tugged on it—locked tight.

Tiny Clemshaw had been the last person incarcerated in the cell Cal now occupied. A few years ago her dad had thrown him in overnight for running over Meg Foster's poodle, Pepé, after too many whiskey sours at the Buckhorn.

"Did my dad put you in here?" she asked Cal.

"Nope."

"Who then?"

He looked up at her with sorrowful eyes. "That'd be me."

The source of the clang she'd heard. "Have you done something wrong, Cal?"

"Not yet."

"Not yet?"

"Come unbuttoned, I tell ya. 'Fraid I might."

"Might do what?"

"Somethin' wrong."

"Like what?"

"Hook somebody in the eye."

"Best not to do that," she agreed.

"Best not." He looked back at his cup.

"I'm glad you came down off the roof. That looked dangerous."

"Weren't bitin' no how."

"Where's everybody else?"

"Pest House."

"Where?"

"Nervous water out there. Mathers says the devil's gonna put a stop to it."

"You're not making sense, Cal."

"Told ya my bait's been stripped. Told ya that already." He stared at his worms.

"You planning to stay in here then?"

"Yep. Aim to keep myself outta the way of all those fish."

Hazel sighed. *Not a bad idea.* Briefly, she considered joining him.

Instead, she slogged back to the front of the bank and kicked open the door, then stood on the sidewalk and loudly asked, "Now what?"

After an empty minute or two, she headed aimlessly up Fortune Way, thinking about just going home and crawling into bed and pulling the covers over her head.

It wasn't until she'd passed Buckhorn Tavern and nearly reached the Mercantile that she noticed Tiny Clemshaw's shotgun trained on her chest.

"I won't have you stealing from me!" Tiny howled.

As heavy as her flashlight weighed in, it was no match for the shotgun. "I just want to pass, Tiny, that's all…" Hazel began to cut as wide a swath as possible around him.

Tiny held his ground on the sidewalk in front of the store's broken display window, hair sticking out at all sides, infuriated features stuck in that cotton ball of a face. "I won't have anybody stealing from me anymore!"

Hazel was quicker to recognize the symptoms now; clearly Tiny Clemshaw was going insane on ergot. "I don't think you're feeling yourself," she tried. "Maybe you should put down the gun."

He did not put down the gun. Instead, he tracked her, pivoting on the knee he threw out last winter shoveling snow. "Maybe now you'll think twice about stealing beer from me."

"I won't come into your store. Never again if that's what you want." What *she* wanted was to move much faster—to turn and flee—but she worried he'd panic and fire.

"I want you to send the sheriff over. Right away." His aim on her was steady.

"I'll find him, Tiny, and I'll send him." She realized she was holding her good arm up in the air, *stick 'em up.*

"He's at the Rhone place." He pointed up Fortune Way with the shotgun, then quickly trained it back on her. "Go fetch him."

She dared take her eyes off Tiny to look toward the bakery. Trucks—including her dad's Jeep—were parked in front of the Rhones' house with their lights illuminating the yard. Hazel returned her gaze to the gun. "I will. I'll go right now."

And then she did turn and run, certain she'd hear the crack and feel the rip and burn of shot filling her back at any moment.

"Hurry," he yelled after her but didn't need to waste his breath.

Her sore ribs and elbow protested, creating shocks of pain with each footfall as she pounded past the bakery and up the rise to the bowed house. She was relieved as rain to spot her father standing next to the clothesline. White sheets hung slack in the breezeless night.

Her father was looking down with a puzzled expression. *What's going on here?* she wondered.

"Dad!" She continued running toward him.

He looked up in alarm and held up his hands, crossing them back and forth in a frantic *no, no* gesture. "Stay back, sweetheart. *Don't* come over here!"

She did anyway, she couldn't will her legs to stop moving until she was almost upon her, and she forgot all about Tiny Clemshaw gone vigilante at the Mercantile.

If it weren't for all those red curls, Hazel would've never

guessed it was Melanie Rhone. Wouldn't have had any idea to whom those mounds of split flesh belonged. Blood glistened wet in the lights of the Jeep; bone shone white and cold.

Poor, sweet Melanie. If Hazel had had anything in her stomach besides hard candy, she would've lost it. *Did Violet and Daisy see this?* She truly hoped not. But that would explain the blood on their dresses. The grass surrounding the body was soaked. It was hard for Hazel to imagine that the small woman had contained that much blood.

"I came to ask if she'd seen any more wolves." Her father's stare was fixed on Melanie but his face displayed no emotion, as though he were looking at a stack of dirty laundry. He shoved his hands into his pants pockets, a gesture that said, *I don't quite know what to do about it.*

"Who did this?" Hazel asked. An ax lay in the dandelions a few feet away. She might vomit after all.

He met her gaze with a befuddled expression. "Wolf?"

Hazel wanted to reach over, shake him, scream, *A wolf didn't do this! Wolves can't swing axes!* But his eyes had gone vacant, he was somewhere else, not seeing her at all, she suspected. She glanced down at his hands to see if they were swelling or turning color with gangrene but they remained hidden inside the pockets of his khakis.

"No, Dad," she said, "not a wolf."

"Is that you, Anabel?" His eyes glinted with surprised delight.

"No! Not her—I'm *me.*" And suddenly she was furious at her mother for not being here when she needed her.

"Anabel…what should we do?"

That's it, Hazel thought, *he's done,* and the earth may as well have split open and sucked her in. Because any hope she'd had that she wasn't completely alone in this now drained away.

"Nothing in the house except bloody shoe prints." Her Uncle Pard came up behind her. "Size eleven, I'd say." He ignored Hazel, sidestepped Melanie, and loomed in front of her father. "What we need to do now, Sheriff, is get things cleaned up."

"We can't clean this up." Her father's autopilot seemed to switch on. "We need a proper investigation."

"Do you really want people seeing what a mess you've made?" Pard clutched him by the upper arm. "There'll be charges against you—*criminal* charges—for allowing this to happen."

Her father's face twisted with uncertainty.

Hazel stepped up. "He's lying, Dad. He's trying to scare you."

She pulled her uncle off her father and glared at him. "We need doctors up here, Uncle Pard."

He shook his head as if to say, *No can do.*

"Doctors *and* vets. You know there's something wrong with the feed, don't you?"

He placed a fist on his hip and leaned close to her. "I'm going to say this for the *last* damn time—my beef could not and did not make anybody sick."

"You don't get it—the *feed* is making the *cows* sick. Maybe a vet from Stepstone who hasn't lost his mind like Simmons can help your herd."

Pard appeared to consider that for a moment, and Hazel hoped his certainty was finally beginning to waver. But then he said, "We wipe up our own spills. You know that better than anyone, Hazel. You, your father here…and Sean Adair."

No, she mentally shook her head. *He's not still using what happened at Hawkin Rhone's cabin against us. He can't be. Not now. Not with another dead Rhone on our hands.*

Her uncle pushed his cowboy hat up off his forehead so she could see straight into his hazel eyes. "I've been to the bakery."

Cold fingers squeezed Hazel's heart. "Do not threaten me."

"Only telling the truth. Besides, folks are on the mend."

"They're getting worse."

He squinted hard at her. "I've got things under control."

Hazel gestured at pieces of Melanie. "*This* is under control?"

"Listen to me, girl—let me handle this."

"You're *not* handling it! What happened to the phones? Where's the radio?"

"Don't know anything about any radio."

"Damn you, Uncle Pard! I'm taking the Jeep and getting outta here."

"You won't get far. And don't swear at me."

"Why not?"

"Because the bridge is closed. And because it's not lady-like."

"What are you *doing?* Have you completely lost your mind too? We need help! Not quarantine. I'm leaving whether you like it or not."

"Cut and run? Didn't realize how much you take after your mother."

"Don't say—" she started to protest.

"Though I can't say I blame Anabel." Pard looked at her father with obvious disdain.

"Don't say that!" Hazel cried. "Don't you ever say it was our fault she left!" She thought about picking up the ax and lodging it in her uncle's thick skull. Instead, she hit his chest with her fist several times but he was a big man and it had no effect. When she swung at him again he caught her by the wrist and squeezed.

"Be careful," she told him, fast running out of steam. "That's the one Hawkin Rhone broke, remember?"

He let go and she fell on her rump in the grass, landing just inches from the body.

Her dad hadn't moved a muscle. He simply stared. Hands growing gangrenous in his pockets, she supposed.

And she wondered if Tanner made it out before they closed the bridge.

Hazel glanced up at the old apple orchard, at the leafless trees' misshapen branches. "Where's Zachary Rhone?" she suddenly thought to ask.

Her father looked at her with that now familiar helplessness and her uncle glanced away.

Returning her gaze to the pile that was once Melanie Rhone, former Winslow rodeo queen, mother of two young daughters, she realized, *They think Zachary did this.*

The gravity of Tanner's remark that Zachary Rhone is looking for Sean crashed down on her then with stark horror and ice-cold panic.

She shot up and stumbled fast down the hill, away from her dad, her uncle, Melanie, passing right by the Jeep without even thinking about jumping in and leaving town.

Because now her only thought was, *I must find Sean before Zachary Rhone does.*

4:30 A.M.

KILLING SEAN ADAIR was the only thing Zachary Rhone allowed himself to think about.

When the flash of images lit through him—splashes against the white sheets hanging on the line, that blue eye staring unblinking into the sun—he forced himself to refocus.

"I'll hunt you down," he repeated, "and make you pay."

Melanie, my Melanie. Why had he married a woman so pretty, so sweet? The boy had tried to steal her right out from under him.

"Focus!" Zachary was desperate to clear his head. "It's so hard to think anymore."

Pard Holloway had paid him a visit earlier. Today? No, yesterday. He'd made accusations.

Zachary had protested, "How do you know it's not your beef that's making people sick?"

"So what if it is? Six of one, half dozen of the other, wouldn't you say?"

Zachary had nodded, having no idea what Holloway meant. "Don't you worry, Rhone," Holloway had assured him, "the one responsible will get his due before this is through."

Again Zachary had nodded, this time with understanding. And fear of being found out.

But Holloway wanted to keep it quiet. He'd told him, "Let's keep it between us."

Or else, Holloway didn't say, but Zachary had heard it loud and clear all the same.

After Holloway left, Zachary felt as though he'd bought a

pig in a poke. Like he hadn't been quick enough on his feet and Holloway got what he came for but left nothing in return.

The blue eye flashed; red splashed. *Don't think about it.*

Zachary never expected it to turn out like this. When he'd finally taken a good look—after the baking, after the delivery, after everyone had already eaten the bread—the flour looked off. Only slightly, but what a difference that made. So he'd cleaned it all up and pretended it never happened because by then it was too late.

And now I'll be shunned like my father. The apple doesn't fall far from the tree.

Eyes searching the black orchard, he realized, *But apples don't fall from these trees. Did they ever?* Not since his father was sent away.

"Shut up! Shut up and focus!"

It's that boy's fault, he reminded himself. Zachary loved his family, would never hurt his family the way his father had hurt them. *My sister, poor Missy.*

So it was the boy's fault then. *Why didn't Sean tell me the flour was off?* It had to be his fault.

Zachary should've never hired him, should've never given that rotten apple a chance. But he'd felt sorry for Sean when he came looking for work, pitied him because his old man was a drunk. *I know what it's like to be ashamed of your father.*

Then Zachary wondered where his daughters were.

The eye stared; the sheets stained.

"Are you hiding from Daddy?" he spoke to the orchard. "Are you ashamed of me? Because of what happened to Mommy?"

Think about Sean, don't think about that. Think about hunting him down and making him pay for the loss of your family and your mind. Zachary's rage against Sean flared anew. "I'm going to find you, and when I do, you are not going to like it. No sirree."

DAISY

HAFTA STAY HIDDEN, hafta mind Violet, no getcha gotcha. What daddy do to mommy why daddy do to mommy? Dark can't see, but oh Hawkin Rhone's gonna getcha, he's gonna getcha! Don't be ascaredy-cat...

SEAN FOUND HIMSELF lying next to Three Fools Creek, not sleeping really. *Just resting,* he thought, *waiting out the dark.*

The sounds of water streaming over rocks and hemlocks shedding their needles to the forest floor kept him company. He gazed up through a break in the tree canopy: still dark, still night.

He rolled over and sat up. Taking in the woods, the creek, the moon, he suddenly felt as if he were living a fairy tale. That at any moment an ogre or witch or talking wolf would emerge from between the trees and take him on a journey beyond his imagination—one he hoped would end with a kiss from a princess instead of his head in an oven.

In the moon shine, the surface of the water undulated like quicksilver. He got down on all fours before a small pool and drank and drank like a dog, and when he got up his belly sloshed. He'd been doing a lot of that: drinking and pissing, his body trying to flush out the poison.

It was coming and going enough now for him to realize it comes and goes.

He stood up on the bank and moved forward a few steps to plunge his bare feet into the cold water. The shock succeeded in bringing him to full alert.

Okay—think now while it's gone. Think back to before any of this started.

The water rushed strong against his calves. He watched a school of tiny silver fish swarm around his right ankle, trying to take bites out of him with their miniature mouths. No fools bobbed along the creek, but a two-foot section of branch journeyed past, knocking into rocks, becoming wedged before popping back out to continue downstream. It reminded him of chopping firewood on the stump behind the hotel and then loading the logs into a linen sack and delivering them to the ballroom fireplace like a bundle of severed arms.

Sean wondered if he was starting to come out of it or if he was just getting used to feeling this way and learning how to function in it. He stared into the water at the fish. His focus seemed less swimmy than it had been, and his legs felt less noodley.

Maybe I'm getting better, he thought and his spirits lifted. He raised his eyes to the crooked cabin across the creek, where on the porch Hawkin Rhone was busy skinning a raccoon.

His focus sharp now, Sean smiled to himself. *Yeah, I'm definitely getting better.*

Feeling relieved, he shook his head, tried once more to concentrate.

Okay. I was in the bakery Saturday morning, he remembered, *when Hazel came in with Jinx. But what was I doing before that?* He rubbed his temples hard as if the gesture would gather his thoughts. *I tried to tell Zachary about the flour, that the bread didn't turn out right.*

"He wouldn't listen to me," Sean called across the water to Hawkin Rhone. "Told me to taste it. Told me to get in that delivery van. And later accused me of making time with Melanie."

Sean kneaded the sore muscles of his arms and felt thirsty again already. Why did Zachary think he was after Melanie, anyway? She was the one always ogling *him. I don't go for rodeo queens.*

Leaning down, he cupped his hand and scooped more water into his mouth. He remembered being here with Hazel Sunday afternoon, back when Hawkin Rhone was still in his grave.

And he remembered hugging her, jokingly begging her to protect him. And she'd been scared of Bigfoot in the woods. Sean couldn't remember a time when he didn't love Hazel Winslow, and he wondered why she was always so scared of that, too.

Then when he'd been hunting for Hawkin Rhone that afternoon, Sean saw Hazel climb on the back of Tanner Holloway's motorcycle on Park Street. He'd watched as they rode out of downtown together toward the bridge, thinking, *She won't come back.* Why would she?

He missed her already, felt as though he'd been missing her his whole life.

Somehow the creek bed shifted direction beneath his feet and he swayed to keep upright. Then he sank back down to the ferns and dirt, curled up into a ball, and buried his face in his arms. The loneliness felt spiky. *Are we the last ones here?* he wondered with sure dread. He wished he had his shirt.

"Them bones, them bones gonna walk around," Hawkin Rhone sang across the creek, "disconnect them bones, them dry bones."

Sean knew the headstones for Hazel and Aaron in the Winslow family graveyard weren't real, that it was just his mind playing tricks on him. But these tricks were punishing. Not that he didn't deserve them. Hazel might be sick by now. Aaron and his mom definitely were. Patience Mathers, Melanie Rhone and the little girls, and everybody else in Winslow for all he knew.

I deserve to be punished.

Sean sat up again—it wouldn't let him rest—and looked back at the cabin. Maybe he'd just stay here forever, thinking about what he'd done. He only hoped the animals wouldn't get at him like they'd gotten Hawkin Rhone. Then he realized he'd probably starve to death before that happened.

The old man kept singing while he scraped meat off Bandit's carcass. "Head bone connected to the neck bone..."

Except for his creek-numbed feet, Sean hurt all over and wondered if he'd been beat up or hit by a car. *I'd remember that, wouldn't I?*

Staring into the dark driving water, he smelled trout. *Try to concentrate.*

He remembered being completely pissed at Zachary Saturday morning. Remembered the smell of bacon frying when Zachary slammed the door in his face. Saw himself removing the hot-dog bun bags from the large drawer where they store the pink bakery boxes, saw himself standing and staring at a loaf of bread and thinking, *So what?* The flour was a little sticky and gray. Sean didn't know what that meant. How could he have possibly known?

Then when I rolled in there on Monday, Zachary was in the bakery and he barked at me to go home and it was clean and nothing was baking. So it was that morning that Sean had realized the bakery was responsible for the food poisoning going around town.

Zachary had then told him, "Don't say anything to anybody."

And Sean thought that sounded like a pretty good idea at the time.

Only that was before things got worse...

Then it hit Sean like a ton of bricks. He gasped, held it, slowly exhaled.

It was clean.

Abruptly he stood.

The bakery was clean like I've never seen it before and he wasn't baking any bread.

And finally Sean understood: *Zachary knew.*

Zachary knew *even then* that it was worse than food poisoning. He knew even then that things were about to get so much worse than mayo left out too long in the sun.

Sean shoved his wet feet into his tennis shoes and left Three

Fools Creek, heading down the dark trail toward town, back
to the bakery to find Zachary Rhone.

FINDING SEAN WAS the only thing Hazel allowed herself to
think about.

Leaving her father and uncle and the carnage at the Rhone
house behind, she forced herself to focus on just one thing:
finding Sean before Zachary Rhone did.

Her stomach was in turmoil at the thought of him sick and
alone. *Does he even know he's in danger?* She remembered
him driving the bakery delivery van Saturday morning, the
sunlight pouring through the windshield lighting his eyes and
kissing his hair.

She would not let herself cry. She would not fail him again.

With nothing to go on except what Patience had told her in
the park, Hazel decided to follow the path of the ghost hunt
and was resigned to sweep the whole mountainside with her
flashlight if that's what it took.

First stop: church cemetery. The cow was gone, Hazel
noted with odd disappointment. The wrought-iron fences
looked shiny in the beam of her flashlight, the headstones
dull and cold. She turned in a slow circle, cutting swaths of
light through the area surrounding the cemetery, and recalled
Rose Peabody saying in a sermon on tolerance that at one time
those deemed not respectable weren't allowed to be buried
here. Instead, their bodies were taken to the woods and buried in graves with no markers.

There was still activity up at the church—she could hear
the organ and see figures moving in the light of the candles—
but she had no intention of going in there again and knew
Sean wouldn't, either. He never went to church even if Honey
begged. When he was little she'd bribe him with the promise
of ice cream afterward but that hadn't worked for a long time.

He's not here, Hazel determined and moved on.

She hurried up Civic Street—barely registering the wreck-age of dented trucks and downed streetlamps along the way—and turned onto Ruby Road. Near the end of the street she passed beneath the glare of The Winslow. All four floors of the hotel blazed with yellow light. *Don't even look,* she told herself. *I am not going back there—I am never going back.*

She ducked into the woods and found the trail that would take her away from the hotel and east to the Winslow fam-ily graveyard, a path so familiar she could easily navigate it under the light of the moon. *Don't be scared. Don't think about things in the woods. There's nothing here. But even if there is, you'll brain it with your flashlight. Don't be scared...*

Yet she couldn't help but think about the Sasquatch bigfoot-ing it around the woods at Three Fools Creek Sunday after-noon. There had always been a lot of talk about the creature lumbering through the forests of the Pacific Northwest. And a lot of replay of the Patterson film showing the half man/half ape strolling—sorta *casually,* in Hazel's opinion—between the trees. Though she had never thought he looked particu-larly threatening, right now she was scared as hell because whatever had been in the woods with her both Sunday and yesterday afternoon was not shy—reputedly Bigfoot's most endearing quality.

Fortunately, she reached the Winslow family plot with nary a rustle from beside the trail. Exhaling relief, she aimed the flashlight across the rise and saw familiar headstones and crosses: Ruby Winslow, Jim Adair, a smooth log resting near the pond like an unburied bone, but no Sean.

She walked forward a few feet—her tennis shoes tangling momentarily in the blackberry brambles—to the edge of the pond where Sadie Mathers had drowned. *Poor Sadie...*

The flashlight beam penetrated the water and for a horrified instant she thought she saw Sean submerged in the pond. The flashlight hit the water and sank out of reach before Hazel realized she'd let it slip from her hand. "Damn, damn, dammit!"

The flashlight came to rest upright in the muck at the bottom of the pond, casting pale light upward through the water. What she'd mistaken for Sean turned out to be blackened tree roots.

"I am such an idiot!" She angrily stomped her feet on the ground, which made her elbow and ribs explode in pain. "Ouch," she whimpered. "Damn."

Hazel could not afford to let herself get bogged down like this. *He's not here, keep going.*

She noticed that the sky was lightening at last—the long night finally nearing an end. Her heartbeat hadn't slowed since she'd come upon Tiny Clemshaw guarding his Mercantile, the shotgun targeting the rainbow across her chest. Not when she'd run to Rhone Bakery to find her father, or laid eyes on the remains of Melanie, or fought with her Uncle Pard.

And certainly not now. *Because I have to hurry.*

In the gray light of predawn Hazel looked up at the opening to the Second Chance mine shaft: a black mouth that had long ago spit out the mounds of wrung earth still littering Silver Hill. *The perfect hiding spot.*

She gazed longingly at the flashlight nestled deep underwater before she left the pond and goose-stepped through high brambles, heading uphill toward the mine.

When Sean was seven and got fed up with his dad, Samuel, he ran away from home carrying a hobo sack (fashioned out of a potato bag and croquet mallet) that he'd filled with three Milky Way bars, his slingshot and five bologna-and-cheese sandwiches.

Hazel knew this because he'd stopped by her house on the way out of town to try and persuade her to come with him. "I can't," she'd refused him. "*Buffy* is on tonight."

And she remembered how small he looked as she watched him disappear, alone, down the sidewalk on Park Street.

It was after dark by the time Samuel and Honey Adair realized Sean was missing, and they searched every floor of The Winslow before ending up at her house. Then Sean's parents tricked it out of her by saying Hawkin Rhone was sure to get Sean unless Hazel gave up his secret spot. But Sean forgave her the betrayal because by then he was lonely hiding up in that mine all by himself. *He's lonely now, too,* she speculated.

Trudging up Silver Hill, Hazel tried to imagine the cacophony of hard rock blasting and drilling when the mines were active in the late 1800s…and how quiet it must have seemed once it all stopped. A dry hush, like now.

She skirted past signs reading Danger and No Trespassing, then paused beneath the square set timbers at the entrance to the mine. It had long been boarded up tight, and reinforced each summer to keep the kids out. Now a good-sized section was pried away as if someone had recently entered.

"Sean?" she called into the hole.

Silence.

"Please answer me, Sean—I *really* don't want to go in there."

No answer. So she forced herself to crawl between the wood slats.

Only a dozen yards into the mine, she rounded a corner and found herself immersed in complete darkness. It was cool in there, too—she'd expected it to be hot like a furnace. Her neck started creeping and crawling and she clasped her left hand together with the right in the sling, holding them close to her body lest something nip at her fingertips.

Sally forth, she ordered herself. In school, Gus Bolinger told them he'd made a mantra of those two words, repeating them to himself and his comrades when things got gnarly during the Battle of Bloody Ridge. Hazel sallied bravely forth.

"Sean?" she called again. Completely blind in the cave, she wished like mad she'd held on to that flashlight.

Don't lose your bearings, she thought as she continued deeper.

It was something her dad always warned her against. "Don't ever lose your bearings in the woods, Hazel, or you'll get lost."

What are bearings, anyway? she wondered. *Don't know, but don't lose 'em—*

"Who's there?" a man's voice cleaved the silence.

Hazel jumped and jerked all in one motion. She peered in the direction from whence the voice had come, but all was black.

"Who's there!" Deeper, more insistent now.

Her heart pounded out hard, fitful beats. "Hazel Winslow?" She hoped that was the right answer.

"I'm here…" The man sounded distressed now—as if he'd wanted to be found but nobody had bothered to look. "The little ones ran me out with sticks and rocks," he whined.

"Who are you?" Hazel couldn't help but think *Hawkin Rhone,* and her heart thumped even harder.

"They hurt me!" The anger returned to the voice and she took a step back.

Or was it to the side? She was turned around; it was that dark. "I didn't mean to disturb you, I'll leave you be."

Which way is out? She darted blind eyes all directions. *Help me—which way is out?*

As she turned what she bargained was the right way, a hand popped out of the blackness and grabbed her arm, ripping the sling, and she screamed from the terror and pain of it. He yanked her down to him—he was so strong.

Maybe he's a vampire, she horrified herself, and any second she'd feel long, fat teeth sinking into her neck, followed by the weak, warm feeling of blood draining from her body.

"I beg you," he whispered in her face with breath that smelled of something dying inside.

And her mind shrieked, *It is him! Fucking Hawkin Rhone vampire!*

He pulled her even closer, biting distance now. "Please kill me," he said. "It's unbearable."

Hazel screamed and kicked and batted at him with her left hand for what seemed like minutes before he finally released her tortured right arm, and she kept screaming as she ran, her cries echoing back to her so that it sounded like a madhouse full of girls screaming, and she could no more outrun that smell than she could her screams. It was on her now, in her hair: his morbid exhalation.

"Beware the Pest House," he bellowed.

She careened off the dirt walls, bouncing her way out of the pitch-dark mine like a pinball, and fought through the hole in the timbers that had somehow shrunk while she was inside so that now she barely fit back out, terrified the whole time that she'd feel the vampire's bony fingers wrap around her ankle so he could drag her deep inside his tomb.

When she did finally emerge from the mouth of the mine, the day's first light sliced into her pupils before they had a chance to contract.

She veered blindly—a white blindness now—her hand shielding her eyes, and then sprinted across Silver Hill through dry yellow weeds that scratched her calves mercilessly, racing for the tall water tower with its enormous *W* painted on one side of the rusty tank, desperate to reach it and hide before the Hawkin Rhone vampire caught her and sank his teeth into her neck.

At the ladder, she didn't look back or hesitate. Instead, she started up fast. *I won't come back down. Ever.*

She climbed carelessly, hysterically. *If I stay up here, I'll see as soon as help comes. Somebody must've made it out before they blocked the bridge. Or come up and now they're missed. Maybe Tanner will send help after all. His parents will wonder what he's doing back, won't they? They won't buy his story. They'll want to talk to Uncle Pard.*

When she reached the platform, she leaned out to glance down the ladder, half expecting to see the vampire scrambling up right behind her, like a spider closing in on its prey.

But he wasn't there. Panting furiously, she crawled across the metal platform and then defensively tucked her back against the tank like a wounded animal.

We're just a bit out of sorts is all, she thought, aware that she'd finally been driven to hysteria. Anything that had begun to heal in her elbow was now ripped asunder and raw nerves all along her battered body screamed their distress.

We'll just stay put until help gets here. It has to, right? It has to—

The vampire's death smell retouched her nose, and forced her to ask the question she'd so desperately been avoiding: *Is this fatal?*

The image of a duck flashed in her mind, the dead duck that ate ergot-infested piecrust.

Hazel hung her head and began to sob.

Is everybody going to die?

WEDNESDAY SUNUP

"IT'S NOT A good idea," Aaron whispered to Violet.

Maybe he was right, but she caved in to Daisy anyway. They'd been cramped in their hiding spot for hours and hours and they couldn't sleep 'cause it was too uncomfortable and they couldn't cry 'cause it makes too much noise and Daisy would not stop poking her that it was *time to get out!*

Besides, nobody was around.

Violet peeked again through the gap in the boards and could see that nobody was around. Plus the sun was coming up so everything wasn't scary like before when it was so dark. Hawkin Rhone only comes out at night *(I think maybe).*

So she pushed open the big lid and raised her head and still didn't see anybody. Her legs were sleeping and pins and needles tried to wake them up.

Aaron tugged on her dress, trying to pull her back in. "Hazel said to stay hiding."

"Don't be such a baby," Violet told him and stepped out of the fruit storage bin and into the very first sunbeam to hit the apple orchard Wednesday morning.

ZACHARY

I'M LOST.

How am I supposed to find the boy when I can't even find my way out of this place? This place made my father do what he did. Now it's making me. Don't look at that eye. Blueberry. Maybe it was my father who did it. Again. Missy, we missed you after you were gone. So maybe it wasn't me after all. Wait! Remember? It's the boy's fault. Sean Adair. I'm lost. My bones hurt—will they ever stop hurting me? It's daybreak. Maybe I'll find my way out now. Getting light fast. The eye will burn under the big sun. I ought to go down and close the eyelid. Already lighter and I can see him there. There—my father. Hawkin Rhone. Has he ever left? The apple doesn't rot far from the tree. I am he; he wants me to be. He needs me to tend the orchard.

And now the children have come to me.

They're here, waiting for me to let my guard down...waiting to pluck apples with small hands.

"Bluebells, cockle shells, easy ivy over!"

From where Aaron floated above the orchard, he watched Violet and Daisy jumping rope in their long colorful dresses. He tried to yell, "Stop singing!" but no sound came out because his voice was down there with his body, which was slumped in the dirt next to that ugly dead apple tree.

Violet and Daisy's red hair bounced and waved, calling even *more* attention to them.

"Stop! Hide!" he tried again but still his body only laid there.

The girls' daddy was moving fast though: sneaky and slithery around the trees like an eel, his face stuck on mean. Meaner than Aaron ever saw his own dad's face, meaner even than the worst bad guys in the video games his mom didn't like him to play.

Get back in! Aaron ordered himself. *Get back in!* The closer Zachary Rhone got, the surer Aaron was that he'd better get back into his body. What if Mr. Rhone hurt his body when he wasn't in it? What if he hurt it really bad? Panic seized Aaron: *Where would I go after that?*

Then he saw the other kid: a girl with a long dark ponytail, the little girl named Missy that Hawkin Rhone poisoned to death.

"Apples, pears, peaches and plums," Violet and Daisy chanted, "tell me when your birthday comes."

"Be quiet!" Aaron tried to warn them. "He's close!"

Mr. Rhone continued to creep through the orchard, slower now, trying not to scare them off.

"January, February, March…"

The ghost girl skittered around Mr. Rhone. Aaron could tell that she was trying to distract him, to keep him from finding his daughters.

"April, May, June."

But he's so close now, Aaron saw.

Though the ghost girl skipped in front of him, trying to change his direction, she couldn't stop him from heading straight for the other girls, the ones who were still alive.

"July, August…"

And then Aaron saw Sean. His big brother was down by the bakery.

"Sean!" Aaron tried to call to him and saw his own body convulse. "Help us," he was finally able to whisper from the inside out.

DARTING HERE, DARTING THERE—children children everywhere. Stealing apples. Taunting. *How can I tend the orchard when they won't behave?* wondered Zachary Rhone.

All the while, the morning grew hotter. *Am I in hell?* He looked straight at the sun and marveled at its enormity.

But that didn't explain the heat, not all of it. He placed one hand against a tree—its bark warm and rough against his palm—and bowed his head, trying to collect his thoughts.

When he swiveled his head to one side, he discovered something extraordinary: *The bakery's on fire.*

Bright orange flames shot out the back window; smoke poured through the screen door.

Fire! He swung the ax he'd been lugging around against an apple tree, sinking the blade into soft rotted bark clear through the trunk. After the treetop spilled to the dirt in a cacophony of cracking branches, he managed to wrench himself free from the orchard's grasp. "Let. Me. Go!"

Leaving the ax to the tree, Zachary ran. On the way downhill he fell twice and scraped his chin in the dirt once. "Put it out," he panted. "Save it. My father left it to me—the only good thing he left to me."

When Zachary rounded the corner to the front of the bakery, he found him.

Finally, he found him.

Funny thing was, Sean Adair stood to one side of the entrance as if he'd been waiting for *him.*

Zachary peered through the glass door. Inside, flames curled in waves from the rear oven area, over the prep counter, to the shelves in the storefront. The donuts and pastries on fire in the display case reminded him of pinwheels.

He turned his back on the bakery to face Sean. Incredibly, the boy said nothing about the fire, just stood on the sidewalk with his legs apart and his arms crossed, as if Zachary had to mind him, as if Zachary weren't the boss anymore.

"The children are misbehaving," Zachary explained. "Anybody can see that." He wished he'd held on to that ax.

"Not them." Sean stared straight at him. "*They* didn't do anything wrong."

He's staring into my head, Zachary realized. *Stop it! Can't let him see in here.* Hotter and hotter he felt.

"You knew," Sean said.

Unbelievable! Zachary thought. Insolent boy. And to think Zachary had felt sorry for him because his old man had no control over himself. Only Zachary felt out of control of himself, too. "The bakery's burning," he told Sean. "What should we do?"

"Did you know before I delivered bread to my mom at The Winslow? To the Mercantile? The Crock?"

Zachary was shaking his head rapidly back and forth.

"Did you know—" Sean leaned within inches of Zachary's face "—before I gave my little brother a fucking poison apple fritter!"

"After that! I swear on my father's grave!" He shot a look over his shoulder. It was his father's establishment burning behind them. *Rhone Family Bakery since 1924,* said the door. Suddenly suspicious, he pointed at Sean. "Did you start this fire?"

"Why didn't you warn anybody?" Sean ignored the question.

"We have a reputation to uphold," Zachary sputtered.

"Don't you get it?" The boy put his hands to his head as if his brains might leak out his ears. "Everybody in the whole town is sick!"

"I couldn't think straight," Zachary explained. "It's impossible to think straight anymore."

"If you'd warned people, things wouldn't've totally spun out like this."

"This is your fault!" Zachary screamed. "*You* delivered the bread. Not me!"

"I tried to tell you."

"Tried to tell me? How do you *try* to tell somebody something, Adair? You either tell them or you don't—no try about it."

"If you'd listened to me, none of this would've happened."

"I knew why you were sniffing around."

"Dammit, Zachary!" Sean put his hands to his head again as if it hurt, then went quiet.

The bakery continued to burn behind them. Hotter and

hotter. Zachary turned and looked through the glass door. Flames licked pine floorboards; paint boiled on the walls.

Finally, Sean asked, "Where's Melanie?"

Zachary ground his teeth hard before responding in a low growl, "*Don't* ask me that."

With a look of disgust, Sean shook his head. "You didn't help anybody. Why didn't you do something? Nobody but you knew what was happening."

"It was too late."

"No! It wasn't too late then." He gestured toward Fortune Way. "Do you know what's happening out there *now?*"

"The bakery's on fire," Zachary whined. "Do something."

But Sean only continued to stare inside his head; Zachary could feel him rooting around in there. *Get the hell out!*

When Zachary heard the glass door behind him cracking, he finally felt it needed to be said, "My father didn't mean to poison those children."

Looking confused, Sean cocked his head. "What?"

"I know what it's like to be ashamed of your father. Nobody'd go fishing with me after that, nobody even saw me anymore. A ghost. Until Melanie—" Zachary felt his heart coming apart. "Oh, Melanie, my sweet Melanie."

"Zachary, that's got nothing to do with what's going on now."

"It's got *everything* to do with it!" he screamed in Sean's face and the boy took a step back. "My father never meant to hurt anybody except those camp robber jays. They kept pecking at the apples. They'd knock 'em off the trees then leave 'em to rot in the dirt. 'A damn waste,' Daddy said. What else could he do? He told Missy and me not to pick any more apples, explaining that he'd sprayed the trees but good to teach those little bastards a lesson and we were to stay out until next spring. 'Do you understand me?' he said. Wasn't his fault Missy didn't understand anything well enough to mind him.

Especially because it was her share day at school so she went into the bakery and asked him for a dozen donuts to take for the class because she knew everybody liked donuts and nobody liked her because she was slow. But Daddy said, 'If they want donuts they can come in here and pay for 'em like everybody else.' And I saw she looked hysterical when she said, 'I need them! It's my share day!' But he refused, saying, 'A man's gotta make a living and he sure as hell doesn't do that by giving donuts away.'"

Zachary was weeping, choking on fat tears. "Missy must've gone to the orchard after that because the next day she snuck out for school with her basketful of apples. Then when her classmates were hurting like the poisoned birds I was scared to tell anyone and get her into trouble. I should've anyhow, because after it was over nobody wanted to hear that my father had meant no harm to anything except those robber jays. Not even our mother."

He paused, wiping his wet face with his hands. "Only by believing he'd meant to punish the children for stealing apples out of his orchard could townsfolk make sense of the tragedy. And it helped everybody cope to see him pay for it."

He noticed that Sean's face was twisted up as if he were in some sort of pain. "What's the matter with you?" Zachary sniffed hard and hawked spit to the sidewalk. He'd expected no sympathy from Sean Adair, desired none, only wanted the truth out in order to set things right.

"I killed him," Sean said.

"What?" *So hard to think a straight thought anymore.*

"I had no choice." Sean passed a shaking hand across his mouth.

From the heat and confusion, Zachary swayed on his feet. "What are you saying?"

"We were across Three Fools Creek from his cabin, and

we dared each other to go over there. It looked quiet, like he wasn't around. Otherwise we never would've done it."

"Done *what?* What did you do?" Without glancing over his shoulder, Zachary knew the fire was growing larger, felt it reach the front of the bakery.

The boy trembled all over now. "He had Hazel by the wrist so hard I heard her bone snap and she's screaming and he looks crazy as shit so I picked up a log and hit him on the head to make him let go of her."

Zachary retched, his stomach corkscrewing and trying to make its way up through his throat, only there was nothing left in him but the horror.

"We couldn't tell if he was dead or not," Sean said quietly.

Zachary could barely hear him over the fire.

"We didn't wait around to find out. After he let go of Hazel we ran back to town and told Sheriff Winslow and he got Dr. Foster and when they came back from checking on him they wouldn't tell us anything."

Feeling as bewildered and betrayed as when his father had first been forced across the creek, Zachary hung his head. "They led me to think he was done in by a bear." Zachary had known there were bear out in those woods; his father told him so during one of his rare and uncomfortable visits to the old cabin.

"I had no choice," Sean insisted again.

"This is all your fault."

"That was. This isn't."

"You need to make it right."

"How am I supposed to make this right?"

"You'll take your share of the blame. That's how."

They were silent for a moment, listening to the fire consume the bakery behind them with a disinterest more befitting a wienie roast.

Then the insolent boy said, "Look at your hands."

"Why did you have to say that?" The force of it rocked Zachary on his heels. *I won't look, he can't make me look.* He tried to wipe his hands clean on his T-shirt and saw the blood there, too, encrusted dark in white cotton. *Help me—whose blood is it? Whose?*

Zachary backed away from Sean. "They'll hang this on somebody. And it won't be a Rhone this time, no sirree."

"Don't get so close to the fire," Sean warned.

"Never again!"

"Stay back, Zachary."

"I've lost everything and I won't cross that creek, too. No Rhone's taking the fall this time."

"You're too close!" Sean yelled.

But it was too late—always too late—and Zachary watched as his skin reddened and blistered. *I never expected it to turn out like this.* He lunged for Sean.

"Don't!" the boy cried as Zachary latched on to his forearm and pulled. The impact of Sean's blow against his right temple left him momentarily stunned and he did let go. Then he grabbed him again with both hands and this time didn't let go even when Sean slammed him in the eye and he was blinded on that side, nor when his teeth collapsed into his mouth beneath the boy's fist. The force of it hurled him back against the door of the bakery, which imploded on impact, and Zachary fell inside in a shower of frosted glass. Still, even then, he held on.

No air in the bakery, nothing to breath but smoke, and Zachary felt himself burning alive in a fire fueled by his own rage and remorse.

But Sean was there with him, at least, so the anger quickly subsided and Zachary let himself think about red curls and pink apple blossoms and porch swings and fresh laundry pinned to the line...clean sheets and bright eyes dancing in a blue breeze.

Arriving at the granite wall, Hazel finds that Sean has erased I'M SORRY. In place of that, he wrote, HW → SA TFC X HRC. She easily deciphers his message: Hazel Winslow meet Sean Adair at Three Fools Creek across from Hawkin Rhone's cabin.

She fights her way down the overgrown path and hears the first helicopter as soon as she reaches the creek. Squinting west, she sees the forest service chopper hovering over the bridge. But that's no matter to her right now. What matters is that she knows she'll find Sean here. What she doesn't know is if she'll find him alive.

She wavers at the edge of the water—petrified. Every truth she's ever known and every wild imagining she's ever had about this place play together in a symphony of terror. She peers across the creek at the moldering cabin. What will she see when she gets there? What if it's an animal-mauled mess outside the cabin door, like when her father found Hawkin Rhone? What if just a few locks of Sean's brown hair plastered to the rough-hewn logs are all that's recognizable?

Bigfoot is loose in the woods, she shudders. *Hungry wolves.*

She's afraid to go, afraid to find out. *Don't think,* she thinks, *go!*

She looks back to the turbulent water: The creek is full and raging, tossing logs around like beach balls. *How did he get over there?* she wonders.

She's out of her mind, she realizes, to even *consider* crossing the creek.

She steps into the water anyway—

And it happens surprisingly fast.

Her left foot slips off a slimy rock and she's sucked into the cold torrent, and with only one arm to fight with, she's losing the battle and thinking, *I made it all this way only to be the fourth fool to drown in this fucking creek?*

Just as suddenly, Sean is there, pulling her out of the water and up onto the opposite bank. As happy as she is to be alive, she's even happier to see him again. He looks unharmed. Strangely normal. She grabs hold of him and won't let go, spitting up creek water and trying to catch her breath, and crying with relief.

Crying, crying, I'm crying...

Crying not with relief, but in pain.

No, I don't want to leave him. Let me stay here.

But it felt like her arm was on fire.

Goodbye, Sean, goodbye helicopter, goodbye dream.

Hazel shifted her weight on the water-tower platform and cried out at the burning pain consuming her shattered elbow. She opened her eyes, bleary with agony and tears.

The sunshine was still soft so she knew she had slept only a short while, and as she squeezed more tears from her wide-awake eyes, she felt glad for the dawn that continued to rise behind her and bathe Silver Hill in light the color of orange sherbet. It had been a very long night.

She had no plans to leave the safety of the tower. Her back to the tank, the position made a perfect cat perch: high in the air and sheltered from behind, so nothing could sneak up on her, and shaded from the monster sun that by midmorning would bake the mountainside crisp. But her body insisted she stand up, having grown stiff and sore from sitting on the metal platform.

All her aches and pains shifted into high gear as she hobbled to the railing for a better view. There were men on horseback riding around downtown. Holloway ranch hands, it looked like, kicking ass and taking names. *Go back to the ranch,* she wished. *Mind your pigs and cows and leave us alone.*

Prospect Park looked empty, while a handful of people darted along Fortune Way. Pursued, she hazarded a guess, by Tiny Clemshaw and his shotgun.

Sniffing and wiping her face, she watched a brown car swerve up the driveway to The Winslow. She figured that her grandmother must still be in the hotel, somewhere Hazel hadn't thought to look. Regret gnawed at her—she should've searched harder. It was so much safer up on the tower, if only her grandmother were here with her, instead of hiding in that insane asylum.

She turned her back on the town and stared at her right arm. The lunatic in the mine had ripped away the sling, so she cradled her injured elbow against her bruised ribs. Naked now, her arm revealed a swollen kaleidoscope of color: blue black purple and red. Seeing it made it hurt so much worse, made her feel as though all her blood really had been drained by the vampire. Even the wrist broken five years ago by a different madman throbbed in aggravation.

Ice would help, she knew, but not enough to compel her to climb down from the tower. So instead she thought about milk-shakes and cold water creeks, about Sno-Kones and the snow that come November would drape the entire mountain range, cloaking the sins of summer in pure white.

Snowflakes, corn flakes, I scream for ice cream—

She spied a matchbox wedged inside a hose bib. After snaking her fingers in to retrieve it, she slid open the box. Her lucky day. Nestled inside was a half-smoked joint, tightly rolled, Tanner Holloway-style. Matches, too. She had yet to strike a match when she smelled smoke.

Serious-smelling smoke.

Ignore it.

Where was it coming from?

Just stay put.

That lasted all of two seconds before she turned back to the railing and glanced down...beyond Silver Hill, past the apple orchard—to Rhone Bakery. Red flames caressed the immutable stone wall at the rear of the bakery, but mostly it was smoke—a skinny funnel pouring through an opening in the disappearing roof.

Panic struck with such ferocity that Hazel recoiled from the railing. With her good fist she pounded the side of the metal tank in frustration, crushing the matchbox and its precious contents, while Tanner saying, "Zachary Rhone's looking for him," looped in her mind.

"Where *are* you, Sean?" she screamed at the town, across the mountainside.

Then it occurred to her: maybe Sparks Brady would see this fire. Maybe he'd see the smoke and respond with help and helicopters.

She peered in the direction of the fire lookout tower so many miles away, then back at the white smoke coming off the smoldering bakery, where Cal Allison and Hap Hotchkiss, both armed with hoses, were spraying the last of the flames.

Her father had taught her that white smoke means a fire has been doused in water and is on its way out. *Of course Sparks knows that,* she realized with despair, *which means no helicopters, no help.*

Suddenly her heart seized up. Violet and Daisy and Aaron were hiding in the apple orchard—not far from the fire. It hadn't been tricky to figure out where they planned to hide because it's where Violet always hides when they play hide-and-go-seek.

Hazel knew then that she had no choice but to leave the safety of the tower. Sally forth. Only she wasn't a brave soldier, she was terrified. She walked toward the ladder anyway, her weight causing the metal platform to warp and clang with each step.

She stopped just short of the ladder, gripped the railing. *I can't do it.*

Looking over the side of the tower, she released the matchbox and watched it fall…and fall. *I can't.* It was so far to the ground she'd never make it all the way down; she'd break her neck trying and land in the dirt in a lifeless heap.

Besides, what could she even do? She'd tried already, hadn't she?

But yesterday she'd deluded herself into thinking everyone would be better today.

Today, Melanie Rhone was dead.

Today, the bakery was on fire.

Today, the children were waiting for Hazel—waiting for her to finally call, "Olly olly oxen free!"

She swung herself out into thin air, her left hand clutching the ladder, the right worthless and throwing off her weight until her feet found purchase on the rungs and she started climbing down—one-armed and reckless—wondering what that Hawkin Rhone vampire had meant by, "Beware the Pest House."

THE BRIDGE

I CAN'T BELIEVE I'm stuck here, thanks to that stupid bitch.

All night Tanner Holloway had been forced to ride rough-shod over the town with Kenny Clark and Old Pete Hammond, rounding up sickos (as Kenny called them) and dumping them at The Winslow. Then once the streets were clear they'd started knocking on doors and dragging people out of their houses if they looked like they might have the sickness.

Now Tanner was crusted-over tired and his leg hurt like hell. But he was glad the night was finally through, and wondered when someone would get wise to what was happening in Winslow. Tanner could understand nobody driving up here with the rodeo over, but wouldn't somebody at least try to call and then question why the phones were dead? *Nice going, Uncle Pard, real nice.*

Sitting on the El Camino's tailgate he watched Old Pete and Kenny descend the steps of the hotel. They wore bandannas tied over their noses and mouths, and thick suede cattle-rustling gloves. Kenny slapped his hands together as if rubbing away dirt. They'd just dropped off Patience's parents. They'd really fought, those two, claiming they didn't have it.

He hadn't seen Patience around. Too bad. He realized she'd been right, of course, when she told him that nothing good would come to him.

"Headin' out." Pete clapped Tanner hard on the shoulder, as if Tanner were a lazy cow that needed a good shove to get it moving.

When Tanner climbed into the truck bed, his left leg pain-

fully crackled and popped. And as they drove down the driveway, the hotel still looming large, he thought, *At least I'm not
stuck in that hellhole.*

He wiped his face on the sleeve of his already damp T-shirt.
It hadn't cooled off—all night long he'd sweated like a roasting pig.

They cruised down Civic Street, Kenny driving moroni-
cally slow and Pete with his rifle poised out the window, ready
to fire at anything that moved.

But all was quiet. If people knew what was good for them,
they'd keep quiet. And not answer their door.

Kenny swung a sudden hard right onto Fortune Way and
gunned it, causing Tanner's head to snap forward and then
back against the window with such force he worried his skull
might crack. Then Kenny eased up, crawling slowly by Clemshaw Mercantile to Rhone Bakery. Where the bakery used to
be, anyway, wasn't much there anymore.

"Whatever happened here is over now," he heard Old Pete
say.

Kenny flipped around at the corner of Park Street, then
punched it again down Fortune Way.

As they passed back by the smoldering bakery, Tanner
imagined he saw charred bones piled up in front of the blackened oven that stood alone amid the ruins, and he supposed
maybe he smelled something like cooked meat. *Maybe Sean
got deep-fried in there.*

He thought about Sean puking his guts out over the railing of the water tower Sunday night and even then acting as
if he were better than Tanner. And the last time Tanner saw
him, Sean had just stood there going "uh uh uh" when Tanner asked him why the hell he was talking about mayo and
deliveries. It was almost as though he *wanted* to be responsible. The guy had a guilt complex or something. But if that's
the way Sean wanted it, who was he to argue?

Tanner wondered how Hazel was faring. Wondered how surprised she would be to see him again. And wondered how sorely he could make her regret that he was stuck here, thanks to her holding him up for so long.

He shifted his weight off his aching, burning leg. As soon as he got a chance he intended to whip that horse Blackjack for doing this to him.

They left town on Winslow Road and drove past the church cemetery, into the tunnel of trees, back toward the bridge. *Time to relieve the troops,* Tanner thought with great weariness. He threw back his throbbing head and watched the sun speckle in and out through the branches. *I could sleep for a hundred years—Rip Van Winkle*...and he did semisnooze in the truck bed for a couple of jostled minutes.

But there was trouble at the bridge when they pulled up— screaming yelling guns-raised trouble.

Kenny slammed on the brakes, spinning the El Camino in a complete one-eighty before it jerked to a stop that nearly flung Tanner out the back. Then Kenny leapt out to join the fray.

Old Pete got out slow, him and his Winchester, no rush... just stretchin' his legs. "C'mon, kid." He gave Tanner that shoulder shove again and Tanner knew he'd better cooperate.

But he didn't like the looks of it. Didn't want any part of it. In front of the barricade—which now included the fat man Fritz Earley's truck—the nervous vet was arguing with Uncle Pard. Behind Doc Simmons was the red truck Tanner knew to be his since he'd seen it parked next to the barn the day Simmons came to slice Indigo apart. The Doc didn't have his glasses on but his hand kept going up to the bridge of his nose anyway, pushing at the rim that wasn't there. Obviously Pard Holloway was winning this argument: he was the one with the gun.

Tanner hadn't seen his uncle since the wake-and-bake in the south pasture yesterday morning, when he'd told Tanner that drastic situations call for drastic measures, then forced him to light the cattle carcass bonfire. He realized that Pard looked haggard now, sort of diminished. His uncle noticed him climbing off the truck bed and gave him a nod. Tanner felt glad for that in a way.

Kenny loped up to the red truck and pulled a knife out of his boot. *You are a complete moron,* Tanner thought. The truck was dented, its windshield cracked on the driver's side. Kenny stabbed the left front tire, sinking the long knife deep before he rocked it back and forth.

Simmons didn't notice; he was too busy blustering at Pard. "You can't keep me here."

"Where're you aimin' to go?" Pard asked.

"Stepstone."

"What for?"

"Supplies."

"What kind of supplies?"

"Medicine."

"What kind of medicine?"

Simmons stammered and sputtered, "Just…you know… medicine."

"Only place you're going is to The Winslow so you can do your job, Doc. Now get your scrawny ass up there and start treating people."

Simmons shied back from Pard. "I don't want to get involved."

"You're involved, all right. Whether you want to be or not is none of my concern."

Tanner was walking behind Pete and wondering what chance he had of making a break for it. He'd have to leap up and scramble over the flatbed and then run like hell, dodging bullets no doubt. But it'd take them a while to untangle the trucks and give chase and by then he'd already be across the bridge and hiding in the woods. There was just one problem:

his leg was bad, his foot was even worse. He wasn't sure how fast he could run, if at all.

While Old Pete joined Pard, Tanner continued to the north side of the bridge where the Kawasaki had been wedged to block the pedestrian path. Someone had sliced the clutch cable in two. *Big surprise, wonder who?* He shot a hateful glare at Kenny Clark.

Pete asked Simmons, "So will you be driving yourself up to the hotel or riding with me?"

Simmons shook his head fiercely. "I'm leaving. Got to go now. Right now."

Tanner could see how desperate the vet was to get out, but couldn't tell if he was babbling because he was sick or due to that nasty-looking crack across his forehead.

Ignoring the vet, Pard asked Old Pete, "What's the situation in town?"

"Rhone Bakery burned clear to the ground. No sign of Zachary Rhone anywhere around."

"Who'd want to burn down the bakery?"

"Maybe Rhone himself." Old Pete glanced at Tanner. "The kid says it's the bread making folks sick."

Now everybody turned to look at him.

"That right, Tanner?" Pard asked.

Tanner tried to sound casual, "Yeah, it all came from Rhone Bakery. They used bad flour to make bad bread."

Tanner saw Doc Simmons's face tighten with panic. But his uncle's very slight smile told Tanner that he was pleased with this offering, relieved to finally have the heat off Holloway Ranch.

"Damn good thing we stick to Maggie's soda sinkers," Pard said, and Maggie and the other cowhands laughed.

Damn good thing...only Tanner had eaten more than ranch biscuits over the past few days. There was that ham on rye at the Crock early Saturday. Hazel had taken his order and called him a stoner when he asked for double fries. Then there were those donut holes Sunday morning: ninety-nine cents a dozen—here, take two for a buck and a half, Sean had convinced him.

If I didn't know better, Tanner thought dully, *I'd think they were trying to kill me.*

Pard addressed Simmons, "What's in the bread? I know that you know—I can see it in your eyes."

Simmons closed his revealing eyes. "Ergot."

"What's that?"

"A fungus. Grows on grain crops if they're rained on too heavily."

Tanner decided he might as well help his uncle along. "Maybe the same fungus found its way into your feed as Rhone's flour."

Pard squinted at him one-eyed.

"Kid could be right," Old Pete said. "Could be ergot is what's got into the herd. I've witnessed it before—a cow loses the tip off its ear, half if it's real bad, sometimes a tail. But never to this extreme, never seen the animals go strange before, and I've certainly never seen it happen to folks."

"That sonofabitch!" Pard made tight fists. "Get Fritz Earley and bring him to the Buckhorn. And act friendly, Pete. I don't want him showing up there all balled up. I'm damn near worn out trying to figure out what the hell we're up against here and need some honest answers out of him."

Suddenly Pard lunged for Simmons and grabbed the frightened vet by the shirt. "I need some answers out of you, too. What happens if it is this fungus? What do we do about it?"

Simmons went white. "There's nothing we can do about it."

"Don't give me that!"

A brown cow with white puzzle-piece markings strolled up to the mouth of the bridge and stopped next to Simmons. Then she looked directly at the vet and mooed.

Pard released Simmons and turned to Maggie Clark. "Take care of that, will you?" He lifted his hat and sopped up sweat with a bandanna. "Cattle wandering the streets. Who's leaving gates open?"

Simmons finally noticed the hiss that was his tire hemorrhaging air and swung around. Then he strode to the truck with Pard yelling after him, "Where do you think you're going?"

The vet hauled himself into his truck and started the engine with a foot heavy on the accelerator. He reversed wildly for thirty feet and then sat for a moment, both hands gripping the wheel. Clearly he intended to crash into the barricade—try and smash through it—and take as many cowboys with him as he could.

Tanner backed up to the bridge railing. Everything shone stark in the clear morning air, the sun glinting off metal and glass.

"Dammit it, Simmons!" Pard bellowed. "Get the hell out of there!"

The vet gunned his engine. Tanner could see the madman's gleam in his eyes. Then Simmons floored it and screeched toward the barricade.

The ranch hands scrambled off the road and onto the pedestrian walkways. Old Pete and Pard ended up next to Tanner in front of the bike. On the opposite side of the bridge Kenny Clark raised his rifle and shot into the cab and Simmons ducked below the windshield. Casings caught sunlight as they flew off the bridge and Pard shouted, "Hey hey whoa! Hold your fire!"

The red truck collided with the barricade and smashed Maggie's Chevy aside in a scream of twisting metal. Simmons and his truck slid across the bridge, slammed into the railing, and wobbled precariously over the edge before banging back down on all fours.

Kenny started in the direction of Simmons' truck but Pard shouted. "Hold up, Ken. Did I tell you to fire?"

"The Doc's gone crazy." Kenny held up his hand and looked at Pard as if to say, *What else was I supposed to do?*

"You're never to let fly unless I order it. Understood?"

Kenny took on a hangdog look. "Yeah, boss."

Simmons' engine shuddered to a stop and Pard turned and scrutinized Tanner for what felt like a long time. Finally, he clamped his dry hand across the back of his nephew's neck. "Go and get Simmons out of there."

Tanner accepted the revolver his uncle handed him. Then Old Pete gave Tanner that cow shove again. His heartbeat ramped up as he approached the vet's truck. *Why does he want me to do this?* And why did it seem so quiet all of a sudden? He sucked in his breath and peered into the cab.

Curled up on his side, the crazed glint in Simmons' eyes had been replaced by sheer terror. Tanner let out a long breath before he looked back at the ranch hands standing at the barricade. They were all staring at him.

I'm gonna puke. He was sure of it, felt it right there, but swallowed hard instead and stepped onto the running board.

Simmons sat up and scooted across to the passenger's seat.

Tanner aimed the gun at the vet's head, but his hands were shaking so bad he'd be lucky to hit the sky. "Get out."

"I can't." Simmons shook his head.

"Get out, you cowardly piece of shit."

The vet made a bleating noise a lot like the calf had at Holloway Ranch the other night right before Kenny blew its brains out.

Tanner raised the gun to point above Simmons' head. He pulled the trigger. A resounding boom and the bullet punched through the roof of the cab. Tanner's ears popped first, then settled into a roaring *ziiinng.* He lowered the gun and took shaky aim at the vet's astonished right eye.

"Okay okay." Simmons mouthed but Tanner couldn't hear him. The vet scrambled back to the driver's side and Tanner stepped down and opened the door.

"Take him to The Winslow," Pard barked from what sounded like a million miles away. "And bring me that sono-fabitch Fritz Earley."

Simmons shrank back, giving Tanner a look that seemed to say, *I know what you're hiding.*

Kenny Clark shoved Tanner aside to grab Simmons out of the cab. "C'mon, Doc," Kenny said in a faraway voice. "It's to the Pest House with you. Time to take care of the sickos."

Tanner's damaged hearing made him feel as though he were deep underwater and all this commotion was occurring distantly above the surface.

Simmons tried to squirm free but Kenny held fast. "I can't hear you!" Simmons screamed. "I'm deaf! I can't hear you!" Tanner noticed blood trickling out of the vet's left ear.

Sickos... Tanner's fingers went to his own ears to see if they were bleeding too but they came away clean. *You're the ones who are sick.* He turned around to find his Uncle Pard and the other ranch hands eyeing him with something like approval.

But damn did his leg hurt. The pain had been shifting toward a burning sensation, and the heat kept getting cranked up.

He hobbled over next to his uncle and through the ringing in his ears barely heard him ask, "What's that smell?" Pard sniffed the air. "Like meat gone bad. Do you smell that?"

Tanner forced his eyes to meet Pard's, terrified he'd betray himself. "I think we scared the shit outta Simmons. Literally."

Tanner glanced around at Uncle Pard and Old Pete missing a few teeth and Maggie Clark, all laughing in their rough way, big heads lolling on thick necks.

And finally he had to admit it to himself: this was worse than a rodeo injury. Something else was wrong with his leg.

something worse than wounds suffered from the spill he'd taken off Blackjack. Tanner felt his throat closing up with panic and his mouth went so dry he gagged when he tried to swallow.

I fucking have it!

His eyes darted from unfriendly face to unfriendly face—it seemed as though the cowhands were surrounding him now—and he realized then that he couldn't beat 'em so he sure as hell better join 'em before he was found out and tossed in the Pest House, too.

He handed his uncle the gun. "Let's go rustle us up some more sickos." Then he managed to force a cold laugh past the fear wedged in his windpipe.

His Uncle Pard regarded him with a shifting mixture of skepticism and favor, then Old Pete clapped Tanner on the shoulder again but this time in a more fatherly way, less lazy-cow ass-slap.

THE WINSLOW

THE CREEKS AT high water never bode well, Sarah Winslow thought, *neither does everybody getting themselves all riled up like when Samuel Adair—such a fool—poked the end of his broomstick into a nest of yellow jackets beneath the porch eave.*

Sarah sat before a rosewood vanity among the other retired furniture in the attic of The Winslow. A collection of spent history. *What clutter,* she thought. *How much can we hold on to before we can no longer bear the weight of it?*

When Hazel and Patience were small girls, they used to fuss at this dressing table. Donned in Sarah's old gowns and musty furs, they'd edge each other out for the spot in front of the mirror, puckering on lipstick and piling on costume jewelry. Once thus adorned they'd emerge and dramatically descend the hotel's wide staircase to the parlor where Sarah sat waiting. She'd pretend they were fine ladies visiting from San Francisco and welcome them to sit, "Won't you take tea?" and offer them Vienna Fingers (Hazel's favorite).

Patience would always say, "Why, thank you."

And Hazel would proclaim in a ridiculous British accent: "I do say you have a lovely place here, although it is a bit *tired.*" Her granddaughter had overheard a guest say that, Sarah guessed. Nonetheless it was visible even then: the hotel layered in a dank patina that wouldn't rub clean—the exhausted past.

Sarah sighed. They still found thirsty yellow jackets in the bathrooms and laundry room on the first floor. Not sure how they were getting in, they seemed to find a way.

Studying her reflection in the vanity's beveled glass mirror, she thought, *I've watched myself grow old in this mirror...will my granddaughter be afforded the same luxury?*

There was no point in continuing to cower in the attic; it wasn't doing her or anybody else any good. So Sarah rose, pushed open the attic door, unfolded the stairs and stepped down with the care old women take.

She now saw what the crunching noise had been earlier: a crystal glass lay crushed. Underfoot, it would seem. She had heard her granddaughter calling her but willed herself not to answer. She'd suspected that Hazel would insist she come with her, and Sarah didn't care to leave or argue about it because she was too old and too tired for either. Relieved once Hazel left the tower, she then hoped that her granddaughter would leave the hotel altogether, for Sarah was not so convinced that the ghosts were friendly here.

Now as she reached the second floor-landing of the servants' staircase, she sensed things stirring. Decidedly unfriendly things.

The hotel is too full.

A helpless sensation washed over her.

The same helplessness she had felt after she'd watched Randall get out of their bed and collapse, and her husband was gone to her forever in the two seconds it took her to reach where he lay on the soft pine floor. It'd been different with Lottie Mathers because of all the blood. Sarah could never bring herself to remember how much blood there'd been, nor could she ever stop mourning the loss of her friend.

The adage proved true that summer, she realized. *Death came in three: first Lottie then Hawkin Rhone then, worst of all, Randall.*

Voices rose to Sarah from the kitchen as she continued

down the staircase from the second floor. She recognized those of Honey Adair and Owen Peabody, but didn't know to whom the third voice belonged until she reached the bottom stair.

Fritz Earley, the distributor from down mountain, sat eating at the table. Honey hovered over him, spoon in hand, waiting to refill his bowl from the pot she cradled in the crook of her arm.

Squatted before the breakfront, drenched in sweat and holding a stack of saucers, Owen was peeling off the saucers one at a time and placing them on the floor. "Ten. Eleven," he counted. Shards of porcelain surrounded his bare feet—broken pieces of Ruby Winslow's French china. He shifted position and left smears on the tile where his cut feet had bled.

When the final step creaked beneath Sarah's weight, Fritz and Honey looked up in alarm, as though she'd caught them in an illicit act. "Oatmeal?" Honey offered.

"No, thank you, dear." Honey looked even worse than the last time Sarah had seen her. Her dress sagged like a hand-me-down from a much bigger sister, her brown curls wilted around her face. So fond was Sarah of Honey and the boys that they were the sole reason she kept The Winslow running. (Samuel Adair she could just as well do without but it was a package deal.)

Only now she wished she hadn't kept the hotel open... wished she'd closed it for good after Randall died. Boarded it up like the old mine shafts and left it to the ghosts. *Because things are stirring,* she knew. *Things not properly laid to rest in the past.*

The sound of a saucer breaking was followed by Owen's "Oops."

Sarah took the chair across the table from Fritz Earley and quickly assessed his state. His face was bruised but he was not ill. Nervous, though. No—frightened. He looked at her with the same critical eye and she doubted his conclusion was any different.

"What's happening up here isn't right," he stated the obvious.

"No, it's not," Sarah agreed.

"Where's your son?"

"In the woods."

"Isn't he Sheriff?" Fritz Earley kept eating. He appeared to be a man who ate often.

"Yes, he is."

"Then where is he?"

"In the woods."

"We need to do something." His eyes took on shiny panic. "Things have gone too far."

"What are we to do?"

"People need medical attention." He continued to eat that oatmeal as if it were the last meal of a condemned man. "*Immediate* medical attention."

"And if they don't get it?"

"People are going to die."

He said it with such certainty that Sarah knew it must be true.

"Four, seven, six, five..." Owen kept on.

Honey moved to sit next to Sarah, relinquishing the spoon to the pot and the pot to the table. Sarah could hear Samuel rassle-frasseling upstairs. Arguing with someone, it sounded like. Another piece of Ruby's precious china shattered against the tile. It'd always been intended that the set would go to Hazel.

"Rare nowadays," Fritz was saying, "but before anybody identified the cause, epidemics of ergotism weren't uncommon. Whole towns would go stark raving mad. People imagining that their limbs are on fire, others hallucinating that they can see and talk to the dead, others bizarrely compulsive." He rolled his eyes Owen's direction. "Obsessed, even. Animals bashing their heads against walls as if possessed. Women accused of witchcraft."

"So I've heard," Sarah said. Randall had once told her about a convent that lost its collective mind after eating ergot-contaminated bread. The nuns began to curse and spit and raise their habits and make lascivious gestures. Their priest was accused of bewitching the entire convent and for that, the sorcerer was burned alive at the stake. The Devils of Loudun, Randall had called the hysterical episode. And Sarah had asked her husband where he got such stories.

"Happened in southern France in the early 1950s," Fritz continued. "Doctors thought it was food poisoning at first. Took them a week before figuring out that the grain used to mill flour for the bakery in the small village had been full of ergot. Bread of madness, they called it."

She watched him eat for another moment, then asked, "How could you let this happen?"

"Look." Fritz waved his spoon and a clump of cereal fell to the table. "I'm just the middleman here. I don't grow the grain. I don't harvest the grain. I don't mill the grain. Hell— I don't even *see* the grain outside of the bags. And even if I did, how would I know what ergot looks like?"

Sarah raised her eyebrows. "Nothing more than a delivery boy then?"

"Distributor," he corrected.

"So there was no way for you to know."

"No." Fritz quickly looked away from her, down at his bowl, then spooned in another mouthful. "But I *do* know that if ergot sickness goes left untreated—" He stopped chewing and squeezed his brows together. Sarah thought he was considering the repercussions of rampant ergotism but then he reached his thumb and forefinger into his mouth and pulled out what looked to be a raisin. He held it up before his one unswollen eye but could make no sense of it and tossed it aside, spooning more oatmeal into his mouth before going on.

Sarah glanced down at Honey's hands, which lay like dead chicks in the lap of her apron. The very tip of her right thumb was missing.

Things were stirring. *Things are coming back to haunt us all.*

BEN MATHERS WAS reasonably certain he was getting through to Samuel Adair. Ben had figured it might take some convincing, except perhaps if the person he was attempting to persuade was given to drink—was, in fact, plastered now—and had a propensity toward the bitter and a willingness to take advantage of the situation. But for the moment Samuel slept on the sofa, snoring loud enough to wake the dead.

'Cept the dead never sleep in this wretched place, Ben remembered. If only they would.

Samuel had passed out in mid-sentence ("Not my fault that—"), his gesturing hand dropping to his lap before he slumped over on his side.

Thus here Ben sat in an uncomfortable chair in the living room of the Adairs' apartment on the second floor of The Winslow, waiting for Samuel to come back around.

Ben had sworn he would never return, since clearly the hotel intended to consume him, too. *Murder haunts here.* His father shot in the head, his aunt drowned, his wife poisoned and stabbed and now his granddaughter was sick and possibly dying.

But Ben had changed, his fear shoved aside by his determination to finally finish what *she* started. So when he'd approached The Winslow this time, there'd been no hesitation. Even after he'd pulled up the driveway and the hotel glared its rapacious intent, he'd maintained his resolve.

All out in the open now, he'd thought as he strode through the yard without a hitch to his step. Then he'd pushed open a heavy walnut door and marched up the main staircase as though he had every right in the world to be here.

Clearly it'd been left to the Mathers family to take control of this situation and get things back on track. He'd have to stay out of Pard Holloway's hair but that shouldn't be difficult—the man was preoccupied. No matter, Ben felt spryer than he had in years and fully capable of finishing (once and for all) what was started a long time ago.

Samuel stirred. "Huh, what?" He blinked at Ben Mathers five times before it registered that the old man really was sitting a few feet away, watching him. Samuel sat up and rubbed his face with both hands while blubbering something incoherent. Then he announced: "I'm awake."

Ben leaned forward in his chair. "Do you remember what we were discussing?"

"What do you want, Mathers?"

"We decided that with her out of the way, it could be yours."

Samuel grimaced as if he had a rotten taste in his mouth. "Yeah—I remember."

"That the way to rid ourselves of this scourge is to clean the Pest House," Ben said. "Remember?"

"Yeah, yeah. Vile. The whole stinking place."

"Then you're up to it, right?"

Samuel stared at Ben for a moment before he threw up his hands. "To hell with it. Hope the roof caves in. Could, you know? Nearly impossible to fix that dry rot. Who cares? It's not my rotting hotel, where the sick come to die and the dead won't ever leave."

Beneath the red in Samuel's bloodshot eyes, Ben thought he saw greed. "So you understand what we're going to do then, right?"

"Right, yeah, *yes* already." Samuel reached for his bottle of bourbon on the coffee table.

"Now isn't the time to be drinking," Ben said.

"Now isn't the time *not* to be drinking."

Ben stood, intending to tell Samuel to lay off the booze, then thought better of it and left without another word.

But he would need to recruit more than Samuel Adair. And there was the possibility that Samuel could sober up and reconsider. Tiny Clemshaw, perhaps; he didn't much care for her, either. Ben was confident that Cal was on board. What about Doc Simmons? Maybe. Ben decided to head first to the Mercantile to firm things up with Clemshaw. If he planted enough seeds, some were sure to take root.

I warned her, didn't I?

THE WOODS

I SMELL YOU...

It smelled of damp possum fur, and urine.

Nate Winslow knew how to hunt. His dad taught him like every good father teaches his son what he knows about recreation and survival. But he'd never enjoyed killing. Even as a boy, he'd felt custodial toward the wildlife in the forest.

This was different. This creature meant them harm. This time he would relish the kill. And he would strap the carcass across the hood of the Jeep and drive up Fortune Way and down Ruby Road for everyone in Winslow to see how well he's protecting them.

The revolver felt good in his hand now, natural, as though the longer he held it the more it became a part of him.

Pausing along the trail that parallels Ruby Creek, he quieted his feet, body, mind...and listened. Except for the whir of bugs in the air and murmur of water running in the creek, the woods were silent. He bent at the knees and scanned the forest floor—looking for tracks, scat, clumps of fur, anything peculiar—but saw nothing unusual.

Could be deer, he'd supposed more than once. But he dismissed it again. Judging by the trampled low branches he'd come across, it was larger than even a mature buck. And there was that dank scent that reminded him less of deer and more of an animal of prey.

He returned upright and popped open the cylinder of the Smith & Wesson. Two rounds spent. *Where did they go?* Maybe it wasn't fully loaded to begin with? But he knew that wasn't true. Then he remembered being at Dead Horse Point with the chocolate Lab, the Peabodys' good sweet dog. He'd had to put her down. No other choice. He retrieved two cartridges from his belt, loaded the cylinder, and pushed it back into place.

Despite the old-growth mountain hemlocks shading his path, Nate felt the temperature rising and the air around him growing heavy with heat. *The creek will be cooler* was his only thought as he headed right, leaving the trail and tree cover for the banks of Ruby Creek.

When Nate saw the deer lying dead—half in, half out of the creek—his first thought was *I shot it.* But as he got closer he knew he hadn't. This was something else entirely.

He crouched next to her. The young doe had a foot-long gash in her side that still bled into the clear water. *What did this?* Nate didn't know what would do this. He could see clear into her. It didn't appear as though anything was missing; she remained intact. So this kill was not for food.

Paranoia crept up on him. He lifted his eyes to the shady woods, then back up the creek bed where the water rushed toward him, threatening to overflow the banks. He swiveled to glance over his shoulder at still more forest, more water. *It could be anywhere...watching me. Lurking in that stand of hemlock, concealed behind that boulder.*

When Nate returned his gaze to the deer he was shamed by her unblinking, incriminating stare. *Why didn't I help you?* He ran his hand across the patch of white adorning her chest. "I'm sorry." He felt himself choking up. "Why did this happen?" *If I couldn't save Melanie Rhone, who can I save?* Nate swallowed his tears and swiped angrily at his stinging eyes with the back of his wrist. Three murders he lay witness to now: the doe, Melanie and Hawkin Rhone.

The last, a while ago. Five years. After the children had confessed what happened, Nate and Jules Foster had hurried out across Three Fools Creek and found what was left of the baker in a wet pile next to the cabin's only door. It appeared the man had been trying to crawl into the shelter of the cabin but something got him before he could make it through the doorway.

"Was it an animal that killed him?" Nate had asked the doctor hopefully.

"Could be animals got at him after he was already dead," Jules replied.

Either way, Hawkin Rhone's remains were a snarled, soaked pile and even Dr. Foster couldn't sort them out.

But that was hardly murder, Nate reminded himself. If Sean Adair hadn't hit the man, had instead run away to get help, who knows what Hawkin Rhone would've done to Hazel? And nobody missed him when he was gone. Zachary Rhone had seemed almost relieved when Nate went to him and said that he was sorry, but he'd been to the cabin and while he couldn't be certain, it looked as though a bear had gotten the better of his father.

Sean had protected Hazel, and nobody ever saw a good reason to punish him for that. Nobody had ever even brought it up again. Until now. Now an exhumation felt imminent. Pard Holloway had threatened as much to keep Nate from getting the help from down mountain that Nate was convinced they needed. "We are the authorities, Winslow," Pard said Monday night, back before it was too late, "and we clean up our own messes around here. You know that better than most."

So Nate had had to go along with the quarantine, with not radioing for a doctor, because now it was his turn to protect Hazel and Sean.

Staring at the wound that gaped along the doe's side, he felt devastated.

He placed the Smith & Wesson on a flat rock, grabbed hold of the deer beneath the rib cage, and pulled her out of the creek. He could do that at least. Corpses pollute. "I'm sorry," he repeated as he released her into the ferns.

He returned to the creek bed and plunged his hands into the cold water, scrubbing his palms together and then wiping them dry against his pants.

When he turned and reached for the gun, it was gone. *Oh, no.*

Defenseless, he jerked his head from side to side. Where was the gun? Where was the *creature?* Nate knew it could rip him to shreds in seconds, his only shield his bare hands, and the thing would bite off his fingers before tearing through his tendons with its barbed claws.

Feeling it at his back he spun around—not ready to face it but left with no choice—and there it was.

The gun. Right where he'd left it.

He stooped to pick it up (too relieved to berate himself) and offered one last apology to the doe before turning away from the creek.

Calm down. Your heart's beating too fast. You'll have a heart attack like Dad.

Then what good will I be to anyone? You're no good now. You know that.

Have I moved? My feet are stuck in these bristlecones. So crunchy and dry. I hope there's not a fire. I'm hot. I'll get in the creek. The water smells clean. No—don't get any closer to the edge. Stay here. Keep the revolver out. It's safe here. But while I'm out here, nobody's safe.

Okay. Then I'll track it down and make sure it doesn't hurt anybody else. I smell you...

Nate climbed up the embankment to the trail. "I'm sorry, Anabel, that I let you down. I'm sorry, Melanie. I'm sorry, Hazel."

Go find it. He resumed hiking down the path, heading east toward the ponds. *Go now.*

"Don't lose the scent," he instructed himself. "That's what Dad would say. Don't lose your bearings."

Bearings. Nate suffered a sinking sensation. *Losing...* He blew out his breath. *Lost.*

I wish I didn't know. Now he felt his brain weeping—twisting and wringing with sobs. *Better not to know. And if only I'd lose it a little bit more, then I wouldn't have to know anymore.*

What am I thinking?

He kept his eyes on his feet, trying to stay on the path and not lose himself to the trees. But he knew; he understood: "I'm thinking it'd be better not to know that I'm losing my mind."

MATHERSTON
GHOST TOWN

A RING AROUND the moon means soon it will rain. A red ring
heralds something worse. Once the moon rose last night Pa-
ience Mathers saw the red ring. There was no use denying it:
the ill omen that misfortune would soon befall her or someone she loves.

Patience clapped her hand around the charm bracelet on
her opposite wrist and walked toward the tourists waiting at
the entrance to Matherston. It seemed even dustier than usual
so she looked down and saw her pony-hair boots kicking up
dirt, and she was almost there when she realized she didn't
have on her Victorian dress. Too late now, she'd have to give
the tour in the rodeo outfit she'd changed back into after Hazel
abandoned her in Prospect Park.

I don't want to do it, I don't want to...

When she reached the half dozen tourists she said, "Look—
'm shaking."

And they looked at her shaking.

She said, "Welcome to Matherston."

And they said, "Give us the ghost town tour!"

"If you'll follow me—" Patience turned and led the group
up Prospectors Way "—we'll start with the blacksmith shop
on the right and the livery stable next door where you'll see a
collection of mining equipment, including the original Bur-
eigh drills and rolling mounts."

But they passed the livery without stopping, clomping along
the warped plank sidewalk.

Patience felt faint. It was too hot and she felt thirsty and empty and weak. "Hazel told me I'm looking for more trouble," she said, "but that's not true. Trouble is coming even if we close our eyes." She glanced back and saw the tourists spread out all over the place, not even listening to her. "Pay attention!" she reprimanded. "Stay with the group!"

Hazel never pays me attention, except when I said he wanted me.

"I begged her don't leave me, I need you," Patience told the tourists. "She knows what the crystal ball said, but doesn't care. She only says, 'Where's Sean? Where's Sean?'"

"Where's Sean? Where's Sean?" the tourists echoed.

"I could tattle on him, you know? Tell what he did that summer across the creek."

"What did he do?"

"But I crossed my heart and hoped to die." *I don't want to die—*

Patience abruptly halted in front of Holloway Harness. *It's so simple,* she suddenly realized. *I'll find him first.*

She faced the group. "I'll find him first—he's so sick, I could see that when he tried to kiss me—and then she'll know how it feels to be low fruit nobody wants even if they are easy pickin's and she'll pay me attention and she'll help me then."

"You're not giving us the tour!"

"Oh." She glanced around at the false-front buildings up and down Prospectors Way before pointing at the Chop House Restaurant across the street. "Thickest steaks and…and something else-est in the West courtesy of Holloway Ranch…" she trailed off.

"What now?" the tourists demanded.

Patience suddenly felt sick to her stomach all over again and bent at the waist and dry-heaved over a hitching post. Then she stood, took a deep breath, straightened her suede vest and looked into their expectant faces. "Now Hawkin Rhone is back to punish us for what Sean Adair did."

"You're scaring us!" the tourists cried.

"Me, too," Patience agreed and then led them through batwing doors into the Mother Lode. "This is one of three saloons in Matherston—"

The dog, Hazel Winslow's familiar, was crouched beneath the cursed poker table, red fur matted, ears forward, wet eyes narrow. "Easy, boy, easy." Patience held up her hands to placate the dog as he drew back his lips to bare sharp teeth. He smelled like mushrooms, which sent her stomach roiling again.

"What's wrong, Patience?" the tourists behind her asked.

Then Jinx snapped his jaw.

She spun around and pushed past the tourists and through the doors, stumbling off the sidewalk onto the dirt road.

"What's wrong?" they called after her.

But she was already running down Prospectors Way, crying and thinking, *Why did she tell me to shut up? That's no thing you say. Things are cooking. Now we're cooking with gas, like Gramps always says. If only she would hear me, I know what's cooking in that vile place. Gramps tells me and she should know, too, and be afraid.*

Patience paused at the timber-framed entrance—soaked in sweat, hair hanging in her face—to look back at Matherston.

"I warned everybody," she whispered, panting. "Dogs death, smoke fire, creeks rain. Cows on fire, bread on fire."

She closed her eyes to it all. "I warned them they'll come in threes."

HIDE-AND-GO-SEEK

"OLLY OLLY OXEN FREE!"

Hazel's voice had gone hoarse calling to them. She'd been searching everywhere and all she wanted was to see their little heads pop up from their hiding spot, to see them weaving their way to her between the apple trees.

In fact, she wished everyone would come out of hiding. She found it entirely odd: in a town so small, how could so many people be lost?

Her body thrummed with tension, nerves taut with paranoia. "Come out, come out, wherever you are!"

The orchard was hot and still and smelled of rotting fruit, although no apples clung to the branches or littered the ground. *These trees are dead,* she realized. She grasped a narrow gray branch and snapped it off. *Ought to be chopped down and burned for firewood.*

The bakery still smoldered down the hill. She'd skirted it first before looking for the children, trying to determine if Zachary Rhone were lurking about. But she hadn't seen him or anybody else. *Come out, come out...*

The front door to the Rhone house had been hanging open like a slack mouth but there was no way in hell she was going in there. The second story appeared even slopier than she'd remembered, the paint more severely blistered. From the recent heat wave, she supposed. *Not going in there—uh-uh, no way.*

Continuing now through the orchard graveyard, each tree a brittle corpse, she reached the far side of the orchard at the base of Silver Hill and yelled again with all she could muster, "Olly olly oxen free!"

Then she waited…while not a creature stirred.

Last night, the woman in the ballroom had cried, "Where are the children?"

"Hawkin Rhone got 'em," Kohl Thacker had answered without hesitation.

That made Hazel's pulse race as she approached a long wooden bin, appropriately kid-sized. Hoping coiled snakes didn't spring out at her, she lifted the lid. Empty except for a dark red gemstone—the garnet ring she'd given to Daisy. She bent to retrieve it from the floor of the bin, mindful of her vulnerability since all anyone would have to do is kick her from behind and she'd tumble in. She snatched up the jewelry, then hopped back from the bin and let the lid bang shut.

Rubbing the cold stone of her grandmother's ring, she blew out a long breath. "You aren't here anymore," she decided. "The fire scared you away."

Then she noticed the ax lodged in the trunk of a decapitated apple tree. Her heartbeat skidded as she wondered if it were the same weapon that had been abandoned to the dandelions next to Melanie's body. She averted her gaze, not wanting to consider it any further.

Instead, she glanced west toward the bridge, thinking that when Daryl came with the mail tomorrow and saw the bridge closed, she'd know something was really wrong.

Hazel clicked her tongue against the roof of her mouth, "Ticktock, ticktock."

Can we wait that long?

"Tick." *No.* "Tock."

A lot could happen in one day. She thought about gangrene, about suffocated tissue and split black skin. Can spread to the rest of the body, the encyclopedia warned.

No, too much could happen in only one day.

Unable to stop herself, she looked at the ax again and thought, *Who else will die if no help arrives?* Her chest constricted painfully. *How soon?*

Panic propelled her forward. "Come out, come out!" Her voice rang shrill with desperation.

And then she prayed that they hadn't taken to the woods, because Bigfoot eats children for breakfast.

WHEN HAZEL REACHED Dead Horse Point, she expected to see the barricade blocking the bridge that spanned the Lamprey River canyon—the one way into town, the only way out. What she *didn't* expect to see was the grain distributor's flatbed truck wedged beneath the first truss.

"So much for Fritz Earley to the rescue." Frustrated, she kicked dirt and rocks over the side of the cliff, wondering if anybody knew he was up here. If anybody cared. She imagined him living alone, eating cold cereal for dinner in front of his television.

Doc Simmons's red Ford was crammed against the bridge railing and that didn't sit well with her, either. Did that mean that Daryl and her mail truck would simply be added to this collection? No help, no rescue, just a growing blockade until the bridge collapsed altogether under all that vehicle tonnage?

She watched five ranch hands mill about the barricade, and tried to suppress the panic she knew would do her no good. *Trapped. Trapped like rats.* The cowboys bore arms.

The sun continued its ascent in the cloudless sky, growing hot on her back. This day would bring no relief from the heat, no relief of any kind, she speculated. The pine trees looked dry and unhappy—braced for the misery of another afternoon in the furnace. The river below remained in shadow, but she could hear it: dark water slipping past as if there were nothing peculiar going on above its banks…just another ordinary Wednesday morning.

Every bug on the side of the mountain awoke then and mobilized to buzz around Hazel's ankles and ears. Swatting at them, she paced along the edge and debated where to look next.

Her miserable arm was begging for mercy so she inventoried the contents of her pockets: Daisy's garnet ring, the matchbook she took from Honey Adair in the kitchen of The Winslow, the bottle of eyedrops, a half-empty box of candy, but no more Percocet. If only she'd known how desperately she'd need it, she would've taken the whole bottle from her grandmother's medicine cabinet. As it was, not even the promise of a reprieve from pain could compel her to return to The Winslow—nothing seemed worth that.

Despite the turmoil of sugar that was her stomach, she sucked on a mouthful of hard candy as she stood on the brink, sensing the altitude and sheer nothingness all around. Nothing except Yellow Jacket Pass, empty of vehicles, just the narrow blacktop indifferently and unhurriedly bending its way down the mountain. When she turned to glance at the ridge that rose behind her, she felt the void beyond those mountaintops as well, and recalled Tanner saying that they could all eat each other over the winter and nobody would even know. *A Donner Party waiting to happen,* she had agreed then.

I'm alone, she thought now, with both wonder and dread. *We are so alone.*

She noticed for the first time how precariously the boulders were balanced in their haphazard formations up and down the mountainside. And across the canyon, the leaves on the aspens shimmered in the sunshine as if the trees wore sequined gowns.

Then it occurred to her: *Maybe this isn't just happening here—maybe it's happening everywhere, the whole country, the entire world.* Somehow, the notion brought her comfort.

She popped more candy into her mouth, wondered how

many horses really had toppled over this point to their deaths. After inching closer to the edge she peered down into the ravine. And the lure of gravity pulled, willing her to fall off and plunge into the Lamprey River below…and the candy box slipped from her fingers and went bouncing down the rocky side. *So this is how it happens.*

Snapping her body out of gravity's grip, her jaw clamped down on a piece of hard candy and her right rear molar cracked with an ugly sound and a bolt of pain, followed by a shiver of shock chasing down her spine.

"Help me!" she screamed at the top of her lungs across the chasm, and drawing her breath through her mouth brought fresh agony as air brushed the exposed nerve.

Tears flooded her eyes. Maybe she should just leap off. It'd be quick, and at least she'd know what to expect. *No skeleton but my own.*

Instead, she plopped down, defeated, into the dirt.

There was no stopping it now, the messy shaking kind of sobbing like when she was seven years old and fell out of the big oak in Prospect Park. Like then, she was crying more from fear than pain. And she felt that same eerie sensation: free-falling backward through space out of the tree, dreading the landing but wishing it would finally come all the same. When she'd at last hit the ground, all the wind had whooshed out of her as she smacked down flat on her back. After her breath had returned, she ran home hysterical to her dad, who scooped her up and hurried her over to Dr. Foster's to get her all patched up.

Who can I run to now? She adjusted her arm where it lay against her rib cage, wincing at its objection. *Who will patch me up now?*

She became aware of a presence just behind her, something that had snuck up as she cried on the precipice. It breathed hot against her shoulder. *Trapped.* There was nowhere for Hazel to go but down.

"Brraghh," the breathing thing noised in her ear.

Hazel turned and caught a hairy mouth against her cheek and one huge brown eye staring into hers. "You again." She recognized the creature from the church cemetery. Hazel pushed the cow's gigantic head away so she could stand up without tumbling into the river. "Are you following me?" With her left hand, she kept her right cheek pressed into her mouth so her breath wouldn't twinge the bare nerve again when she spoke.

"Brraghh."

Hazel smiled a painful, lopsided smile. "Okay, let's go find them."

The cow followed her only so far, losing interest when she happened upon a patch of clover.

"Bye…" Hazel wiped her wet face with the hem of her tank top, already missing the company, and wishing Jinx were by her side like he always used to be even when she'd tell him to get lost.

Intending to go and erase Sean's puzzling apology, hoping to find the kids along the way, she headed for the woods to continue on the path that would take her to the granite wall. Only to stop a few feet away when her right tennis shoe smacked into something disturbingly soft.

She forced herself to look down.

Molly.

She cupped her hand across her mouth and squeezed her eyes shut. Rose and Owen Peabody's dog, Jinx's girlfriend, whose favorite leftover at the Crock was turkey potpie.

Hazel bent over her and pushed aside tall weeds. The Lab had been shot once between eyes that looked more like marbles now.

Hazel popped back up and scanned the tree line. Who would shoot her?

Returning her gaze to Molly, she noticed the dog's mouth was bloodied, and broken teeth lay scattered in the dirt around her body. Hazel made a whimpering noise as her stomach lurched and her bones turned to marshmallow.

She suddenly felt exposed, a sitting duck, and headed for the cover of the forest.

Molly had been sick; that much was clear. So maybe somebody had put her out of her misery?

Oh, no. Hazel's paranoia ramped up. *What if somebody's putting* people *out of their misery?* She thought of Rose and the others in the ballroom of The Winslow: sick, helpless, scared out of their broken minds. *What can I do about it?* Hazel felt horrified. *What can I do?*

Shaking, she forced herself to push all thoughts out of her mind except finding Sean and the kids. All else would have to wait.

If it will wait, she thought with renewed alarm.

"Don't think about it," Sean told her that July day a million years ago, right before he gave her a gentle shove to keep her moving through her fear. "Just go."

Don't think, she thought now. *Just go.*

She waded through the woods until reaching the ruins of Matherston Miner's Camp, a tilted assortment of hand-hewn log cabins smothered beneath eighty years' worth of brambles. Once she stopped crunching down the trail, she heard singing. She ducked behind a rusted-out wagon and watched.

Half a dozen people were gathered around an unlit fire pit, singing some hippie-sounding song, while Hap Hotchkiss pushed his lawn mower in a big circle around them.

They're happy, Hazel marveled and stood up. Nothing to fear here, she picked her way toward them, avoiding rotted boards and rusty nails. Closer, she saw that inside the pit, they had piled stones, pinecones and wildflowers.

Emily Bolinger, James's tall mother, who taught the occasional art class at their school, greeted Hazel with a warm smile. Then she frowned. "You're hurt, Hazel Winslow." Gently, Emily stroked her blood-encrusted arm, then touched the hand that Hazel held pressed against her cheek to protect her tooth.

"I'm okay," Hazel lied. "How are you?"

Emily cocked her head. "I'm different than I used to be."

"Is that good?" Hazel couldn't tell.

"I haven't decided. I also haven't decided whether or not I'll fly off the bridge."

"*Don't* do that, Emily. That would *not* be good. Okay?" Hazel waited for Emily to nod convincingly before she asked, "Have you seen Sean Adair?"

Emily finger-combed Hazel's long, tangled hair, looking as if she might cry out of pity. "You poor girl." Emily caressed Hazel's cheeks. "There, there."

Hazel wanted to beg Emily to adopt her, beg her to do and say more motherly things because she found it so comforting. Instead, she asked, "You knew my mother, didn't you?"

The question seemed to puzzle Emily. Then she replied, "None of us really knew her. Did we?"

Sighing, Hazel found it impossible to imagine Emily ever leaving her own son, or locking him out of the house for that matter, as James claimed his parents had done on Sunday night. But right now, she needed to stay on track. "Have you seen Aaron Adair? The Rhone girls?"

"No, but I've seen Heaven." Emily twirled away, taking all of that comfort with her.

Hazel turned to Hap Hotchkiss. "Have you seen—"

He shook his head, looking sympathetic.

No use, Hazel thought.

As she walked away, back into the trees, Hap called after her, "You can stay with us, Hazel, if you like. You're welcome to."

She continued toward the trail. This was confusing. They were *happy*. Were there others like them? She realized some people must be holed up in their houses, sick or otherwise like Constance and Chance Mathers, and maybe they have *no idea* what's going on.

Maybe I should stay with Emily and Hap—

Hazel halted. A figure stood on the trail up ahead. From so far back it looked to be half man/half ape with long dark hair.

And she had to wonder: *Am I hallucinating, too?* The cow, Molly, the hippies…now a Sasquatch?

The shape dashed away. Hazel could trace its movement by the upset of low branches as whatever it was cut a path through the woods and then disappeared over the rise.

Am I hallucinating?

Maybe her arm was infected and causing delirium. Maybe she was losing her mind, too.

The horror of it struck then—maybe she'd already lost it. Or worse: *Maybe I'm the only one and none of this is even happening. Maybe I'm straightjacketed in the rubber room at Stepstone Sanitarium loaded on Lithium and drooling like a toothless hag.*

"That's too easy." She laughed a little, like a crazy person would. "That's *way* too easy."

Besides, what difference would it make? There was no getting off this ride now.

IMPOSSIBLE AS IT WAS for her to believe, her tooth hurt even more than her elbow. Dueling agonies now, engaged in fierce competition for her attention.

Rooftops of ramshackle buildings on Prospectors Way came into view as the trail climbed toward Matherston. Five nore minutes and she'd reach the granite wall. Five more hot, exhausted minutes.

Matherston. Her breath caught and her heart hiccupped. *I bet that's where Sean is, with the kids. That makes sense. They're probably all together in the assay office eating ice cream sandwiches.*

The first pleasant thought she'd had in days, she held on to it as she hurried toward the ghost town, embellishing the image until everybody was there, kicking along Prospectors Way, feeling better and licking the ice cream that melted down their arms. Sean and Aaron—Aaron imitating Sean's every move in that worshipful way he has. Violet and Daisy chasing each other around the hitching posts. Her grandmother with the calm returned to her eyes. And her dad, confident and brave in his uniform, his arm sure and strong across Sarah's shoulders. Owen and Rose Peabody awake and looking like their old Popeye and Olive Oyl selves again. Even her mother Anabel (why not?), still young because Hazel didn't know what she looked like now. And Jinx running elated circles around the girls...

Hazel scooted up the road, excited to see them, Sean especially. *I'll tell him everything. I'll make everything the way it was before. Better even.*

She passed under the timber-framed entrance to Matherston and struck dust with each step in the dry dirt as she continued up Prospectors Way. When she reached midway through town she stopped in front of Hank's Boarding House to squint up the road, then back down the way she had just come.

Deserted. Not a soul, dead or alive, greeted her arrival.

But an action figure (Wolverine, it looked like) lying on the wood-plank sidewalk in front of the blacksmith shop told her someone had been here recently. Aaron Adair, she hoped. And when she glanced back up she caught the tail end of a diminutive figure disappearing between the Never Tell Brothe and the Mother Lode Saloon.

"Olly olly oxen free?" she called.

Meat cooked nearby. The smell of it reached her and sent her stomach into a ravenous growl.

She followed her nose to the Mother Lode Saloon and peeked inside.

Empty. Then she stole a look down the space between the Chop House Restaurant and the saloon, found it empty as well, and tiptoed between the buildings.

She heard voices now—light, small voices.

A section of the restaurant's siding had decayed away so she could see clear inside the Chop House as she passed. Round tables and broken chairs still cluttered the interior, along with game heads plastered against the wallpaper. *Appetizing.* That roasting meat.

When she reached the end of the building she stopped to listen.

"I can't wait anymore," a boy.

"It's done when I say it's done," an older boy.

Hazel eased her head around the corner of the saloon.

So this is where the children are. A whole clan of them, twenty or so, possibly all the kids in Winslow. Except for her three, the three children she most wanted to see were not among them.

James Bolinger was the older boy she'd heard. Cynthia and Nicholas Thacker, Penelope and Tim Hotchkiss, Lindy Spainhower and Collette Dudley were all gathered around the fire pit despite the heat. What cooked above the pit looked like a cat carcass and Hazel's innards turned over.

Boo, she thought and her stomach slid back the other direction.

Penelope Hotchkiss wept silently by the fire, shoulders

shaking, while her younger brother Timmy tried to comfort her, his small hand patting her shoulder. Hazel recognized Penelope's battered green Schwinn propped up against the back of the Chop House.

Gunner Spainhower emerged from between the saloon and the brothel—the figure she'd caught a glimpse of earlier. "I'm thirsty," he declared and made a beeline for the gallon jug crammed in with a hoard of other supplies on the back porch of the Mother Lode.

Other small forms rested beneath sprays of hemlock within the split-rail fence enclosure.

Nicholas Thacker sat too close to the fire, sweat dribbling off his eager face, transfixed by the cooking cat, literally licking his lips. "It's done," he told James.

James stood back from the group, leaning on a long board he'd fashioned into a walking stick, or a weapon. Clearly he was their leader. "It's done when I say it's done."

Hazel stepped out into view. James tensed and raised the board, but then relaxed when he saw it was her—the love of his life. He reached her in six long-legged steps.

"Hazel…" James's young face seemed to have been aged twenty years by circumstance—like his grandfather Gus at the hotel—and his black eyeliner had smudged all around his eyes, giving him a ghoulish appearance. "What happened to you?" he asked.

"I wouldn't know where to start." And then she was crying again. She couldn't believe it. But the look of sympathy and concern on his face got the better of her and it came pouring out. She'd never been like this. It was embarrassing and made her feel like an idiot.

"It's okay." He hugged her lightly. "It's okay."

After sniffing it all back in she sighed. The other kids were staring at her, curious and frightened. Realizing she must be quite a sight she tried to smile at them but knew it was weak.

She looked at James. "Are any of them hurt?" She glanced at Penelope. "Is she okay?"

"Yeah," James followed her eyes. "They're all hanging in there."

Turning away from the group of urchins, she whispered to James, "Let's go talk."

"Go ahead and eat," James told the kids and Nicholas lunged for the meat. "But don't burn yourself, for crying out loud."

James followed Hazel, who led the way back between the structures and continued into the Mother Lode. She went to the bar and leaned against the smooth wood, one foot up on the rail, as if expecting a bartender to bring her a whiskey. But there were only empty beer cans scattered around. Behind the bar, shards from the mirror Tanner broke Saturday night still clung to the sticky wallpaper. *Guess we shouldn't have let him do that,* Hazel thought wearily.

James joined her at the bar to wait for his whiskey, too.

She turned to look at him. "What was that?"

"What was what?"

"What was that cooking?"

"Rabbit."

"Oh, good."

"Do you have it, Hazel?" He wrinkled his smooth brow.

"No." She searched his face for signs and symptoms. "How are you feeling?"

"Hell if I know. I can't remember what normal feels like." He ran a hand through his hair, flattening his disheveled Mohawk. "But at least I'm not as bad off as most people. Not even close."

"That's good," she said, grateful for that. "How many of the little kids have it?"

"Ten. They keep scaring the shit outta themselves and then run outta juice for a while."

She decided against asking him if there were any signs of gangrene. "Tell them not to eat any more bread."

"How come?"

"There's mold in it—it's what's making everybody sick."

"Seriously? How did that happen?"

That question made Hazel wonder for the first time: *Who really is to blame?* She had been so caught up in Sean's role she had never even considered that most basic of questions.

She frowned at James. "Seems to me like it's Fritz Earley's fault. His flour, his feed. It all came from him. Shouldn't he know moldy, gonna-make-people-sick-as-hell flour when he sees it?"

"You'd think so. When does he come up with deliveries, anyway?"

"Fridays, usually. But he's already here. Somewhere." Hazel pondered where that might be. If her Uncle Pard had figured it out, she imagined he'd have something major in store for Fritz Earley. She turned her attention back to James. "How long have you been out here?"

"Since Tuesday."

"That's only yesterday, you know?"

He looked puzzled for a snap moment. "I guess you're right. Seems longer."

"Sure does. Who knows you're here?"

"Nobody, I don't think. Except some sick carny guy we chased out."

"Who?"

"Some greasy-haired guy and his moustache wandered in totally messed up and we told him to get lost, we didn't want him here. But he didn't get it so we chased him and threw stuff at him until he ran up Silver Hill and disappeared."

Hazel would have laughed if she weren't so scared. Instead,

she nodded. "The vampire. He's holed up inside the Second Chance mine shaft. Stay away."

"Don't worry." He blew out a sharp breath. "But I seriously hope nobody else knows we're here. Don't tell anyone, Hazel."

"I won't," she promised. Then she said, "The bridge is closed."

"I know—your uncle's henchmen have it barricaded. My mom and I tried to take off but they turned us back." He winced as if the memory pained him, then he looked sadly at Hazel. "Do you think anybody's coming to help us?"

She wished she could tell him yes, that at any moment they'd be rescued, she was sure of it. But she wasn't. "I honestly don't know, James. I hope so. If some of the tourists or carnies came down sick after the rodeo, maybe somebody will trace it back here."

His expression told her how disheartened he'd become. "But how long will that take?"

"I have no idea." She sighed, suspecting that it might take a while—probably too long. Plus, she'd read in the encyclopedia that ergotism is caused by *excessive* intake of ergot, so people have to eat infested bread repeatedly. To her, that meant that even if tourists had eaten some of the bread, they wouldn't be anywhere near as sick as everyone here who'd kept eating it.

James sighed, too, a defeated sound. "The ranch hands are patrolling the streets," he said, "rounding up everybody and taking them to The Winslow. Did you know that? It's really scary up there."

"Really scary," she agreed.

"Everybody's gone completely psycho. I hope they don't find us, Hazel. I hope they don't drag us up there." He was looking at her with profound worry.

The last time she'd seen James was at the Crock and he'd been worried about his upset stomach. Now he was worried about insane parents and ruthless cowboys and haunted hotels.

"I hope they don't find you, either," she said, her unease so great that she was incapable of reassuring him. "Hey, I just saw your mom and she's feeling good. She's with other people tripping out in the woods."

"Really? I'm so glad you saw her. She almost jumped off the bridge before she took off and then I couldn't find her." He shook his head, looking relieved. "Isn't it weird? My mom's acting all groovy while everyone else is having a bad trip." But the relief on his face was quickly displaced by the worry again. "I wish I knew where my grandpa is."

Hazel didn't have the heart to tell him she'd seen his grand-father Gus at The Winslow and that he wasn't feeling good at all. Instead, she asked, "Why did you come to Matherston?"

"Better here than in town. Except that all the little squirts followed me."

"Cool of you to look after them."

"Yeah, guess so. What happened to your arm?"

"Wiped out on my YZ. Bike's completely tweaked. Crazy Doc Simmons shot at me and Jinx and we ate it."

"Oh, that sucks, Hazel. That totally sucks." James put a hand on her shoulder and she winced. "Maybe we should sling it, take the pressure off?"

"Okay…" She didn't have the energy to tell him about Aaron's Vanpire T-shirt and how the vampire in the mine had ripped it apart. "Got any good drugs?" she asked as he took off his own shirt and tried to figure out how he was going to accomplish the sling. It was his vintage Mudhoney concert T-shirt—a sacrifice beyond measure.

"Just dirt weed." He pulled the collar of the T-shirt over her head and gently swung her arm away from her body, then ran her hand through one sleeve and eased the rest of the shirt around the back of her arm to cup her elbow.

"Ice?" Tears stung her eyes. The pain registered different now, deeper and more acute.

"Let's try the assay office."

They retook the sunlight and dusty road and headed for the far end of Prospectors Way.

"Why was Doc Simmons after you, anyway?" James asked.

"We went to his place for help but he was out of his mind, completely bug-eyed with it. He killed Jinx." That last part rode out on a whimper.

"Jinx is here."

"What?"

"He showed up last night when we were roasting hot dogs."

Hazel shook her head in confusion. "Is he okay?"

"He's acting hurt but I looked him over pretty good and couldn't find any gushing wounds or anything. And he ate three hot dogs so I figured he's all right."

She was afraid to get her hopes up. "Are you sure it's him?"

"Oh, I'm sure. He scared the hell out of Patience Mathers."

"Wait, wait, back up—when was Patience here?"

"About an hour ago. She gave us the ghost town tour. She wasn't looking too good though. Had on her barfy rodeo clothes."

"Did she say where she was going?"

"No, just flew down the road screaming like a total freak. But before she ran into Jinx in the Mother Lode, she said something really bizarre."

"What?" Her gut got that doomy feeling again.

"That she's gonna tell everyone what Sean did."

Hazel froze.

"What did he do, Hazel?" James was holding open the door to the assay office for her.

She wasn't surprised to see it empty inside. No Sean, no Dad, no dripping ice cream. It had been a nice daydream. Avoiding James's question, she asked him the one she felt doomed to repeat the rest of her sorry life: "Have you seen Sean?"

"No." James shook his head. "But his brother showed up a little while ago."

"Aaron?" Her heart leapt. "Are Violet and Daisy with him?"

"Yeah, they're all here. I think something bad might've gone down at their house though, but they don't seem to want to talk about it."

"Where are they?"

"Second floor of the Never Tell."

They stepped into the assay office. She'd expected it to be cool inside because of the refrigerators, but the air was hot and stale. She went to the white porcelain freezer and grabbed the handle. *There could be body parts in here,* she thought, suddenly sure and horrified. *Blackened, rotted feet.*

"Is it stuck?" James asked behind her and she jumped. Reaching around her, he pulled up the lid. Ice cream sandwiches were nestled inside, like they always were, and little sundae cups with wooden spoons wrapped in paper. No hands, no feet.

"These are perfect." James grabbed two ice cream bars and turned her around. Carefully, he stretched away the T-shirt and positioned the frozen bars in the sling, one above and one below her elbow.

Hazel raised her eyebrows, impressed. "Thank you." Looking up at him, she saw how pleased he was to have helped her. So she stood up on her toes and kissed him, knowing that since people were dying and the whole town was imploding it was a good thing to do.

When she stepped away they both smiled, hers saying, *It'll be our secret,* and his, *I'll take what I can get.*

She reached into the freezer and grabbed four ice cream sandwiches. "If Sean shows up, please take care of him, he's really sick. Tell him to stay put, tell him I'm looking for him."

James didn't reply but the dubious look on his face said it all. Why should he provide comfort to the enemy?

"Please, James." She was stuffing the ice cream sandwiches into the top of her sling.

"Okay, I will." He reached down and straightened the sling. "Stay with us."

"I can't. I have to find him."

He considered her for a moment, maybe thinking he should knock her on the head and drag her by the hair back to the safety of his fire pit. Finally, he said, "I'd go with you but I have to stay with the squirts. In case anyone comes."

She nodded, marveling at his selflessness.

"No matter what, Hazel, don't tell anybody we're here."

"I won't tell, I promise." She gestured across the rainbow on her chest and smiled. "Cross my heart and hope to die." Another promise. This one she'd have to keep. No matter what.

It was hard to walk away from James—he of relatively sound mind and strong body, he who actually cared about her. She did it anyway. She walked out the door, alone, back into the brutal late-morning sun.

The brothel sat catty-corner from the assay office. *Must've been convenient,* Hazel thought. *Cash your lode, then—*

"Here, Jinxy, Jinx." The high voice sounded like Daisy's, and it chilled Hazel's spine.

The Never Tell had lost its door at some point so she stepped right in. The brothel had a lurid history. Patience once told her that during the ghost town tours, no story played better than that of the night a miner, Dinky Dowd, shot dead the upstanding purveyor of dry goods, George Bolinger, over a beautiful prostitute's favor. The town's founders had done their best to keep civilized folk separate from the miners, yet nobody could stop the gentlemen of Winslow from frequenting the Mother Lode to gamble or from paying a drunken visit to the Never Tell.

"C'mere, boy, c'meeeere."

Daisy was definitely upstairs. Without allowing herself

time to contemplate the staircase's obvious lack of structural integrity—let alone the entire second story, which sagged down into the first—Hazel hauled herself up the steps.

"Doggie, c'mere."

Amateurish paintings lined the hallway of the second floor: portraits of rouged women in dark velvet dresses, displaying cleavage and garter belts. Hookers with hearts of gold, Hazel supposed. The rooms she passed were tiny, all stood empty.

"Jinxy!"

"Daisy, be quiet!" Violet's voice.

Last room on the left. Hazel hoped the ice cream hadn't completely melted. The room they occupied was larger, she saw, and still contained a bed on which Aaron lay in his cowboy pajamas. Though he faced the doorway, eyes open, he didn't acknowledge her when she entered.

Hazel had never been happier to see three snot-nosed kids in all her life.

"Hazel!" Daisy ran up and grabbed her around the thighs.

"Hey, string bean." She tried to pry her off so she could get into the room, and at the same time smiled at Violet, who looked about to cry with relief. Disengaging Daisy, Hazel pulled the ice creams out of her sling, soft now inside their foil wrappers. She handed one to Daisy, another to Violet and held out the third to Aaron on the bed. "Eat. It's good for you."

He sat up and took the ice cream sandwich from her, holding it by his fingertips as though it was something foreign and possibly dangerous.

"Eat," she ordered again and sat down on the edge of the soiled bed.

The girls didn't need to be told; they were already in, Violet taking deliberate nibbles (she'd never finish before it turned to complete mush) and Daisy going at it full bore, mouth ringed in chocolate.

Hazel opened the last one and took a big bite.

The kids' eyes flew wide open in alarm when Hazel screamed.

"What! Are you okay?" Violet held up her little hands, fingers splayed, in a gesture that said, *Help! I don't know what to do!*

"I'm okay. Give me a second." Hazel cradled her jaw in her hand, thinking, *Sonofabitch!* She had hoped the cold would numb the pain of her broken tooth. Instead, it had the opposite effect and sent her nerves—and her—shrieking.

A loud whimper issued from beneath her.

She threw her head between her knees to look under the bed and found a hairy red haystack. Jinx. The dog scampered out and sprawled his body across the doorway as if he did not intend to let anybody leave the room.

Swallowing the ice cream that felt like a rock in her throat, Hazel went to her dog, leaned on her left arm all the way down to the filthy floor, and placed her chin in front of his muzzle so she could look straight into his dopey eyes. "I'm glad to see you," she said.

He chuffed in her face as if to ask, *Where have you been?*

"Such a good boy." She touched her nose to his. Wet, as usual, which she took to be a good sign. She sat up on her knees and gingerly poked and prodded him in order to assess the extent of his injuries.

"Lemme eat your ice cream if you're not gonna!" Daisy bossed Aaron.

Jinx whined when Hazel touched his rib cage.

"I took one in the ribs, too, buddy," she told him. "I know it hurts." Gently she pulled back his lips to check his teeth. All there, she let out a loud *phew.* But one floppy ear had an inch-long tear in the side, cleaved and wet with blood. She leaned down and kissed the soft fur on his other ear and murmured, "I know it hurts, but you're going to be fine."

He whined back at her, *maybe,* while his wagging tail thumped up small dust explosions.

How am I going to tell him Molly is dead? she thought. And when she looked back at the girls, who were watching her with big eyes, red curls framing round faces, she wondered, *How will I ever tell them their mother is dead?*

She didn't have to.

"I know why you're sad, Hazel." Violet came over and stroked Jinx on the head with tiny, gentle fingers. "You're sad because now none of us have mommies."

And with that, Daisy went from joyous ice cream eating to wailing despair.

"It'll be okay," Hazel tried to calm Daisy.

"It'll be okay," Hazel told Violet next.

But to herself she thought, *How will it ever be okay again?* Gazing into their sorrowful eyes, she said, "If you two keep being so brave, my dad will make you his deputies. Does that sound good?"

Mouths aquiver, the sisters both nodded.

"*I'm* not a scaredy cat," Daisy insisted.

"No, you're not." Hazel's heart ached deeply for the girls, knowing firsthand the pain and loneliness that their motherless existence would bring. At least they had each other. At least their mother had loved them. "You're good, brave girls, both of you."

She stood and gave each girl a long hug despite the misery it caused her arm and ribs. Then she went to Aaron on the bed, where he was still holding the limp ice cream sandwich, a sour look pasted on his face. Hazel took it from him and handed it to a sniffling Daisy.

"Did you ever find Sean?" she asked him.

"Yes," he whispered.

Her heart sped up and she grabbed his hand. "You did?"

"He found me."

"When?"

"When we were in the apple orchard and mean Mr. Rhone came for us."

"Daddy's not well." Violet shook her head dolefully.

"Sean saved us." Aaron's mouth twisted with despair.

"Why are you so sad? That's good, isn't it?"

Aaron nodded, eyes downcast.

"Where's Sean now?"

"He was just gone," Violet said, "after the bakery caught fire and Daddy didn't come back out."

Hazel let out a long, relieved breath. *Zachary didn't come back out...* And instantly she felt ashamed—truly horrified—at her relief because the girls had already lost their mother.

Aaron added, "The little girl ghost kept us safe until Sean could get there."

Little girl ghost? Hazel did not like the sound of that. "But where did Sean go after that?"

He wouldn't answer, wouldn't look at her.

"Aaron—tell me."

Finally, he raised his eyes to hers. "Sean's a ghost now, too."

Terror stabbed Hazel. "Don't say that!"

Aaron began to cry, tight and squelchy as if he were trying hard not to.

Realizing she had been squeezing his hand too tightly, Hazel let go. Then she put her arm around him, pulled him close. "I'm sorry, Aaron. I am so sorry." She laid her cheek on top of his head, against his shiny brown hair that smelled like puppy, and let him cry.

After a minute, she pulled away. "I'll find your brother and bring him back. You'll see."

He didn't seem to hear her. Hazel touched his cheek. Still burning hot. *Are you ever going to get better?* she worried.

Daisy had stopped sobbing long enough to eat her second ice cream and now stood in front of Hazel, wringing her hands in that nervous way she always did when she had a question she wasn't sure she wanted the answer to. At last she asked, "Is Hawkin Rhone gonna get us?"

"No. Don't worry." Hazel dug into her pocket and retrieved the garnet ring, which Daisy promptly snatched from her hand. "He's not here," Hazel continued, too exhausted to argue the truth. "He's out there—across the creek."

Hazel heard Aaron gasp. Thinking that talking about Hawkin Rhone had frightened him, she turned toward him.

He was staring at something above her head with terror in his eyes.

"Aaron," she said, alarmed, "what is it?"

"Blood is pouring from the sky," he whispered. "We are going to drown."

NOON

A LOT OF MEN DIED during the short time the mines were active: mangled in accidents, struck with typhoid fever, murdered over a misdealt card game or perceived slight. Their graves in Matherston Miner's Cemetery were identified by wooden markers, epithets burned in pine.

The boneyard was full of ghosts today and it was all Sean could do to stay out of the way.

So he sat at the top of the rise between two grave markers, his back against the granite wall, and wondered when Winslow had gotten so crowded. There were a lot of people wandering around town all of a sudden, whom Sean didn't know but who bore unsettling resemblances to people he did.

At present, on Sean's right, unrested the spirit of George Bolinger / Outstanding Purveyor of Dry Goods / Shot Dead / Never Tell / Oct. 13th 1889. And to Sean's left: the ghost of Dinky Dowd, hanged for the murder of George Bolinger, Oct. 14th 1889, by order of the Hon. E. A. Winslow.

Sean, George and Dinky all preferred to keep to the shade of the purple-leaf plum tree. Sean wished like hell that he had something to smoke. Something to mellow him out.

George Bolinger looked a lot like James Bolinger, he realized. Half his face had been blown off and his guts hung out of his shirt like uncooked sausage, but still Sean noted the resemblance—tall with big hands and feet. Dinky was skinny and short like he never grew up all the way and had a face marked by toil in the mines.

Sean leaned back and observed the activity in the cemetery. Many more dead miners hustled about their business. They wore ill-fitting denim and sturdy boots, stamping down straw-colored weeds that sprang back in their wake. The rushing men would pause long enough to argue with each other using hostile gestures, or to tell a joke as evidenced by their barks of laughter—not amused laughs, but bitter and knowing. They did not seem bothered by the heat.

George and Dinky and Sean had been discussing the situation for quite some time now. Everyone agreed it was Zachary Rhone's fault that nobody knew how sick they were going to get from eating the bread. And for keeping that a secret— George and Dinky insisted—he'd deserved to die.

Yet none could deny that it was Sean who spread the bread all over town.

"I should've made Zachary look at that nasty flour before I made deliveries." Sean tossed a pinecone at a marker planted beside the tree:

18 Sept 1890
Fourth of July Mine
By accident, most harsh
Here lies what's left
of Guy D. Marsh

"Should've," George agreed and kicked at the pinecone. Then he reclined into the tree, resting one boot against its trunk.

"Should've thrown all that bread into the trash," Sean said. The remorse was voracious, eating away his spirit in fat, greedy bites.

"Yeah." Dinky squatted down next to him. "You really should'a."

Sean examined the singed skin on his right forearm. "I wanted to save him."

"Did yer best," Dinky said. "Weren't yer place to deny 'im his due."

"I thought I had him when he latched on to my arm."

George gave a plaintive shake of his translucent head.

"I tried to pull him out but he pulled against me. Why'd he do that?" They all shook their heads *dunno*. "I had to cut him loose. My arm was burning, the heat on my face. Had to."

"No choice but to cut him loose," George agreed.

"I watched him melt away." Sean exhaled hard and abruptly stood as if the memory of it wouldn't let him sit. "I never wanted him to get hurt. Only wanted to talk, get things straight."

Dinky stood, too, remaining at Sean's side. "But then ya seen the blood inside the house," he reminded him.

"Everywhere." His stomach churned. "In the house, on the sheets outside, all over the grass."

"And heard yer brother, Aaron, callin' to ya."

"Heard the fear in his voice."

"You had to do somethin'," George said. "You saw him—you saw the ax."

"I had to flush him out or else he'd hurt them, too."

Dinky put his hand on Sean's shoulder, but Sean felt no pressure from it.

"Burnin' the bakery was right," Dinky said. "Was redemption in those flames."

"I'm still gonna have to pay." Sean walked out from beneath Dinky's weightless grasp.

"S'pose you will," George said. "S'pose you will."

Then Sean suffered a gruesome thought, *Maybe I melted, too.*

Except the pine needles were sharp beneath his bare feet and his arm hurt where Zachary had grabbed him with burning hands, and Sean didn't think pain carried over to the great beyond. But he could be wrong. After all, why did he run away after it was all over?

"Why'd ya hightail it?" Dinky wanted to know.

"Because I didn't want Aaron to see me this way," Sean said.

"What way?" Dinky asked.

"Toes up," George answered for Sean. "Worm food."

Not caring to discuss it any longer, Sean drifted away to the stand of hemlocks at the base of the graveyard. He shook a branch and brown needles rained down.

Everything's dying, he thought. *And now I've killed twice: two Rhones, father and son.* "I'm going to hell for sure."

When he was here with Hazel on Sunday, it'd been roasting then, too. How long had it been this hot? He couldn't imagine it ever being any other way.

And now his heart felt sick—mottled and thin and weak. She had always made it clear, hadn't she? Made it clear since they were little kids that she didn't want him holding her hand. Made it clear since the first time they swiped rubbers from Clemshaw Mercantile that it meant nothing to her. ("It's fun, Sean," she says, "but don't get emotional.") Why'd he ever let himself think otherwise?

I couldn't stand to see.

But Tanner had forced him to face facts. "Hate to see a friend get suckered," he'd said.

Maybe it was better to finally accept it. Only now he imagined that everyone had been laughing at him behind his back—for years—for being such a slobbering fool. No better than James Bolinger. *Why didn't I have the guts to face it?*

"The thing is, though," he told Dinky Dowd who'd followed him to the hemlocks, "it doesn't even matter if I face it now, does it?"

"Nothin's changed," Dinky agreed.

"I still want her."

"That's nothin' new."

"And she doesn't want me."

"Nothin's changed."

Sean supposed he should leave now. This was his last stop. Time to cross the creek.

When he trudged back up the hill, he was startled to spot Patience Mathers standing at the entrance to the cemetery. He wouldn't have recognized her were it not for her long black hair; all her other features were washed away by the sunlight. Sean was sad to see her, for he knew what it meant.

This is my punishment, he realized then. *This is my hell.*

He could tell she didn't want to be here. That she was scared.

But being dead, she had no choice.

"Patience," he whispered. "I'm sorry I killed you."

PATIENCE DREADED ENTERING the graveyard. It was swarming and repulsive and she was having trouble swallowing, but she had to get to him first. Matherston Cemetery was always the last place Sean searched on his ghost hunt, so this was where Hazel would find them.

She fidgeted with the lucky charms at her wrist. The dice felt huge between her fingers—sixes all the way around. Lucky. *It's all I have.* She felt helpless and powerful at the same time.

Patience forced herself forward.

And they reached each other under the purple tree.

"I'm sorry, Patience." Sean wrapped his arms around her, hugging her tight. "I'm sorry."

Warmth flooded her but then Sean pulled back.

"Sorry for what?" she asked. He was shirtless so she unbuttoned her vest.

"I killed you."

"No, you didn't." She took his hand and placed it over her heart. "See? It beats."

"I'm dead," he said.

"No, you're not." She placed her palm flat against his chest. "See? Warm." Then she slid her fingers down to his belly but he stopped her and took her hand in his.

"It isn't like that with us," he said and she could tell from his eyes that he meant it.

"What does it matter, Sean, if we're dead?"

HAZEL PULLED THE melted ice cream bars from her sling and tossed them onto a fern beside the path. Her arm wasn't killing her for the first time since the Percocet wore off. The relief would be short lived.

After leaving her dog and the kids safely ensconced in the Never Tell Brothel, she had picked up the trail and continued west, growing hotter with every step as the sun rose to its most offensive position of the day and even the tall pines could no longer shield her path. She sucked in a long breath, careful to hold her tongue against her tormented tooth so as not to irritate the nerve. She was almost there.

When she arrived at the white granite wall Hazel retrieved a piece of blue chalk wedged at its base and scratched out I'M SORRY. Beneath that, she scrawled: SA → HW TFC X HRC.

The message turned out to be unnecessary because when she rounded the corner of the wall and saw a pair of black tennis shoes lying in the dirt, she knew she'd finally found Sean.

In her excitement, she forgot all about her battle wounds. She couldn't wait to see him and she marveled at how completely she'd missed him. She hadn't seen him since he came looking for her at the Crock on Monday morning, when she told him she didn't have time for him.

I don't have time for you? It was impossible for her to believe that she'd said that to him. *What the hell!* He was sick and confused and she couldn't make time for him? *How could I do that to you?*

She fully realized then how much her loneliness for him had drained her spirit; it was a wonder there was anything left of her. And as she ran to the entrance of the cemetery, she thought, *I have all the time in the world for you, Sean. The rest of my life, if you want it.*

As soon as she reached the wrought-iron gateway, she saw them.

"They move like ghosts," she whispered and wondered briefly if Aaron was right.

But their bare torsos appeared all flesh and blood.

The graveyard stood bleached beneath the noon sun. The weeds, the grave markers, the trees—all the same bleak tone. Hazel felt delirious from the blank heat and brilliant shock.

The charm bracelet reflected sunlight as she touched him and he took her hand. He spoke, but from so far away, Hazel could not hear what he was saying.

Hot and high, the sun washed Hazel's world away in an achromatic wave and she swayed on her feet, wondering what happened to all the air on the mountainside.

Then Sean saw her over Patience's exposed shoulder and his eyes took on a look of bewilderment.

Patience turned, followed his gaze to where Hazel stood in the wrought-iron gateway, and smiled that exquisite rodeo queen smile.

Hazel felt like somebody else entirely as she marched toward them at the plum tree, as if another entity had taken over her body and all she could do was keep out of the way and watch.

Sean appeared stunned to see her. He pulled away from Patience and released her hand.

Patience did not look one bit surprised, like when they were kids and she'd been following them.

This isn't happening, Hazel thought. *This. Is not. Happening!* She kicked a flat wooden grave marker in her path, splintering the word *Hanged* in two.

Sean reached for her, as if he wanted to touch her to verify that she was real the way his dad, Samuel, had thrown the candy dish at her in the hotel hallway. "I thought you left with Tanner," he said.

She dodged his grasp. "Does it look like I left, Sean?"

He staggered and shook his head like a boxer who'd taken a sucker punch.

"I stayed for *you.*" She poked a finger against his bare chest. "I've been looking for *you!*"

"What happened to your arm?" He reached for her again, eyes dark with concern.

"Don't touch me! Don't ever touch me again!" She noticed red slashes across his right forearm as if he'd been burned, but all she could think of was that arm around Patience. *This isn't happening.*

She glowered at Patience, who hadn't moved from Sean's side. Her eyes held that same hollowness as when Hazel had encountered her in Prospect Park the night before, made creepier still by the bright light in the cemetery.

"Hazel," Sean said softly, "you are so wrong—"

"I *saw* you," Hazel cried. "I've been looking for you everywhere and finally I really saw you!"

"Don't do this…" He wore that same helpless look he used to get when he was still small and couldn't defend himself against Kenny Clark or his drunken father.

"I was so worried about you." Hazel placed her hand over her stomach as though the thought of it sickened her. "But now I see that you're fine. The two of you are just fine and dandy."

Patience said nothing, only scratched up and down her redstriped arms with that maddening sound.

"Hazel, come over here with me." Sean wrapped his hand around her fingers and pulled her away from Patience.

"Let go of me!" She squirmed out of his grip and then pressed her hand against her cheek.

"What's wrong with your mouth?" he asked.

"Nothing." She let the hand drop. "I broke my tooth."

"Were you eating candy?"

"Yes—damn you." The urge to cry nearly overwhelmed her, but she would not let them witness her heart breaking.

His face drawn with empathy, Sean said, "I would never do anything to hurt you, Hazel."

She narrowed her eyes at him. "I don't care enough about you, Sean, to get hurt."

The corners of his mouth shot down and he blinked hard against watering eyes. "Don't get close, don't get hurt. Is that how it works?" He grabbed her hand again. "So nobody will hurt you like your mother did?"

She shook him off, refusing to respond.

"It would never be that way with me." His eyes flashed anger. "Why don't you get that?"

"Hazel!" Patience screamed shrilly enough to wake every dead miner in the graveyard.

Hazel spun around.

"Look at me!" Completely nude now, Patience stood with her arms held out toward them, shaking and shivering like a wet cat. "Do you see me, Hazel?"

"I see you," she replied, "and you look pathetic."

Patience wrapped her arms across her chest, her respiration rapid. "I have to tell on him—what Sean did at the cabin." Her eyes glazed over. "'Cause Hawkin Rhone will punish us unless we tell the truth."

Hazel charged up to Patience and grabbed her by the hair. "If you say anything to anybody about what happened, I'll drown you in the deep pond. Do you understand me?"

At last the blank look in Patience's eyes broke; now her eyes registered surprise and fear. She nodded, gasped, "Understand."

Hazel let go of her and turned to face Sean, knowing she was about to start bawling and not caring anymore. "I was looking for you." She whimpered, wanting more than anything to touch him, to touch his mouth where it turned down at the corners. "Aaron's hiding in Matherston, scared and worried about you. He thinks you're dead."

"I am," Sean sounded anguished. Then he did touch her, traced her tears down her cheeks, along her jaw and under her chin, his amber eyes a swirl of confusion and longing.

She cried harder, tears dripping, nose running. "Tanner told me but I didn't believe him. With *her,* Sean? She told me, too, and I didn't believe her, either. I couldn't. How could you do this to me?" She turned from him, intending to leave because there was nothing left to say.

Until Patience spoke in a voice gone cold: "What's the big deal? I saw you with James Bolinger in Matherston."

Hazel whirled around to see the alarm on Sean's face.

"Hazel," he sounded horrified, "what did you do?"

"Nothing." And although it really *was* nothing, she worried that Sean would suspect there was more to the story. Because he always knew when she was lying. *(Doesn't he?* she thought. *Hasn't he all along?)* So she added honestly, "I gave him a kiss because he fixed my sling."

Sean looked inordinately upset—his face all twisted—as if she had just confessed to screwing Kenny Clark. "*James?* Why are *you* doing this to *me?*" He grabbed the Mudhoney sling where it hung from her shoulder and jerked her forward so that she stumbled against him.

"Sean, I didn't—"

"This is *his* fucking shirt!" He tightened his grip.

"He was only trying to help me." His rage terrified her.

"Never mind—I *get* it." The muscles in his arm tensed as if he were about to rip the sling the way the vampire had.

Now he was really hurting her. "Let me go, Sean!"

Instead, he yanked her close to his face. "Don't come looking for me anymore."

After he released his grip and shoved her away from him, she turned and raced out of the white ghost world of Matherston Cemetery.

She could not have felt more grief-stricken if Sean really were dead.

She wished *she* were dead.

Who knows? she thought, crossing through the iron gateway. *Maybe we all will be soon.*

PART THREE

Sometimes the past needs a good diggin' up if you aim to make peace with the nowadays.

—Dinky Dowd

ONE O'CLOCK

AARON SHRANK BACK against the picture window of Matherston Miners Supply. He couldn't feel the glass, or the frame, only the terror. Because they were *everywhere.*

Loud, rough men, the creases in their unshaven faces filled with grime. Crusty old boots pounded the wooden boardwalk, making the whole of Matherston shake.

Loud women, too, in tight dresses and bright makeup, laughing at the men, slapping away their hands, leading them into the Never Tell Brothel.

Shuddering, Aaron tried to close his eyes and cover his ears. Then he remembered Hazel telling him not to be scared, that they were friendly ghosts. That gave him the courage to move across the boardwalk onto the dirt road, not sensing his feet upon the ground, floating through the noise.

Searching for a friendly face, he looked up Prospectors Way toward the assay office where men whooped and kicked up their heels inside a cloud of silver dust billowing from the open doorway. Then he looked the opposite way, past the blacksmith's shop that was on fire and the people watching just laughed and laughed, and on past Holloway Harness where horses were escaping one by one, clomping and neighing frightfully, trampling anyone in their path.

Aaron's spirit sank: no friendly faces here.

He glanced at the second story of the Never Tell and wondered if Violet and Daisy Rhone were still up there. Suddenly he regretted leaving his friends. Daisy, especially, because she was so sick. What if the ghost ladies found them hiding in the room upstairs? Would they be in trouble?

As Aaron continued to look up, the sky shifted from bright blue to black. Music, fast and tinny, started up inside the brothel.

It struck him as funny that everyone in Winslow always called Matherston a ghost town, yet no one truly believed it.

Until now. No one could deny this was a ghost town now.

An ugly man in too-big jeans brushed against him—knocked into him on purpose maybe—and sent Aaron reeling toward the batwing doors of the Mother Lode Saloon. Once he landed, he scrambled like a crab to the hitching post and attempted to grab on to one leg of the post to keep grounded. As more men strolled past, some regarded him with amusement, others ignored him. None offered help.

The men seemed to know exactly where they were going, so why didn't Aaron know where to go? It would be better if his mom weren't so sick and could tell him what to do, like when she would bug him to come inside and eat his lunch or go outside and do the weeding. Aaron wanted more than anything to be back in his bedroom at The Winslow Hotel, feeling sleepy or hungry or bored. Not chilled to his core. Not afraid because the ghosts were in charge now.

A man who looked like Sheriff Winslow (but not like him at the same time) began to cross the street, heading straight for Aaron, who would've given anything to see the real Sheriff Winslow right then: his bike, his new video games, his allowance for a whole year—anything. Instead, he could only try to hide better, to become even more invisible, to try and keep this ghost from stealing his soul.

The man kept coming, all swinging arms and long, sure strides, paralyzing Aaron with his purposefulness. When he reached Aaron, he leaned into the hitching post, crossed his arms and stared hard at Aaron as if he'd been waiting a long time to give the boy a good talking to.

Aaron's brother, Sean, always said that it's only stories. That the ghosts aren't real. So why did this feel like the most real thing that had ever happened?

Aaron noticed that one of the man's hands was missing, his arm ending at the wrist in raggedy-looking skin and splintered bone.

"Name's Guy Marsh," the man didn't say out loud. He gestured toward his mangled arm with the one hand that he still had. "Mining accident," he offered by way of explanation.

Aaron caught a huge whiff of the man as he moved. Like the other ghosts, this one smelled bad. Rotten, oozing potatoes and soggy black leaves—the smell of a body that has spent time in the ground.

Aaron realized then that he had lost his own body again.

Panic struck. Where had he left himself this time? Was anybody taking care of his body, or was he just lying out in the open where coyotes and wolves could eat him?

"What is it, son?" Guy smiled crookedly, his jaw broken in half. "Cat got your tongue?"

Another terrifying prospect struck Aaron then: What if one of the ghosts stole his body? What if it walked around pretending to be seven years old, fooling everyone and doing stuff it shouldn't be doing? Bad stuff that would get Aaron into bad trouble if he ever got back inside himself again.

"Where am I?" Aaron cried voicelessly.

Guy Marsh regarded him with great sympathy on his dented face. A "now, now, easy there" expression that Aaron knew meant something was really seriously wrong.

Aaron wanted to run away from that look, but he had no legs.

Had he arms, he would have crawled.

The ghost leaned closer to Aaron then, bringing along a fresh wave of old death to smother him. "If nobody's home, son," Guy gently asked, "how long before your body goes cold?"

TANNER

THIS IS HER FAULT, thought Tanner Holloway. *This is all Hazel Winslow's fucking fault.*

He glanced at his new pal Kenny Clark as they clomped along the boardwalk on Fortune Way. Kenny was wolfing down a cold hot dog he'd helped himself to in Clemshaw Mercantile, that look of determination that said, *Get 'em,* still pasted on his ugly mug.

"Stale as shit." Kenny spit pieces of bun when he talked. "Nothing to eat around here."

Tanner blew out a breath. *Guess you were busy scratching your ass while the rest of the class went over that it's* the bread, *you moron.* Tanner had no appetite, hadn't in three days. He was too busy worrying about how much longer he could hide it. Because his limp was getting worse and whenever anyone got too close they'd ask, *What's that awful smell?*

So no matter how well he continued to play the cooperative buckaroo, somebody would figure him out soon. Then they'd take him to the Pest House or trap him in a ditch and light him on fire. And he felt like he was running a fever, too. *Impossible to tell in this heat.*

Passing the Crock, he saw that the dining room sat empty except for tables littered with dirty dishes, and chairs scattered and knocked over.

"I gotta take a piss," he told Kenny. "I'll catch up with you."

"All right, meet in the park," Kenny said. "And don't take all damn day."

Tanner pulled open the Crock's glass door in a cacophony

of bells, then it was quiet inside except for the buzz of gorging flies. Food sat untouched on plates; the heat had baked eggs dry and petrified the bacon. Black coffee sat thick in mugs. The stench of spoiled milk and rotting food nearly floored him. He gagged his way to the back as quick as he could manage, dragging his left leg across the linoleum, shoving chairs out of his way.

This is her fault. He spat on the floor. Caged, while whatever the hell sort of rot this was grew in his leg and the whole town grew even nastier. Hazel Winslow's fault, no doubt about it.

But the rot itself? Tanner flipped over a small plate and two slices of old toast went flying. *That's thanks to Sean Adair.*

"What a dumb fuck." His voice rang loud in the deserted Crock. "What an arrogant, apologizing, moldy-bread-delivering dumb fuck."

Then Tanner had an enticing realization: *All I have to do is tell Kenny.* A smile formed on his lips. *I'll just casually mention it,* a tasty thought, *and let those two jack-offs cancel each other out.*

That'll get her where she hurts. Tanner laughed and spat again. "Whatsamatter, Hazel? Is that knife in Sean's back breaking your cold little heart, cousin?"

He pushed open the men's room door, flipped on the light, and slid the door lock into place. Then he went around the partition that separated the urinal from the can, flung down the toilet seat lid and plunked onto it. Hot stale air enveloped him.

Pausing a moment, he shut his eyes and took deep breaths. *Don't panic, just take a look.*

He lifted his left leg and crossed it over his right knee, then carefully removed his tennis shoe and dropped it to the tile. *Deep breath on three.*

Holding his breath now, he peeled the sock off his foot—slowly, painfully—and as he did, stuff stuck to it…pieces of crunchy skin, pus-filled clumps of flesh, gooey strings of infection.

In a state of fascinated horror, he held up the sock to examine the detritus. *Oh, shit...*

Tanner glanced down at his foot: his ulcerated, blackened foot. The rot had crawled up and over his ankle now, creeping its way up his calf.

And suddenly the pain he'd been suffering for days went times a trillion. His foot looked dead, but his nerves sure as hell weren't. On active duty now, they bombarded his brain with signals that shrieked, *Red alert! Mayday! Do something already!*

Then a slow burn spread through him. *She's gonna pay.*

He turned the soiled sock inside out and then screamed at the agony of easing it back around his swollen foot. All his toenails were gone (stuck to the sock, he saw) except for the one on his pinky toe. One little piggy spared.

She is going to fucking pay.

PARD

"To your health," Pard Holloway toasted Fritz Earley.

"Here's how." Pete Hammond brought his own bottle to his lips.

Fritz sat on a stool at the bar next to Old Pete while Pard stood across from them like a friendly bartender. In the cool dark of the Buckhorn Tavern, they were just a few friends shooting the breeze over a tall one. Pard hadn't bothered asking Fritz where he'd gotten those cuts and bruises on his face. No mystery there. He grinned at Fritz before he took a long draw from his own bottle. The cold beer went down easy. This day had developed into the most blistering yet, the afternoon sun beating down with a matchless fury.

Pard noticed Fritz hadn't touched his beer, only sat there looking as nervous as a pecked hen. "Drink up!" he urged.

Eyeing Pard warily, Fritz raised his bottle and took a sip.

"First of all," Pard addressed both men, "things are fouled up to be sure. But if we keep our heads, we can contain the damage. A lot's been lost, but a lot can be salvaged."

They both agreed, no argument expected.

"'Course we all know that keeping it dry is desirable in these sorts of situations. And I respect a man's right to keep his mouth from shooting off in directions that might harm his own interests. But between us, Earley—" Pard implied that the three of them constituted a convivial *us* "—how, precisely, did this happen?"

"Hard to say." Fritz shook his head and looked even more anxious.

"Strikes me as odd that Zachary Rhone didn't notice anything peculiar." Pard tried to sound chummy. "Does it you?"

"Listen, Holloway." Sweat broke free across Fritz's forehead. "It was an accident. You beat up on me to find cheaper feed, remember? Didn't you tell me either get it cheaper or you'd get yourself a new supplier? Now this happened."

"Let's stop beating the devil around the stump here." Pard maintained his pleasant tone. "We'll all be taking our fair hit, but we'll help each other out as best as we can, won't we? I'd hate to see anybody suffer disproportionately over what you yourself said was only an accident."

Fritz appeared suspicious. "I'll reimburse you for your losses, if that's what you're getting at, above and beyond actual. You and Rhone both." He took a fast swig of beer. "I insist."

"That's generous of you. Don't you think, Pete?"

Old Pete nodded. "Been expectin' you'll pay."

"Does Rhone feel the same about keeping things between us?" Fritz asked.

"Don't worry about him," Old Pete said.

Pard cocked his head inquisitively. "What I'm really interested in knowing, Fritz, is the full extent of this situation."

"It's only here." Fritz looked hopeful now, as if he thought Pard might be glad to hear that. "The situation's contained in Winslow."

Old Pete said, "Difficult to fathom this occurring at all, what with testing these days."

"Oh, it still happens," Fritz quickly defended, "from time to time."

"Apparently." Pard chuckled and Fritz finally loosened up and laughed a bit with him. Then Pard asked, "So what happens next?"

Fritz shook his head again and repeated, "Hard to say."

But Pard could tell it wasn't because Fritz didn't know,

it was because Fritz didn't want Pard to hear it. He stared at Fritz for a long moment before he leaned across the bar and harshly whispered, *"Try."*

Fritz gasped.

"Try!" Pard snatched up his beer bottle and slammed it into the side of Fritz's head. The bottle exploded against the man's scalp and skull and Pard grabbed Fritz by the neck before he could slip under the bar. "Would it be *hard to say* just what the hell you were thinking when you brought ergot-contaminated feed up to my ranch and poisoned my herd?"

Bloody beer ran down the side of Fritz's head and dripped loudly onto the bar.

"Would it be *hard* to say just what the hell you thought you were doing delivering poison flour to this town's only bakery?" Pard continued.

Fritz was slipping out of Pard's grasp, desiring only to pass out on the floor, it looked like, but Old Pete grabbed him by the back of the collar and wedged him against the bar.

Pard yelled in Fritz's face, "Would it be hard for you to say that you'll clean this mess up or die trying?"

Fritz sputtered, "People are looking for me by now."

"What people? Nobody's looking for you. In fact, I'd bargain you didn't tell a soul you were coming up here." Pard looked at Pete. "This get-together is officially over. Take him back."

"To the Pest House?" Old Pete asked. "Sure you wanna do that?"

Pard studied Fritz for a moment; the man did not look good. "Just as well let things run their course. And Pete—leave out the particulars, but make certain they get the gist of our conversation here."

PARD SAT ALONE at the bar after they left. Not drinking, thinking.

Earlier, when he'd returned to town from the bridge and

saw for himself the bakery burned to the ground, he'd thought, *Just what I need.* But the fire had been put out quickly, Tiny Clemshaw had informed him. So the situation hadn't turned into a problem as far as Sparks would be concerned. Though it did worry Pard some to see Clemshaw both sick and on the shoot—that combination could easily turn into a problem. *And the fact that nobody's getting any better is a problem.* If you counted Zachary Rhone, who Pard figured for ash since he hadn't managed to cause Pard any further trouble, that made at least two dead already. Things were fouled-up, all right. And the bloody mess inside the Rhone house and spread across the yard—that was definitely a problem.

His niece Hazel also posed a problem, undermining his authority and asking questions he wasn't keen to answer. *And dammit, she really does look just like Anabel when she's all fired up.*

At five years his junior, Anabel used to follow Pard everywhere and he'd be damned if he'd let his kid sister tag along with him and his buddies. But there she'd be with her fishing pole or baseball mitt or wearing her swimsuit with the yellow daisies—the right equipment for wherever she guessed they were headed. He'd yell at her to get lost and she'd turn fightin' mad, eyes flashing that same green he saw in Hazel's eyes last night when she'd pounded on his chest.

Pard sighed, worn-out tired. *We need to get things tidied up, is all,* he thought. He was gambling that nobody would come looking for Fritz Earley. *Because now we really can't let anybody see the hash we've made of things up here.*

What Pard needed was to get back to the ranch to check on his herd. He *wanted* to get back to his ranch where things were manageable. Because the longer he remained in town, the more he felt the reins slipping from his hands.

He swiveled off the bar stool and left the Buckhorn, shoving through batwing doors and into the brutal sunlight. Blackjack was tied to the hitching post in front of the tavern and Pard started on the knot that would release him.

The town was quiet save for the drone of a vehicle accelerating and what sounded like the car dragging something, its bumper maybe. Peering across the park, Pard saw a brown Plymouth moving fast: Old Man Mathers driving fifty damn miles an hour down Park Street. *He's gonna kill somebody,* Pard worried.

After mounting Blackjack, Pard rode across Fortune Way and into the shade of Prospect Park. When he reached the playground he stopped short of the swings to observe his cowhands working the area. Tanner was with them, bobbing along on the back of Kenny Clark's chestnut Morgan. He and Kenny were shouting back and forth to each other and laughing. Laughing? They were acting real friendly—best buddies. *When the hell did that happen?* Pard wondered.

Making a noise, *"Scheww,"* Pard pulled off his hat and mopped his face with a bandanna. He wanted to make his nephew into a man and maybe there was hope after all. Tanner had been cooperating all day; Pard was truly surprised the kid had it in him. And he wanted to feel pleased—but dammit if those weren't the Marshes over there by the duck pond. The very same people he'd ordered home yesterday at sunset. Pard *scheww*ed again as he replaced his hat and steered Blackjack in their direction.

To Pard's astonishment, Kenny and Tanner suddenly gave chase after Jay Marsh, Kenny twirling a lariat above his head while Tanner crouched out of the way behind him and held on for dear life. Before Jay could scramble under the monkey bars Kenny effortlessly tossed the rope over the man's head and jerked it tight around his bare torso, pinning his arms inside. After turning his horse to yank Jay to the ground Kenny leapt off and then pulled the kid down next.

Pard saw the shock hit Tanner's face when he landed on his

left leg. Pard had noticed at the bridge that Tanner had gotten himself roughed up at some point and was limping pretty bad. Pard had truly hoped then, as now, that the limp was the result of Blackjack dragging his nephew around the rodeo ring and nothing more.

Kenny shoved the rope into Tanner's hands. Then he pushed Tanner toward where Jay lay squirming in the grass at the other end of the rope. The kid hauled himself over and began to hog-tie Jay Marsh, who was yelling, "Stop! I'm a human being!"

They're too rough now, Pard admitted. *How many times has this line been crossed?*

From where he was still working the rope around Jay's ankles, Tanner looked up when Pard reached him. At first the kid's face registered fear—as if he thought he was about to get it. But then Tanner smiled…a huge grin through that mess of pale hair, like he knew his uncle approved, like he was proud of himself. And Pard felt the reins completely slip away.

HAZEL

HEEDLESS TO THE aggravation that running caused her injuries, Hazel pounded down the trail, her ends disturbingly loose.

Fighting with Patience Mathers was hardly unusual. She and Patience had often fought when they were younger: over a game of jacks ("I already did twosies"), over who got the last Louie-Bloo Raspberry Otter Pop, over Patience being so irritating, mainly.

This was only the third time Hazel had ever fought with Sean Adair.

The second was Monday morning in front of the Crock. The first was when they were eleven and Kenny Clark was beating the crap out of Sean in front of the Fish 'n Bait and Hazel intervened by smashing Kenny from behind with her skateboard. But that didn't stop Kenny from pummeling Sean some more and later Sean told her, "I can take care of myself."

And she'd said, "It didn't look like it."

And he'd spat, "Just leave me alone," before ditching her to lick his wounds in private.

Leave me alone... That sounded sorely familiar. *Don't come looking for me anymore.*

When she could run no more, she collapsed to the forest floor. Sprawled on a carpet of pine needles, licking her own wounds, she wished Bigfoot would come and carry her away to his Sasquatch digs, where they'd eat blackberries and communicate using hand gestures and grunts.

But he didn't come for her.

So after she caught her breath, she rose and staggered down

the trail—the sun beating down on her like a different kind of hot-breathed monster—and headed back to town. Nowhere else to go. No idea what to do next. Not even thinking about it, really, just making her way along the path, bleary-eyed, trying not to smash her hurt arm into any branches.

I'm shell-shocked, she realized.

Matherston Cemetery had been another unimaginable nightmare. Like last night when she had seen how twisted and tormented everyone had become at the hotel, or viewing the gruesome remains of Melanie Rhone while her dad stood quietly growing gangrenous, or the vampire attacking her in Second Chance Mine that morning.

Nightmares. Surely not reality. Surely those things did not happen to her.

Unthinkable.

Popping out of the woods onto Winslow Road, Hazel longed to see Sheriff Riley Washburn's patrol car cruising up the blacktop. (Riley and her dad liked to shoot the breeze over a shot of bourbon on the back porch of The Winslow.) An ambulance speeding past with its sirens whirring would've been good, too. Or that forest service helicopter from her dream.

Yet all was still… No vehicles approached, no breeze quaked the aspens, there was only the flat sound of her tennis shoes hitting the road and the incessant drone of insects going about the routine business of their unremarkable day.

She considered hiking to the fire lookout. Sparks Brady would have his radio; her dad yakked with him all the time. ("See those thunderheads forming east of the ridge?") And Sparks was certain to be manning the tower during this heat wave.

There was only one problem. When her dad had taken her to see the tall tower and meet the rangy Sparks a few summers ago, they'd traveled for hours by fire road in the Jeep. How long would it take her to hike to the tower as the crow flies, along rough deer trails and across raging creeks? Would she get lost in the forest?

I'll lose my bearings, I know it. It'd be just a matter of time.

So the idea was abandoned by the time she reached the church graveyard at the edge of town. She half expected to see Sean and Patience among those headstones, too, and flashed on that awful image: everything toneless except her hair, long and black down her back; his, soft and brown across his shoulders. Hazel stared straight into the high sun. *Burn it from my eyes.*

Blinking away sunspots, she entered town and started up Fortune Way, careful to avoid piles of road apples left by horses. *Patience and Sean can rot happily ever after in this shit hole, for all I care.* But no matter how much righteous indignation she managed to drum up, it quickly drowned in her deep sorrow. Everything Hazel thought she knew was turning out to be wrong. Everything.

Life moved up along Fortune Way, ranch hands mostly. She avoided eye contact with them as though they were vicious dogs, refusing to let them see her fear.

At least now that she was no longer consumed with finding Sean, she could tend to other things. Such as her broken body. She decided to hit the Mercantile for drugs—benzocaine for her tooth, some aspirin, something stronger with any luck— and hoped that Tiny Clemshaw wasn't still wielding his shotgun with that same indiscriminate rancor.

Up ahead, a woman who looked like Tilly Thacker with gray hair gone wild gave Hazel a frightened gape before dashing between Mathers Bank and the Crock. Though Hazel had no reason to think this weirdness was directed at her personally, it left her feeling even more unsettled all the same.

Because it felt different in town now. And unnaturally . quiet.

Everywhere, that is, except the Buckhorn Tavern, which

was raucous with country music and shouts and boot stomps and compulsive laughter, as though all the noise in Winslow had been rounded up and sequestered in that one establishment.

Two ranch hands exited Prospect Park right in front of her. To join in the racket at the bar, she guessed. Both men stopped to eyeball her, and after one mumbled something close to the other's ear, they both laughed—the same sort of forced laughter that was coming out of the Buckhorn. Then they continued past her, one on each side so that she was surrounded for several frightening moments.

This business bodes ill, her grandmother's words echoed.

As Hazel continued toward the Mercantile, she grew angrier and angrier: at the cowboys and the fact that they truly were scaring her and everybody else; at her uncle's bullheadedness and her dad's incapacitation; and about nobody but her seeming to care that the whole stinking town had capsized.

Worst of all, Hazel's heart wrenched, *what I most wanted to find wants to stay lost to me.*

Just past Cal's Fish 'n Bait, Hazel was jolted out of her anger when she noticed a still heap in the space between the bait shop and Clemshaw Mercantile. She backed up and took two steps toward the body lying prone in the passageway before recognizing him.

"Oh, Cal…"

He lay crumpled up in the dirt, broken-looking legs tangled in fishing line, the pole snapped in two beneath his hips. Cal still grasped his reel in one hand, the foam cup of worms crushed inside the other.

Hazel groaned, heart-stricken. "Did you fall off the roof?" When she stepped closer, she saw that a crack high on his forehead gaped wide and oozed dark. She whimpered loudly in shock and sympathy. Then she whispered, "I hope you caught the big one, Cal."

She left him for the store. Tiny Clemshaw no longer guarded the front of the Mercantile. In fact, he was nowhere in sight even when she entered. Despite the ceiling fans spinning so fast they looked about to launch, it was smothery inside. And while the store looked empty, it didn't feel it. *Make it quick,* she told herself.

She hurried past the checkout counter with its jars of beef jerky and racks of chips, while the fan blades continued their ineffectual *whomp, whomp.* Then she made a tight right into the last aisle, which contained the medicine and elixirs and cleaning supplies.

That was when she saw Tiny Clemshaw on the second floor of the Mercantile, leaning forward against the railing that overlooked the main floor. The man stood so stock-still—face waxen, eyes void—that at first she mistook him for a mannequin.

He gave no indication that he'd noticed her in the store below, only stared straight ahead, frozen in place by some mysterious force.

Whomp, whomp, whomp.

She snatched a package of paper tablecloths from the picnic supplies shelf and turned and hustled down the aisle. Along the way, she grabbed a bottle of aspirin off the top shelf without stopping or daring to glance up at the second floor. Then she left the Mercantile without Tiny ever acknowledging that she was there.

Returning to Cal's body in the passageway she ripped the tablecloth out of its plastic wrapper. "You were safe locked up, Cal. Who let you out of jail?"

Since her right hand operated only as a flipper sticking out of the sling, she moved awkwardly as she unfolded the tablecloth then flicked it out like a sheet above the body and eased it down to cover him. She had never formally picnicked, yet the red-and-white-checkered pattern made her think of fried chicken and ants. Blood instantly seeped through the white section of paper draping Cal's head.

Trying to swallow the sadness stuck in her throat, she walked away. As she did, she tucked away this incident, completely incapable of processing yet another loss.

I should've gotten a drink, too, she realized once she was back out on the sidewalk staring at the bottle of aspirin in her hand that she'd stolen from the store. But she was afraid to return and risk rousing Tiny out of his stupor.

The din coming from the Buckhorn had increased. Holloway Ranch headquarters, she figured. *Okay,* she tried to steel herself. It was time for everyone to face facts: Melanie Rhone—murdered, Zachary Rhone—most likely burned to death, Cal—dead in the alley. *What's next?*

People are going to develop gangrene. That's what. Maybe they already had; she did not intend to go up to The Winslow to find out. But she was going into that bar. And they were going to listen to her. And they were going to agree that it was time to open the bridge and send somebody down for help.

As she approached, the voices of men carried to her from the tavern, along with the easily recognizable, annoying, high-pitched laughter of one boy: Tanner Holloway.

Sheer panic sliced through Hazel, obliterating all thoughts except for one: *He didn't make it out.*

The realization froze her in place because it meant that Tanner had been on the loose all this time, angry at her for refusing to go with him, pissed-off and mouthy and out on the town.

She placed her hand over her pounding heart. *He's the only other person alive who knows Sean's role in all of this.* With sudden terror, Hazel understood just how dangerous that made Tanner Holloway and his big, fat mouth.

She pitched the bottle of aspirin into the street and marched toward the bar.

After pushing through the batwing doors into the Buckhorn, she spotted him right away. His back to the door, he drank from a longneck bottle of beer next to Kenny Clark at the bar. There were roughly fifteen ranch hands in the tavern, which meant most of her uncle's men. All of them, maybe, except Pard himself and Old Pete and Maggie Clark. Hazel didn't care.

They all watched—amused, it seemed to her—as she stalked up behind Tanner and then struck him with her fist on the side of his head.

He spun around on the bar stool with a stunned look on his face. "What the hell?"

"Why didn't you leave?" she demanded.

"Because *you* fiddle-fucked around too long." He smoothed his hair as if he still couldn't believe she'd hit him.

Somebody pulled the plug on the jukebox and Hank Williams' "Your Cheatin' Heart" *whrooed* to a stop.

"Why did you lie?"

His mouth twitched upward. "Why did I lie about what?"

"The quarantine, for starters."

"I can't imagine what you're talking about." The mouth widened into a shit-eating grin.

He winced when she grabbed a handful of his blond hair. "Why'd you bring up my mother?"

Tanner unfurled her grip on him, then squeezed her hand so tight she marveled her bones didn't crumble. "Thought you'd want to know where she is." He squeezed harder. "Don't you?"

"Not anymore." Hazel really needed Tanner to let go of her hand. "She's been lying to me all along. Letting me believe it was my fault. She's just like the rest of you Holloways. All liars."

The men around the bar leaned in, not wanting to miss a word. Kenny Clark sat cross-armed on the bar stool beside them, a smug look planted on his face as he lapped it up, too.

"I'd never tell a lie." Tanner finally released her to make

the Scout's honor sign with one hand and a simple, middle-fingered *f-you* with the other.

Kenny Clark laughed in her ear and she batted her hand that direction but didn't take her eyes off Tanner's sneer. "I really wish you'd left," Hazel said.

"It's your fault I'm still here!"

"I wish you'd never come here in the first place."

Tanner squinted pale eyes at Hazel before he got off his bar stool to stand in front of her—his face only inches from hers, but she didn't back off. Then he said loud and clear, "Just answer me one thing, Hazel: Why'd that dumb-ass do it?"

Her stomach sank. She glanced around the bar—the cowboys were quiet, staring at them.

She looked back at Tanner. "Shut up."

"Why?" He shrugged as if to say, *Sorry, sucker.* "It's a damn good question, you have to admit."

"Shut up." Her heart was thumping so loud she worried they could all hear it. "Do not say another word."

"But everyone wants to know." He gestured around the Buckhorn, grinning like the devil, and suddenly the men in the bar were snickering at her. "C'mon, you remember what we talked about yesterday. Here, I'll refresh your memory—we talked a lot about flour."

Her stomach dissolved completely. She leaned closer to him and harshly whispered, "Like it or not—and I for one do not—we are family, Tanner, and you *swore.*"

"Gee…" Tanner scratched his head. "Now I'm the one who can't remember. What exactly did I swear to again?" He looked past her. "Do you remember what it was, Kenny?"

Kenny stood up from his cowhide bar stool and climbed onto the bar to better address the eager audience. "Sean Adair knew the flour—"

Hazel sidestepped Tanner to the bar and wrapped her good arm around Kenny's left leg at the knee and yanked hard.

Caught completely off guard, Kenny's balance buckled, sending him crashing against the bar and then the bar stool before he finally slammed down on his back on the hardwood floor. Kenny yelped when he hit the floor, then grunted as he tried to right himself like an overturned turtle.

Before he could recover Hazel kicked him twice in the head, screaming, "I warned you, Kenny Clark. I warned you that if you even *said his name again* I'd kick your ass!"

The ranch hands didn't interfere—but did, in fact, cheer her on to the accompaniment of Tanner's high laughter while Kenny tried to roll out of kicking range and she connected with his rib cage.

Then over the blood rushing through her ears she heard her uncle boom, "What the hell's going on here?" and everyone immediately simmered down.

Hazel gave a solid kick to Kenny's face and his nose went crooked and red. Even then she hardly felt through with him. When she swung back her leg for another go, strong arms grabbed her up and off her feet from behind, crushing her tender elbow in an explosion of fresh agony. Then Pard carried her across the tavern as easily as if she were a tantruming child. He set her back on her feet just inside the doorway where Old Pete stood looking confounded.

With the back of her hand she wiped at the sweat dripping into her eyes. Then, between gulps of air, she told her uncle, "This has gone way too far."

"Obviously." Pard steered her against the swinging doors before moving in front of her to try and block the spectacle of his niece from view of the rest of the bar. "What's going on here?"

She could still see Kenny on the floor, moaning, while blood poured between the fingers he cupped to his face. "She broke my nose!" he screamed.

Tanner sauntered up and stood next to their uncle, keeping his mouth shut for once, but his self-satisfied grin said, *You are dead meat.*

Hazel was shaking so bad she had to grab hold of a batwing door for support. "*Do* something about them," she implored Pard. "You created these monsters."

From what felt like out of nowhere, Old Pete said, "That leg's gonna have to come off."

Hazel followed Pete's watery, old man eyes to Tanner's left leg…to the black and the ulcers and the swelling that were creeping up from his foot and above his sock. *Gangrene,* she refused to speak the word aloud. But the sound of her bare knees knocking together was loud and clear.

"Right away." Old Pete didn't bother to sugarcoat it. "It's got to come off right away."

Tanner shot a panicked look at Pard, who was staring at the leg in horror. When Pard met Tanner's gaze, Hazel could see that for the first time their uncle wasn't in charge. That he wasn't going to fight Old Pete on this. And she actually felt sorry for Tanner, like when Blackjack was dragging him around the rodeo field and nobody did a thing to stop it.

"Fuck that!" Tanner darted between them, knocking Hazel aside and slipping out of Pard's grasp as he fled the Buckhorn.

Pard made a move as if to go after Tanner but Old Pete stayed him with a hand on his shoulder, saying, "He won't get far."

"This is your doing," Hazel shouted at her uncle. "This is *your* doing!"

He didn't seem to hear her; he appeared to be in shock. He looked at Old Pete. "You know what this means?" Pard glanced around at the other men in the bar, clearly avoiding looking directly at their legs and feet. "All of you—do you know what this means?"

"Means any of us could come down with it," Old Pete replied.

"That's right. Didn't I order all of you to keep off the bread?

Back to the ranch! Every last one of you. We've got our own quarantine now."

Kenny yelled, "I'm not going anywhere until I settle up with that Winslow witch." He sounded stuffed up from the blood congealing inside his nose.

If only she were a witch, Hazel wished, she'd cast a spell to make him disappear.

"A Holloway cowboy *never* barks at the boss," Pard shouted. "Got that? Now get your ass up off the floor, Clark. Boys—get him back to the ranch. Then help him pack up his gear and clear outta the bunkhouse for good."

Kenny struggled to his feet, head bowed in humiliation, trying to avoid the stares of the other ranch hands. Once up, he pleaded with Pard, "Give me another chance, boss. I don't have anywhere else to go. There's nowhere else I want to go."

Pard shook his head. "This is not the first trouble I've had with you, Clark. But it's the last."

Kenny glared hatefully at Hazel. *This is not over,* his eyes promised.

"Let's move it out," Old Pete called.

The men rose from their chairs and off bar stools, grumbling and knocking bottles to the floor like *who gives a shit anymore if things get dirtied up?*

"All right, all right, all right!" Pard hollered. "Do it orderly."

Hazel grabbed her uncle by the arm. "You can't leave! You and your damage control! It's thanks to you trying to control everything that everything has spun completely *out* of control."

The steadfast resolve that reliably occupied her uncle's eyes dissolved into uncertainty. "I've done as much as I can for this town, Hazel. Time now to protect what's left of my ranch. You can come with us. That's the best I can do for you."

"Even now?" This was unbelievable. "You saw Tanner's

leg! He can't be the only one and you know it. And have you seen Cal lying dead in the dirt?"

But Pard's eyes had gone impassive again. A bottle broke against the jukebox and he turned from her to yell at the cowboy responsible, "I said orderly, dammit!"

She stared at his rigid back for a moment before deciding, *What's the use?* and pushed her way out of the bar and onto the sidewalk.

Unfuckingbelievable.

Tanner was already long gone. Blinking against the harsh sunlight, she thought, *It must hurt him to run. Really hurt him.*

Then she stumbled away from the Buckhorn, across Fortune Way, and stopped to stare into the deserted park, feeling every bit as empty as it looked.

This was early Wednesday afternoon. Summertime. The little kids should be playing in Prospect Park, running and screaming and pestering the ducks while Ben Mathers shouts from his porch, "Keep it down to a dull roar, will you?" before he slams his screen door shut.

But there were no children, no Mathers on his porch, no sign that anything was the way it should be. She closed her eyes and swayed on her feet, trying to picture the park as it had been on Saturday, filled with people and rides and music... but found it impossible to imagine.

I want things back the way they were. An astonishing admission, she realized, since she'd hated the way things were before any of this happened.

Opening her eyes just enough to shuffle into the park, suddenly too tired to properly lift her feet, she reached the swings and plunked down onto a canvas seat.

The lack of food and sleep, the relentless heat and shocks, had all taken their own greedy toll on her. *Out of service,* she thought, *down for repairs.*

Holding one chain, head bent because it felt too heavy to

hold up anymore, Hazel stared at her feet. Her tennis shoes were caked with dirt, the fabric coming apart at one heel, and it looked like blood had stained the rubber by her left big toe. Melanie's, maybe. Cal's, too, she supposed.

A moan issued from deep inside her chest.

She'd need new shoes after this was over. Her dad would take her down to the valley as soon as he felt better. They'd shop, not for long because they both hated it, but he'd be feeling a lot better and they'd get lunch at Gino's, which was always a big deal because there was no pizza place in Winslow.

She began to swing but it proved too tricky using only one arm so she skidded to a stop. Then she wondered, *Who else has gangrene?* Stretching away her sling just enough to steal a glance inside, she was relieved to see that while still colorful, her arm wasn't black with gangrene.

Using one foot in the dirt, she pivoted the swing around like she and Patience always did whenever they tired of swinging, and remembered her mother pushing her on this very swing the day before she left for good. Hazel shot an angry glance westward, figuring her mother must be somewhere that direction, and cried, "How could you even look at me, knowing what you were about to do?"

All at once Hazel felt as laid bare as she had that day, when she was waiting for her mother to come home for lunch, having no appetite for SpaghettiOs in her absence. Then dinner came and went with still more uneaten SpaghettiOs because that was all her dad could think to cook for them.

Now Hazel kept turning with her foot, twisting up the chains. Finally, she pulled both feet off the ground and the swing spun her in circles until the chains broke free of each other.

Feeling dizzy, she thought, *I've lost my bearings. Thanks to you, Anabel, I lost them a long time ago.*

With some effort, she pulled herself up from the swing and

went to the little red merry-go-round. Climbing onto the metal platform, Hazel imagined her mother giving her a good spin. Round and round, faster and faster. Only now her mother's pushing seemed cruel. She was only a small girl, why did her mother push so hard? Maybe Anabel hoped that if she spun fast enough, Hazel would fall off into the dirt and crack her head open, or be flung through the air and hit a tree. Then Anabel wouldn't have to leave Winslow just to get away from her daughter.

Hazel felt the anger that had been simmering for years bubble to the surface, as if all the terrible things that were happening now had turned up the heat. "How could you leave me?" Hazel gripped the metal handle so hard her wrist ached, as if the merry-go-round were spinning too fast and she had to find a way to hold on. "How could you let me think it was my fault?"

Her rage finally boiled over. "It's *your* fault! And it's *your* fault Sean left me, too—*you* made me this way!"

In her despair, Hazel realized that she should've said goodbye to her dad before racing off from the Rhones' place to look for Sean. Her heart filled with regret. What if she never saw him again? *I should've told him goodbye. My mother should've told me goodbye.*

Feeling ruined, she pushed off from the merry-go-round and headed for the duck pond, intending to dip her feet in the water, rinse the blood from her shoe, maybe dunk her miserable head.

Sunlight glinted off something in the grass a dozen feet ahead. Hazel approached slowly, the object sparking more golden light as she neared. She stopped just short of it and gazed down. A miniature pair of dice, a wishbone, a golden horseshoe. *Oh, no.* Patience's charm bracelet.

She visualized Patience's wrist, bare and fragile without the bracelet. And imagined that, bereft of her lucky charms, she would feel helpless and vulnerable. Then she remembered the brutal red welts she'd seen all over Patience's pale skin, remembered how annoyed she'd been by the sound of her scratching.

Hazel suddenly felt ashamed. "Oh, Patience," she whispered, "I am so sorry." *Why didn't I see how sick you are? Why didn't I care? I should've helped you bury the broken mirror in the moonlight.*

She bent to retrieve the jewelry from the grass, wondering why Patience had come this way after leaving the cemetery. Staring at the bracelet in her hand, seeing all the charms she had given to Patience over the years, it suddenly dawned on Hazel: *It wasn't Sean you wanted attention from.* She rolled the charms against her palm. *It was me. All along, it was me.*

She shoved the bracelet into her pocket, hoping she'd have the opportunity to return it.

Hazel slogged over to the duck pond, where she stepped on the heel of first one then the other tennis shoe, pulling her feet out. Then she eased the dirty shoes into the water.

There were no living ducks around. But several dead ones lined the top of the wall at the far side of the pond. And Julie and Jay Marsh sat on the low wall surrounding the pond, legs in the water up to their knees. Since neither wore clothes, it struck Hazel that the pile she'd encountered in the park last night had indeed been theirs.

Jay gave Hazel a smile that seemed to say, *Well, here we are,* as if things were destined to come to this. He had some nasty bruises on his face, and his right cheek was sunken and dented in a way that looked painful. He also had what appeared to be rope burns on his arms.

Hazel felt no compulsion to ask how he'd sustained these injuries. Instead, she sat down on the wall a dozen feet away, plunged her feet into the pond, then put her hands into the water and rubbed them together in a cleansing motion.

When she leaned back up, she peered across the park to where her house sat forgotten.

Then she stared at her toes in the pond, her mind empty now. There was nothing left to think about. And as she sat, a welcome numbness began to fill the empty spaces, leaving her feeling nothing at all...not panic, nor fear, not the throbbing of her arm or ribs, not even her tooth. She had nothing left with which to feel. *All used up,* she thought dully.

She swished her feet around, sending ripples across the water. It was warmish but still felt good. Shallow, the pond was no good for swimming, only wading. But the ducks liked it. Usually. Not today.

Too sunny at the pond, she decided to head over to the shady oak—the tree she had never climbed again after it had spit her to the ground. First, she plucked her shoes out of the pond and set them on the wall to dry. Then she pulled her feet from the water and stood. Her limbs had filled with concrete while she'd briefly rested, so now she moved stiff-jointed like one of Aaron's action figures.

When she reached the cover of the expansive oak she dropped to her knees and swiveled to plop onto the cool grass.

Glancing up at The Winslow, Hazel remembered the brown car she'd seen pulling up the driveway while she was up on the water tower platform, then recalled her grandmother telling her Ben Mathers had paid her a hostile visit. He was such a blustery old fool that Hazel had dispelled the notion that he might be a threat to her grandmother.

Now she wondered if that may have been a mistake.

I am so incredibly tired, she thought, realizing that her eyes were barely open. She looked across the park toward Ruby Road, then her focus softened and she must have nodded off because the next thing she knew her head jerked and she couldn't remember what she'd just been thinking.

A large figure was tromping around on the flat roof of the

hotel. It turned in a slow circle, pointing up and down, counting all the trees in the forest. *Owen Peabody,* she guessed. *Or Bigfoot.* Same squat legs, same gorilla arms.

Tired... She surrendered and flopped down on her side in the grass.

Head cradled in her arm, she thought, *Julie and Jay naked in the duck pond. Sean would think that's completely hilarious,* and then she slept.

TANNER

DRAGGING HIS LAME leg up Silver Hill, trying to outpace the smell of rot that threatened to choke him, Tanner searched for a safe place to hide.

There was no way in hell he was letting them chop off his leg. *No way.*

He could picture it: Old Pete holding down his arms, Kenny clamped around his ankles, grinning like an imbecile, happy to help. Pete and Uncle Pard would swap a look—the one they always exchanged right before they lit animals on fire or beat some poor bastard—then Uncle Pard would loom over him wielding that same circular saw Doc Simmons had used to slice open Indigo's skull, with bits of the bull's hide and hair still stuck to the sharp metal blades. And right before his uncle fired up the saw, he would give Tanner a look near remorseful and say, "Drastic situations call for drastic measures."

No fucking way. It was so Civil War. *They're totally insane.*

The climb up Silver Hill seemed as difficult as scaling Mt. Everest. He glanced down at his useless leg. The black had crept up to his knee.

The thought crossed Tanner's mind that things that turn black are usually dead. Oranges left on the ground. Possums trapped in trash cans.

But not his leg—it'd be all right. The doctors would do their doctoring thing and fix him.

If they ever get here...

His fever must be raging, he figured, because the sun pounded the mountainside, yet he felt cold—his confused body producing sweats and chills at the same time. More worrisome, foamy spit kept collecting at the corners of his mouth. He'd wipe at it with his hand but more kept coming.

He looked again at his leg trailing in the weeds. The black moved a lot faster now, having gained a completely fucked-up momentum somewhere around late morning. Maybe it was his rapid heartbeat accelerating everything out of control. And recently the burning pain had given way to numbness. While a relief, he suspected it might not be such a good sign.

Dead things turn black, he couldn't help but think. *Smashed fingernails. Charred cows.*

He neared the gaping hole he knew to be Second Chance Mine. Sean had pointed it out to him Sunday when they were up on the water-tower platform.

Tanner wasn't sure why he had wanted to see Sean taken down from the start. Maybe it was the way Sean had scoped him out when they'd first met a few weeks ago. He hadn't missed Sean's look of dismissal, the one that says, *You're more mouth than motor, I can already tell.*

Tanner never missed that look. But whatever. *Who even cares what happens to Sean?*

Picking his way toward the mine around loose timbers and signs that warned, Danger and Do Not Enter, Tanner thought, *These signs are in the wrong place. Oughta be before you enter Winslow, before the bridge even.*

He caught his numb foot between a couple of boards but didn't even notice until he nearly yanked it out of its socket. Would he ever have feeling in that foot again?

He sighed. "Shit."

At Buckhorn Tavern, when Old Pete would not shut his pie hole about hacking off the leg, Hazel had looked at Tanner with that woe-is-you expression, as if he were pathetic. But she was the one who was pitiful—shaking and scared like she was a little girl again and Mommy still hadn't come home to tuck her beddy bye.

Okay, so maybe everything isn't totally Hazel's fault, Tanner conceded. Maybe if she hadn't dismissed him too he would've gone easier on her. Too late now.

Who cares anyway? He'd be back to riding his skateboard down the paved sidewalks of civilization in no time. His parents would come and get him, take him to Mercy Hospital where he'd had his tonsils removed, and then he'd never have to see any of these freaks again.

When he finally reached the entrance to the mine, he crawled through a hole in the boards that someone had pried clear. Tanner shivered after stepping in. It felt tombish inside—dark and dry and cool. But a decent hiding spot, he confirmed. He continued deeper, drawing his foot through the dirt, until he rounded a bend into total darkness.

"Far enough," he said aloud. The enclosed space distorted the sound of his voice. He crossed toward what he sensed to be the far wall, desiring a defensive position should anyone come back here.

He reached blindly for the wall but still fell short. Pulling his left leg up from where it lagged behind, he took another step forward. This time he hit something with his dangling right hand. But it wasn't the wall. It was soft and smelled even worse than his leg. He reached out with both hands now and his fingers touched hair, rubbery flesh against stubborn bone, the collar of a shirt.

A body. A dead-ass corpse.

Tanner didn't scream, didn't dare utter a word for fear of waking the dead. He backed away, trying to minimize the scrape of his dragging foot and the choke of his breath, until his back hit the opposite wall and the corpse groaned. Tanner bolted, running as best as he could—a hop, skip, and a jump sort of run that got him out of the mine quick anyway.

Climbing back through the hole, he heard something rip but didn't feel anything and kept going, his heart pounding angrily at his chest: *let's go let's go let's go!*

Once outside the mine, he blinked in sun blindness and confusion. Where should he go? He was covered in sweat and now both legs felt weak. Knowing he couldn't make it much farther, he hitched his way down Silver Hill to the remnants of the old mill where he collapsed in the shade of a rusty mine car.

They'll come get me, he thought, eyes closed and chest panting, *and lay me across the backseat of the Subaru. And Mom'll tell me to hang in there, baby, like that cat poster in the laundry room, and Dad'll drive like a bat outta hell down the pass to get me to Mercy...*

Tanner opened his eyes to look at the leg stretched straight out before him. Where the skin had split open along the length of his shinbone, a watery discharge frothed pink at the edges. Muscle visible inside his leg wept dark red.

Uncle Pard will tell them I did good up here. He averted his gaze to the mountaintops. *That he'll have me back anytime I want.*

With eyes that felt glazed he stared at the top of Stepstone Ridge, where pine trees stood motionless, looking dead, as though Christmas has been over for a long, long time...and realized his fever was climbing. He should've picked up that bottle of aspirin he saw discarded in the street after he ran out of the Buckhorn. *Maybe I should go back for it.*

But suddenly it was impossible to move.

So he lay there, alone, for what felt like a whole other lifetime, and thought he heard the Subaru pull up just before it all went black.

PATICE

"I'M THE QUEEN, I'm the queen!" She flapped her arms up and down in frustration. "The whole town's counting on me!"

"Is that why you made her cry?" he asked.

"Go away, Hawkin Rhone. You. Are. Dead!"

The red ring around the moon had been for Hazel. Patience felt terrible about that, but there was nothing she could do to change it.

Patience had been so afraid Jinx would chase after her from the Mother Lode Saloon, all the way to the miners' cemetery, that he'd ruin everything. Or worse, that he'd rip her apart one bite at a time, pausing to gnaw on her flesh, eating her in front of her own eyes.

Instead, Hawkin Rhone had been waiting for them in the graveyard, and he had sat beneath the purple tree, watching them with a curious bent to his smashed-in, dried apricot pit of a head. Just as she'd dreaded, Hawkin Rhone had found Sean first—and now Sean would be punished.

She picked up the pace. "Go…a…way!"

And then Hazel had been in the cemetery, too, wearing the rainbow tank top her dad had given her on her birthday (they'd both laughed when Hazel first showed it to her), crying green-eyed tears, streams of them running down her freckled cheeks, and Patience was reminded of the time they were playing jacks on the front porch and Gram Lottie leaned out the screen door and called, "Hazel—run and ask your mother if you can stay for lunch," only to trail off with, "Oh, I'm sorry, dear. I forgot."

Patience always thought that was when Hazel realized her mommy was never coming back because Hazel was crying so hard when she took off running for home that Patience wondered how she could see where she was going.

But this time Hazel cried because of me. I did that to her. Through her tears, she finally saw me.

"Look at me!" Patience shivered intensely.

When she recovered, she said, "I told her you're back but she didn't listen."

"Did hurting her make her hear you?"

"Be quiet—you're dead. You're dead and now you're a ghost. Don't try to confuse me just because I'm sick."

After Patience and Sean had wandered away from each other in the cemetery, both set adrift by Hazel's departure, Patience had skimmed past the soulless houses on Loop-Loop Road, then cut through Prospect Park, trying to ditch Hawkin Rhone along the way but he caught up with her anyhow. She felt weightless, gravity's familiar pull relinquished. If she were any lighter, she'd float away.

"When are you planning to tell?" he asked, not gently.

"Why should I? We're already punished."

"I'll make it worse."

"No." She shook her head, refusing to look at him. "Go away—you're scaring me. You're dead, not here, so go."

"You witnessed my murder."

For once, anger overtook her fear. It was all going wrong. He was making everything go so wrong. She hissed at him, *"So what?"*

"So that obligates you."

"Nobody will believe me anyway. Nobody ever believes me."

"They will. Because they need— No, they *crave* something to believe."

"I won't tell." Her stomach tightened and her throat constricted. "I've told too much."

Hawkin Rhone stepped in front of her, forcing her to stop and look at his mummified face. "You will or else I'll keep after you until you do."

"You can't make me!" She shut her eyes tight. "I crossed my heart and hoped to die and I don't want to drown in the deep pond and be dead like you! Now leave me alone!"

When she dared to open her eyes, he was gone. Patience stood alone on Ruby Road.

She'd expected to feel relief once that happened. Instead, she felt buried, the shame smothering her spirit and crushing her bones beneath its weight. She knew she should tell the truth. It was the only way to keep Hawkin Rhone from coming back.

But I won't because I'm already ashamed. Patience pushed at the oppressive feeling with her fists, trying to fight it off. *Ashamed I make such a spectacle of myself, ashamed I make Hazel cry, ashamed I'm so sick.*

Sensing something skulking up behind her, her heart seized. She listened for a tense moment…then asked, "Jinx?"

And when Patience reached across to touch the charms on her opposite arm, her wrist was bare—her lucky bracelet gone.

AHH, STOP CRAWLING on me—get off. I'm thirsty, I'm choking. Listen— I'm crying.

Patience crawled along the trail behind The Winslow, heading east toward the ponds. Sharp pine needles poked her palms, sweat dripped freely from her brow into the dirt. She took it slow: one hand forward, then a knee, then the other hand…

Somebody had stolen her lucky bracelet. *Somebody who wants me weak.*

She moved forward, pausing to scan the ground for the four-leaf clover, the tiny horseshoe.

Pink and blue. A small object in a pink-and-blue wrapper. She picked it out of the dirt with her fingernails: an ancient piece of bubble gum. Every Labor Day holiday, Sheriff Winslow would set up a scavenger hunt on the grounds of The Winslow to keep all the kids in town busy while the adults drank gin in the park. She stared at the gum for a while, willing it to become a lucky charm.

Jinx growled.

Shooting her head up, she expected to see his red muzzle in her face, yellow teeth bared.

Nothing stood on the trail. She blinked sweat from her eyes. She didn't think the dog was capable of stealing her bracelet, yet she wouldn't put it past him, either. He was clever. He was having no trouble tracking her through the woods. Whenever she'd stop crawling, she'd hear his paws crushing pine needles.

She seesawed a few more feet down the path. Maybe Hawkin Rhone swiped her bracelet. He was tricky, too.

She had to find it. Without her charms, she was defenseless. And she needed protection against what she knew waited for her farther up the path—her shame burning so intensely that she no longer had any choice but to take it there and douse it.

Patience sat up on cut knees, wiped sweat off her face with dirty hands and surveyed the woods. She couldn't remember at which point her bracelet went missing or when she'd gotten so lost. She had no idea which part of the Winslow woods she wandered now. *Why can't I see the hotel anymore?* Her thirst was extraordinary.

The dog's next low, deep threat shook her frame.

"Go away!" she screamed.

Then she saw it.

A few feet off the path, something glistened. She leaned forward for a better look. Several wet drops shone red in the dirt. Looking closer, she saw a slight rivulet snaking along the forest floor, bending and curving around rocks and slugs. Still bent at the waist, she pushed herself up and followed the flow but couldn't determine its source.

The flow trickled wider. Fear snatched at her. *Where's my bracelet? Which way is out?*

Again, she felt the same choking panic that had plagued her ever since Gramps Ben told her Hawkin Rhone was back in Winslow.

She spun around on the path. Which way had she come? She felt trapped and exposed at the same time. She hugged her arms across her chest. She had no means to protect herself.

Now the red flowed in a small stream down the middle of the trail and she stepped carefully back and forth to either side of the path to avoid getting her feet wet. But then she cut one side short and her left foot splashed in, immersing her leg up to mid-calf. And seeing it on herself, running down her white skin in narrow squiggles, she understood.

It's blood.

"Help me," she cried, splashing through the widening stream that grew deeper with every high step. Up to her thighs now, she tried to climb off the trail, only there was nowhere to go as it welled up on both sides and she realized she was going to drown in this river of blood.

Her shame forced her forward, wading thickly through, and soon the level rose to her waist. And the roar of it swirling around her—it felt like *through* her—deafened Patience to everything except Sadie saying, "Come into the pond."

Choosing to join Sadie at last, Patience marveled at the sensation of liquid wrapping around her legs and running between her toes. Weak arms fluttering, she turned in a slow, heavy circle. The forest floor was gone. Everything had disappeared but the red and the wet and the trees sticking out of the rushing blood that splashed against their trunks and sent crimson spray high up into the branches. Dripping back down off the pine needles, the sun caught the drops, lighting them like thousands of brilliant rubies, and Patience thought, *It's beautiful.*

When the level reached her chin, she finally accepted what Sadie had been telling her all along: *This is our fate,* and she succumbed to its warmth and inevitability.

NATE

TRACKING THE CREATURE that butchered the doe and Melanie Rhone, he'd thought—for one brief hair-and-gun-raising moment—that he'd finally found it. But when it had turned out to be Patience, he had dropped the revolver to his side, grateful he hadn't shot the girl.

Nate hadn't felt right approaching her and ordering her to leave the woods. She was already scared, that was plain. But his job was to protect and he would not allow the creature to harm her as well. So he'd trailed quietly behind as she'd sleep-walked (it seemed to Nate) and then crawled on her hands and knees toward the ponds.

When she leapt into the deep pond, he had to move fast, because he knew Patience Mathers had never learned how to swim.

There was no getting her out without going in himself so he tossed the gun and shed his shoes as he ran to the water and then plunged in feetfirst. Putrid and warm, the pond was thick with roots and slick twigs of every size and he had to fight just to keep moving toward her.

She hadn't been under long so he was surprised when he reached her to see that she wasn't even struggling. Holding his breath, he dipped down a few feet and grabbed Patience around the waist and pulled her up until both their heads surfaced out of the water. Then he gripped her beneath her arms and dragged her through the muck.

Climbing out was a challenge—the edge of the pond was soft mud—but Nate managed to carry Patience out in his arms like he used to carry Hazel upstairs to bed after she'd fallen asleep in Anabel's overstuffed chair.

Once clear of the water, he set Patience on a thatch of ferns just as he'd done with the doe and as he did, she coughed and sputtered and groaned, much to his relief. Then he plopped down beside her and there they both sat, the girl spitting up foul water and Nate catching his breath, and he wondered if maybe the bad blood between the Winslows and the Mathers had finally been cleansed. If perhaps Ben Mathers could now find his peace.

Once his breath was caught, Nate stood, dripping wet, to search for his revolver. After finding it in the shadow of a boulder, he returned to Patience and sat back down, gun at the ready, intending to wait out the heat and their exhaustion, listening for suspect footfalls in the woods…until his mind drifted off to a pleasant place where creatures do not hunt and the sun does not scorch.

Upon his mental return, Patience was saying, "The unburied are cooking up terrible things for us."

"Unburied?" Nate did not like that word, or the frightened intensity in her eyes.

"The creeks are full of rain. Old murders boiling over. Gram and Sadie—"

"You're not feeling well, Patience. It's all in your mind."

"Sterling Mathers and little Missy Rhone."

Those bad apples, Nate shivered. "It's only in my mind."

"Do you see the trouble coming in your mind, Sheriff Winslow? Trouble in threes."

The delicate tendrils holding Nate's sanity in place were losing their grip. "Trouble?" he croaked.

Leaning close to his face, black hair wet and stringy, cheeks scratched red through the mud, she breathed, "Blame burns there."

Unwilling to ask where, he shivered again. "That's enough, Patience."

"Cows on fire. Bread on fire."

"Enough."

Abruptly she stood. "Then I'm going."

"I can't go with you." Nate rose, slowly scanning the ridgeline. "It's out here. I can't leave these woods until I catch it." He looked at her. "Stalk it. Find it. Kill it before it hurts anybody else."

She nodded her understanding. "He's been following me. Dogs are death."

"I can protect you."

"I have to go there. She'll need me."

Nate watched Patience Mathers dribble pond water onto the trail and then disappear.

Later he would regret staying in the woods. Because he was not there to help his daughter. And later he would discover no peace was found. To the grave it goes.

SARAH

AFTER TALKING TO Fritz Earley about the bread of madness, after seeing bloody footprints across the kitchen floor just as there'd been that night Lottie died, and after hearing what could only be that old brown car pulling up the gravel driveway again, Sarah Winslow had once more retreated to the safety of her broken furniture and dusty memories in the attic of The Winslow.

Facing the pull-down stairs attached to the hatch door, Sarah sat tensely on the vanity stool, shotgun across her lap, and listened. Listened for footsteps pounding up the servants' staircase, listened for accusing voices in the circular room just below the attic, listened for any indication that, right or wrong, they were coming for her, too.

They had come for Hawkin Rhone in the dead of night.

Sarah's husband, Randall, had wanted no part of it, insisting it wasn't their place to mete out frontier-style justice. But Jules Foster had been the only one to agree with Randall.

The rest took up arms—all too eagerly, in Sarah's opinion—and marched through the night certain that two wrongs could make a right. Even after they roped the man's wrists behind his back while his young son protested in horror, even as they escorted the penitent man from town, his head hung low with a remorse that could not have been made any greater no matter how they devised to punish him, even then, they remained certain that his suffering would somehow bring tragedy to an end.

Sarah thought then, as now, that placing blame and enacting punishment only made it all worse—made everyone guilty to one degree or another.

"All are guilty," Randall used to say, including once to his granddaughter after he discovered her trying to set fire to the gazebo. Then he'd winked at his wife before scolding Hazel in a mock grave tone, "But some are guiltier than others."

Sarah sighed, missing her husband, as always, with a painful longing made worse still by her blossoming fear. She wondered if his heart had hurt this bad right before he died.

I can't handle this alone, Randall. Why did you have to go without me?

Faint at first, the unmistakable sound of footsteps climbing the wooden staircase quickly grew louder, more urgent, until Sarah heard the door to the room below her rattle in its frame. She raised the shotgun with trembling hands. Earlier, she'd dragged a chair in front of the door and propped it under the knob as she had seen done in movies. But the crashing noise she heard next told her the chair had only held for a moment.

Her breath was coming in quick, shallow gusts; blood coursed rapidly through her veins.

Heavy footsteps were crossing the room, approaching the attic hatch.

She had pulled up the stairs behind her and secured the hatch, but the pull-down door couldn't be locked from inside. Her only solace was the fact that few people were aware the attic even existed, and even fewer knew about the folding stairs. Her son and granddaughter knew, perhaps Honey, and, of course—

"You up there, old woman?"

Samuel Adair.

SEAN

SEAN RAN A hand across his torso. His ribs protruded, his stomach was sunken. *I starved to death,* he thought.

Then he remembered he wasn't dead yet.

Normally he ate a lot of food: huge sandwiches that Owen Peabody let Hazel make for him at the Crock, stacks of his mom's blackberry pancakes, donuts when Zachary wasn't around.

But now he was too pissed off to be hungry. *James Bolinger. Seriously?*

Sean stomped down Prospectors Way into Matherston, the spectral figures of Dinky Dowd and George Bolinger on either side of him. As they passed the livery stable, Gunner Spainhower burst out the door onto the street and performed a jig, churning up dust and screeching like his feet were on fire.

"Havin' a difficulty, kid?" Dinky asked.

"Red-hot!" The boy bobbed and jerked. "Red!" *Bob.* "Hot!" *Jerk.*

"Hot as a whorehouse on nickel night," Dinky agreed. They continued past and Gunner moved his hoofing up to the boardwalk where he proceeded to make an even louder racket.

It had been Hazel's fury at Matherston Cemetery that made Sean realize he and Patience weren't dead yet—she wouldn't have reacted that way to two forlorn ghosts. And his sense of loss had been so deep his bones ached with it. Until she confessed what happened here in Matherston.

The red dog loped across the dirt road to Sean and sniffed

his pockets as if hoping that Sean might have an apple fritter or two hidden inside.

"What's up, Jinx?" Sean kneeled then to examine the rip in the dog's ear—and his anger exploded. "Who did this to you?"

Jinx didn't answer and Sean rose, feeling irate now that he knew someone had hurt the dog.

"C'mon." Sean and his ghosts and the dog continued past Holloway Harness to Hank's Boarding House, where more ghost miners streamed in and out of busted-out windows.

George leaned across Sean to tell Dinky, "Haven't been back here since you shot me in the Never Tell, you filthy bastard."

"I do apologize for that, Georgie." Dinky grinned. "But I'll be damned if she wasn't worth it."

"Dreadful pretty," George agreed. "Like a Mathers woman, only without the crazy."

Dinky chuckled. "I shouldn't've gut-shot ya, though, Georgie. Ya hardly deserved that."

"Tiger on my tail!" Penelope Hotchkiss screamed. She rode fast down the road toward them, legs pumping, wind in her tangled hair, eyes huge, green bike wobbling wildly beneath her. *"Tiger!"*

When she got closer, they stepped to either side to let her pass but she swerved and nearly hit Sean anyway with her bike.

Jinx took off after Penelope, barking joyfully while she screeched maniacally.

Sean called after her, "Slow down before you wipe out!"

Then he noticed James Bolinger standing in the middle of Prospectors Way across from the Chop House, wielding a ragged, three-foot-long board.

Sean figured he must look mad as hell marching up to James because the tall, skinny kid seemed nervous, saying,

"Guess it's a good thing it's hot, seeing as neither one of us has a shirt anymore."

Sean came in close to him. "I saw *yours* on *her,* you weaseling bastard!"

James backed up, raising the board. "Listen—she's in bad shape. I did what I could to help."

"I should pound your face right here and now, but I think I'll save it for later when I can take my time and *really* enjoy it."

"Aww, let fly," Dinky urged. "Dry gulch 'im!"

"Later," Sean told Dinky. Then to James: "I came for Aaron."

"No." Sweat broke out on James's upper lip, dotting his peach fuzz moustache.

"Where's my brother?" Sean demanded.

"Why do you want to know?"

"I'm taking him out of here."

"To where?"

"Home, asshole."

"The Winslow?" James asked as though Sean was out of his ever-loving mind. James shifted his weight back and forth between his feet. "Over my dead body."

Sean noticed that the board shook a little in James's hands. "James, I'm more than willing to step over your dead body."

"Sean!" a boy yelled.

The voice sounded like Aaron's so Sean swung around to look in the direction of the shout and heard *craack* when the board slammed hard against his head.

This is how Hawkin Rhone felt, Sean thought as he went down, down, down—the sun spinning sparks across the sky—until he fell into the dark.

ONE CHEEK PRESSED into the road, Sean came around with a banging head, a mouthful of dirt, and Jinx barking loudly in his ear.

James stood looking down at him, poised with the board. "You calm now, Adair?"

Sean rolled over onto his back and sat up, sending his bruised brain crashing against the front of his skull and bright lights flashing behind his eyes. "I cannot believe you nailed me with that thing."

"I can't let you take Aaron. And you'd better not go back there, either."

"You're holding my brother hostage? Isn't it enough you finally got what you wanted?"

"You have it completely backward! Hazel made me promise that if you showed up, I'd take care of you."

"You're doing one helluva job." Sean closed his eyes against the pain. "*Damn,* James."

"Sorry, man—you gave me no choice. They've all gone psycho at The Winslow. You can't take him there."

"It's where we *live,* you dumb-ass."

"Not anymore. Just be cool. Stay here, we'll take care of you."

"I feel better."

"No you don't—you look like shit." He raised the board again. "And you're not taking Aaron."

Out-weaponed, Sean decided to try a different tactic. "Okay, we'll ask Aaron what he wants to do. If he wants to come with me, you'll let him go. Deal?"

IN A FILTHY room on the second floor of the Never Tell Brothel, Sean could see Aaron struggling. "I wanna go with you, but not there." The poor kid visibly shook.

"Mom and Dad are at home," Sean said. "I bet they miss you."

"Daddy!" Daisy chimed. "'Member Mommy hollered at us to eat our eggs?"

"We all got yelled at that morning," Sean said.

Daisy pounded Sean's knee with her small fists. "You go make those deliveries right now, mister, and I mean right now!"

"He shouldn't've made you," Violet said. "It got moldy."

James turned from his watch out the window. "Hazel said that grain guy is in town."

"Fritz Earley?" Sean stood. "Where?"

He shrugged. "The Winslow, probably. That's where everyone ends up."

"I have to talk to him."

"Bullshit you do. Don't go there, man, unless you're spoiling for some serious nastiness."

"I need to see how my mom's doing."

"Don't go, Adair."

"And I need to tell everybody what happened."

"They call it the Pest House now—did you know that?"

"The truth. I want the truth out for once."

"Trust me—you don't want that. Why do you think they call it the Pest House, Sean?"

"Patience Mathers is gonna rat me out anyway."

"Because they're all sick and insane. That's why."

"It'll be better if they hear it from me."

James sighed in frustration. "Fine. But if you want your brother to stay safe, you won't tell anybody we're here."

"Why would I? Don't worry."

"Sean, don't go!" Aaron cried.

"I'll come back for you later." He mussed up the kid's hair. "I've got things to do."

Sean pounded down the stairs and out the empty doorway of the Never Tell, sure that there was only one way to put Hawkin Rhone back in his grave, the only way he'd finally rest in peace.

Like shadows, Dinky and George rejoined him on Prospectors Way.

Sean turned to George. "Will you give me a hand?"

George frowned. "Not sure what you've got brewing is such a smart idea, my friend."

"Aww, c'mon, Georgie." Dinky grinned. "You've heard the scuttlebutt rattlin' this burg like they's blastin' up at Fourth of July Mine. Let's get a wiggle on." He rubbed his hands together in anticipation. "Sometimes the past needs a good diggin' up if you aim to make peace with the nowadays."

3:00

ALL THE DUCKS are dead—their heads impaled on stakes lining the driveway to The Winslow. Black eyes stare. They drip from the neck. And Hazel twitches in fright.

"Wake up, Hazel."

Sean lags behind her, still down on Ruby Road. He is barefoot and Hazel thinks maybe the gravel hurts his feet. Hurry, Sean, she thinks. Hurry.

"Hazel!" Somebody shakes her shoulder. "You have to wake up."

Stop it, she tries to say. Wait for him to catch up to me. Her back to the hotel, she cannot see it. She only sees him. But she hears screams erupt behind her each time the car rounds the third bend and the skeletons jump out of their graves.

Fingers dig into her cheeks, moving her head from side to side. "Wake up, wake up!"

Just as Sean starts toward her, reaching for her, brown eyes smiling, Hazel leaves him there and wills her own eyes to open, struggling to wake up in Prospect Park.

Marlene Spainhower's head blocks the sun. "You'd better come quick!" Marlene gasps.

Hazel bolts upright, blinking away ducks and wondering how much time has passed since she collapsed to the grass, unable to take another step.

Marlene stands then and the sun hits Hazel full in the face. "He's acting crazy." Marlene can't seem to catch her breath. "He took over the hotel."

Hazel tries to swallow but her mouth is too dry. "Who?"

"Mathers." Rapid, shallow breaths. "Ben Mathers."

Hazel squints past Marlene at The Winslow.

She doesn't want to go back. She swore she'd never go back. She stands anyway.

Because she cannot leave her grandmother alone in the hotel any longer. Not now. Not after the way Ben Mathers had stared straight at Hazel in church when he preached that wrongs must be righted, wicked acts atoned for. Not after the way Patience's eyes had taken on an especially haunted look last night when she whispered, "Gram and Gramps told me other forgotten things, Hazel, about you and your family."

Hazel grabs Marlene's forearm. "Is my grandmother okay?"

Marlene is still breathing hard. "Is anybody okay?"

Hazel releases Marlene's arm and hurries to the duck pond to retrieve her tennis shoes. She'll need them. Otherwise the gravel driveway will hurt her feet.

Jay is still sitting on the wall with his feet in the water. "Don't go up there, Hazel," he says.

She doesn't answer him because she knows she's going and he knows she's going, so what's the point? Instead, she stands before him, dangling her shoes by the laces. "Help me with these, will you?" she asks because she's unable to tie them with one arm in a sling.

She doesn't complain after Jay knots them too tight. And as she leaves the pond, she wonders where the ducks are hiding. Though she doesn't wonder why.

The sun is high, shadows short, so the world stands in stark relief: no fuzzy details, no soft edges. When she reaches Ruby Road, she checks both ways before crossing. Just to be safe. *Because, please, please, I can't take any more pain.*

Then she pauses at the driveway and stares up at The Winslow, trying not to think about the things she saw the last time she was here, trying her best to forget Samuel Adair raging down the hallway, wielding Sean's baseball bat or Honey Adair sobbing in the kitchen or Gus Bolinger and Rose Peabody and all the others quarantined in the ballroom—the sick growing sicker while spiteful ghosts riot in the tower.

The House of Horrors, she winces. *The scariest ride in Winslow.*

Although skeletons popping out of their graves would be amusing by comparison.

She shakes her head, tries to shake off the paralyzing fear. *Don't think—go!*

And that's that. And that gets her feet moving. *I'll go in and get my grandmother and we'll leave.*

Her tennis shoes feel snug, as if they'd shrunk while drying in the sun.

There are no duck heads impaled on stakes. Likewise, Sean is nowhere to be seen and she is relieved at that. This is no place for him. He doesn't live here anymore. Nobody does. Only the ghosts belong here now.

She plods up the long driveway concentrating on nothing more than putting one foot in front of the other, her tennis shoes going *crunch crunch* with each step in the gravel. She hitches up her loose shorts—she's been running around so much, not eating, her hips barely hold them on anymore.

A chestnut-brown horse tethered to a weathered post swings his big head to watch her pass.

Left, right, left, right, left, she marches until she reaches the stone steps. *Don't think. Go.*

Cautiously she climbs, her eyes glued to her feet, and then she's moving through the soft yard where each step releases a green-grass smell that reminds her of Saturday mornings and trying to sleep in late but it's impossible with her father's lawn mower already going outside and a football game blaring from the television downstairs.

At the porch steps, she looks up. Sunlight glints off tall windows in spikes that stab at her eyes. It's her family's hotel: the mansion her great-great-grandfather built with marble fire-places carved by a hysterical Norwegian stonemason, where countless summer mornings she and Sean ate blackberry pancakes together in the kitchen nook, where her grandfather fell dead to the floor in his bedroom upstairs, where likely her grandmother now hides, afraid.

With sudden sorrow, Hazel realizes that never again will her family lay claim to The Winslow. As if corrupted by the bedlam occurring within, the structure has developed a nasty personality and now stands beneath the baking sun, sweating out absorbed malevolence.

Dark red *X*'s adorn both walnut doors and each ground floor window.

Beware the Pest House, the lunatic in the Second Chance mine shaft had warned her yesterday.

And suddenly she remembers: plague. Gus Bolinger had taught them about plague during history class. The Black Death, he called it, and she flashes on the gangrene crawling up Tanner's leg. Gus told them the authorities would shout from the streets, "Bring out yer dead!" and mark the doors of the afflicted with *X*'s to warn away visitors.

Keep away, she shudders, yet forces herself to climb the steps to the porch.

Passing beneath the double-arched entry, Hazel's legs begin to quiver like the sick cow at Holloway Ranch before she buckled to the ground, like Indigo before they dragged him thrashing and bellowing off the rodeo field and shot him dead behind the corral, and like Gus Bolinger when he'd tried to flee the horrors of the ballroom on plague-weakened, old-man legs.

Keep going.

There are dead animals on the porch. Just two, but that's enough. A pair of tawny goats lay limp across the wide boards—their throats cleanly slit. Nearby rests a pail their executioner had used to capture blood as it poured from their wounds. *Some 4-H kid is gonna miss those goats,* is all she can think.

She wishes it weren't so bright out, that there were shadows to hide such things.

I'll go in and get my grandmother. That's all I have to do. Only she's backing away, unaware she's doing so until she bumps against a pedestal gas lamp—and her first startled thought is that somebody is grabbing for her, anxious to slit her throat, too, so they can paint the rest of the hotel red.

Trying to steady her breathing and slow the pulse that threatens to pop out her eyes, she pushes away from the lamp pole and softly chants, "Go in. Get her. Leave."

To reach the front doors, she must first stretch a long step over one of the goats. Then she reaches for the door, vaguely aware of her own helpless, terrified mewling over the swell of voices coming from inside the hotel.

Her hand shakes wildly as she turns the cold silver doorknob. *Go in, get her—*

Hazel snaps her hand away from the knob.

Not this way. Foolish to fall for it, like Sean said at Three Fools Creek.

She steps carefully back over the goat and descends the steps, then cuts right and crosses the yard toward the side of the hotel. When she rounds the corner, she's struck by the stench of blackberries rotting in the sun. Hand over nose, she rushes past the bushes to the kitchen door. Locked. She cups her hand against the glass and puts her face up to peer inside.

As she had hoped, Sean's mom is alone in the kitchen. Hazel lightly taps the glass and the woman startles before hurrying over to open up.

Honey Adair is a portrait in misery. Covered in sweat and cooking oil and specks of food, she looks as though she's lost twenty pounds since Sunday. *What happens if she doesn't eat something soon?* Hazel panics. *How long does it take a person to starve to death?*

"Come in, come in," Honey urges Hazel inside.

Hazel scoots in and then shuts and locks the door behind her. Platters and bowls overflowing with food cover the counter-tops, the table, the floor.

"Did you find my boys?" Honey's eyes are wild with hope. It's obvious to Hazel that she's getting worse, that every time she sees her she's much worse.

"Yes, I saw them both. They're fine." Hazel pictures Aaron in his cowboy pajamas on the whore's bed in the Never Tell, and Sean—sick and furious and barefoot—standing in the weeds among the grave markers of Matherston Cemetery. But she realizes she can't let herself get distracted. "Where's my grandmother?" she asks.

Honey purses her lips together and closes her eyes.

"Honey, please tell me."

She shakes her head back and forth.

"Dammit, Honey." Hazel could strangle her. "Tell me where she is!"

She opens her eyes, looks pained. "Samuel's holding her for the trial."

Hazel's breath escapes her. "What trial?"

"The Pest House trial." Honey lowers her voice, "Ben Mathers made him do it."

"Do *what?*"

"Hold her for the trial. Mathers says he's been waiting a long time to clean Sarah Winslow's Pest House."

Hazel reels with panic. "Honey, you need to get out of here."

"No, I need to stay in case my sons come home."

"You'd better hope they don't—it's not safe here."

"Not safe." Honey wipes her hands on a dish towel, eyeing the closed dining-room door with a look of apprehension. "Not safe inside."

Hazel pulls away from Honey and heads toward the dining room. As she rounds the kitchen island, she slips, one hand latching on to the freezer door handle to keep from falling. She looks down: two dark smears run parallel along the tile all the way into the dining room, as if somebody with bloody feet had been dragged, resisting, across the floor and out of the kitchen.

"Owen Peabody," Honey explains. "He was taking inventory when they came for him but he fought hard because he *has* to take the inventory. Only then there were even more men and they removed him to the ballroom where all the sickos have to go."

Hazel stares at the bloody streaks, thinking about the way Owen teases her to at least pretend to be nice to the customers in the Crock, feeling guilty that she made no attempt to deter his obsession to count every last thing in town…and an urgent, awful certainty sets in that she cannot let this go on.

"Okay, okay." Hazel sucks in a long breath, huffs it back out. "Go out to the garden, Honey. Pick the blackberries. Stay out of the kitchen for a while."

Honey cocks her head. "Why?"

"They're ripe," she tells the sick woman. "They need to be picked *right now* or else they'll die."

"Yes, okay." She nods and scurries for the door. "But come get me if my boys come home."

"Promise," Hazel says, thinking, *Not a chance.* Then she rummages through the drawer next to the stove until remembering she already has what she needs in her back pocket.

Is there any other way? she wonders before heading to the dining room door.

From the exterior doorway, Honey calls, "Why don't you leave, too?"

"I will. Soon." Hazel doesn't look back. "Don't worry about me." She rests her hand flat against the swinging door, imagining the opposite side splashed in Lottie Mathers's blood, and realizing that no matter how hard they scrubbed, it would never truly go away.

"I wouldn't go in there if I were you." An aching sadness infuses Honey's voice. "It's unclean."

I have to, Hazel thinks. *I need to find my grandmother. I need to put a stop to this.*

Heart pounding, she eases open the door and enters the dining room.

Empty. And clean. Except that most of the chairs lay over-turned and away from the table, as if something unexpected and terrifying had suddenly occurred, upsetting the dinner party and sending the guests scrambling away. Perhaps the butler had lifted the lid off the platter to reveal the evening's entrée: human head surrounded by carrots and boiled potatoes.

Hazel lets the door swing shut behind her and the move-ment of air brings the odor of maple syrup from the kitchen.

The pocket doors leading from this room into the lobby are shut tight. It's the only way. As Hazel picks her way around the chairs and across the dining room she hears voices and the scuffling sounds of movement on the other side of the doors. She has a weird taste in her mouth, she realizes. Acidic like the black ant she once ate, curious how it would taste. That had been against her better judgment.

So is this. She curls her fingertips into the pull handle of the door and hesitates long enough to allow the fear to pen-etrate her marrow.

She slides open the door. The wheels moving along the track sound like faraway thunder.

Hazel gasps.

Somebody is hanging by the neck. A raw, chafed neck en-circled by a noose at the end of a rope slung through the chan-delier in the center of the lobby.

The back of the body is to her, its head bent at an unacceptable angle.

Who is it?

The sickeningly sweet smell of syrup retakes her. Her stomach pitches and rolls.

Dark curtains have been drawn against the afternoon sun and the lobby is dusky save for the light of the chandelier. Hazel stands frozen in the doorway, watching people maneuver around the body. A woman bumps it and sends the Austrian crystal chandelier swinging, illuminating secrets in dark corners.

Another woman hisses at Hazel, "Shut that door! They'll get in. Don't you know? They'll get in and they'll butcher us!"

Too late, Hazel thinks as she rolls the door closed. *They're already in.*

She starts toward the middle of the octangular lobby, all sides bordered in black tile, a black star dead-center beneath the chandelier. She cannot stop herself. But her ratty tennis shoes scuff against the polished floor, resisting forward, the rubber protesting progress toward the hanging thing.

Who is it?

The chandelier settles back in place above the black star. Only to be knocked again when Hap Hotchkiss cuts the body too close and the light show begins anew. "Why didn't you stay at the miners' camp?" Hazel asks Hap, but he doesn't hear her over the din in the lobby. *You were happy there.*

Five steps, six, she wishes she could stop—turn back the way she came and run all the way down Yellow Jacket Pass until she reaches Stepstone, until she reaches help. Only she has to know. *Who is it?*

She moves with the acceptance that this has already happened. That she's already seen the face. Time has flipped, running sideways and backward. She's afraid she'll pee her pants.

The chandelier eases back into its gentle sway, the faint

shadow of its passenger moving against the portraits of Evan and Ruby Winslow that hang on the opposite wall.

Hazel swipes at the sweat running down her cheeks.

When she reaches the body she grasps it by one khaki pant leg.

She spins it around.

Everything else disappears except his face stuffed above the rope at that impossible angle.

He did not go lightly, she sees, *he fought it.*

For he is not pale and waxy like the other dead people she has recently seen. He's purple and angry looking, his tongue protrudes black and huge.

And it's a wonder that she recognizes him at all.

Fritz Earley.

The distributor from down mountain. Whose feed and flour have lain waste to Holloway Ranch and Winslow.

Hazel puzzles over the people simply brushing past, not seeming to care that Fritz Earley hangs dead from the chandelier. She scans the lobby for an ally, a person of some sanity.

Marlene's brother, Caleb Spainhower, lies curled around his guitar on the sofa. Ivy Hotchkiss is sprawled on the floor at his feet, propped against the couch like a rag doll, staring blankly with button eyes. Hazel imagines that if Caleb starts to play his guitar again, Ivy will reanimate—jerking back to life and dancing puppetlike around the corpse in the center of the lobby. Others shuffle in and out of the lobby on the errands of zombies.

Hazel makes her way over to Hap Hotchkiss who is now parked on the third step of the stairway. When she reaches him, she gestures at Fritz Earley. "Who did this?"

Hap's glassy eyes peer past the body, toward the ballroom. "I guess we all did."

"Because it's his fault?"

Hap shrugs. "Guess it's his fault." His eyes widen. "I *hope* it's his fault."

Sharp shivers shave her spine. *This has already happened,* she senses again, *backward and sideways.* She looks back at Fritz Earley. "They're assigning blame now, aren't they?"

"Don't know what else to do."

She cannot peel her eyes off the rope where it's digging into the neck. The flesh surrounding the noose is red and raw and ragged. Quietly, she says, "And they're doling out punishment."

"What else is left?" Hap agrees.

Forcing her gaze away from Fritz Earley, she looks up the staircase toward the tower and thinks, *Another ghost for The Winslow.*

She runs her hand along the smooth, curved banister, then skips her fingertips across silver stair rods...and feels the hotel cracking open: things that have been simmering for years are seeping up beneath the hardwood floors, soaking through the hand-blocked wallpaper.

Why have I never seen it before? She is stunned by its obviousness. *The stain of every miserable thing that has ever happened here.*

Feeling dazed, as though she has taken one too many blows, Hazel hauls herself away from Hap and out of the lobby, past Fritz Earley swinging, over Ivy insensate on the floor, across the hallway and into the ballroom.

The stench hits her first. She never knew anything could smell this bad. Sweat, urine and all the other revolting odors that ripen on the ill and unbathed. *Bring out your dead...* She places her hand over her nose and mouth and enters, jolting to a stop again just inside the wide doorway.

The ballroom has turned to bedlam—teeming with bodies and the murmurs of the unsound. *A madhouse,* her very soul cringes. Vertical shafts of brilliant sunshine leak through cracks in the drapes at either end of the long room, illuminating a wretched tableau of suffering. Tangles of human beings overflow sofas and chairs, or sit slumped against the walls. The worst off lay strewn across the floor, writhing and restless. She guesses eighty people in all, a good portion of the population of Winslow.

Except for the children. *No place for children,* is all she can think.

She's always pictured hell to look like this, especially during one of Ben Mathers' long-winded Sunday sermons on how the whole lot of 'em are headed straight there in a handbasket. No longer looking the harmless old coot, Ben Mathers now appears to be meting out earthly justice from the podium at the head of the ballroom, his back to the window so that the sunlight stealing between the drapes shoots out behind him. "All out in the open now!" Mathers bellows.

I shouldn't stay long, she thinks. *Only long enough to make sure there is no other way, only long enough to get my grandmother out before Mathers hangs her, too.*

She presses her hand harder over her nose. Nobody else seems to notice how entirely foul it is in here. Or that nestled in his wing-back chair, Gus Bolinger suffers from gangrene to both his hands, the skin black and open and oozing at the knuckles. Survived the Battle for Bloody Ridge only to be struck handless by tainted bread. "They burn," Gus groans.

Impossible to take in all at once, Hazel's mind breaks down the panorama into macabre snapshots. Rose Peabody curled tight as a roly-poly pill bug, bare patches revealing irritated pink scalp. Kohl Thacker bashing his head against the fireplace mantle. The whites of Laura Dudley's eyes showing. Bald Billy heaped against fleur-de-lis print wallpaper, his white T-shirt soaked in blood.

Hazel does not see her grandmother.

"Don't stay," Jay told Hazel yesterday.

Don't stay, she thinks now.

Then she whispers, "Yesterday…was that only *yesterday?*"

She spots Owen Peabody tucked into the corner across from Ben Mathers at the lectern. Owen's thick arms and ankles are strapped tight to the legs of the chaise lounge formerly occupying her grandmother's bathroom. Neck stretched beyond conceivable limits, he gnaws on the wide band of cowhide wrapped around his left wrist. The soles of his bare feet are encrusted with dried blood.

What are they doing to you, Owen? She remembers her dad once telling her that an animal will chew off its own leg to escape a trap. Hazel dashes into the ballroom. Rushing, she trips over someone on the floor and they squawk in pain. "Sorry!" she cries. When she reaches Owen, she crouches beside him and gently pushes his head back from the strap. "Don't, Owen, don't."

Blood drips from one corner of his mouth. "Hazel," he sputters, then gives her a gap-toothed grin.

"Hey, Owen," she tries to sound calm. "I'll get these straps off for you." *One, two, three,* she silently counts the number of his white teeth embedded in the leather restraint.

Ben Mathers loudly demands, "You've heard the evidence, now who's with me?"

She glances up. The old man is trembling with exuberance. *I shouldn't have dismissed it when my grandmother told me he'd come to see her,* Hazel realizes. *I should've known Mathers meant trouble.*

Darting her eyes around, anxious as hell to leave, especially now that she's deep inside the ballroom, she tries to loosen the strap. Men spook the perimeter of the room: Tiny Clemshaw, Doc Simmons, Chance Mathers, others she can't make out in the gloom. They rest against the walls in casual poses but with guns conspicuously drawn. Evidently they're the bailiffs of these proceedings, present to keep order in the court. And they're watching her.

She's doing something wrong—the strap won't give. What she wouldn't give to be fully functional again. Everything's so difficult one-armed.

Owen moans frightfully.

She really shouldn't stay a second longer.

Two hands join her one on the leather restraint.

Muddy hands, with chipped pink polish on long finger-nails packed with debris.

Hazel raises her eyes to take in the Queen of the Rodeo. Long hair plastered in leaves, skin mud-streaked, the corners of her eyes and mouth caked in dirt, the most beautiful girl in Winslow grimaces and grunts with the exertion of trying to undo the fat strap binding Owen's wrist.

Patience seems to sense Hazel's gaze upon her and looks up. "I knew you'd need me," she says. "I'm sorry I made you cry."

Hazel feels about to cry again, touched by her friend's self-lessness. "I'm sorry I didn't help *you* when you needed *me*." She fishes the bracelet out of her pocket. "I'm sorry I didn't believe you."

Patience stares at Hazel's hand, transfixed by the charms she holds. "I'd rather be wrong. I never wanted any of this to come true."

"If only I'd listened to you," Hazel says. "Terrible things *are* happening here."

"And Hawkin Rhone *is* back." Patience totters drunkenly. "You didn't tell anybody what happened at Three Fools Creek, did you?"

"No." Her expression is soft. "Never."

Hazel hands her the bracelet. "Here you are, I'm sor—"

Ben Mathers booms, "Who can deny that the Winslow

family has brought ruin to this town?" His sudden change in tone brings people in the ballroom to attention.

"What is he talking about?" Hazel asks Patience.

Patience looks scared. "I warned you."

"Ruin!" Mathers shouts.

As though he's ruining her nap, Rose Peabody uncurls herself on the sofa and gets up to a wobbling stand. "What on earth have the Winslows ever done to harm you, Ben?"

"What have they done?" Mathers echoes, sounding utterly incredulous. "They're murderers!"

You're the murderers, Hazel thinks. *You murdered Fritz Earley.* Her need to find her grandmother grows even more desperate.

"I don't believe that," Rose says, aghast.

"Believe it." Tiny Clemshaw steps forward, looking even more pie-eyed from ergot poisoning than the last time Hazel saw him. "Sheriff Winslow locked Cal up in jail. I sprung him but the next thing you know, Cal's lying stiff in the dirt. Punishment for escaping, I suppose."

"And Sheriff Winslow ordered quarantine but won't let any doctors into town," claims Mathers.

"Turned them away at the bridge, I heard," Doc Simmons adds.

"That is not true," Hazel says quietly, catching the looks of surprise that flash her way.

Patience places her arm around Hazel's waist. It's hard to tell who's trembling more.

Just as Hazel readies to voice her protest, she spots Kenny Clark by the fireplace—and freezes.

What has he been telling them? Dread dawns with terrible certainty. *About me?* She puts shaking fingers to her lips. *About Sean?* Her grandmother's words shriek across her mind: "Once placed, right or wrong, blame is hard to shake."

Kenny looks much worse for it at least, from the kicking

she gave him in the Buckhorn Tavern. Blood cakes the nostrils of his swollen nose and he's got a rag bandaging his head like a wounded Civil War soldier. But he's practically salivating, giving her a look that says, *Here comes the icing on my cake.*

And Hazel realizes—*he's going to kill me.* Her lungs clamp shut. *Breathe, breathe, keep breathing or else you'll pass out and then they'll strap you down like Owen.* She manages a staccato inhale. *I have to get out of here.*

"And where the devil is Nathan Winslow now?" Mathers demands.

That's a good question, Hazel thinks. *Where are you, Dad? I need you. I really need you. Come out, come out, wherever you are.*

"Sheriff Winslow's protecting us!" Patience cries. Leaving Hazel's side, she approaches her grandfather at the podium. "Protecting us from the dogs!"

Tiny Clemshaw says, "Honey Adair told me Sarah Winslow plans to shut the hotel for good after this. What will happen to us then? No hotel means no tourists and no income for anybody."

Hazel glares hatefully at him. Why must he keep stoking the fire?

Kenny shouts, "The Winslows think they own this town! Ever notice that?" Slowly he turns to look at Hazel. The way he taps his rifle against his thigh makes her think he's enjoying himself, that he sees no cause to hurry this savory situation. Kenny's completely off the leash now, and she recognizes the brutal irony that it's largely her fault that her Uncle Pard cut him loose.

Ben Mathers has followed Kenny's gaze to where Hazel is trying to shrink into the corner. "About time you showed your face, Miss Winslow."

"Stop this, Gramps." Patience stands before him, sobbing.

Hazel edges toward the doorway. *Don't ever let yourself get backed into a corner,* her dad had taught her.

She musters bravado. "Careful, old man—if Winslows kill Mathers, then aren't you about due?"

More people turn to look at her, then all commence to talk at the same time.

"Everybody—settle down!" Mathers says.

Places, everyone, she thinks, her back against the wall. *All of you know your parts.* In fact, Hazel suspects that some of them have been waiting years for this show to begin. She watches Mathers, hunched over the lectern, eyes shiny with anticipation. *He has his role down pat,* she sees, *been preparing for some time.*

As she continues to slink along the wall she notices that another hangman's noose dangles from the chandelier in the sitting area, hovering between twin velvet sofas. This one doesn't look like it has been used. Yet. Or maybe it's the same one they used to hang Dinky Dowd in 1889. The courtroom is the same.

She flashes on Fritz Earley's dead eyes bulging with the question, *Who's next?*

Clearly there has been a shift in power in the tower. A bloodless coup. For different ghosts haunt the hotel now: Sadie, Sterling and Lottie Mathers. Fritz Earley and Zachary Rhone. Looking to settle their scores, since all other scores seem to be coming due right here, right now. *This business bodes seriously ill.*

She keeps her eye on Kenny across the room. His posture makes clear he intends to give chase if she tries to dart away, his rifle shot sure to catch up to her no matter her lead.

"How do you plead, Miss Winslow?" Mathers asks in a perversely gentle tone.

"Gramps, please," Patience pleads. "Let's just go home." She looks around for support.

But everyone is staring at Hazel.

She stops her crabwalk toward the doorway and searches the ballroom for a rational face. Patience and Rose are the only ones who don't glance away when their eyes meet.

Except for Kenny Clark's rat eyes daring her to make a quick move. How she wishes she'd kicked his rat ass into an irreversible coma back at the Buckhorn.

"We're waiting." Mathers taps his fingers on the podium with a sound that's enormous over the sudden hush.

Despite the high ceiling, the ballroom closes in on Hazel and claustrophobia tightens around her throat, squeezes—she can't breathe, she has to get out.

"I'll start for you, then," Mathers says in a voice so mockingly mild and sympathetic she wants to tear his face apart at the mouth. "We all know how greatly you dislike our town. Hated it ever since your mother left you."

Hazel's head is spinning.

"And Doc Simmons told us you knew the bread was making people sick," Mathers continues the inquest. "You came to him at church and told him all about it. How could you know such a thing?"

Her heart pounds so hard she's amazed it doesn't burst free and scamper away without her.

"And why," he asks, "pray tell, didn't you tell us *before* our friends and neighbors took sick?"

"No, no, no!" Tiny Clemshaw shouts. "Owen Peabody's been saying all along it's the water. Haven't you, Owen?"

Hazel glances over at Owen in the corner. The Popeye muscles of his arms strain against the leather restraints; his face contorts with effort.

"And a dozen people saw her up on the water-tower platform," Tiny continues. "Opportunity, that's what that is. Isn't that right, Ben?"

Hazel refuses to defend herself to this kangaroo court; sees how entirely hopeless it is.

"That's right, Tiny," Mathers agrees. "So what do you have to say for yourself, Hazel Winslow?" *Tap. Tap. TAP.*

Puddles cover the maple floor, of what she doesn't want to know. Dark smears defile the white marble fireplace. And the reflection of Fritz Earley's body swings in the gilt-framed mirror over the mantle.

"What do you have to say?" Mathers says.

That you're murderers, she thinks again. Then she notices that Kenny Clark has begun to skulk across the room toward her.

Does Uncle Pard know what's going on here? She doubts it. She doubts he has any idea the climate he's fostered. But as furious with him as she is, she'd give anything to see him right about now. He may be harsh and stubborn and dead wrong, but he's not completely deranged.

Gus Bolinger stands and hoarsely shouts, "This has got nothing to do with the Winslows *or* the water, for crying out loud, and everything to do with Rhone Bakery. Remember?" He gestures with his blackened hands. "Remember, Mathers? All of you? We've already got things figured out—as far as we're going to for now anyhow—so let's give it a rest!"

"Which is why we've moved on to the business of the Winslows," Mathers says in a choked voice. "The other's been settled out there in the lobby."

"The feed man got what was coming to him," Tiny says. "The baker, too, in the fire."

Mathers waves his hand impatiently. "Then let's get back to—"

"They're looting in town!" a man yells from the hallway.

"Who's stealing from my store?" Tiny shoots a round into the ceiling and plaster showers down.

People rise from the floor and off the furniture, upset and excited.

"Listen to me!" Mathers pounds the lectern with his fist. "Do you see anybody else in charge here? No! So listen to me!"

"For the luva Mary," Gus Bolinger calls, "give it a rest, Mathers!"

Everyone is moving fast and confused, as though the hive has just been hit by a rock.

Kenny's a lot closer now.

"See what you've done, Mathers?" Hazel shouts to be heard above the clamor. "You set this in motion and now you can't control it."

Patience rushes the podium and pulls her grandfather away. "No more, Gramps!"

"Stop making such a spectacle of yourself, Patience Charlotte! You shame our family!" He pushes her and she falls—awkwardly and hard—against the base of the podium.

Hazel runs to her, shoving at zombies who won't move out of her way, screaming at Ben Mathers, "Shame on *you* for not looking out for your own granddaughter!"

When she reaches Patience, she pulls her up off the floor. "Are you okay?"

Though Patience nods, Hazel worries about the way her eyes seem unfocused.

"What are the three?" Hazel asks her, thinking, *Zachary, Fritz*...

"Huh?"

Hazel's scalp creeps and she shoots a glance behind her. Kenny Clark is watching them from where he now straddles the middle of the doorway—the only way out of the ballroom—and she realizes that now she *is* cornered.

She turns back to her friend. "I need to know, Patience. Who are the three?"

Her gaze remains distracted. "Apples, cows, bread. Creeks, rain, drown."

"Please try to make sense." Hazel gently shakes her. *"Please."*

"Shame blame—" Patience's eyes flit to a place over Hazel's shoulder, then they widen, as though she's trying to take in something larger than life.

"What is it?" Hazel asks.

Patience returns her eyes to Hazel's. "Sean."

Hazel spins around and her breath locks in her throat.

Oh, Sean, why did you come here?

He's passing Kenny in the doorway, covered in sweat and dirt, dragging a canvas bag so heavy and full it takes both his hands to pull it along.

Why, why, why?

As Sean goes by him, Kenny laughs. "What've you got there, Adair?" Rifle slung over his shoulder, Kenny is laughing his rat ass off. "What the hell have you got in there?"

Sean shoots a look of annoyance at Kenny as he continues past, and all is chillingly quiet across the ballroom except for the sound of Sean's bag scraping along the wood floor. He's not heading to where Hazel and Patience stand stunned at the head of the room, but rather to the fireplace opposite the doorway.

Every eye lay curiously upon him.

Who's next? Hazel thinks. *Step right up.*

Sean looks so slight to her as he weaves himself and his plunder around the human obstacles on the floor.

Drop the bag! she silently screams. *Turn around! Run!*

When he reaches the fireplace he releases his hold on the bag, exhaling from the effort of lugging it all the way from who knows where.

"Can we help you, son?" Ben Mathers asks, and more men laugh.

Then they begin to move in Sean's direction. *Step right up. Gather 'round.*

Sean kneels and splits open the sack. Dirty yellow bones and a big skull tumble out onto the floor at his bare feet.

"What," Kenny says, "is *that?*"

Sean stares at the pile of bones. They *all* stare at the pile of bones.

"Hawkin Rhone needs the truth told—" Sean's voice reveals his resolve "—so we can give him the proper burial he deserves."

Hazel and Patience swap looks of horror.

"Good Lord. Is that—" Mathers points at the skull. *"Him?"*

Doc Simmons comes forward for a closer look at the remains. Indicating a caved-in section of skull at the left temple, he says, "See this depressed fracture? Bet you that's what did him in."

Patience moans and knocks against Hazel on her way down to her knees, hands covering her face, attempting to shield herself from this worst of all possible nightmares come true.

Still kneeling before the bones, Sean glances at Patience, then at Hazel, and pushes tangled brown hair out of eyes polluted with remorse.

Hazel shakes her head at him—slowly, clearly—while mouthing *no.*

He pinches his face at her, *I have to.*

No. She lifts her gaze to the rope dangling from the chandelier, hoping his eyes will follow hers, so that he'll see the noose and understand what's going on here.

But when she looks back at Sean, he's studying Hawkin Rhone's skull, running his finger along one of the cracks. Then he staggers a bit when he stands and announces, "I killed him. So it's up to me to set things straight."

"Don't," Hazel says.

She sees Kenny push off the doorway and head for the fireplace.

"Hawkin Rhone didn't poison anybody on purpose," Sean says, "except for the birds."

Doc Simmons dives his arm into the mound of Hawkin Rhone and rummages around, and the bones clatter and clack against each other like an upset bag of golf clubs.

Hazel's stomach lurches.

"He ordered Missy not to pick any apples," Sean goes on, "to stay out of the orchard till spring. But she didn't mind him, even when she saw the birds dying beneath the trees. Because none of you liked her, did you?"

"Missy Rhone was not popular," Rose Peabody's voice quivers in sad admission. "Always a little sickly and that hair in a big snarl." Rose rubs her pink scalp where a swath of her own hair has gone missing. "None of us wanted to play with her."

"That's why she disobeyed her father," Sean says. "It was her day to share and she wanted you to like her. If only he would've given her donuts, she wouldn't have brought those apples."

Rose joins Sean at the fireplace and frowns at the bones. "I haven't felt this sick since then. Like I'm coming apart." Rose searches the faces across the ballroom. "You were there, Marlene, and Ivy and Hap, all of us schoolmates fell ill. The Holloways, too. Anabel, still here then. Where did Anabel Holloway go?" Her eyes land on Hazel. "And Nate Winslow? Where did he go?"

"So all of you got sick," Sean said, "but only one died, right? Missy Rhone."

With the toe of his boot, Kenny prods the skull. "What was wrong with the apples?"

Tiny Clemshaw replies, "Hawkin Rhone soaked them in poison."

"He never intended for anyone to eat them," Sean insists. "Only wanted to stop those robber jays."

"Outcome is all that matters," Mathers says. "And nobody wanted him in town after that. Not then." He narrows his eyes at the bones. "Not now."

Sean spreads his hands, imploring. "Why did you punish him when losing his daughter, Missy, was punishment enough?" Looking increasingly haggard, Sean falters on his feet when he takes a step forward. "It wasn't right to bury him across the creek. We need to bury him in the church cemetery—it's the only way he'll keep to his grave. Otherwise Hawkin Rhone will haunt this town forever."

Kenny pokes the end of his rifle through the mouth of the skull, then lifts it to eye level for closer inspection.

"Knock it off, Clark! That's disrespectful!" Sean snatches the skull off the end of the gun and Hazel's heart clenches when the rifle swings to point in Sean's face.

Laughing, Kenny lowers the rifle. A bit.

As Hazel watches Sean set the skull on the mantle, it dawns on her that if this goes on much longer, she will go completely insane, too.

Hand over belly, Marlene groans miserably. "Why did I eat Missy's apples again?"

"Is that what happened to Melanie and Zachary Rhone?" Doc Simmons appears utterly confused. "Is that when they died?"

"What?" Gus Bolinger looks startled. "Are they dead?"

Simmons glances around. "Do you remember when all the children were dying?"

"Where are the children now?" asks Marlene.

Simmons looks bewildered when he replies, "Gone."

Gone into hiding, Hazel thinks. *Hiding from you.*

Kohl Thacker sputters through split and bloodied lips. "The children of Winslow have been poisoned all over again!"

The room explodes with exclamations of shock.

Then Simmons asks, "Who poisoned them this time?"

Standing before Sean, rifle lowered but hardly at ease, Kenny Clark casually and loudly asks him, "What'd you do with them?"

"Do with what?" says Sean.

"All the little bodies."

"What do you mean?"

"I mean after you poisoned them."

Sean's jaw drops.

Kenny turns to face the increasingly agitated crowd. "Sean Adair knew the flour was bad, but he delivered poison bread all the hell over town anyway."

When Kenny's eyes find Hazel's, he mocks a face at her: surprise!

Damn you, Tanner! Hazel thinks. She curses Tanner Holloway—wills *both* his legs *and* his arms to turn black and rot off. The slower and more painful the better. Kenny's, too. Or better yet, she hopes Kenny's rat head crusts off at the neck and plops to the floor where she can squish it underfoot like a grape.

Hazel starts for the fireplace, shaking off Patience who reaches for her, trying to stop her. Only Sean seems so far away all of a sudden—half the length of the ballroom. She'll never reach him in time.

"I didn't think the bread would hurt anybody," Sean says. "I was wrong."

Hazel yells, "Sean—don't say anything else!"

"Is that why you wrote 'I'm sorry' on the granite wall?" Kenny asks.

"That you?" Mathers raises an eyebrow.

Sean's nod is made heavy by his utter contrition.

Stop! Hazel's brain sobs. *You're digging your own grave. Not Hawkin Rhone's—yours!*

Kenny pokes Sean in the bare chest with his rifle, forcing him back against the fireplace. "And that's why you told Tanner Holloway that it's a lot worse than food poisoning and people will get a lot sicker?"

Again Sean nods, his expression one of total defeat. "Zachary told me to keep quiet. He was afraid you'd run him out of town like his father."

"Sean, no!" Hazel is not getting there in time. Her feet are moving, but not nearly fast enough, and people won't get the hell out of her way.

"I'm sorry I didn't figure it out sooner." Sean looks diminished and feverish and gravely unaware. "By the time I did, it was too late to change anything. I'm really sorry."

"You *knew* something was wrong with the bread?" Doc Simmons shakes Hawkin Rhone's femur at Sean.

"The flour looked kind of grayish, but I didn't know why. How could I know?"

"Shut up, Sean!" Hazel cries. Deeper and deeper he digs.

"You should've known." Doc Simmons scolds with the bone. "You work at the bakery."

Hazel screams at Simmons, "Should've known? You *did* know, you lunatic. And what did you do about it? You're a coward, Simmons!"

"You knew, too!" Simmons yells back. "What did you do about it? Either of you?"

"Enough of this nonsense!" Gus Bolinger shouts. "This is ridiculous—"

Tiny Clemshaw strikes Gus on the nape of the neck with the butt of his shotgun and Gus drops. Clearly Tiny and his shotgun have had enough of Gus Bolinger's nonsense as well.

"I tried. I'm sorry. I tried," Sean is saying.

But it's difficult for Hazel to hear him over the gasps and accusations and the rope creaking in the breeze of the fans and the men checking the loads in their guns and the clang-

ing in her own head: *Blame.* Clang. *Will.* Clang. *Be placed!*
Clang-clang!

At last she reaches Sean at the fireplace and shoves him
behind her, as if her slender body might physically protect
him. "Don't say another word," she hisses at him under her
breath. Then she addresses the crowd, which seems to grow
larger and uglier with each passing moment. "Let's get this
straight. It's Fritz Earley's fault the flour was bad and Zachary Rhone's that the bread got delivered."

"Mighty convenient," Mathers says, "seeing as neither one
is alive to defend himself."

"Did Rhone hold a gun to your head?" Tiny Clemshaw gestures at Sean's head with his shotgun. "What about you?" He
points the gun at Hazel. "I saw you in the delivery van, too."

Feeling helpless, Hazel looks at Sean, but he's busy staring
at Fritz Earley's body in the lobby. She sees firearms sited on
them from every direction and wonders, *Where did all these
guns come from?*

"Let's see this bad flour!" Kohl Thacker can't stand still.

"Too late for that." Kenny narrows his eyes at Sean. "Seeing as Adair here burned the bakery clear to the ground."

"Did you set the bakery on fire, son?" Mathers asks Sean.

"Yes, but not to—"

"He burned the bakery to destroy the evidence!" Kenny says.

"And killed Zachary and Melanie Rhone to keep them
quiet," Clemshaw adds.

"He's killed before," Mathers says. "Told us so himself."

"Stop, stop, stop!" Hazel screams. Backed against the fireplace, she shields Sean with her arm, trying to deflect their
words. "He was forced to hurt Hawkin Rhone to protect me.
But Sean has never hurt anybody else."

Doc Simmons is toying with the skull. "Except for all those
little children he poisoned to death."

"There are no dead children!" Hazel shouts.

"Hazel," Mathers's tone takes an especially grim turn, "we saw you with the Rhone girls right before they disappeared, too."

"Tell us where their little bodies are stacked," Kenny orders.

Hazel's eyes drift to the empty noose…and she suddenly worries that the promise she made to James Bolinger in Matherston will prove unbearable to keep. *"Don't tell anybody we're here,"* he'd beseeched her in such desperation. *"I can't let them get us—it's really scary there."*

Hazel returns her attention to the really scary mob before her. "The children are safe," she says, willing her voice to sound more commanding and less terrified. "And they'll keep safe only if they stay hidden from you until you're feeling like yourselves again."

"She's telling the truth," Patience cries. "I swear on my Gram Lottie's grave!"

Kenny steps close enough to Hazel that she can smell his sour milk breath on her face when he says, "Prove it. Show us one kid and we'll believe you."

Hazel swings toward Sean, tightly pursing her lips at him, *We cannot tell.*

And yet when Sean nods his understanding, she's tortured by how soft and exposed his throat looks—not red or raw or ragged. Uncertainty slices through her.

"Where are they?" Kenny asks almost cheerfully.

Sean gives Hazel a slight shake of his head.

So she takes his hand in hers and says to Kenny—says to them all— "I won't tell you."

Hazel sees Patience ducking out of the ballroom and immediately understands that she's headed to Matherston to retrieve a brave child or two in an effort to dampen the fervor. But as Patience disappears through the doorway, Hazel feels the corners of her mouth tugging down, her eyes filling with tears. Because she knows that it's already far too late. She strengthens her hold on Sean's hand.

"Go on, Hazel," Kenny says, "what are you waiting for?" Then he grins.

And in that horrible instant Hazel realizes that Kenny knows exactly where the kids are hiding and how desperate they are not to be found. And that if she won't reveal their location, he will—but only after Sean has already been punished for killing them.

A few dismal groans and the scritch of the rope chafing against the chandelier save the ballroom from total silence. Hazel has caught Kenny glancing at that empty noose many times. His mouth set in a calculating pose, his rat eyes look at the rope, then at Sean. Rope. Sean. She can feel Sean's exhaustion in the hand she tightly holds—he's so weak from the sickness and the strange things he's been up to over the past few days that he's shaking. *Protect me—*

With a howl of terror like Satan is reaching for his soul, Owen Peabody snaps free of the restraints around his wrists and reaches to unbind his ankles. Rose hurries toward her husband only to be mowed down by men rushing over to quash Owen's liberation.

Hazel sees that Kenny is torn. He looks longingly across the room, itching to join the fray, but his reluctance to let his guard down on Hazel and Sean keeps him rooted to the spot.

"You're sick, Kenny," Hazel states overly loud.

He startles, turns to her.

"Aren't you?" she asks.

People swivel to look at him, surprised.

"You're one of the sickos now," she continues. "I can see it in your eyes."

Those eyes flash fury. "Shut up, you scheming bitch."

"Hazel…" Sean pulls her protectively against him.

She releases Sean's hand and pushes him back from her. "Let's see your feet, Kenny." She steps away from the fireplace. "Are they turning black?"

He lunges for her.

She dodges him.

Then runs.

Darting out of the ballroom and through the lobby, Hazel skips over Ivy's legs and shoves Fritz Earley's body out of the way like a punching bag—not slowing to look over her shoulder, not letting herself think about him giving chase, not daring to consider the bullet that might split her spine at any moment. She dodges Hap Hotchkiss on the lower stair and takes the steps three at once, climbing the red-carpeted staircase of The Winslow for the last time, thinking, *She's up here, she has to be, it's the only way.*

Hazel hits the landing and starts down the hallway, her mind racing: lure Kenny away from Sean, find Sarah, get her shotgun, put an end to this madness, and most of all keep out of Kenny's clutches. She's well aware of him pounding up the stairway behind her.

She's faster than he is, so she might make it—unless he shoots her in the back.

She keeps running, refusing to glance over her shoulder, afraid that if she does, he'll be right there, reaching for her hair.

Hazel bursts through the door into her grandmother's quarters, praying that Sarah will be right there, ready to blast this maniac to kingdom come and that'll be the end of him.

Instead, Samuel Adair is sprawled on her grandmother's sofa, a nearly empty bottle of Scotch clutched in one hand. He gawks at her in drunken puzzlement.

The baseball bat rests on the coffee table.

Panic seizes Hazel by the throat. "Where's my grandmother? What did you do to her?"

"In there." Samuel swings the bottle to indicate the bedroom.

Hazel can't see a thing—the lights are off in the bedroom, and the darkness fills her with dread.

"Grandma?" She steps forward, fearful of what she might find.

Closer, her grandmother comes into view. Her frightened, fragile-looking grandmother, shrinking into her rocking chair.

"Hazel," Sarah fervently whispers, "you shouldn't be here!"

Boot steps clomp down the hallway, floor-shaking thuds.

"Grandma—where's your gun?"

"They took it— Run!"

Hazel whips around to face the doorway.

He's here. Kenny, his rifle, his hungry wolfish grin. And he says, "I've got a score to settle with you, Hazel Winslow."

"I've got a score to settle, too!" Sean shouts from the hallway.

"Sean, no!" Hazel screams. "Go back!"

Kenny turns just as Sean comes into view.

"You've had this coming for a long time, Clark," Sean growls. "Drop the gun and let's go!"

Instead, Kenny raises the rifle. Sean dives forward and punches him in the face.

More blood flows from Kenny's ripe tomato nose. He looks stunned.

Before Kenny can recover, Sean hits him in the gut.

Kenny doubles over, groaning.

Sidestepping Kenny, Sean heads for Hazel in the doorway. "Did he hurt you?" he asks, his eyes full of concern.

Behind him, Kenny is rising, and Hazel shrieks, "Sean!"

Sean turns and Kenny smashes the butt of his rifle against Sean's jaw.

Looking as though he might pass out, Sean staggers down the hallway, back toward the staircase, leading Kenny away.

Hazel darts into the sitting room and grabs the baseball bat. Samuel doesn't try to stop her, only looks confused.

By the time she returns to the hallway Sean has reached the top of the staircase.

Kenny is right behind him.

Sean falls to one knee, head bent, clearly struggling to remain conscious.

Taking aim, Kenny says, "I never did like you, Sean Adair."

"I warned you never to say his name again!" Hazel sprints for Kenny.

He turns toward her.

"And I meant *never!*" She swings the bat and connects with Kenny's rat head.

The crack of wood against bone is a sound she remembers all too well.

Her broken elbow bursts into flames; the bat suddenly weighs a thousand pounds.

Kenny stumbles. His left eye rolls back into place, but the right roams and pools with blood. "I got fired," he slurs. "Your fault!" His finger twitches at the trigger of the rifle.

"Stop!" Hazel orders. "You're hurt—you need to stop this right now."

"Pard said I can never come back." He wobbles, white as a ghost, his right pupil zooming in and out like a camera seeking focus.

"Stop now," Hazel says forcefully.

"Your fault!" He squeezes off a shot.

The bullet whizzes past Hazel. The wall sconce behind her explodes.

Kenny fumbles with the rifle and manages to chamber another round.

Hazel charges and buries the bat in his belly.

Kenny flails backward. His feet tangle. He trips over Sean.

Then Kenny is tumbling down the staircase, hand reaching for the banister that eludes his grasp.

People in the lobby scatter. Kenny lands flat on his back on the cold marble.

This time neither eye rolls back into place.

Hazel wants to run screaming from this Pest House of horrors, wants to grab her grandmother and Sean and take them far from this place. All she manages to do is start shaking. Hard sobs escape her. The bat slips from her hand and rolls in a semicircle around the floor, leaving a crescent moon of blood.

Sean reaches her and wraps his arms around her trembling body. "It's okay," he whispers. "It's okay."

"He was going to shoot you." Hazel bites her lip, tries to stop the sobbing.

"Yeah, he was," Sean says.

"That Clark bastard had it coming," Samuel says.

Hazel spins. He has joined them in the hallway. Her grandmother, too, looking exhausted.

"You had no choice, Hazel," Sarah says. "Never second-guess what you had to do here."

Hazel rushes to give her grandmother a one-armed hug. "Honey told me Samuel was holding you for trial." Hazel shoots a look of anger at Samuel.

"What the hell, Dad?" Sean is massaging his jaw.

"He came for me, all right," Sarah says. "All it took was a bottle of Randall's aged Scotch to buy him off."

Samuel looks hurt. "I protected you, old woman. I would never let Mathers hurt you."

Sarah nods. "I know that, Samuel."

Hazel glances down at Kenny's body. Red blossoms from his cracked head, yet more blood soaking into The Winslow.

Sarah must be looking at it too because she says, "We'll never get it clean."

Hazel sighs. "We can't let this ghost live here." She looks

at her grandmother. "Remember what you told me about the Silver Hill Hotel in Matherston burning to the ground?"

A glint of understanding sparks in Sarah's blue eyes.

"And about how that night finally put an end to the reign of lawlessness in Matherston?"

Her grandmother nods, slowly, sadly.

"There's no other way," Hazel says. "I am so sorry."

Sarah shuts her eyes, and Hazel imagines the flood of memories that must be playing behind those closed lids. At last her grandmother reopens them. "All right, sweetheart. But be *careful.*"

"I will." Hazel turns to Sean. "Take my grandmother and your dad out. I'll be right behind you."

"No way am I leaving without you," he protests.

"Please, Sean, we have to hurry!" Hazel turns him by the shoulders and points him toward the stairway. "I need to be sure that you'll all be out. I promise I'll be right behind you."

With obvious reluctance, Sean takes Sarah by the arm. And as soon as they start down the hallway, Samuel pulling up the rear, Hazel dashes back into her grandmother's quarters.

She beelines it for the mantel and grabs the wick lamp that's always there next to the photograph of Anabel smiling and Hazel ogling her dad. *Third time's a charm,* she thinks, remembering the delight on her mother's pretty face, both of them giggling as Anabel plucked her out of Ruby Creek after Hazel succeeded on her third attempt at a somersault on a hot day like today.

They'll come in threes, Patience predicted. Three days, three murders...

She throws the lamp hard against the window ledge and the glass base bursts open, soaking the cranberry velvet drapes in kerosene.

Three fires: Holloway Ranch, Rhone Bakery, The Winslow—it has to be next.

From her pocket she retrieves the matchbook she took from Honey yesterday, the one with the pig in a bib eating ribs. She strikes several matches at once and lights the drapes at the hem.

The whoosh that follows sucks all the air out of the room with a sound like diving underwater.

All are guilty, but some are guiltier than others, she thinks, and laughs out loud. Her grandfather had easily foiled her attempt in the gazebo; this time she has to succeed. The drapes go up so easily she cannot believe that in over a hundred years it never happened by accident. The fire leaps from floor to ceiling in one fluid motion and Hazel watches, fascinated, as flames stretch greedily to the next set of curtains before fanning out across the carpet.

She beats the flames to the mantel—she has to save the photograph. Because now, it's the only part of Anabel she wants to hold on to, the only memory worth saving. After snatching the picture, she races out of the burning room.

The fire is spreading so much faster than she imagined it would. She bolts and the fire chases her not down the hallway, but through the rooms—like ghosts walking through walls—devouring bone-dry timber, moving unimpeded toward the staircase, up to the tower and down to the first floor, snapping like a million firecrackers.

"Fire!" Samuel is yelling at the top of his lungs as Hazel flies down the staircase toward her grandmother in the lobby. People scream and run around pell-mell. Frantic, they pour out from the ballroom—some limping, some crawling, Owen dragging the chaise lounge by one ankle—and cram into the lobby where they bottleneck at the black walnut doors. When the jam loosens everyone funnels out, including her grandmother and Samuel.

Except Hazel doesn't see Sean with them, and she vows then and there never to lose sight of him again.

She races back into the ballroom where Ben Mathers is still pounding the podium, bellowing with upraised fist, "Where are you going? We're not finished!"

Then she spots Sean in front of the fireplace, gathering bones. "Sean!" she screams and he looks up, startled. "Let's go!"

"I can't leave him here!" Sean plucks the skull from the mantle, shoves it inside the canvas bag, then rushes to bundle it all up.

"Hurry!" she shrieks.

She runs to Mathers and grabs him by one loose-skinned arm and pulls him out of the ballroom just behind Sean who is dragging the big bag. All around them, wallpaper bubbles and the ceiling warps down, as together they cross the lobby, pass over the threshold, and leave the hotel forever. In their wake, history crashes down in an explosion of red embers.

There was no other way, Hazel thinks as she leaps across the dead goat on the porch and trips down into the yard. It was the only way to get everybody out—the lunacy was feeding on itself, growing hungrier. It was the only way to alert the rest of the world that something is *very wrong* up in Winslow.

There's shrieking and outrage as people spill across the yard with hot cinders and ash sticking to their sweaty bodies. Many dash for the shelter of the gazebo to escape the rain of debris.

Trailing Sean, Hazel flies down the stone staircase and lands on the gravel driveway, where they watch in silence as windows explode in protest of the heat and the weight of the past bearing down upon aged frames. The smell is caustic and sulfurish and the leaves of fall burning all at once. In the blistering heat, Hazel wonders if the whole mountainside might erupt, spewing bits and pieces of itself all over Stepstone Valley.

Ornate eave brackets detach from The Winslow's flat roof

and crash into the porch balustrade, while old-growth siding warps and buckles. When the tower collapses, Hazel thinks, *The only way.* The crackling grows louder, the heat intensifies. Her throat and lungs feel seared.

After the top floors cave in, the staircase hangs for a moment in open space—its steps leading to nothing but thin air—until it too relinquishes to the growing mountain of cinders in a deafening crash.

Then the fire eats the southern portion of the ground floor as though it were tissue paper, pausing to gnaw on the parlor where her grandfather used to pop out waving his arms high over his head and shouting at her and Sean, "Bogeyman's gonna get ya!" and they'd run out back screeching until they'd reach the safety of the giant oak where they'd split their sides laughing.

The bay window bursts into the yard, sending shards of glass into the trunk of the birch tree her father planted when he was a Boy Scout. Her dad and Samuel Adair had already worried about the prospect of fire during the dry season and had consequently cleared brush and trimmed the other trees away from the hotel. As a result, the fire is starved for fuel after devouring the tall birch and refocuses its fury on the remaining structure.

At least the kids don't have to worry about this place anymore, Hazel thinks. *The Pest House of Horrors is no more.*

"Get the fire hose!" Tiny Clemshaw shouts.

"It's too late for that," Hap Hotchkiss says.

"Let it burn," Hazel whispers, "just let it burn."

She glances at her grandmother standing next to Honey and Samuel at the entrance to the gazebo. Honey's hands are full of blackberries, the juice staining her fingers purple and dripping on her feet. Together, the three of them watch their home and livelihood burn to the ground.

Catching her grandmother's eye, Hazel grimaces apologetically.

Sarah dismisses Hazel's second apology with a stern shake of her head. Then she places a hand over her heart and closes her eyes, her breast swelling with a deep breath. A gesture of relief.

The cloud of smoke billows beautifully black, thick and high into the clear sky.

Hazel squints south in the direction of the fire lookout. "This time, Sparks, you'll see. You'll see and you'll send help."

At Hazel's side, Sean is wiping his sweaty, sooty face with the back of his filthy hand. "Guess we'll both be sent across the creek now."

"Can't think of anyone I'd rather share exile with," she says. Their voices sound hoarse from all the smoke. "We'll fix up Hawkin Rhone's cabin. New curtains, a little paint. Adopt Bandit. And eat lots of berries and squirrels."

"I'm in," he says. Then he looks her over. "Nice shirt."

She glances down at the rainbow on her tank top—the sign of hope emblazoned across her chest since Monday night. "Thanks. I think so. Where's yours?" She laughs. But just as suddenly, she's sobbing. "I wouldn't blame you, Sean, if you'd let me drown in Three Fools Creek."

"Drown? Why would I? You protected me, just like you promised you would." He puts his arms around her and pulls her close, careful not to crush her arm. "I think I'm starting to feel better already."

"Good." She wishes they could stay like this forever.

But he pulls back. "Let's go."

"No." She hugs him to her again.

He gently pushes her away. "Let's go."

Hazel raises her head to look at him. "Go where?"

Sean pulls a handful of teeth out of his pocket and hands them to her, then stoops to pick up the bag of bones. "Let's go put Hawkin Rhone to rest for good."

THREE WEEKS LATER

"Want to check out my tooth?" Hazel pulled back her cheek to expose the shiny gold crown her cracked molar had earned her from the dentist that morning.

Sean came in for a better look. "Cool."

She let go of her cheek. "Makes my mouth feel weird. Like my tooth's too big."

"Let me see." He leaned even closer and kissed her.

Then he shrugged. "Feels all right to me."

They were stalling, Hazel realized, standing outside Hawkin Rhone's cabin, reluctant to go inside. And for what? After all they'd been through, certainly this was nothing they couldn't handle.

Emboldened, Hazel climbed the steps to the porch, clearing away cobwebs with her good arm as she did. Her other arm was still in a sling—a real, hospital-issue sling this time—and the doctors had cautioned her that it might take yet another surgery to set her elbow right. At least now she was armed with a full bottle of Vicodin.

She glanced back at Sean where he remained at the foot of the steps, eyeing the door to the cabin warily, as if the bogeyman himself might suddenly burst out.

"Don't worry," Hazel told him, "I'll protect you."

He laughed before joining her on the porch. "You know what? I believe you now. At least when it comes to the ghosts."

"Oh, yeah? What else is haunting you?" she asked.

"The long arm of the law." He shot a look over his shoulder

as if lawmen might close in on him at any moment. Then he returned his anxious gaze to Hazel. "That's what."

She hated that he still felt distressed; he'd suffered enough. She rested her hand on his shoulder. "Sean, I told you not to worry. It's business as usual around here. My dad said that since no one's talking, there's no way for Riley Washburn to sort it all out, let alone determine any fault beyond Fritz Earley. Even Ben Mathers is smart enough to keep his mouth shut."

"Guess you're right. Besides, *nobody* was in their right mind. Washburn would have to arrest every single person in town." He grinned, his brown eyes clear and bright.

Hazel couldn't get enough of seeing Sean, sturdy and sound again. It had taken him, her father and the others seven to nine days to crawl back into their minds. Aaron had been the worst off—it took him two weeks to settle back into his body for good. But everyone still alive at the time the forest service helicopter responded to the fire did eventually recover.

Though Hazel knew that nobody in Winslow would ever be the same.

She turned from her boyfriend and placed her hand on the cabin's rough-hewn log door, saying, "Last one in has to be rodeo queen."

She pushed on the door but met with resistance. Putting her weight behind it, the door finally swung open and she stepped inside, Sean right behind her.

It was obvious that nobody had been in the cabin for years, probably not since Hawkin Rhone himself was last inside. On the cooktop of the potbellied stove, a single plate and rusted-out percolator sat next to a metal mug stained dark with dried coffee. Positioned in front of the stove was a chair with most of its stuffing scavenged by rodents. A tattered blanket was wrapped over one arm of the chair, and on top of that lay an open book, facedown: *The Tales and Poems of Edgar Allan Poe.*

When she glanced at Sean, the look of wonder on his face

told her he was thinking the exact same thing she was. "Look at this," she said. "I can't believe we were so afraid of him."

"Us, and every other kid in Winslow," Sean marveled. "Before and ever since."

This was the scene they had interrupted that summer day. This was what the man—driven mad by isolation and remorse—had been doing right before they dared each other to cross the creek, to trespass and steal a souvenir, surely frightening him when they'd clamored onto his porch. This was how he was spending his afternoon right before they killed him.

Hazel's heart filled with pity as she imagined Hawkin Rhone sitting beside the little stove, the blanket warming his old-man legs, reading his poems for probably the thousandth lonely time and eating a lunch of berries and squirrel.

Sean walked slowly to the chair. Digging into his pocket, he pulled out a gold, heart-shaped pendant on a chain, reached to the shelf behind the chair, and gently hung the necklace around a frame containing a photograph of the Rhone family: mother and father, Zachary and Missy, all young, all smiling. Sean had discovered the pendant among the bones after he dug them up; Hawkin Rhone must have had it on him when he was buried the first time. Later, when Hazel and Sean had read the engraving, *For Missy, Love Father,* they had both felt that it belonged here—the site where he paid his penance—rather than reburied with him in the church cemetery, burdening him for all eternity.

Sean turned back to Hazel, relief softening his features. "You know who's next, don't you?"

She nodded. Before Violet and Daisy Rhone had left to go live with their aunt in Gig Harbor, Hazel heard their dread-fueled whispering about Gus Bolinger. The old veteran had lost a hand to gangrene and had his wrist fitted with a large steel hook. At that, a new bogeyman was born in Winslow.

"Gus the grappler," she said, repeating the kids' dark words.

"Nice." Sean grimaced. "Real nice."

"Don't forget the vampire in Second Chance Mine. They still haven't figured out where that sick maniac came from."

"A carny, probably. Hope it wasn't Cyclone Clyde."

"I hope not, either," she agreed, wondering what had become of their bag of weed that Tanner had with him. "And the most ghoulish bogeyman of them all…" Hazel winced. "Tanner Holloway's leg."

"You're right." Sean's eyes reflected the horror of that image. "That amputated leg's gonna be walking around in the nightmares of every kid in Winslow for a long time."

"Poor Tanner." She shook her head. "You know, I'm surprised, but ever since he went home, I actually miss him a little."

Sean frowned. "I don't."

Feeling as though they were finished here at last, Hazel left the cabin. Once back outside, she paused, titled her face up to the sun, and released the pent-up breath she'd been holding for years.

Then she glanced at Jinx, where he was taking a nap in a sunny spot of dirt, wearing a gigantic plastic cone around his neck because he refused to stop scratching at the stitches in his ear.

Coming up behind Hazel, Sean wrapped his arms around her and bent his head to hers. "I'm glad you stayed," he said. "You, I'd miss."

Hazel thought about her own mother not bothering to pack anything, not bothering to say goodbye before leaving everything and everybody behind. "Don't worry, Sean. Before I go anywhere, I'll give you plenty of time to pack your bags, too. And bring extra bologna and cheese for our—"

Hazel gasped and Jinx shot up, barking his furry head off.

Something was coming, gnashing and crunching its way through the woods across the creek.

She whipped around to face Sean. *"Bigfoot,"* she mouthed, and pushed past him to get back onto the porch. The whereabouts and whyabouts of the creature in the woods had yet to be discovered. Wolf, bear, Sasquatch, nobody knew for sure.

"Hey!" a high voice called.

Hazel turned to see Patience emerge from the trees on the opposite bank, a colorful beach towel draped across one arm, the other arm gesturing to them with a scoop.

"That's it!" Hazel placed her hand over her pounding heart. "That is the last time I let anything on this mountainside freak me out."

Sean squinted at her with skepticism. "We'll see."

"You guys coming, or what?" Patience shouted.

As if she'd meant him, Jinx was already loping her direction, tail wagging, cone bobbing.

Hazel held out her hand to Sean, which he took in his own and pulled her down from the porch.

Then they walked to the edge, kicked off their shoes, and waded into the cool, calm waters of Three Fools Creek.

Time to teach Patience Mathers how to swim.

* * * * *

REQUEST YOUR FREE BOOKS!

2 FREE NOVELS
PLUS 2 FREE GIFTS!

W⊕RLDWIDE LIBRARY®

Your Partner in Crime

YES! Please send me 2 FREE novels from the Worldwide Library® series and my 2 FREE gifts (gifts are worth about $10). After receiving them, if I don't wish to receive any more books, I can return the shipping statement marked "cancel." If I don't cancel, I will receive 4 brand-new novels every month and be billed just $5.49 per book in the U.S. or $6.24 per book in Canada. That's a savings of at least 31% off the cover price. It's quite a bargain! Shipping and handling is just 50¢ per book in the U.S. and 75¢ per book in Canada.* I understand that accepting the 2 free books and gifts places me under no obligation to buy anything. I can always return a shipment and cancel at any time. Even if I never buy another book, the two free books and gifts are mine to keep forever.

414/424 WDN F4WY

Name _____ (PLEASE PRINT)

Address _____ Apt. #

City _____ State/Prov. _____ Zip/Postal Code

Signature (if under 18, a parent or guardian must sign)

Mail to the **Harlequin® Reader Service:**
IN U.S.A.: P.O. Box 1867, Buffalo, NY 14240-1867
IN CANADA: P.O. Box 609, Fort Erie, Ontario L2A 5X3

Want to try two free books from another line?
Call 1-800-873-8635 or visit www.ReaderService.com.

* Terms and prices subject to change without notice. Prices do not include applicable taxes. Sales tax applicable in N.Y. Canadian residents will be charged applicable taxes. Offer not valid in Quebec. This offer is limited to one order per household. Not valid for current subscribers to the Worldwide Library series. All orders subject to credit approval. Credit or debit balances in a customer's account(s) may be offset by any other outstanding balance owed by or to the customer. Please allow 4 to 6 weeks for delivery. Offer available while quantities last.

Your Privacy—The Harlequin® Reader Service is committed to protecting your privacy. Our Privacy Policy is available online at www.ReaderService.com or upon request from the Harlequin Reader Service.

We make a portion of our mailing list available to reputable third parties that offer products we believe may interest you. If you prefer that we not exchange your name with third parties, or if you wish to clarify or modify your communication preferences, please visit us at www.ReaderService.com/consumerchoice or write to us at Harlequin Reader Service Preference Service, P.O. Box 9062, Buffalo, NY 14269. Include your complete name and address.

WWL13R